Pierre Lemaitre worked f   ıre
before becoming a noveli   rs'
Association Internationa   *eat
Swindle*, the first volume i   gy,
which also won the Prix

Frank Wynne is an award-winning writer and translator. His previous translations include works by Virginie Despentes, Javier Cercas and Michel Houllebecq. He chaired the jury of the 2022 Booker International. Most recently his translation of *The Art of Losing* won the 2022 Dublin Literary Award.

Praise for Pierre Lemaitre's novels:

'*The Wide World* is one of his best . . . Compellingly plotted, stuffed with great characters, thought-provokingly situated in history – honestly, what else do you want from a novel?'
The Times

'Lemaitre's hard-boiled style of writing is perfectly matched by his translator Frank Wynne, who avoids any trace of sentimentality . . . but there is also a great deal of psychological depth in the storytelling'
Financial Times

'Pierre Lemaitre skilfully captivates and stuns the reader'
Le Figaro Litteraire

'Storytelling with never a dull moment'
Le Figaro

Also by Pierre Lemaitre in English translation

THE
WIDE
WORLD

Pierre Lemaitre

Translated from the French
by Frank Wynne

TINDER
PRESS

First published in the French language as *Le Grand Monde*
by Éditions Calmann-Lévy – Paris 2022

First published in Great Britain in 2023 by Tinder Press
An imprint of HEADLINE PUBLISHING GROUP

First published in Great Britain in paperback in 2024 by Tinder Press
An imprint of HEADLINE PUBLISHING GROUP

ISBN 978 1 4722 9212 4

Typeset in Sabon by CC Book Production

Printed and bound in Great Britain by Clays Ltd, Elcograf S.p.A.

Headline's policy is to use papers that are natural, renewable and recyclable products
and made from wood grown in well-managed forests and other controlled sources.
The logging and manufacturing processes are expected to conform to
the environmental regulations of the country of origin.

HEADLINE PUBLISHING GROUP
An Hachette UK Company
Carmelite House
50 Victoria Embankment
London EC4Y 0DZ

www.tinderpress.co.uk
www.headline.co.uk
www.hachette.co.uk

To Pierre Assouline with my friendship
For Pascaline

There will be novels to write.
Lucien Bodard,
La Guerre d'Indochine

But if anything is certain it is that no story is ever over.
Robert Penn Warren,
All the King's Men

I
Beirut, March 1948

Since you have decided to leave

Over the years, the annual Pelletier family pilgrimage down the avenue des Français had known many variations, but never before had it taken on the air of a funeral cortège. This year – if one ignored the inconvenient detail that she was still very much alive – it looked as though Madame Pelletier was being conveyed to her final resting place. Her husband, as was his wont, led the procession, his tread all the more solemn since his wife, now lagging far behind, kept pausing to glance at her son Étienne like a dying woman pleading for the coup de grâce. Behind them, Jean, known as Bouboule, being the elder son, walked stiffly while his little wife Geneviève trotted alongside. François, accompanied by Hélène, brought up the rear.

At the front of the cortège, Monsieur Pelletier smiled and greeted the hawkers selling watermelons and cucumbers, waved to the bootblacks; anyone would have thought he was a man heading to his own coronation, which was not far from being the truth.

The "Pelletier pilgrimage" took place on the first Sunday of March, come rain or shine. To the local children, it was an institution. One might miss a neighbour's wedding, the New Year's celebrations, the Paschal Lamb, but to miss the birthday of the soap factory was unthinkable. This year, Monsieur Pelletier had even paid for return tickets from Paris to ensure that François, Jean and his wife would be present.

The ritual consisted of:

Act I: the slow procession to the factory, principally intended for neighbours and acquaintances.

Act II: a tour of the factory that everyone knew like the back of their hand.

Act III: the return, along the avenue des Français, with a stop-off at the Café des Colonnes for an aperitif.

Act IV: the family dinner.

"This way, we're bored senseless four times instead of one," François would say.

Admittedly, at the café on the way home, it was tiresome to be forced to listen to Monsieur Pelletier – since he was standing drinks for everyone – as he reminded the assembled company of the principal chapters of the family saga, an edifying tale that began with the first Pelletier on record (who, it had apparently been proven, had fought alongside Marshal Ney) and concluded with himself and his empire, "Maison Pelletier et Fils", which, in his eyes, was the realisation of a dynasty.

Louis Pelletier was a placid man, one who did not easily lose his sangfroid. Above a finely delineated mouth he had passed on to all his children, the perfectly straight line formed by his little salt-and-pepper moustache, a counterpoint to his silvery locks, was his pride and joy. "Every man in this family is bald by the time he is forty!" he would haughtily proclaim, as though the fact that he was not proved that, in him, the Pelletier line had reached its acme. His narrow shoulders contrasted with his broadening hips. "I could model for Badoit," he would quip, referring to the distinctive bottle whose slender neck grew ever wider as it reached the base. He radiated an energy that was serene and faintly, discreetly smug. True, he had been a success. In the 1920s, he had acquired a modest soap factory which he had developed "by wedding quality craftsmanship to industrial efficacy". He was fond of slogans. In his mind, the factory situated a stone's throw from the place des Canons was destined to become the city's chief industry. Within a few years, the Pelletiers would be to Beirut what the Wedels were to Lorraine, the Michelins to Clermont or the Schneiders to Creusot. Since then, he had somewhat scaled back his claims, though still boasted about being the figurehead of the "flagship of Lebanese industry", something no one had the heart to contest. Over the years, he had never ceased to innovate, adding oils of copra, palm oil and cotton to traditional recipes, refining the drying process, altering the balance of oleic acid, etc.

4

The thirties had proved profitable for the Maison Pelletier, which managed to buy up a number of small soap factories in Tripoli, Aleppo and Damascus. The Pelletier family fortune was doubtless much larger than their relatively modest lifestyle might lead one to suppose.

While the day-to-day running of subsidiaries had been devolved to managers, Louis Pelletier refused to relinquish responsibility for overseeing quality control. Accordingly, he considered it his duty to visit his various businesses, sometimes arriving without warning, taking and analysing samples, making changes to the production process.

He claimed not to enjoy these travels. "I'm a bit of a home-body . . ." he would say apologetically. He sometimes travelled to Paris, where he had some hazy role with the Federation of Overseas War Veterans, but these clearly were of little importance to him, since he channelled all his energy, his talent and his pride into his factory and the quality of "his soap". He was never happier than when surveying the great steaming cauldrons whose temperature was regulated day and night by a team of master soap makers, admiring the tubes that channelled soap paste into the plodders. The very sight of the soap being cut into cakes and bars could bring tears to his eyes. "I'll take over from you for a while," he would suggest to the man at the end of the production line who had not asked for help. And so, as workers looked on, the proprietor of the factory would sit in front of the cutting machine as it turned out bars of green soap and with a judicious blow from a soap mallet – neither too forceful nor too feeble – would stamp each with the seal of Maison Pelletier: a silhouette of the factory flanked on either side by cedar leaves. Madame Pelletier managed the staff, oversaw the deliveries of raw materials and the dispatch of the finished product, and dealt with the accounts. Her husband's domain was the factory floor. It was not unusual for him to get up in the middle of the night and cycle to the factory (he had never learned to drive a car) and take samples which he and the *maître savonnier* would discuss into the early hours.

He insisted that the Maison Pelletier had been born on the day they fired up the first "great cauldron", which he called La Ninon, an allusion, he claimed, to *La Niña*, the first of Christopher Columbus's three ships, whose name, together with the company seal, were engraved on a copper plaque fixed to the base of the tank. When, two years later, her husband named the second vat La Castiglione, Madame Pelletier raised an eyebrow: she could see no connection to the discovery of the Americas. When the third cauldron was installed and christened La Païva, she was completely befuddled, and turned to her son François, who was considered the intellectual of the family, having passed his baccalauréat at a precocious age.

"They are the names of famous courtesans. The first is named after Ninon de L'Enclos, the second after Virginia de Castiglione. The third, La Païva, comes from the name adopted by a *demimondaine* called Esther Lachmann. People used to say 'Qui paie y va' – 'You pay, you play'."

Madame Pelletier's lips formed a perfect O.

"You mean they were . . ."

"Yes, Maman," said François imperturbably, "they were."

"Pish tosh!" protested Monsieur Pelletier when confronted by his wife. "These women were sophisticated courtesans, Angèle. I named the vats after them because they are my darlings, nothing more . . ."

"Whores, that's what they were . . ."

"Well, that too . . . But that was not why I used the names."

Madame Pelletier liked to give the impression that her husband was a philanderer. Perhaps she found it flattering. In reality, Louis had never been unfaithful to her, but publicly she never missed an opportunity to deplore indiscretions that she knew to be completely fictitious. She made much of the fact that, when visiting Paris, he always stayed at the Hôtel de l'Europe. He regularly praised the hospitality of Madame Ducrau, the proprietor whom Madame Pelletier only ever referred to as "my husband's mistress", or, when speaking to her children, "your father's mistress". "Oh, Angèle," Louis invariably objected, "Madame Ducrau must be at least a hundred!", a protestation she would dismiss with a little wave that meant: "A likely story!"

Just now, however, Madame Pelletier had a more pressing concern than her husband's mistresses or the soubriquets of the three great soap vats: surviving.

Nothing, she felt, could be less certain.

They had only just passed the Al-Majidiyyeh Mosque. The factory seemed far beyond her reach.

"Go, Étienne, leave me, I . . ."

She almost said: "I shall die here," but was restrained by some vestige of lucidity and the fear of appearing ridiculous (one so often encountered people one knew). Instead, she merely slowed her pace and dabbed her temples with a kerchief. A sea breeze enfolded the city in the cool embrace of spring; no one, not even she, was perspiring. Even so, hearing the clinking cymbals of a passing street vendor, she gestured to Étienne to stop him and buy a glass of cool tamarind water which she sipped stoically as though it were hemlock. Aside from raising her hat a little and running her fingers over her brow, she had no other way to express her overwhelming exhaustion. She paused once more, one hand on her heart, struggling to catch her breath. Étienne turned and shot Hélène a fatalistic look; there was nothing to be done. The successive departures of her children had been so many nails buried, one by one, in their mother's heart.

"But Angèle, our little ones are all grown-up," argued Monsieur Pelletier. "It is quite normal, surely, that they should leave home."

"They are not leaving home, Louis: they are fleeing!"

Monsieur Pelletier gave up. His wife was gifted with a talent for sophistry whose depths he had never sounded.

"Go, go . . ." wheezed Madame Pelletier, "don't worry on my account."

No longer troubling to reply, Étienne gently squeezed his mother's arm, encouraging her to carry on in spite of her fatigue. One step and then another; eventually they would get there. The task of supporting his mother fell to Étienne because, on this occasion, he was at fault, he was the guilty party.

Previous leave-takings were engraved on the family's memory. When, two years earlier, François had announced his desire to move to Paris and apply to study at the École Normale Supérieure, Madame Pelletier had collapsed in a dead faint on the tiled kitchen floor.

"It's quite remarkable ..." equivocated Doctor Doueiri, who, it should be said, had never treated a complaint more serious than sunburn and bronchitis (a rather obtuse man, alarmed by his patients' health problems, he excelled only when playing belote).

François had had to spend a whole day at his mother's bedside and listen as she railed, even in her sleep, against her ungrateful son and this family she said would be the death of her. "And you say nothing," she chided her husband, "you never say a word."

"All the same, my dear, the École Normale ..." he muttered vaguely, as he quickly straddled his bicycle and headed for the factory.

When Madame Pelletier finally consented to rise from her bed, François had to endure a further ordeal, no less painful than the first, that entailed watching his mother "pack his trunk". "Since you have decided to leave ..." she would mutter a dozen times a day as she gathered, sorted and selected articles of clothing and provisions. Begun with all the ceremony of preparing a wedding trousseau, the process gradually slowed to a crawl. Madame Pelletier obsessed over minor details, roughly set things down, as her anguish gave way to rage. François was no longer a young man whose departure she viewed with sadness, he was a churlish son being shown the door.

In truth, Madame Pelletier was settling an old score with her son. It still stuck in her craw, the letter he had left on the dresser in May 1941 when, at the age of eighteen, he ran away to the camp at Qastinah and enlisted in the First Light Division of Général Legentilhomme's Free French Forces. Curiously, she had better understood this first leave-taking. He had been heading off to war, an honourable venture all things considered, rather than leaving to study when he could just as easily study in Beirut.

"No, Maman," François would explain, "it's just not possible here."

"No, of course not! Beirut isn't good enough for 'monsieur'!"

When François boarded the ship, preceded by two trunks crammed

8

to bursting point, Madame Pelletier had appeared calm and serious. "You will take care of yourself, won't you?" she whispered into his ear. Louis feared that his wife would linger on the quay until the ship completely disappeared but, as soon as it moved away, she took him by the arm and said: "I do hope that he'll write . . ."

She went back to her routine. Little by little, the incident lost its ability to wound. Especially when François passed the entrance exam to the ENS. It was as though the statute of limitations had passed and she was once again proud of her son; she all but claimed the credit for his departure and his success.

It was shortly afterwards that Jean, the eldest, announced that he and his wife were leaving Beirut for Paris. François had barely been gone eighteen months.

"Really? You too?" murmured Angèle.

She took to her bed and refused to see anyone, even Jean.

Doctor Doueiri, muttonheaded as ever, prescribed baking soda footbaths. "Doueiri is an imbecile," thought Louis, a fact already apparent to everyone.

Angèle was not as grieved by Bouboule's departure as she had been by that of François. For months before he left, Jean had been utterly miserable; he tried to stay out of her way, and she understood. If she kept to her room, it was because she did not want him to think she was less upset by his leaving than she had been by his brother's.

While he waited for her to reappear, Monsieur Pelletier stopped off for a Cinzano at the Café des Colonnes on his way home from the factory.

The waiter who spent all day listening to Umm Kulthum proposed a game of backgammon, since there were few customers.

"My word . . ." said Louis.

Questioned about the state of Angèle's health:

"Better, much better . . ." he said. "She'll soon be back on her feet, in spite of Doctor Doueiri."

No one would have refused the services of the doctor, who had become an institution, even if they never knew whether the illness or the doctor would prove more dangerous.

"The man's a fool," said the waiter.

"No, he's a damn fool."

"It's the same thing."

Monsieur Pelletier stopped playing.

"No, it's not at all the same thing. If you explain something to a man three times and he still doesn't understand, he's a fool. But if, at that point, he is confident that he understands it better than you do, you're dealing with a damn fool."

The waiter gave a wry smile.

"Well, in that case, there's no question that Doueiri is a damn fool."

When the game of backgammon finished, Louis drained his Cinzano and sat a moment, brooding. He knew Angèle better than she knew herself and he knew that she would need some pretext to emerge from her room. He went back to the factory, then cycled home with a sheaf of invoices he had just paid. Angèle glanced through them.

"Louis!" she said, scandalised. "Please tell me that you have not paid these!"

"I . . . I shall do my best to recover the cheque before it is sent," he blustered shamefacedly and rushed out of the room.

He returned to the factory ("Hell's teeth," he mumbled as he pedalled, "this had better be an end to it!"), wrote out a cheque, ripped it up, carefully placed the torn scraps in an envelope and left it on his wife's desk.

The following morning, Madame Pelletier returned to work.

Jean and Geneviève sailed two days later. "Take care of yourself . . ." Angèle whispered in Bouboule's ear. As the ship pulled away from the quay, she took Louis's arm and said: "I do hope Geneviève will write . . ."

And now Étienne . . .

Once again Madame Pelletier stopped to catch her breath.

"Indochina! There's a war on over there!"

Étienne had already explained this a thousand times, yes, there was a war, though not exactly, how could he make her understand?

"It's an armed conflict, Maman."

"An armed conflict in which people die is a war."

She blew her nose affectedly and gazed up at him.

Though even with a gun to her head she would not admit it, she had always thought Étienne the most handsome of her three sons. Burning questions scalded the tip of her tongue but, from her slumped shoulders and her vacant stare, it was clear she would not ask them; she already knew the answers.

Indochina, his friend Raymond, the letters that had been arriving for months now ...

When he first invited Raymond to the house, she had said: "I can see why you like him, he's a handsome young man." Oh, if everything in Étienne's life could only be as simple as it was with his mother ... But this was far from being the case. From his schooldays to his work at the bank, he had endured humiliations, overheard insinuations, experienced insults ...

He was a slender lad, his light brown hair almost blond. Smiling eyes and a certain insouciance in his gestures and gait betrayed a sensual, voluptuous character. His talent with numbers had earned him nothing more than an accountancy diploma since he had no professional ambition.

What mattered most to him was love, which was unfortunate. The select social circle in which the Pelletier family moved was too civilised to reject him because of his sexual proclivities, but too bourgeois to accept him without some ulterior motive. And so Étienne felt torn between two worlds, of which his family was a microcosm. The women (his mother, Hélène) worshipped him. The men (François, Jean) loved him, but from a greater distance. This left only his father, his most devoted admirer, who forgave him everything and loved him with an awkward gruffness that expressed a slightly pained helplessness. Étienne was an "ethereal" creature, Angèle could think of no other word. He seemed to float in the air, one could never tell what he might do next. He was an idealist, but had no ideals. Life itself was not enough for him. Which is probably why he has these passions, his mother thought, these tumultuous desires. Sometimes, she would take his face in her hands and ask: "When will you be content with what life has to offer you, Étienne?" and he would laugh and say, "Tomorrow, Maman, cross my heart."

He had met Raymond a year earlier while he was garrisoned near Hadath. They had had a passionate affair that lasted six months. Although Étienne had always been a joyful soul, his mother had never seen him as happy. Then, Raymond was posted to Indochina, where he was to serve out his tour of duty. He was Belgian, and had no desire to return to his native land. Before enlisting in the Legion (for reasons he never disclosed to Étienne), he had been a schoolmaster. "But that's all over," he wrote after a few weeks. "When my tour is over I'd like to stay on here, there are so many opportunities ..." In their letters, they discussed various possible projects, from transport companies to plantations. Before long, Étienne began to look for employment in Indochina, though with few expectations, but then, four weeks later – it was scarcely believable – a letter arrived informing him that his application for a post at the Indochinese Currency Exchange in Saigon had been accepted.

"You'll end up catching yellow fever, that's what will happen."

"Absolutely not, Maman, you know yellow doesn't suit me."

"Go ahead, make fun of me ..."

Monsieur Pelletier had been more encouraging than his wife. He had an excellent working relationship with Lecoq & d'Arneville, a company based in Saigon, and while sales of Savons du Levant in Indochina were modest, they were not insignificant. "Étienne will always have a warm welcome there." Then, when his wife failed to see how a company like Lecoq & d'Arneville could be useful to his son, he added: "It's a fallback plan, Angèle. The French abroad share an esprit de corps. Lecoq is a fine fellow!"

Étienne, pressed to his mother's bosom, chuckled. "After all, Maman, anyone with a name like Lecoq can hardly be a bad Frenchman ..."

*

Weaving its way along the street, the little group, its members now strung out like riders in a *stage* of the Tour de France, finally came to the soap works.

By the time the last laggards had reached the factory door, Monsieur Pelletier – arms outstretched, gripping the handles – was gaily bellowing: "Watch carefully!" as he prepared to throw open the double doors leading to the main workshop. Intoxicated by his own enthusiasm, he hesitated a moment, prolonging a suspense felt only by him. Angèle felt he was making a meal of things. His four children simply waited; they were inured to the ritual.

François was clinging to the wrought-iron railing. His ship had docked only the night before after a two-day crossing during which he had been acutely seasick, and the smell of soap was making his stomach heave.

"If he doesn't hurry up," he whispered to Hélène, "I'll be visiting the vomitorium before we even sit down to lunch."

Hélène stifled a giggle that earned her a black look from her mother.

Monsieur Pelletier glanced over his shoulder, surveying his beloved empire.

"So? Any guesses? Well, here she is!"

"She" was a new vat. The fourth. Made of cast iron. Monsieur Pelletier scuttled over to the small copper plaque affixed to the base: "La Belle Otero".

"Another harlot, I knew it! This isn't a soap factory any more, it's a brothel . . ."

"Maman . . ." warned Étienne.

But Monsieur Pelletier had already moved on to a detailed explanation of the purpose of the new tank, which entailed a complete description of the manufacturing process. The children trailed after him; no one was listening.

Jean could not stop his father from grabbing him by the arm and pulling him aside ("Come take a look, Bouboule, you'll find it fascinating!") before launching into one of his interminable explications.

As he stood on the threshold, Jean felt a rising panic.

His wife, Geneviève, painted and powdered like a marquise, glanced up at the great doorway. "Not a terribly fetching colour, that green, don't you think?"

Jean said nothing. He swallowed hard and stepped inside this place that symbolised his failure.

To have his father lecture him now was a reminder of the torment of his time here, an ordeal that had ended thanks only to an escape without glory or merit.

It had always been ordained that Jean would take over the family business. From the instant he was born, his fate had been sealed: sooner or later "Maison Pelletier" would become "Maison Pelletier & Son". And that son would be he, Bouboule, who had not balked at the prospect. In the small French community of Beirut, it was accepted that a child took over his father's business – ideally, as in a monarchy, the eldest son.

Contrary to common practice, Angèle and Louis Pelletier had never thought of enrolling their children in religious schools, entrusting their sons to the Jesuits and Hélène to the Sisters of Nazareth. They were in favour of the Secular Mission School, where Bouboule had proved a thoroughly lacklustre student. He passed his baccalauréat exams by the skin of his teeth, though this did nothing to undermine his father's confidence in his future as a soap maker. Louis Pelletier believed that the head of a factory was, first and foremost, an industrialist, so he steered Bouboule towards the sciences. To study chemistry. It was at this point that things began to go awry. Jean was not a brilliant student, or even average; he was staunchly mediocre. His father was untroubled by his grades, which were routinely described as "poor" or "inadequate". The lycée was a private school, and the exorbitant nature of the fees and the social standing of the parents (that is to say, the customers), meant that teaching staff were loath to make more brutal (and more realistic) assessments, not that this would have shaken the faith of Monsieur Pelletier. "Book learning is one thing," he would proclaim with unshakeable conviction, "soap making is another." He was convinced that, once Jean left school, and had spent a few months working in the various areas of the production line, he would become an expert in the field.

A cursory glance at Jean was enough to belie his father's faith. He was a chubby, clumsy boy, although he possessed surprising physical strength. He was withdrawn, something of a dreamer, with a tactlessness that owed much to his shyness. Even as a baby he had been pudgy. His father thought he was the spitting image of Ribouldingue, a comic-strip character in *Les Pieds Nickelés*, which Angèle thought was hurtful, but the nickname Bouboule stuck. Since he had no particular passion, and few interests, Jean had resigned himself to following the path marked out for him, but the path had seemed terribly long and littered with disappointment, and this was only a foretaste of what was to come, since, after he was awarded his degree (no one knew how much Monsieur Pelletier paid for it), he suddenly found himself working in the factory where he was expected to become the resident expert.

"I'm not sure it's a good fit for him," Angèle ventured. "I cannot help but wonder whether he really has a technical bent ..." But Louis remained confident. "Once he discovers how this factory really works, he'll grow to love it, how could he not?"

But while Monsieur Pelletier would arrive at the factory at the crack of dawn and lustily breathe in the smell of oil and lye – "the perfume of the trade" – Jean was impervious to the delights of the soap-making process. Consequently, he learned nothing, remembered nothing.

It was 1946.

During the thirties, the Maison Pelletier had successfully exported products to Europe. Savons du Levant quickly established itself as a brand, and there was a constant demand. When the war ended, the factory, which now had a huge workforce, was snowed under with orders. Since its foundation, the factory had been based on the rue de la Marseillaise, on a cramped plot of land opposite the Customs Offices. When an adjacent site became available, Monsieur Pelletier was eager to buy it.

"Are you sure you're not paying too much for the land?"

"It's an investment, Angèle! We'll make our money back in less than two years!"

And so, after Jean had served an apprenticeship lasting only a few weeks, during which he singularly failed to shine in any of the various manufacturing roles, his father entrusted him with the extension, which would be a decisive step in the company's future. The hedges separating the newly acquired land from the soap factory yard were ripped out and plans were drawn up.

Jean was appointed general manager, and immediately found himself out of his depth.

He rarely made bad decisions because he seldom made any decisions at all. He never knew what to do. He pored over plans and elevations, palms sweating, open-mouthed, unable to make sense of the figures or the diagrams. The project manager did as he pleased since Jean never asked questions or made even the slightest demand.

Then came the day when Monsieur Pelletier realised that the new workshops were too small for the equipment they were intended to house, and everything had to be demolished, the foundations enlarged and the workshops rebuilt. This incident was only the first of many: the loading dock turned out to be too shallow, the drying sheds were poorly oriented, making it impossible to take advantage of the wind to speed up the drying process; problem followed upon problem like a string of worry beads. Whenever someone raised a question, Jean would say: "I'll think about it", and never mention the subject again. When some issue became problematic, he would roar: "We'll deal with it later!", masquerading as the man preoccupied with much more important tasks. He would hole up in his office for days on end, wringing his hands, knowing various people were waiting for him to emerge. He would sit, paralysed, for what he considered a decent period of time, then throw open the door, catching everyone unawares, and head down the stairs and to his car, calling to the waiting crowd: "Can't you see I'm in a hurry?" He knew he had to make decisions, but when – miraculously – he managed to understand the problem, he had no possible solution. The trade association pestered him for guidelines. Now and then, facing pressure from all sides, he would democratically solicit opinions, only to abruptly decide on some initiative that invariably proved disastrous. Behind the scenes, his father seemed seriously concerned, but, determined not to give up hope, he would reply to questions with a fervent pride: "You know perfectly well that this is something you need to take up with Monsieur Jean!" Talking among themselves, the long-suffering staff would say: "We have to take it up with *Môssieur* Bouboule."

Jean spent his days trembling and his nights waking up in a panic, throat constricted by terror. He would get up, run to the toilet to vomit. He began to bite the inside of his cheeks until they bled, to slash his forearms with his fingernails, and later a straight razor. He always wore his sleeves buttoned to the wrist, and people assumed that he felt the cold. In the evenings, he would listen to his father talk about his grand ideas for revolutionising domestic laundry; he could not bring himself to hate the man, so turned the hatred on himself. He often wished he might die. At night, he was overwhelmed by the fact that he was incapable of achieving what was expected of him. When he was alone, he would pound his head against the wall. His room overlooked the inner courtyard, while the rooms of his parents and siblings were at the far end of the corridor, so no one would hear. It was a muffled beat, like the piston of some obscure, tenacious engine. He would sit on his bed for hours, slowly banging the back of his skull against the wall, until sleep finally came.

Work on the extension became mired in problems, which in turn affected production. Relations between factory staff and building workers became strained. Steel girders took up space in storerooms reserved for soap oil, while trucks drove round in circles looking for a space to unload their cargo. Several tonnes of perfumed soap contaminated by sawdust carried on the breeze had to be destroyed . . . Faced with the abject incompetence of the man being heralded as their future boss, foremen silently cursed, labourers worried and everyone prayed for their jobs. Increasingly, the company began to struggle. The arrival of "Monsieur Jean" had not simply failed to produce his father's hoped-for "great leap forward", the business had gone from bad to worse, and there was no end in sight.

The situation dragged on for almost a year; a year of worry, torment and fear, which was not helped by Jean's unhappy marriage to Geneviève.

Alone of the postmaster's four daughters, Geneviève was not pretty; her sisters were so ravishing that this accident of genetics mystified one and all. Actually, she was not unattractive, but compared to her sisters, her unremarkable looks made her seem ugly. She had rather coarse features, inexpressive eyes and a rather lumpen physique whose individual components were difficult to distinguish. She was very cheery, and that might have been her salvation. But because she smiled all the time, no matter the situation, her smile was a permanent, frozen rictus intended to please everyone and succeeding only in making them uncomfortable.

Perhaps as reward for her thankless position within her family, she burned with wild ambitions. One day, she would be fabulously wealthy. It was difficult to imagine how she thought this might be achieved before she married Jean, the heir apparent to Maison Pelletier – whom she had always refused to call Bouboule, considering that the vulgarity of the nickname somehow tainted her. She was a post-office clerk working for her father with an intellect limited to the mundane, a little cruel, as designing women often are, yet she had an advantage over the other young ladies in Beirut's French community: she had a certain expertise. Jean was as much a virgin as they came. On their second date, when she laid a hand on his crotch, Bouboule bucked in surprise, then she got on her knees behind a grove of trees and assiduously wrung him dry. Bouboule went home exhausted and defeated.

They were married four months later. Only then did Jean learn – he was the last to know – that Geneviève had something of a reputation. There were few neighbourhood boys her age who had not enjoyed a pleasurable fifteen minutes behind the beech grove with her; many were regular visitors, and all were happy to spread the word.

Since Geneviève's talent was fellatio, when she came to the altar, she was a virgin. Just like Bouboule. From that point, their relationship became complicated. There ensued a series of embarrassing attempts, doubtful penetrations, polite orgasms, such that neither knew quite when they lost their virginity. They remembered only that their sexual relations were difficult, and they became increasingly rare because Geneviève felt that, by failing to take over the family business, her husband had failed to keep his part of the bargain. She still sometimes knelt before Jean, but he doubted that the gesture was intended for him. Geneviève would suck him off with the dispassion of someone leafing through a photograph album. Within a month of their wedding, they had stopped having sex.

This hiatus was one that would last indefinitely.

As a married man, Monsieur Jean proved no more successful at the factory than the bachelor Bouboule. The business continued to crumble. Disruptions to production and deliveries prompted disgruntled customers to threaten to buy elsewhere, while long-standing workers began to talk about quitting. Finally, Madame Pelletier decided to stand up to her husband.

It came as a relief to everyone.

Monsieur Pelletier adopted a pinched expression befitting his new role as a husband whose wife has burdened him with regrettable decisions. He set about resolving the problems but it took him more than a year to get the business back on a sound footing and build the famous extension, which, like a tree that has grown crooked, still retained various structural defects, a reminder to all those who had lived through the black period when Monsieur Jean, the heir apparent, had – for want of a better phrase – been in control. Monsieur Pelletier did not suggest that either Étienne or François "take up the torch", for fear his proposal would be met with an embarrassing rejection. (Hélène was quite another matter, she was a girl.) And so, as he checked the thermometers at the base of the great vats, he took to meditating on the fate of family businesses in general and the future of his business in particular.

A free man, but mortally ashamed, Jean resolved to leave Lebanon: they would move to Paris. Geneviève, though deeply disappointed in her husband, was happy to set off. Her father, the postmaster Monsieur Cholet, assured her that he would invoke bilateral accords and secure her a post in the French civil service, though this would take several months, at best. Which was a godsend, since Geneviève loved doing nothing. Indeed, neither she nor Jean ever imagined that it might be necessary for her to work. Surely any self-respecting husband should be able to provide for his family without forcing his wife to take a job? Moreover, for Geneviève, the thought of doing nothing in Paris was a dream come true. To give the full picture, Bouboule had another reason for leaving the country: two weeks earlier, he had beaten a nineteen-year-old girl to death with a pickaxe handle and he was terrified the police would catch up with him.

With a heavy heart, Monsieur Pelletier found his son a job with Monsieur Couderc, an old friend in Paris. Such was the state of things. The job did not pay very much. Geneviève was bored: without money, life in Paris did not live up to her expectations. Everything she wanted to buy was available only on the black market, and well beyond her means. She who had so loved idleness almost began to dream of securing a position in a Paris post office, of rejoining the social whirl that she bitterly missed now that she was shut up in their apartment. She dreamed of it as a fresh humiliation she could inflict on the second-rate husband who was incapable of earning enough to support them both.

As the date of the "Pelletier pilgrimage" loomed, despite his father sending return tickets for the boat, Jean refused to go back to Beirut, "especially for that idiotic anniversary". He did not say as much, but he was now terrified of the city. But he had not reckoned on Geneviève, who very much wanted to return.

"I want to visit my parents."

"You despise your parents! You've barely written twice in the six months we've been here!"

"Perhaps, but they are still my parents! And then there are my sisters ..."

"You can't abide them either! When your elder sister gave birth and I suggested that we send a gift, you said: 'I hope she dies'!"

"I know, but they're still my sisters ..."

Jean was more surprised than anyone by her determination.

"Regardless, it's out of the question," he said decisively. "We're staying in Paris."

The matter was closed.

Geneviève folded her arms; she had only just begun her siege.

Her greatest weapon was an ability to wreak havoc in everyday matters on a daily basis that shocked Jean. Essentially, it was a sit-down strike. No housekeeping, no shopping, no outings. She did not water the plants, pick up the post or even open the windows. From early morning she would sit enthroned at the head of the table, silent and motionless, dressed to the nines, her makeup perfect, smiling (it was a pose that she adopted so frequently that Étienne had once remarked: "Bouboule should have taken her and one of her sisters, that way he'd have a pair of bookends . . .").

In the morning, Bouboule would make his own coffee. Geneviève would sit, her chubby hands folded on the oilcloth, and watch him bustle about. In the evening, he would find her exactly as he had left her, as though she had not moved all day. The larder was empty. Before long, there was nothing in the apartment.

Worn down, Jean resigned himself to asking his manager for annual leave.

Jean, who did not for an instant believe Geneviève's protestations about seeing her family, quickly realised why she was so intent on making the journey.

They met up with François in Marseille. The brothers stiffly shook hands; they had never had much to say to each other. Geneviève pressed her right cheek then her left against François's, then walked on, eager to get to the quay. When they saw the *Jean-Bart II*, Geneviève's joy turned to jubilation.

Since Monsieur Pelletier had sent them first-class tickets, Geneviève immediately began to behave like a millionairess. Not the sort of rich woman who was impulsive and capricious, no; she was a modest millionairess. All day long, she orchestrated a ballet among the stewards with cries of "Could I trouble you to fetch me a little cocktail, young man? This heat is positively killing me." It took less than three hours for the cabin boys, the chambermaids, the waiters, the cleaning staff and even the deckhands to get the measure of the chubby, cheerful passenger who had them run off their feet with her blithe, benevolent tone. "I'm so sorry to ask,

21

mademoiselle, but would you mind changing the bedlinen? Perspiration, you understand . . ." And she had the trait of the truly rich in that she never offered a tip, never seemed to have any money on her, but let it be understood that she would settle up at the end of the voyage, which elicited a smile from those who knew the routine.

Jean was exasperated, but did not let it show. His wife strolled about the decks, asking crew members to move a steamer chair, to fetch the sunhat she had left in her stateroom – "Oh no, not that one, the other one, if you wouldn't mind, mademoiselle, thank you, you're such a dear, oh, while you're here, could you perhaps . . .?"

On the morning of the second day, she disappeared. Jean reluctantly set out in search of her; no one had seen her.

In the foyer on the first deck, he heard the sound of hurrying footsteps and found her, behind a pillar, her face flushed.

"I've been looking for you . . ."

"Have you?"

She smoothed the front of her dress with one hand while with the thumb and forefinger of the other she stroked the corner of her mouth as though considering some weighty matter.

Jean was dumbstruck.

François, having briefly thought her little charade amusing, quickly began to find the situation painful. Not Geneviève's airs and graces, but noticing the waiters' meaningful looks, the sailors' knowing smiles, the barman offering her cocktails, the chief purser who insisted on showing her the engine room, the officers' quarters, the captain's stateroom. On the last night, when the pasha invited the better classes to his traditional banquet, everyone knew Madame Pelletier; it was she who introduced her husband to the officers and the purser, several of whom she addressed by their first names.

But for the fact that he was so seasick, François would have intervened. As for Bouboule, he paced the length and breadth of the deck, running his hand along the ship's rail and staring out to sea. It was not enough that he had to return to the city where he had been so miserable; even the voyage, it seemed, was destined to be sheer hell. He gripped the railing fiercely, his knuckles white, his face a mask of anguish.

Try as he might, he could not think of a single moment in his life when he had not been an object of ridicule.

François joined him on deck. He had always felt rather distant from Jean, but suddenly felt the need to console, to comfort him.

When they were boys, an unspoken hostility had grown up between the brothers, a hostility that neither of them truly understood; it worsened during their teenage years, culminating in the tragic events surrounding the running of the soap factory, as one brother secretly resented their father's favouritism while the other considered himself unfairly victimised. As the years passed, the rivalry between them faded, only to give way to an awkwardness that made them clumsy and self-conscious. So, when François found his elder brother on deck, he could not say a word, but simply laid a hand on his shoulder. Bouboule immediately turned to him and smiled. "Seagulls must lead a bloody boring life, don't you think?"

*

Jean had been unsettled by his father's insistence on taking him on a private tour of the workshops. The factory was a testament to his failings.

"It's almost midday, Loulou," called Angèle.

"We're coming, we're coming!" roared Monsieur Pelletier from deep inside the hangar.

Louis emerged into the daylight accompanied by Jean looking pale as a church candle and Geneviève, elegant as ever, who burbled inanities, rhapsodising about anything and everything.

As they left, she gripped Jean's arm.

"Your father is marvellous . . . Such an enterprising man! Though it's hardly surprising, everything he does is a success!"

Having used her parents as a pretext to persuade Jean to make the trip home, Geneviève had barely spent two hours with her family, but spent all her time with Monsieur Pelletier, gazing at him in admiration as though she saw him as a surrogate father.

On the return journey, the order of the procession was changed.

The cortège was now led by Madame Pelletier and Étienne, the slowest members, for fear they would be left behind. They were followed by François and Hélène, next came Monsieur Pelletier, who was eagerly responding to Geneviève's incessant questions. Two steps behind came Jean, always the afterthought.

Seeing a police car drive past, he trembled.

He slowed almost to a standstill and held his breath until the car disappeared around a corner of the avenue, then exhaled, though he was still nervous. Up ahead, Hélène and François were engaged in a heated discussion. He could see his little sister was fuming, but she was speaking in a whisper between gritted teeth. François merely walked on, giving a little nod that seemed to say: "Everything will be fine."

"I really can't do it," Hélène was saying. "I swear, it's more than I can bear. If Étienne goes and I'm left with our parents, I'll throw myself out the window."

"Well, do what Bouboule did, get married," said François with a smile. "At least you've got an excuse."

Hélène turned back towards Geneviève and Jean.

"The woman's a complete imbecile. I have no idea what he sees in her."

"I don't think he knows either."

"But seriously, François, what's to become of me?"

"Pass your baccalauréat and you can worry about that later."

Hélène could not help but laugh: this was the dictum their father had drummed into all his children at her age.

"I'll die here . . ."

At eighteen, Hélène was as pretty as her mother had been in her youth; she had the sort of beauty that turned men's heads. She had a particular talent for literature – she was a voracious reader – and for drawing, and was still torn between going to university or to art school.

Whenever her father spoke of Hélène's talents, his mouth would gape like a goldfish for one long breathless moment, then he would say: "Personally, I'm flabbergasted."

A few weeks from now, she would pass the second part of

her baccalauréat "without having to lift a finger" according to Louis. Whether she chose literature or art, she was destined to be a schoolteacher. Together with nursing, it was the only possible profession for a girl.

Hélène did not care one way or another. She did not know what she wanted, but she knew that this life, trapped with her parents, was something she could not bear at any price.

She was sleeping with her maths teacher, Monsieur Lhomond. He would take her to a room at the opulent new Hôtel Kassar; she dreamed of far-flung places, new horizons.

Just ahead of Hélène in the cortège was Étienne, who, though he was five years her senior, she thought of as her twin. She felt a certain admiration for François and great sympathy for Bouboule, but her relationship to Étienne was completely different, it was something like a fusion. The two were inseparable. Even now, it was not unusual for her to sleep in his room; they would tell each other stories and share secrets. And now he was leaving! She did not hold it against him, it was simply that she felt alone, abandoned. The idea that she might join him in Indochina was unthinkable, he had his own life to lead. From the moment they were introduced, she had adored Raymond, a tall, strapping lad with gentle eyes and a graceful poise (whenever she saw Étienne gazing at him devotedly, she would say: "Close your mouth, Étienne, you'll catch flies . . .", which made him laugh) but she knew there was little room for her in their relationship, and she understood. But the thought of staying here, shuttling between her parents and the soap factory, was a prospect she could not imagine.

As though sensing her misery, Étienne turned around. He rolled his eyes to heaven, then nodded to the "queen mother": she was behaving exactly as they had predicted. That morning he had said to Hélène: "I'll be the death of Maman, but not before she serves the meal and does the washing up." He had been right: the homeward journey was taking half the time as the procession to the factory – they would sit down to lunch by one o'clock.

At the Café des Colonnes, the regulars awaited their visit by the pilgrims. The marble-topped tables and the black rattan chairs had been pushed together and, to the joyous clack of billiard balls from the back room, hookahs were brought out, aperitifs ordered for everyone present as they listened once again to Louis recount the legend of the Pelletier family.

Meanwhile, Étienne and his mother headed home, where the exhausted Angèle collapsed into an armchair.

"You'll be the death of me," she said, then abruptly: "Could you go and relight the cooker, please, but don't turn it up too high ... The last thing we need is for the stew to burn."

On the day of the Pelletier pilgrimage, Angèle always served a ragout aux haricots *blancs*.

The vast apartment was peaceful, the windows had been open since morning. Before long, there came the hiss of gas and Étienne strolled back into the living room where the table had been laid before they set off.

"Tell me something, Mamounette," said Étienne, "don't you think La Belle Otero is a little plump these days?"

Angèle smiled. The boy had always been able to make her laugh; he never took anything seriously. And yet she knew, or at least she sensed, how much he had suffered, she had often heard him cry himself to sleep, even as an adult.

Étienne knelt down next to the armchair and laid his head in his mother's lap. Joseph slipped between the two of them. Joseph was a tabby cat, about eight months old with long legs, who looked as though he walked on stilts. He had a head that was more triangular than the usual stray cat ("He's one of the master race," insisted Étienne) and an inscrutable stare. Raymond had rescued him from a building site, and Étienne had inherited him. He and Hélène had fed and pampered him, and at the first opportunity Joseph would curl up next to them.

While Étienne stroked Joseph's fur, Angèle stroked her son's hair.

"I know, I know," she said, "I'm just a foolish old woman ..."

"No, no, Maman, you're not old."

She rapped him on the skull.

"I'm afraid you'll get ill ..."

Étienne lifted his head.

"Oh, that's a foregone conclusion, with all the rice they eat over there, I'm bound to get constipation."

"They eat dog there, apparently."

"You're confusing them with the Chinese."

"No, no, I'm sure they do it in Indochina."

"As long as they don't eat Joseph ..."

He laid his head in her lap again. They had spent many hours in this pose, it was their private space, something that everyone could see yet no one could enter.

"How long is it since you've had word from Raymond?"

It had been exactly eighteen days.

"A week," said Étienne.

Angèle pretended to believe the lie.

"A week is nothing at all."

She could not help but wonder whether her son was making the journey for nothing. What if this Raymond – who seemed like a nice young man – did not want her Étienne? What if he had stopped replying to her son's letters because he had changed his mind? Madame Pelletier vaguely hoped this was true, since it meant her son would come home, but was ashamed of the thought. But her thoughts about his departure were tainted by so many prejudices ... It was said that Indochina was a country of debauchery and fornication, the favourite destination of libertines, failures and degenerates. When it was announced that Étienne would be travelling to a country of lechery and vice in all their forms, Angèle had noticed the sardonic smiles of some of their acquaintances, like the Cholets, who never missed an opportunity to sneer. But she worried that this preconception was shared by some members of her own family, Jean for example, and this filled her with despair.

Finally, the rest of the family arrived back from the café.

Angèle rose from her armchair with some difficulty, brushed aside the offer of help from Hélène and François – "I don't want anyone in my kitchen." It was clear that she was in much better spirits. Geneviève, having quickly touched up her makeup, was the first to take her seat. She sat alone at the dining table as though she had invited the others to a banquet in her honour.

To counteract this impression, Jean went and sat next to her while Monsieur Pelletier fetched bottles of wine. François and Hélène joined them at the table.

The moment had come to propose the toast.

As soon as Madame Pelletier emerged from the kitchen, her husband would get to his feet to raise a glass to the family. Traditionally, the toast was brief and succinct. He had been mulling over possible topics for several weeks, he needed a subject that would bring them together, he drew up a list of ideas, adding some and crossing out others right up to the last minute.

At last Madame Pelletier appeared, removing her apron. Étienne began to applaud, the others joined in and she could not help but smile – though only a faint smile, the circumstances were not propitious to expressing joy.

She took her seat, glancing around the table at each of them, then unfolded her napkin, laid it across her lap, planted her elbows either side of her plate and, since these days she rarely had all the family together, contemplated her children. They all got along well with each other, with the exception of Bouboule. "None of them has ever really understood him . . ." she thought, embarrassed by the feeling that she had fared little better than they. She studied him for a moment. His face was already jowly, though he was not yet thirty. To her as to the others, Bouboule was a mystery, for although they could list the things he disliked (the soap factory, his wife, etc.), none of them could say what he wanted, what he desired, what he expected. She shifted her gaze, quickly passing over that foolish ninny Geneviève to rest on Hélène, her face pressed against Étienne's shoulder, giggling. They were well matched: she was rebellion incarnate; he was insolence. Next to Angèle was François, who spent too much of his life eaten up with worry. While Monsieur Pelletier uncorked the bottle and moved around the table, filling the glasses with the panache of a perfectly trained sommelier, she leaned towards François.

"Did you wash your hands, my darling?"

"Maman, please!" he said, laughing good-naturedly.

Madame Pelletier nodded sceptically. His grubby fingernails and grimy knuckles did not measure up to her idea of a student at the École Normale.

Monsieur Pelletier poured the Château Musar gently, righting the bottle with quick precise gestures so that the last drop did not stain the tablecloth. François gritted his teeth and waited; Hélène looked as though she longed to overturn the table. Étienne was lost in thought. "A week is nothing at all," his mother had said, but eighteen days was something.

*

Usually Raymond would write, even if only briefly, every Sunday and post the letter on Monday. It took ten days to arrive in Beirut. The last letter had been dated 22 February. "We're setting off on a mission tomorrow," it said. The regularity of Raymond's letters was the subject of much amusement in his unit. "My bunkmates tease me: 'Are you writing to your lover-boy?' and I say: 'Yes, but don't get jealous.'" In the Legion, relationships between men, provided they were discreet, were not condemned or punished as one might imagine. There were a few couples in the squadron, everyone knew this, no one said anything. Comradeship won out over morality, because in Indochina, as every soldier was told the day he arrived, no expeditionary force would last more than a few weeks without it.

Despite the agonising pain, it was this thought that allowed Raymond to cling to the hope that someone would come to their rescue.

By now Commandant Lachaume would have marshalled his troops, thought Raymond, the boys would be keyed up and baying for blood. He had heard planes pass overhead, but the dense jungle terrain made reconnaissance impossible. It was the eternal problem: the Việt Minh could build a whole city deep in the jungle that would be invisible to anyone two kilometres away. From the sky, all that could be seen was a dark canopy of foliage so thick that sunlight barely penetrated. And when, by some miracle, they finally tracked down a Việt Minh camp, everyone had fled, the underground tunnels were empty, the shacks deserted. Everyone knew that the Việt Minh would bury themselves in the mud, breathing through a bamboo straw; they could hold their position for hours ...

Obviously, the battalion would have sent out a search party to look for them, thought Raymond, not for the first time. By now, it had probably reached the point where the convoy had been cut off, the spot where, some days earlier, a huge tree trunk had suddenly fallen and blocked the road in front of the truck at the head of the column. No sooner had the trucks stopped than gunfire erupted all around, as though the trees themselves were firing, as though every branch were a gun barrel. Within seconds, the French machine guns returned fire, raking the whole area. With a vicious tug on the steering wheel, Raymond had managed to tip the truck he was driving into the ditch, grab his machine gun and leap out. The soldier in the passenger seat, who had hesitated for a split second, wound up with a bullet in his throat. Now shielded by the body of the truck, Raymond glanced to his right and saw the other drivers who had jumped out onto the verge.

It was a masterful ambush.

The Việt Minh creeping up behind them had nine men in their sights, all lined up behind their trucks.

The battle raging on the far side of the road intensified; the diversion had worked exactly as intended. Within seconds, each driver had a muzzle pressed against his temple, his neck, his back, and had been disarmed. Within three minutes, the Việt Minh had bound their hands and, shoving them with rifle butts, forced them to march into the jungle where they disappeared like pebbles in a pond. The undergrowth was so dense that the roar of gunfire quickly faded and died away. A little further on, the hostages were gagged and forced to kneel. The Việt Minh leader was a thin man of uncertain age. His face was gaunt, his eyes blazed. Each French soldier received a flurry of blows, it was an unambiguous message: don't try anything, we are prepared to be ruthless.

The legionnaires were hauled to their feet and so began the long,

long march. Raymond recognised only three of his comrades; the other soldiers were unknown to him. Directly in front of him was Chabot, who had suffered a wound to his leg, but the Việt Minh had not given him time to fashion a tourniquet or a bandage.

After an hour of staggering through the muggy jungle, tripping over roots, falling and scrabbling to get up before the blows rained down, Raymond was already exhausted. They carried on marching all day, he was streaming with sweat. Far ahead, Chabot's breathing was laboured, he whimpered constantly and from time to time let out a howl of pain. Raymond would recognise the voice, but the screaming never lasted. The Việt Minh at the head of the column were clearly brutal.

As they trudged through a swamp, the young soldier felt leeches cling to his legs. At nightfall, he ripped them off and crushed them underfoot; there were forty of them.

Now, six days later, here they were, their legs shackled, imprisoned in cramped bamboo huts.

In the daytime, the sweltering heat and humidity left them drenched. At night, with no blankets, they curled in a corner of the cabin, shivering against the freezing cold.

Two of his friends were dead; Raymond had seen the Việt Minh drag the corpses away by their feet, their arms tracing ruts in the muddy ground. He had recognised Caporal Vernoux, a likeable fellow, always ready to help. Where had they buried the bodies? At night, he could hear animals growling. Had the bodies been dumped in the underbrush for wild beasts to devour?

Already they were reduced to seven men.

Every day, they were given a single bowl of rice and a rusty can filled with water.

In another hut somewhere to his left, too far for communication to be possible, Raymond could hear Chabot shrieking. His wound had gone untreated and now, burning with fever, he was doubtless watching as his leg became gangrenous. Sometimes Raymond thought he could smell the stench of rotting flesh.

Another captive, Vertbois, a caporal-chef notorious for his "interrogation techniques", was likely praying that the Việt Minh would not recognise him, since, if they did, he would be put through hell. Whenever a Việt Minh soldier was captured, it was Vertbois who conducted the interrogation. Two years in the field had given him time to explore many different approaches, and he had whittled these down to two "techniques": A and B. He would stand in front of the prisoner, look him in the eye and bark: "A or B?" His men knew exactly what to do. "A" meant they hung him from the ceiling by his toes while Vertbois did the honours, beating him with bamboo canes, applying electrodes to his private parts and taking a cudgel to his stomach and his kidneys. "B" meant they had to handcuff the prisoner's wrists behind his back and lay him on his stomach. Vertbois would squat on the back of the prisoner's neck and brutally force his arms upward so the elbows touched the ears, then squeeze his ribs, triggering an involuntary muscle spasm that caused blood to gush from his nose, his mouth, his anus. The Việt Minh called it *lan mé ga* – "guts turned inside out". Raymond, who had never participated in these interrogations, could not even begin to imagine what the Việt Minh would do to Vertbois if they found out who he was. There were rumours that they had once bound a young man to a tree, cut open his stomach and tied his intestines to the tail of a water buffalo before leaving the animal to slowly wander away.

In truth, every one of the prisoners was hoping against hope that the cavalry would come to their rescue.

Twice, they had heard the roar of airplanes somewhere to the north, but it faded after a minute or two.

They all understood the situation. Usually, roadside ambushes were set with the intention of capturing a handful of soldiers in the "colonial army", but this was different. They would not be ransomed in exchange for a few thousand piastres or some American weapons. A week earlier, French soldiers had razed a communist stronghold using flamethrowers while some of the residents were locked in their huts.

In reprisal, the Việt Minh would present their oppressors with an unforgettable spectacle: the maimed and tortured bodies of soldiers of the Expeditionary Force.

It would serve as a visceral example. Raymond's mind swirled with rumours, images and monstrous stories, he was torn between panic and crippling physical pain.

The Việt Minh had flayed lengths of skin from the front and back of his thighs while he screamed in agony. Back in the bamboo hut, with nothing to cauterise the area, the wounds had begun to weep; he too was now in danger of contracting gangrene. The night was filled with the whine of mosquitoes, and the itch from their bites could be soothed only by scratching himself until he bled in areas where his skin had been flayed. The previous night, he had been woken all of a sudden by something crawling over him. It was a luminous millipede about twenty centimetres long, the sort of creepy-crawly that could bite and leave you with a raging fever.

Raymond did his best to identify the positions of the other captured soldiers. The huts were so far apart that it was impossible to call out, to talk to each other. On the first night, from a bamboo cage close by, he heard the Dutchman singing in Flemish, a tune as simple as a nursery rhyme, in a high, clear voice that starkly contrasted with his heavy build. He was a thuggish man who never expressed any feeling. When the Việt Minh guards came and banged on the bars of his cage, he would fall silent, but before long he would start up again, always the same tune, day and night. The guards would go into his cage and beat him senseless, but it was useless: an hour later he would start singing again. He slept in two-hour intervals and could sing the same song twenty, thirty, fifty times a night. The Việt Minh were not the only ones whose nerves were frayed, there were boos and jeers and even insults from the bamboo huts; even Raymond, though exhausted and in agony, joined in the heckling. After three days and three nights, the Việt Minh had had enough. They entered his hut and while two of them restrained his arms and legs, a third strangled him with a rope, winding it tight, as though wringing out a bedsheet. The Dutchman carried on singing as his voice became a ragged gurgle and then petered out completely.

On the sixth day, when Raymond came back from a torture session, bleeding, bruised, gasping for breath, his voice a hoarse whisper from his screams (the Việt Minh had flayed two large strips of skin from his back), he understood how wise the Dutchman had been in choosing to quit the game before he regretted his dogged perseverance.

But Raymond was not ready to leave. He did not easily give up hope. He calculated. The rescue party would have questioned every Việt Minh soldier they knew, and everyone they met along the way; they were bound to pick up some piece of information, and from there, one thing would lead to another ... They were bound to be found, they had marched less than a day from the place where they had been captured, they could not have travelled very far.

As his fever rose, Raymond became delirious, he could no longer tell night from day. He no longer knew whether the groans he could hear were his or those of comrades in the other huts.

Then, for the first time, the Việt Minh took all the prisoners from their cages.

The legionnaires stared vacantly at each other. Each had been subjected to a different torture: the message to their rescuers would be crystal clear. Raymond had been skinned alive, Vertbois had had both hands amputated, Chabot, who was carried on a stretcher made of bamboo and banana leaves, had had every joint in his body broken.

The Việt Minh loaded them into the back of a truck. They longed to talked to each other, but they needed every ounce of strength to steady themselves when the truck went over a pothole or hit the aerial roots of the banyan trees. Raymond spent the whole journey trying to keep Chabot on his stretcher.

Suddenly, there was light. The trucks juddered to an abrupt halt.

A small clearing. On the far side, two water buffalo, their muzzles lowered, were slowly drawing a harrow.

The Việt Minh beat them with rifle butts as they clambered down, then threw them to the ground.

Suddenly, everyone froze and glanced up at the sky.

This time the roar of engines was not far away but almost overhead.

A Morane-Saulnier appeared, the fighter plane nicknamed

the Locust; it was flying very low. Raymond's heart leaped into his throat. It was inconceivable that the pilot would not see the clearing, and the fifty or so men gathered there. The plane banked sharply and flew back over the area.

The French soldiers turned to the Việt Minh in terror. Had they been taken by surprise? And what would they do, now that they knew they had little time, that the Locust had already signalled their position and a paratroop unit would already have been dispatched?

The Việt Minh gazed at the sky, but they seemed neither panicked nor concerned. Almost as if they had been expecting the plane.

As the Morane flew off and the roar of engines began to fade, the little commandant began barking orders.

The Việt Minh converged on the prisoners and, with boots and bayonets, forced them to stand up.

Only two of the men were able to walk unaided. The others were roughly carried by the Việt Minh, with no thought for their wounds.

They came to a row of nine narrow pits, deep enough to hold a man, spaced a few metres apart. Three had already been filled by lifeless bodies that had begun to rot. Raymond recognised the tattoo on the neck of Caporal Vernoux, killed some days earlier, and the body of the Dutchman, the first of the prisoners to die.

With his arms tied behind his back, each prisoner was pushed into a pit. Raymond, being broad-shouldered, did not fall to the bottom so the soldiers beat him down with rifle butts. He felt his collarbone snap. Then two or three of the Việt Minh tossed shovelfuls of earth over the prisoners. Now, only their heads were visible. From a distance, they looked like a row of pumpkins.

The reconnaissance plane reappeared, almost skimming the treetops, but Raymond could not see it for the sweat streaming into his eyes.

Was there a squadron of paratroopers close behind, preparing to jump?

Vertbois started to scream.

35

Looking away from the sky, Raymond was horrified to see the water buffalo slowly shambling towards them.

Overhead, the plane passed again, flying ever lower.

In front of him, the huge beasts dragging the harrow were closing in.

The image that flickered into his mind was of Étienne, who in that instant was smiling up at his mother in Beirut.

Angèle had deigned to raise her glass like the others.

She even smiled, as they did, given the occasion.

Monsieur Pelletier had finally decided on his toast.

He turned to Étienne with a joyous cry:

"To Saigon!"

Everyone raised their glass and echoed:

"To Saigon!"

2

The Exchange issues all authorisations

A month later, Étienne still had no news, and, magnified by time and distance, the phrase "on a mission", which had sounded so routine when he first read Raymond's letter, began to take on sinister, even tragic connotations. Dreams alternated with nightmares. Sometimes, Raymond would join him on a café terrace, his mission accomplished, his army contract at an end. Wearing civilian clothes, he would explain his future plan: a sawmill, a rubber plantation, a rice farm, and Étienne would nod, offer to keep the accounts, and Asia would seem like an earthly paradise. Sometimes the silence would drag out for months until one day someone, a comrade-in-arms, would appear, nervously clutching his white képi, and tell him that Raymond was dead. The soldier, a hazy figure whose features Étienne could barely make out, was always framed against a deep blue that made him seem ghostly.

Étienne had studied a map. According to his letter, Raymond's unit had been heading "towards Hiến Giang, as far as I know". It was somewhere north-west of Saigon. But what was it? A village? A region? It was difficult to tell. The place names on the map all looked alike. Inexplicably, to Étienne's ears, the name Hiến Giang had the grim toll of tragedy.

His terror was as great as his joy at meeting Raymond, a luminous moment that had made up for all the disappointing or sordid encounters he had had since adolescence. Étienne had never been swept along by an all-consuming passion. Love, yes, and certainly desire, but never passion. So the tall Belgian legionnaire, smiling and self-assured, had appeared to him haloed in light.

In the rare moments when he was not panic-stricken by Raymond's unexplained absence, Étienne was haunted by an image suspended in time: a bearded Raymond, wearing a khaki "bush hat", its snap brim held in place by a cord, marching single file through dense jungle. It was a frozen image loaded with silent menace.

What with Joseph mewling in his basket and the other passengers constantly complaining about the cat, Étienne barely slept during the flight.

When the airplane door was opened and Étienne descended the steps to the tarmac, the sweltering humidity of Saigon hit him as though he had stepped into an open-air sauna. Within a few steps, sweat was streaming down his back. Their faces flushed, the women feverishly fluttered fans while the men brandished broad-brimmed hats. Those family members waiting to greet the arriving travellers were gingerly embraced from afar as sweat stains blossomed in every armpit.

Crippled by the heat, the travellers trudged toward their cars, eyeing the huge louring clouds rolling across the pale sky with a mixture of worry and relief.

"Monsieur Pelletier? I'm Maurice Jeantet, director of the Currency Exchange."

He was a tall man in a white linen suit, his face careworn, his hair almost white. Everything about him – his tone, his eyes, even his handshake – exuded a profound weariness. He stared in disbelief at the basket Étienne was carrying.

"What is it?"

"My cat."

Jeantet heaved a sigh of dismay.

"Come on, it's this way ..."

He said it as though eager to be rid of a burden.

"I have to wait for my trunk," said Étienne.

Jeantet shrugged as though this was of no importance. Étienne hurried after him and they jumped into the waiting taxi.

"We'll drop off your luggage on the rue Grivelle, we have an apartment there we offer newcomers. I should warn you, no one has ever stayed there more than a couple of days."

"Why?"

Jeantet flicked his hands as though shooing a fly.

"You'll see for yourself ... My God, that cat of yours stinks."

"It was the long flight ..."

"I'm sure."

Étienne quickly realised that the man's demeanour was marked not by fatigue but by fatalism. Proof, if it were needed, came when, as much out of politeness as curiosity, he expressed surprise that the director had personally come to meet him at the airport.

"Pff, it gets me out of the house. So, where exactly are you from?"

"Beirut."

Jeantet's eyes opened wide as saucers.

"Beirut? Really? Well I never ... You should have told me. No one ever tells me anything."

"It was on my application form."

"I never bother to read the applications. Besides, there's no point, I'm not the one who makes the decisions – can you believe it?"

He seemed to expect a response, but as Étienne struggled to think of something, Jeantet forged on.

"I have fond memories of Beirut."

His eyes misted over as he talked about his military service. One his way to Africa, he had spent a day and a half in Beirut, but his short stay in the city had left an enduring memory, though it was difficult to understand why. "Ah, Beirut, Beirut ..." he dreamily repeated, then, after a brief silence, abruptly asked:

"Is the weather nice there?"

It was a curious question, though one perhaps related to the climactic conditions here in Saigon. Indeed, Jeantet leaned his head out the car window and gazed up at the sky, now black with thunderclouds.

"Mark my words, when they burst ..."

The taxi had just reached what appeared to be the centre of the city when the torrential downpour came.

"What did I tell you?"

For an instant, his face lit up at his accurate prediction, then just as suddenly his expression returned to one of fatalistic desperation.

Fat raindrops hammered on the taxi roof like pebbles, the street had become a wall of water streaked by vertical sheets of rain, the car had slowed to a snail's pace. They could sense rather than see the other cars, blurred shadows that seemed to waltz along the road in water that had risen to their mudguards. Étienne instinctively hunched his shoulders as though fearful the taxi roof would suddenly cave in.

Jeantet nodded grimly at this sorry spectacle.

"This is nothing – just wait until the rainy season, you'll see . . ."

Suddenly he turned to Étienne.

"I have three children."

It was impossible to tell whether this was a boast or a complaint, or even why he had troubled to mention it, since by now he had moved and was issuing orders to the driver in Vietnamese. Perhaps he found it difficult to concentrate.

Before long, the taxi turned off the broad avenues and into what looked like a poorer neighbourhood. It finally came to a halt, coasting towards the pavement like a ship gliding up to the quay. They got out of the car and raced to the building, splashing through puddles a metre wide.

The few steps from car to building had been enough to leave them drenched. Étienne shook himself. Jeantet carelessly swept his hair back with the palm of his hand.

The hall was rather ugly. Beneath the flaking paintwork, the walls were crumbling.

"It's on the second floor."

The large, soulless room was furnished with a wrought-iron bed, a chest of drawers that tilted to the right, and threadbare straw matting on the floor. What was most surprising was the billowing steam that smelled of laundry starch and washing powder that drifted through the half-open window.

"You can't say I didn't warn you . . ."

Jeantet shook his head as though faced with some new calamity.

"I have no budget. This is all they'll give me."

He nodded to the window.

"That's from the laundry down in the courtyard. Steam rises, there's nothing you can do about it. Except close all the windows, but then you'd suffocate . . ."

Étienne put down the basket and opened it. Joseph, who looked as though he had lost at least a kilo, scurried out and hid. Étienne found a small bowl, filled it with water and what little dry cat food he had, bent down and set it on the floor next to the sink.

As he stood up again, he heard loud voices from the stairwell, and a series of dull thuds echoed along the landing. Moments later, two men appeared awkwardly carrying his trunk, bashing it against the banisters, the landing walls, the doors. Both had broad smiles. Drawing themselves up to their full height, they dropped the trunk on the floor, satisfied with their mission, and stood as if at attention, staring confidently at Étienne. He fumbled in his pocket for change, found none, and was about to apologise when Jeantet unleashed a torrent of abuse on the porters, who raced out onto the landing and hurtled down the stairs.

"They've already been paid," he said, "but they always want more . . ."

"By the Exchange?

Jeantet said nothing.

"Right, we'll pay for the first two nights, I'll be surprised if you decided to stay longer than that. I'll ask Diêm to find you somewhere else."

With that, as though seized by a fugitive impulse, Jeantet turned on his heel and left, giving a small impatient wave. Étienne rushed to follow him, locking the door behind him. The director plodded down the stairs muttering: "Putting a bloody apartment above a laundry, have you ever heard the like . . .?"

By the time they reached the street, the clouds had cleared and the late afternoon sunshine cast long shadows across the street. Étienne was overcome by the smell of damp earth, spices, grilled meat and herbs; the sky had cleared and the city felt cool after the downpour. They got into the waiting taxi. There was a grinding of gears.

They headed back to the city centre, the tall, ostentatious buildings, the broad pavements teeming with people, the impossible chaos of cars, bicycles and cycle rickshaws through which Vietnamese and European pedestrians weaved their way. The taxi pulled up in front of an office building. Next to the door, a bronze plaque read "Indochinese Currency Exchange".

Jeantet made no move to get out of the taxi.

"Right, this is it . . ."

It was as though he were the new recruit arriving for the first time and getting cold feet. Étienne did not know what to do.

"I've asked Gaston to show you around," Jeantet said, then, realising Étienne had no idea who he was talking about, he added wearily: "Gaston Paumelle!", and as he opened the car door, he muttered to himself: "I've got more than enough on my plate."

Étienne got out and trotted after the director, who strode purposefully into the building.

They stepped into a vast banking hall with a long counter behind which a dozen European clerks were hard at work. Their echoing conversations created a permanent background hum, peppered with the occasional strident exclamation. "But yesterday you said . . ." protested one. "No, no, that's a *pro forma* invoice!" said another.

On the other side of the counter, the thirty or so chairs were occupied by men in suits, elegantly made-up women, Indochinese men in tortoiseshell glasses, Vietnamese shopkeepers, matrons in long silk dresses, each of them clutching the yellow ticket that had been handed to them by a plump elderly porter at the door. Some distance behind the line of tellers there were more desks groaning under the weight of documents, clerks buried under paperwork, and, sitting opposite them, those customers who were permitted to enter the *sanctum sanctorum*.

"Come on, come on!"

The director looked permanently infuriated; everyone simply had to put up with it.

He led Étienne into his office piled high with files and folders and, on his desk, an extraordinary number of photo frames, all turned such that, to the visitor, they presented only an array of doggedly impersonal backs.

Étienne remained standing while Jeantet went around and settled himself in his executive chair. Étienne's personnel file lay on the desk. He opened it, and put on his glasses.

"Franco-Lebanese Bank, excellent, excellent ... Legal department ... Excellent."

He closed the file, leaned forward, picked up a small frame and turned it towards Étienne.

"Itsou."

It was a photograph of a German shepherd.

"Died last year. The weather, obviously ... Right, I need someone in the transfers department, that's where you'll be working. Now, here's Gaston ... He's the one who'll ... Well, you get the picture ..."

*

Paradoxically, although Étienne was now in Indochina, he was so completely caught up in the upheaval of his arrival that Raymond seemed further away than ever. Everything seemed to push them further apart: the plane journey, the director, the apartment that reeked of turpentine, this shimmering city, the aromas and the lassitude that once again overcame him now that the rain had passed.

To say nothing of the young man with the big nose, who was putting on airs.

Gaston Paumelle was the same age as Étienne, but he wore it very differently, with gaudy shirts, a matching pocket square, a chunky signet ring on the little finger of his right hand. Gaston was about thirty, a smug, self-confident young man with just a touch of the maverick, the sort of guy that always goes for the least obvious solution.

As soon as he came in, he put an arm around Étienne's shoulders and leaned close, as though to confide a secret.

"We're on first-name terms, right? I mean, we're co-workers ..."

Taking his colleague's response as read, he took Étienne by the arm, as though he were an old friend he was thrilled to see again, and whispered in a sultry tone:

"Let's take a tour of the castle, then I'll show you your private apartments!"

He let out a loud, staccato laugh. The joke, which had clearly been made a hundred times, still tickled him.

"So, where are you from?"

"Beirut."

Seeing Gaston's bewildered look, he added: "In Lebanon."

"Ah, with the ragheads ... So, who pulled strings to get you a job here?"

It had never occurred to Étienne that a position in this obscure exchange was so coveted that it required influential connections.

"Sheer luck. I've got no contacts."

Gaston screwed up his eyes and his mouth. In his world there were only contacts, vested interests, services, debts and trade-offs; luck did not enter into it. He lit a cigarette and muttered, "Have it your way ..."

"No, it's true," said Étienne.

Gaston studied his new colleague for a moment and realised he was being sincere; this information was quite unsettling.

"This way," he said as they came to a broad stone staircase that served three floors of vast, identical, high-ceilinged offices with tall sash windows left open in the hope of encouraging a breeze, and ceiling fans that, when not broken, whirled incessantly.

"This is the currency exchange ..."

"Can I change my French francs for piastres?"

Gaston spread his hands, palms up, like an apostle.

Étienne took a few thousand-franc notes from his wallet and together they approached a counter where a short-sighted woman all but merged into the background.

"This is Étienne Pelletier, a new colleague," said Gaston in a stentorian voice.

The woman nodded and screwed up her eyes. Étienne tendered the banknotes, which she slowly counted. Meticulously, she lined the bills up along the counter. He could not tell whether it was his new surroundings, the muggy weather, or the eccentric manager who had not given him time to catch his breath, but Étienne felt a sudden wave of exhaustion. He asked directions to the toilets, splashed cold water on his face, looked at himself in the mirror and found the reflection unprepossessing.

The thick walls of the building and the way it was oriented doubtless explained why the air was less stifling here than outside, but it was pervaded by the smell of sweat, lustred-cotton sleeve protectors, ink, files, old paper and obsolescence.

The staff comprised some sixty men and a handful of women seated behind tables and desks, surrounded by vertiginous stacks of files that, by some miracle, managed to stay upright. At the Exchange, a mislaid document was considered a write-off. Étienne followed Gaston on his tour, shaking hands, smiling, and now and then answering questions that were not really questions only to immediately forget the names, responsibilities and the roles of the people to whom he had been introduced. To him, the Exchange looked like a teeming anthill that was entirely devoted to some futile, fastidious and opaque activity.

They went up to the top floor and stepped into the archive room, a dusty furnace where a wizened old Vietnamese woman wearing a curious blue plastic visor was silently wandering around.

"That's Annie," whispered Gaston, giggling to himself. "So, Annie, when are you planning to retire?"

"Fuck off," muttered the archivist, turning her back.

"She's leaving this autumn," Gaston said as they went back downstairs. "I think she's spent forty years in various departments of the French civil service, always as an archivist. Unbelievable, isn't it?"

Étienne did not see what was so unbelievable about this fact. Gaston jerked his chin as if to say, "Well, *I* get it." Perhaps the director's eccentric tics rubbed off on his employees over time.

"And this is the clearing house . . ."

Again, Étienne felt as though he might faint. He had just stepped into a new world and his head was spinning.

"Are you feeling all right?" asked the young man with the big nose.

He bent his razor-sharp face towards Étienne, who was leaning

45

against a table and dabbing sweat from his forehead with an already sodden handkerchief.

Étienne forced a smile. "I'm fine, I'm fine … It's just the long journey …"

"Come on," he said to himself. "Chin up."

Gaston glanced at his watch.

"Anyway, it's almost clocking-off time …"

They headed back downstairs. It was clearly closing time: the clerks were slipping on their jackets and placing signs marked CLOSED over their windows, while the twenty or so customers who had not been served calmly headed for the door, both parties knowing that they would be back at opening time the following day to take their place in the queue.

"So, tell me, old man, what are your plans for tonight?"

Étienne struggled to think of some excuse, but he was so befuddled that nothing came.

"Well, then, let's have dinner together! We can meet up at Le Rocher du Dragon. Just ask around, everyone knows it. And then" – he winked – "a little surprise. You'll enjoy it."

Étienne did not have time to respond. The clerks were all rushing for the exit, babbling in French and Vietnamese. Gaston donned his straw hat at a rakish angle intended to stress his elegance.

"Can you find your way back, old man?"

Étienne waved and smiled faintly – "I'll be fine" – and Gaston walked away with a skip in his step leaving him alone on the broad pavement.

All around, the city reeled and whirled, cycle rickshaws hurtled along the road, hulking multicoloured streetcars honked their horns, a snatch of accordion music was instantly drowned out by the roar of engines and the cries of street hawkers. It had obviously rained while he was making his tour of the Exchange. The streets and the pavements were slick and gleaming. Many pedestrians had not troubled to take off their raincoats and the carnival of bright colours revolved like a kaleidoscope. It was a constant spectacle. Hardware stalls. Street hawkers selling steaming cups of soup, shiso fritters and individual cigarettes. Somewhere further down the avenue, a car tyre burst, a crowd quickly gathered, and by the time Étienne wandered away, he could already hear the wail of ambulance sirens.

Aimlessly, he turned right, scanning the crowds for a European face. He asked directions from a man in his sixties, who was walking slowly, supported by a heavy bamboo cane.

"The best way would be to go up rue Mac-Mahon. It's up there on your left."

The man had a Marseille accent. So Étienne followed the direction indicated by the walking stick. His clothes were damp and clinging to his body. He felt the heavy key to the apartment jingle in his pocket as he walked. The elderly man had added: "It's a fair distance on foot . . ."

A little further on, he came to a clutch of cycle rickshaws parked haphazardly by the pavement. The drivers were smoking cigarettes and laughing.

"Do you speak French?" asked Étienne.

Four of them pressed around him. He pointed to one at random.

"Do you know where the High Commission is?"

"Yes, yes, Palais Norodom!"

He had already hopped onto the saddle. Étienne squeezed into the buggy and watched the city flash past as heavy grey clouds rolled in.

Ten minutes later, the driver dropped him off in front of the building that was the seat of the French colonial administration and the headquarters of the Expeditionary Force, and demanded an astronomical fare which Étienne divided by three. The rickshaw driver smiled happily.

Through the closed gates, Étienne could see the facade with its wide arches, a Corinthian pediment and a heavy, bluish cupola. Outside the gate, the only sentry box was empty, there was no one he could question.

The cloudburst came without warning, fat raindrops hammered on the pavement and the High Commission vanished behind vertical curtains of rain.

Étienne did not make the slightest movement; he stood ramrod straight on the pavement, like a lamp post. Without Raymond, he felt terrifyingly alone.

The rainstorm washed away the tears streaming down his cheeks.

*

Le Mah-Jong owed its prestige to its incongruity. Its clientele was the Saigon bourgeoisie, French couples who fell into each other's arms; the women wore necklaces, earrings, silk shawls, flourished old-fashioned fans and roared with laughter, the men in rumpled linen suits draped arms around their shoulders and smoked cigarettes down to the cardboard filters, while everyone drank martinis or brandy and soda and talked too loudly. There was a band composed of two accordions, and a singer in a lamé dress. Men wandered in in twos and threes with the elegant indifference of friends who had ventured in by chance to have one for the road. Standing at the bar, the Vietnamese "taxi girls" surveyed the room and whispered in low voices. One might almost mistake it for a bar in Paris.

But, from another point of view, it was a very different matter.

The girls sitting at the tightly packed tables by the coat room were there to perform a dance of a very different kind.

There were always five or six of them, Vietnamese girls in short tunics that rode up scandalously when they sat facing the room, haughty Chinese women wearing dresses slit to their thighs who observed the world with a condescending sneer. It was an intricately choreographed dance between the men who approached the coat check, a cigarette dangling from their lips, with the disinterested air of someone looking for information, and the young Vietnamese girls who agreed to join them for a drink, exchanging stifled schoolgirl giggles. Or the supercilious strut of a Chinese woman followed by a man whose jacket bulged at the waist with rolls of fat. This silent, codified, deceptively discreet two-step was the real draw, the reason people came to the Mah-Jong. It was evident from the affected laughter of the society ladies that they got a delightful thrill from being in this den of vice. Their fans were ineffectual at dispelling the miasma of cigar and cigarette smoke that made the club look like an aquarium. A small lamp on each of the round tables emphasised the air of intimacy.

Gaston had led Étienne to a strategically placed table that offered an unobstructed view of the coat check and the young women waiting there.

Étienne had spent the earlier part of the evening waiting for the moment when he could steer the conversation to Raymond, the only subject that mattered to him. Now, seeing Gaston leer at the girls, he realised that it was unlikely that he would be able to glean any information about troop movements.

*

He had fared little better earlier in the evening at the Rocher du Dragon ("Everyone knows the place!" said Gaston), a noisy restaurant where the flurry of diners were constantly coming and going, calling to one another, sitting down only to stand up again. It was difficult to tell who exactly was doing the serving, since everyone who passed seemed to be carrying a dish or a plate, while money was passed from hand to hand until it reached a sweaty-faced man in a grubby kitchen apron where it disappeared under his pot belly. Without troubling to consult Étienne, Gaston had given their order to the harried woman still wiping down their table. She melted into the crowd and reappeared some minutes later with plates piled high with foods Étienne had never seen, and a spirit stove on which she placed a pan of boiling oil, a dish of Peking duck, crispy noodles, pineapples, mangoes . . . Everything was delicious and, for the first time since he arrived, Étienne experienced a moment of pure happiness, one that was instantly spoiled by the thought that Raymond would have loved it here, that this was exactly the sort of place Étienne had dreamed of when he imagined their reunion in Saigon. Instead, he was sitting opposite Gaston Paumelle, who poked his big nose into the pan and licked his fingers one by one, playing the big man because he knew two or three things Étienne had not yet learned.

Étienne thought about his co-worker's incredulity when he told him that no one had pulled strings for him to get the position.

"What about you?" he ventured. "Where are you from?"

Whenever the opportunity arose for him to talk about himself, Gaston would take a deep breath, as though he did not like the idea, and did so only to please.

"My grandfather lived here all his life. You've heard of the Paumelle plantations?"

He did not pause, since the answer was self-evident.

"Mine was one of the families that built this country. When they first arrived – I'm talking, oh, a long, long time ago – the gooks didn't know how to do anything. Even rice-growing was small-time ... My grandfather used to say: 'The gooks need to be told what to do and then shown how to do it.' Where was I?"

"How you got this job ..."

"Oh yes, my father. He's high up in the Ministry of Transport back in France. So, easy for him to get me a position with the Exchange ... And besides ..."

He dropped his voice to a whisper and flashed Étienne a conspiratorial smile.

"There was this girl. In a delicate condition ... I thought, better to get the hell out, you get the picture ...?"

Étienne got the picture.

"And, well, coming to Vietnam ... It was like taking up the family torch."

"Monsieur Jeantet is a queer fish," Étienne said, casting around for a topic of conversation.

"Oh, he's a decent guy ... Not very resourceful, but a decent guy."

He talked about the director as though he were an underling.

"He doesn't seem to like it here very much," Étienne said.

"He's been running the Exchange for so long it's hardly surprising he's a little tired. But what can you do? Now his wife, on the other hand, she loves it here."

Gaston was wolfing down vast quantities of noodles, but at the mention of the director's wife, he paused.

"Twenty years his junior and still a hell of a looker, let me tell you."

He gazed dreamily, chopsticks suspended in mid-air. If the director's wife herself had walked into the restaurant, he would not have noticed. At length, he shook himself.

"They've got three children, do you understand?"

Étienne wondered what there was to understand.

"They're all grown-up now. So, she's free as a bird."

He winked.

"Always off in Tam Đảo or Bokor, if you know what I mean . . ."

"Um, I don't, no."

"Mountain resorts. Pine trees, waterfalls, that sort of thing, says it reminds her of the Alps. She's from Combloux. But personally, I think there's something more to it . . ."

Absent-mindedly, he ran his tongue over his lips, then looked down at his plate. Since this seemed to be the end of the subject, Étienne seized the opportunity.

"I have a cousin who's a legionnaire here in Saigon . . ."

Since Étienne was no longer hungry, Gaston helped himself directly from the serving dishes, determined there would be no leftovers. He was not fat, but he could put away a phenomenal amount of food. He seized the last helping of noodles, wiped his lips on the corner of the tablecloth, then leaned back in his chair.

"But it's strange . . ." Étienne said.

"What's strange?"

"His last letter came more than a month ago, and we've had no news since."

"Maybe he doesn't like writing letters . . ."

Étienne did not have time to answer before Gaston patted his stomach, leaned over the table and said in hushed tones:

"Now for that surprise I mentioned! You're going to love it . . ."

And he got to his feet.

*

Now here they were at Le Mah-Jong. Gaston's "surprise" involved joining the droves of men who came to ogle the women, dance with the taxi girls and leave with a prostitute.

From the moment he stepped into the Mah-Jong, Gaston, who had appeared supercilious and aloof as he confidently commented on everything and anything, was a changed man. He became a feverish, restless soul whose whole life was focused on a single goal and now he faced the litmus test. He leered at the girls with embarrassing eagerness.

"They charge from three hundred piastres to almost a thousand."

His eyes were constantly drawn back to the coat check, where a couple of young Vietnamese girls were in passionate embrace, giving the impression of a saucy lesbian couple that nobody, of course, believed.

"Those two there," said Gaston, leaning close, "you could have them – both of them – for a thousand piastres. What do you say?"

"Maybe not tonight," Étienne ventured. "I'm tired from the journey . . ."

Gaston stared at him. For the second time, he had proved a disappointing companion. But the powerful attraction of the girls still captivated him.

"Here in Indochina, they're not sluts like they are back in France," he whispered without looking at Étienne. "But pick the right one, and you can do anything with her, so it's much the same. The Chinese women are the most expensive . . . The one on the right in the yellow dress charges eight hundred piastres. To be honest, going with Chinese women is money down the drain. They've no finesse, no desire, they're just lazy . . ."

As a waitress appeared and set down their brandies and soda, Gaston leaned back in his chair, like a member of the landed gentry.

"Since I got here, I've fucked the most beautiful whores in Saigon, and there are new girls arriving all the time. I've got an eye for them. That one on the left, with her blouse open to her belly button, I'll bet you anything . . ."

Étienne was no longer listening. He studied his companion, the signet ring, the watch, the elegant suit . . . These things seemed inconsistent with his modest salary as a clerk at the Exchange.

"You not drinking?"

"No, I am, I am . . ." Étienne raised his glass and smiled. "Thank you for the surprise."

Gaston felt flattered, and the newcomer once again rose in his esteem.

"But even if I wasn't completely exhausted, these girls are too rich for my budget," Étienne said.

"I can advance you some money, my friend. If you're resourceful, you'll be able to pay me back in no time . . ."

This was the second time he had used the word "resourceful".

"How do you mean?"

Gaston was staring at two new girls who had just appeared.

"Just watch what the others do and follow their lead. Take me, for example . . ."

In himself, he had found the only subject of conversation more interesting than Vietnamese prostitutes. He flashed his signet ring.

"Take a look at this ring . . ."

"Very impressive . . ."

"Every time I make ten thousand francs, I trade it in for a bigger one. That way, when I go back to France, I can travel light, you get the picture?"

Étienne's starting salary at the Exchange was fifteen thousand francs a year. Even if Gaston had been here a year or two, and in a better-paid position, he was unlikely to be earning much more.

"Hey!" Gaston exclaimed, as though Étienne had accused him of something. "All the clerks make margins on transfers, I'm not the only one."

He chuckled. This new boy hadn't a clue; well, Gaston would put him right. To him, the prospect was as exciting as taking a virgin to the brothel. He smirked in anticipation.

"So, a piastre is worth eight francs. But in 1945, the French government decided that it was no longer worth eight francs but . . . seventeen! So if you order something – anything – from France, the piastre you use to buy it from Paris is worth double! The French government makes up the difference. Send a hundred thousand francs' worth of piastres to France, it's worth two hundred thousand. A million francs is worth two million. Ten million becomes twenty million. There's no place else on earth where you can double your fortune – regardless of the amount – in a week."

"But who requests the transfers?"

"Civil servants, private individuals, compradors . . ."

Étienne had already come across this word. A comprador was a local intermediary who acted as a representative for foreign companies in their dealings with local people or the Indochinese administration.

"But it can't be that simple!" said Étienne. "These transfers can't be done automatically, there are rules, aren't there?"

Gaston coyly lowered his eyes, as though he had just had a proposal of marriage.

"Yes indeed! In order to receive a transfer, you need an authorisation issued in due form!"

He waited expectantly for Étienne's question, his whole body taut with excitement; this was probably how he looked at the moment of orgasm. Étienne relented.

"So, who authorises the transfers?"

Gaston nonchalantly twisted the signet ring around his little finger as he gazed at the prostitutes strutting around the coat check.

"The Indochinese Currency Exchange, my friend. The Exchange issues all authorisations."

3

It smelled of newspaper

By the end of his shift, François longed only to lower his arms, to let his hands drop like stones. His shoulders and elbows ached, his back was stiff, his legs unsteady. The last bundles glided by more slowly, the infernal racket of the rotary presses gradually faded, a train pulling into a station. When everything had finally juddered to a halt, it was incredible, a tremulous silence fell over everything. At first, no one would say a word, they would look down at their hands, black as those of a coal miner, then shake their heads. But no sooner did one shift end here than another began. As soon as the presses fell silent, the maintenance crew arrived, fresh as daisies, elbowing the print staff out of the way, setting their oilcans on the ground with a clang and prying them open so that the air was filled with petrol fumes as they soaked their oily rags. Now that the air no longer clattered with the deafening roar of the printing presses, some echoes of normal life began to return, people called to each other, they laughed and joked. François stared at the last bundles of newspapers he had strapped onto the trolley now being pushed towards the lift that led up to the loading bay where the trucks would already be waiting, engines idling, accelerators twitching, the drivers eager to be off, none of them wanting to be the last out. It made them feel as though they were already running late when they hadn't even started their round ...

It was 7 a.m. The third edition of *Le Populaire* was hot off the presses.

François went to wash his hands and his forearms. He could never quite get them clean, printing ink embedded itself in every wrinkle, under every nail, he could not get rid of it, even with a pumice stone. "Have you washed your hands, François?" His mother's comment two weeks earlier was still ringing in his head. He could still see that disbelieving look, those eyes round as a chicken's, gazing worriedly into the middle distance. And he had always found her habit of insinuating something without actually saying it exasperating.

He was furious with his mother since she was chiefly responsible for the situation in which he now found himself.

In her classification of discreditable professions and disreputable jobs, Madame Pelletier ranked journalists alongside prostitutes and car mechanics. This stemmed from a story as old as it was preposterous: Monsieur Chamoun had almost run her over while she was pregnant. Monsieur Chamoun was editor and claimed to be a journalist at *L'Orient*, the largest daily newspaper in Beirut. The incident might have gone unremarked had he not just emerged from a café reeking of alcohol. True to her reputation for gross generalisations, Madame Pelletier never questioned her conviction that journalism was the profession of the alcoholic.

Tragically, journalism was the only profession to which François felt suited. He had discovered his passion for reading while poring over copies of *L'Orient* that his father brought home every evening. He was amazed that articles about events that had taken place in his own neighbourhood, practically on his own street, were printed and distributed throughout the whole city, indeed the whole country. One evening, after a minor local fire François had not even noticed, he was astonished to see a photograph of their apartment building in the newspaper. In the sports section he found accounts of bicycle races and boxing matches that people talked about at school. Monsieur Pelletier had even cut out and framed a 1937 article about the soap factory, but his wife would only allow him to hang it in a dark corner of the corridor, because it had been written by that drunkard Chamoun. At home, *L'Orient* was considered a shameful institution. François secretly began reading the daily soap opera, "Tender Corinne", every evening and finishing the crossword puzzle over which his father invariably fell asleep.

When it came to choosing what to study at university, François made a few vague mentions of journalism, but quickly realised it was futile. He cast around for a subject his parents would support, and his suggestion of becoming a teacher was met with approval. "Handing on knowledge is a fine mission," said Monsieur Pelletier. "Yes," said his wife, "you'd be a state employee, that's good."

Being a brilliant student, François was determined to study at the École Normale Supérieure, since there was no equivalent in Beirut. His tactical argument had earned him a ticket to Paris. In the second year of his baccalauréat, he travelled to sit the entrance exam, but, instead, simply gleaned information about the exams from former students, which made it possible for him to write in his letters home about the difficulties he was supposedly facing. His father, who had already begun boasting to regulars at the Café des Colonnes that his son was about to bring unparalleled fame to the Pelletier dynasty, demanded to know all the details. François, who had only the vaguest idea of the requirements of the entrance exam, which he had not even registered to sit, was embarrassed by the protracted lies he told in his letters, but told himself that, in a way, it was journalistic training.

Three weeks later, he sent his parents an excited telegram to say that he had been admitted to the hallowed ranks. An exultant Louis bought a round of drinks at the Café des Colonnes.

That done, François decided he had four years in which to become a prominent journalist, ideally a famous columnist. If he could do this, his parents would be amused by his duplicity, and the story would feed into the family legend endlessly chronicled by his father.

Eighteen months later, things seemed rather different, since he had applied to every daily newspaper in Paris (and a number of magazines) only to be rejected. The sole exception was *Le Populaire*, where he had made the most of a misunderstanding and got a job as a "receiver". He spent his nights stacking newspapers, bundling them up and loading them onto trolleys. Lectures at Normale Sup would probably have been less grimy.

François took the lift upstairs and stood on the pavement, lit a cigarette, and shook hands with friends eager to get home. From

57

his pocket, he took a crumpled note left for him by his concierge, Madame Moreau, known to everyone as Léontine – a regular chatterbox, if you bumped into her, it was impossible to know when you might get away. She had left the note on his doormat and François had found it shortly before midnight, as he was heading off to work. He recognised Gilbert's handwriting: *Can you come and see me after your shift?* He glanced at his watch. Gilbert would not finish until ten o'clock, so François had plenty of time to get to Rambuteau.

The métro was crowded with gloomy faces. When François had first arrived, in September 1946, Paris had seemed to him a grey, worn-out city. The jubilation that had followed the Liberation, a heady mixture of optimism and enthusiasm, had collapsed like a soufflé. Paris looked haggard and old. In the face of deprivation, rationing, transport problems, unemployment, insecure housing and even destitution, the joy of victory had given way to fear, expediency, to the ducking and diving people had known in wartime. François could see the thought etched on people's faces: "What was the point of living through the Occupation for this?" His time in Paris had been marked by strikes; even the police were on strike. And 1947 was a hundred times worse than the year before. Overnight, the price of bread soared from seven francs to eleven and a half, and the bread itself was inedible, indigestible, as yellow as Monsieur Truman's corn. Inflation was expected to hit forty per cent. His trousers sagged at the knees, he hid his patched and darned shirt under a jacket that was missing two buttons, but, looking around, he saw that everyone was in the same boat. Girls did their best to look pretty, but their clothes looked like they had been bought in the sticks a decade earlier. To make matters worse, a bitterly cold winter had been followed by a sweltering summer heatwave. Meanwhile, Renault workers had gone on strike, daily bread rations had been reduced from 300 grams to 250, then 200; petrol pump attendants had walked out, joining railway workers, refuse collectors and civil servants on the picket lines; public transport ground to a halt in October, just before the teachers' strike. French society was constantly on edge, and mass hysteria broke out in December when the derailment of the Paris–Lille train was blamed on union saboteurs. It was now 1948, but things were not improving. The devaluation of the franc by forty-five per cent exacerbated poor living conditions; when the miners went on strike, the government, claiming it was a communist plot, sent in the army. When he first arrived, François had vowed not to touch the twelve thousand francs his parents sent him every month so that, sooner or later, he could pay them back, but the soaring cost of living and his paltry salary forced him to break his vow. Try as he might to curtail his spending, he kept eating into his savings, it was the only way to survive.

François headed down towards Rambuteau and, as every day, strode confidently into the offices of *Le Journal du soir*, where everyone assumed he was on the staff. It was a vast building on the rue Quincampoix, the former headquarters of various collaborationist newspapers which the new owner, Adrien Denissov, had set his sights on during the chaotic first days that followed the Liberation, because it had modern linotype machines and rotary presses. Joining forces with two other Resistance newspapers, he occupied the building. It was little short of squatting. Under his aegis, *Le Journal*, a venerable Parisian newspaper of no interest to anyone, was transformed in a matter of weeks, with a new layout and a new editorial direction. By the time the public authorities became aware that the offices of *Le Journal* were being illegally occupied, it was too late, the presses were running at full speed.

It was here, and nowhere else, that François dreamed of working.

Denissov, a 38-year-old journalist who had fought in the war on the far side of the Atlantic, had come back to Paris bursting with new ideas and projects. He also possessed a staggering amount of energy and a maxim that had a profound effect on François: *Great newspapers must be independent of political parties*. This went completely against the grain. The newspapers that mattered had often been linked to partisan movements. But Denissov wanted his newspapers to be independent, financed entirely by sales and advertising. At a time when governments rarely survived a full term in office, Denissov proclaimed that he wanted "newspapers that last in a changing world". He knew how to set himself apart from his rivals. François, who had been following the news in Indochina ever since his brother left, could see this in practice. When *L'Intransigeant* ran the headline "COMMUNIST ADVANCES THREATEN FRANCE'S POSITION", and *L'Aurore* underscored "PRESERVING FRENCH PROTECTORATES", Denissov dispatched to Indochina reporters who were as much journalists as adventurers, for a report headlined "WITH THE LEGIONNAIRES IN THE HELL OF NAM DINH!"

This was where François had come as soon as he arrived in Paris. It had taken him three days to buttonhole Denissov, who he found somewhat intimidating at first. Everything about him was oversized – his height, his waist, his hands, his nose – like a child who had been stretched at birth and never returned to normal proportions. Behind his round glasses, he had pale grey, piercing eyes; his hair, slicked back on his egg-shaped skull with glossy brilliantine, looked like an otter's pelt. Though Russian on his father's side, he was American in his culture. It was said he had held prestigious positions at the *New York Times* and the *Chicago Tribune*, but no one ever checked: in the press as everywhere, people needed heroes. Denissov confidently put forward ideas that were not his own, but which people were happy to attribute to him because they were new and came from America, which was suddenly all the rage.

"I don't need journalists, my friend, I need …"

Denissov stopped in the middle of the lobby and scowled at François. Being taller than average, he looked down on everyone, and they were forced to look up to talk to him. It did not make for easy eye contact.

"Actually, I need everything. Paper, trucks, advertising, I need readers …"

It was true that François had chosen the worst possible time to try his luck in the press. In a few short months, transport costs had increased by a quarter, paper was sixteen times more expensive, the cost of printing a daily paper was twenty-five times what it had been five years earlier, there was little advertising income, which meant increasing the cover price, and that only served to discourage readers from stopping at the newsstand; it was a vicious circle.

For a moment Denissov seemed to be lost in his own gloomy

thoughts. Then, suddenly, he emerged, as though struck by a tragic realisation.

"Yes, paper is the real problem . . ."

He turned to François.

"Actually, journalists are two a penny."

"I'm a patriot . . ."

"Patriots are even more common than journalists!"

"I was in Damascus in '41 . . ."

Seeing that this had stopped Denissov in his tracks, François added:

"I fought with Général Legentilhomme . . ."

It was a little-known chapter in the history of the Second World War, but Denissov remembered that there had been a battle between the Free French Forces and Vichy France.

"So, no medal, then?"

"No," said François. "It was as though we did nothing."

There was a bitterness in his voice. The battle, which had claimed more than a thousand lives, was deemed a skirmish in a civil war, there could be no question of decorating Frenchmen who had shot their compatriots; no medals, no citations had been awarded.

Denissov was staring straight ahead towards the lobby; his eyes wandered for a moment.

"So, why do you want to work here rather than somewhere else?"

François had prepared an answer, the sentences had rolled around in his mind for so long they had a burnished lustre, but standing here before this giant, who loomed over him like an entomologist over an insect, he did not know what to say.

"This place . . . it's different from other newspapers."

"You don't say?"

He waited for the next part.

"Other people publish newspapers for political parties," François ventured. "You value readers over voters."

"Not bad . . ."

When Denissov smiled, his lips traced a perfectly horizontal line that seemed to span his face. There was something powerfully, irresistibly attractive about him. Was he married? François could see no wedding ring. People said he was a "ladies' man", and François found himself envying him: this was the kind of man he would have liked to be.

"Can you write?"

François nodded to emphasise the humility of his answer.

"I've been told I'm not a bad writer . . ."

Denissov closed his eyes, disappointed.

"If you're a good writer, journalism is not for you. Why don't you write novels instead?"

He walked on through the lobby.

"Do you prefer bad writers?"

Denissov turned. For a moment François thought he was going to slap him.

"Newspapers are full of people who write sentences. Here, we write articles."

"Doesn't that amount to the same thing?"

"No. At *Le Journal*, we don't craft sentences. We tell stories."

It was over. Denissov was already walking towards the lift.

François trudged after him in a desultory fashion, but Denissov's arrival had been expected, and he was already surrounded by a coterie of people, fielding a barrage of questions. He answered everything briskly: yes, no, OK. Sometimes he put on his glasses, took a dispatch, looked it over carefully and handed it back with his verdict. He listened attentively, and hated when people repeated themselves: "You already told me that . . ." Thinking to imitate his energy and his efficiency, some became expedient. "You might want to think about that again," he would say soberly. At *Le Journal*, this piece of advice was tantamount to a slap in the face.

The lift doors opened, the lift attendant greeted Denissov with a cheerful: "Hello, boss," and the great man disappeared without so much as a glance at François.

Since then, François had come to *Le Journal* every day, after his shift.

At first he would stand staring at the wall of classified ads; later he became bolder, and would take the stairs up to the newsroom, or down to the printing presses. At the presses, people assumed he was a journalist; in the newsroom, they assumed he was a typesetter; in the production department, they thought he was a proofreader.

For the first time, he understood his father's passion for "the smell of the trade". Here, the smells were not of oils and lye, but of printer's lead, the ebony of telephone handsets, sweat mingled with a dash of vintage wine. It smelled like a newspaper. Never had François felt such a sense of belonging. As he discreetly greeted the harried men and bustling women, calling, laughing and shouting to each other, and they abstractedly returned his greeting, assuming that they knew him, it felt like a second injustice, which seemed a lot for such a young life. His role in the war had been forgotten, and now the door to the only place where he felt he could exist was closed to him. People assumed François was shy, since he constantly tiptoed out of dark corners as though entering a sickroom. In fact, he was terrified of running into Denissov. Fortunately, the editor's voice carried; the way he bawled and yelled was unbelievable.

François did his round of the departments, scanned the morning news stories; he could not help but try to think up a headline for each. He went downstairs to inhale the atmosphere of the press room, gazed from afar at the typesetting bed as whorls of blue smoke rose from the pipes and cigarettes of the figures poring over the proofs.

François glanced at the large wall clock: half past nine. Time to leave.

He caught the métro. Gilbert worked as a reporter for *La Semaine des sports* on the rue de la Grange-aux-Belles, but dreamed of joining *L'Intransigeant*. "Now, that's a proper newspaper!" He could not understand why François had set his heart on *Le Journal du soir*, that "tawdry rag".

The two had met a year earlier while François was making a round of the newspapers looking for a job, they had had a few drinks, and might not have stayed friends had Gilbert not had a sister, Mathilde, a smart, attractive girl, with whom François became involved. Their relationship was so sedate it was unsettling. Mathilde accompanied him to the cinema, went boating with him in the Bois de Boulogne and slept with him "when she felt like it". She would leave the following morning, making no promises or demands, and while this arrangement suited François, he wondered whether she did this with other men, a thought that did not appeal to him.

The shift had just ended at *La Semaine*. François, being a regular visitor, greeted various people as he strolled through the vast warehouse stacked with the colossal six-tonne rolls of paper destined for the printing presses. Gilbert was in the changing rooms; his face was haggard. Feverishly, he grabbed François by the shoulder – "Come on, come on!" He seemed to be in a tearing hurry. Rather than cross the street to the local bar, Gilbert stopped on the street and leaned against the steel emergency exit.

"Oh, hell," he said. "You can't tell anyone what I'm about to say, OK, promise me?"

He looked shattered.

"*La Semaine des sports* is finished, they're going to close it down . . ."

Gilbert was a well-informed boy.

"It's completely confidential, you understand? They won't make the official announcement for a week or so, because they are afraid of social unrest . . ."

Gilbert was about to lose his job. François almost felt ashamed that he was still employed.

"You could try *Le Populaire*, maybe they're hiring . . ."

Both men knew what the answer would be; it was simple.

"Yeah, I can only ask . . ."

Now that he had confided his secret, he was completely drained. Gilbert was a blond, strapping young man, whom years of boxing had left with a nose that skewed to the right, which made him seem gentle and slightly lost. François was staring at his feet, thinking.

"Come on," said Gilbert, "let's get a drink."

"I can't, I'm sorry . . . There's . . . there's something I need to do . . . I'll see you later?"

Gilbert spread his hands in a helpless gesture, but François was already gone. He caught the métro back to Rambuteau and strode into the offices of *Le Journal* with a determined step. The lift had just arrived, he got in.

"Do you work downstairs?" the lift attendant said with a knowing look.

"Yes, I mean, no . . ."

In a wide corridor thronged with people, double doors separated the editorial office from the newsroom. François moved through the newsroom, amazed by its unique atmosphere. To him, *Le Journal* was not a business, it was a voyage. The people who worked there were not employees, they were pioneers.

"What the hell are you doing here?"

Having managed to avoid him for so long, François suddenly found himself face to face with Denissov.

François grinned and glanced around.

"Thirty six-tonne reels of paper . . ." he said in a low voice, "going cheap . . . Would you be interested?"

Denissov bent his head closer.

"*La Semaine des sports* is shutting down, right now it's classified information, they won't make it official for a few days. Surely selling off their paper stock before they go bankrupt, that would be in everyone's interest."

Denissov gave a short, dry laugh and shook his head.

"Hey, Malevitz, get over here!"

He had grabbed the arm of a passer-by, a heavyset man in his forties with snow-white hair and beard and dark bushy eyebrows that made his gaze unsettling.

"Allow me to introduce . . ."

Denissov turned to François.

"François Pelletier . . ."

"François Pelletier it is, then. Put him on the general news desk. If he hasn't proved himself within a fortnight, kick the bastard out."

Malevitz opened his mouth to say something only to be interrupted by Denissov, who was striding towards his office but turned and shouted back at François.

"It pays nine thousand francs!"

The young man raised his hand by way of a thank you. His monthly salary had just been slashed by three hundred francs.

4

And yet, the end will come . . .

Despite the time difference, or perhaps because of it, Étienne could not sleep. After only a few short hours of sleep, he was sitting up in bed in the dead of night. Joseph opened one eye, rolled over and went back to sleep.

As he had often done since Raymond's departure, Étienne lit a cigarette and set the soft leather binder in which he kept his letters on his lap. Raymond always began: "My dear Étienne". Nothing could seem less intimate, but Raymond was terrified his letters would be intercepted by military censors. "Just write to me the way you would to a cousin in Brittany," Étienne had said, but he was careful not to say anything untoward in his letters, he did not want to get Raymond into trouble.

"The atmosphere here is gruelling," Raymond wrote, and he was not just talking about weather. Granted the heat, the humidity, the sudden cloudbursts could be trying, but there was also a general atmosphere of suspicion. "The local people are volatile and that can be worrying. A cook or a scout you recruited a week ago might suddenly toss a hand grenade into the middle of a group and run for it." But, perhaps to spare Étienne any further anguish, in his later letters Raymond talked less and less about his everyday routine, and when you are done talking about the world, all that is left to talk about is yourself. This he did sparingly. Twice Étienne had questioned him about his army service. It's not every day that a schoolteacher enlists in the army, but Raymond was reticent to offer an explanation. "I'll tell you everything when I see you," he wrote evasively. Although Étienne did not press the point, he could not help but imagine the worst. That Raymond had murdered someone and been forced to flee. He was a strong lad and often talked about fights he had had at school, but that did not make him a murderer ...

Though now a soldier, Raymond still had the handwriting of a schoolmaster. He left a neat five-centimetre margin on the left-hand side and wrote in an elegant cursive hand. He never made a spelling mistake. It was one of the things Étienne had found charming when they first met; Raymond was a cultivated man. When he had to go back to barracks and was running late, he would say: "Thou, Hermes, may act according to thy whims, but I, mere mortal, dare offend the gods!" His expression was solemn and it was difficult to know whether or not he was being serious. They would meet several times a week, on evenings when Raymond was not on duty, and, since Étienne had never read the *Odyssey*, Raymond retold the epic to him. What exactly he was doing serving in the Legion was a question that haunted Étienne. Having his lover tell him the story of Odysseus's journey was disconcerting. So unexpected. So respectful. For Étienne it was an epiphany. He hardly dared believe that he had been lucky enough to be chosen by such a man.

"No, I'll never go back," Raymond had written more recently. He was referring to Brussels, where he had been born and raised. "Would you like to live with me?" Even now, the words brought tears to Étienne's eyes. Now *he* was Odysseus. It was he who longed to recover the love from whom he had been separated; he who made the long journey to find that love.

Would the gods smile on him? Étienne felt overwhelmed by doubt.

*

But for the tropical languor and the Vietnamese accents, the Indo-chinese Currency Exchange in Saigon, with its dilapidated corridors and creaky wooden floors, its closed doors and rickety fans, its overcrowded offices and overworked clerks, looked just like any other department of the French civil service. Étienne found he could not recognise the co-workers he had been introduced to the day before. Whenever someone waved at him, he simply nodded and smiled.

He was ushered into a large office behind the main counter, where he shook hands with his new French and Vietnamese colleagues, though discreetly, since all of them were deep in conversation with a customer. Those applying to make a "wire transfer to France" – i.e. to purchase something in France – first had to present themselves at the counter where a clerk checked that the application had been duly filled out. Then it was Étienne's job to study each file, and to meet with the applicant to solicit further information or to inform them of the Exchange's decision.

He began by wiping down the sticky in-tray on the desk he had been assigned, then refilled it with the stack of files he had temporarily placed on the floor. He settled himself in the chair, which squeaked every time he moved, and set to work.

The majority of transactions involved colonial companies purchasing goods from France. Each application was accompanied by a detailed explanation intended to show the benefit of such purchases to the Indochinese economy. Engines, tools, vegetable seeds, films, sheet metal, cement, washbasins, umbrellas, fertiliser, flashlights, office supplies – it was surprising how many imports Indochina needed if it was to function or develop normally. Étienne spent his first morning checking estimates and invoices. It was deeply tedious, while the sweltering heat and the cigarette smoke did not help.

Having checked them, he stacked the applications that were in order on his right, and those that seemed dubious (he suspected overcharging) on his left.

Before long, this second pile was twice as high as the first.

What was he supposed to do?

He had not had instructions from the director.

Sometime during the morning, he saw one of his colleagues wander out, stretching his aching back. His name was Maurice Belloir – one of the few Étienne had managed to remember – a plump man, with heavy features, grey hair and the sort of prominent ridged brows you might see on lions in the zoo, or on bellicose samurai warriors in Japanese prints. His fingers were yellowed with nicotine. According to Gaston, Belloir's wife took lovers from among the senior officers and her overtures were so forceful that she was nicknamed "the Expeditionary Corps". Belloir kept his Indochinese mistress in an apartment on the rue Catinat, with servants to care for the children he had sired in the past four years.

Étienne got up and, on the pretext that he needed to stretch his legs, joined Belloir on the terrace.

With infinite patience, Étienne chatted to him about the tropical climate ("You'll get used to it, you'll see"), the tedium of the work ("There's only two kinds of jobs in Indochina: bloody boring, and bloody dangerous. I favour the former"), the rainy season ("When it comes, you'll see, it's a nightmare"), then, as they were finishing their cigarettes before heading back into the office:

"I have a cousin in the Foreign Legion."

"Really? Here in Saigon?"

"Yes. And it's very strange, we haven't heard from him in over a month . . ."

Belloir gazed up at the ceiling and adopted the grave demeanour of a man who is always well informed.

"He's probably been sent to suppress the sects. I've heard that the Bình Xuyên are quite restless these days."

Étienne was surprised by the use of the term "sects" here in South-East Asia. The Expeditionary Force was fighting a religious war, was it? His astonishment was written all over his face. Raymond had made no mention of sects in his letters. The Việt Minh, yes, the communists, obviously, but no sects.

Belloir played up his air of omniscience; it was a pose he liked to affect, he felt it gave him dignity and gravitas.

"You do realise that 'sects' are not necessarily religious? How can I put it . . .?"

He seemed uneasy at having to explain, as though reluctant to reveal some higher truth to the lay person.

"The gooks are a very particular race, you'll see. Very superstitious. Desperate to believe. You've got sects all over Indochina. These sects are cults, armed groups, militias, gangs, and they can be very powerful."

"But what exactly is it that they believe in?"

Belloir gave a supercilious chuckle.

"They believe in the sect! Between the colonialism of the French and the terrorism of the Việt Minh, the sects are the only way to get a bit of peace. It started out as a belief system. Later, they formed a militia to protect themselves. They sell opium to make the money they need, and so the sect grows. And the bigger it is, the more its followers feel protected. It's like life insurance. With a dose of mysticism."

"And France is at war with them?"

"It depends. You've got sects on both sides."

"In his last letter, my cousin mentioned Hiển Giang."

"That would be up north . . ."

"On the map, it looks more like it's north-west."

"If it's that close, why don't you just go see for yourself?"

Belloir felt insulted. Here he was giving a lesson in important matters, only to be corrected on some trivial geographical detail. It was very hurtful. He stubbed out his cigarette and headed back to his desk.

Étienne went back to the office and became so engrossed in his work that he was surprised to find it was lunchtime.

"How are you getting on, old man?" said Gaston.

They were strolling out with the throng of co-workers. The customers who had come to apply for transfers did not move; they would wait patiently for the clerks to come back. Étienne was about to ask Gaston the only question that mattered to him when he was approached by a small, chubby man with a mischievous twinkle in his eyes, a childlike mouth, and high cheekbones. On the crown of his head, he had a tuft of thick, black hair that pointed to the heavens, like a cockatoo's crest or a terrified character in a cartoon.

"Duong Khắc Diêm," he introduced himself. "I am here on behalf of Director Jeantet, yes, yes."

He had a high-pitched, slightly nasal voice. Étienne's hand was hot and clammy but he held out a few fingers which the little man gripped, giving a shrill little laugh, hee, hee, hee, revealing immaculate, very white teeth.

"I have nice apartment for you, Monsieur Étienne. If you want to see . . . Very good location, very good?"

His voice tended to rise at the end of his sentences, making them sound like questions.

"You will be most comfortable, yes, yes?"

Apart from these tics of speech, Diêm's French was very good. Étienne resisted the temptation to ask where he had learned to speak it (everyone probably asked) and simply followed the man.

Étienne, who had always had a poor sense of direction, was soon lost. The city whirled around him, the shops spilled out onto the pavement, the street hawkers crying, the passers-by loaded down with bundles and baskets, the milling children; every street looked the same to him.

"You will see, it is not far from the Exchange, yes, yes. Very convenient."

And indeed some moments later they stopped in front of an imposing building equipped with a lift, which looked more like a freight lift, but valiantly fulfilled its function, which was fortunate since the apartment was on the fourth floor.

The flat was clean and simple: two well-furnished rooms with a view of the city and although the bathroom was on the landing, it was private.

"It's six hundred piastres," Diêm said, then, seeing Étienne's reaction, added: "But I got it for four hundred and fifty!"

Étienne smiled.

"To what do I owe the discount, Monsieur Duong?"

"Duong Khắc Diêm, but call me Diêm?"

"Monsieur Diêm . . ."

"Diêm! Monsieur Duong, if you prefer, but Diêm is better?"

"All right then, Diêm, OK. So what about this discount?"

"The landlord owes me one small favour, so this I use to get your discount, yes, yes?"

Étienne took a tour of the apartment. The bed was in good order, the wardrobe had been cleaned and dusted, the kitchen was spick and span; the place evoked a spartan simplicity.

"Is it always as hot as this?"

"In this season, yes, very hot?"

Étienne was wondering how to create a through breeze between

71

the front door and the living room window when his thoughts were interrupted by the sound of muffled thuds and voices on the stairs. Diêm opened the door, and the two wiry movers Étienne had met the previous day appeared, all smiles, and concluded their mission by once again dropping the trunk from their full height. The man on the right was about to drop Joseph's basket but Étienne managed to rush over and stop him. Once freed, the cat scurried away and hid under the bed.

"Well," said Étienne, staring at his trunk which now looked as though it had fallen off a truck, "I think I'll take the apartment."

Diêm entered into a long discussion with the porters, at the end of which he turned to Étienne with a pained expression.

"For the transport of your trunk, Monsieur Étienne, I cannot get the price below twelve piastres ..."

As he rummaged in his pocket for change, Étienne wondered what Diêm's commission was on this transaction.

No sooner had they been paid than the porters disappeared, their hurried footsteps echoing in the stairwell. Étienne took one last look around.

The place was more like a monk's cell than a bachelor's studio. When Raymond saw his living arrangements, he would burst out laughing.

As they were walking back to the Exchange, Étienne said:

"If you don't mind me asking, what exactly do you do for a living – other than find apartments?"

Diêm covered his mouth, hee, hee, hee, and spread his arms wide, palms turned towards the heavens.

"Mostly, I am a comprador, yes, yes?"

Étienne recalled what Gaston had told him about bank transfers.

"But," said Diêm with a little pout, "business at the moment is not good, no, no?"

"So, you find apartments for me ..."

Diêm's face flushed.

"You, Monsieur Étienne, it is not the same, you are a friend?"

Étienne laughed. They had known each other for less than ten minutes.

Making the most of a lull in the conversation, Étienne asked – as though the thought had just occurred to him – about the movements of the legionnaires and mentioned his cousin Raymond.

"Hiến Giang, you say?"

Diêm slowed his pace for a moment.

"The movements of the military, Monsieur Étienne, are most confidential, yes, yes. The Việt Minh, they have ears everywhere, spies, you understand! No one talks about what the military is doing?"

They stopped at a fruit stall and bought slices of pineapple and ate them standing on the pavement.

"A cousin, you say? Private Pelletier?"

"Er . . . no, he is a cousin on my mother's side. From Belgium. His name is Raymond Van Meulen. 3rd Foreign Infantry Regiment."

They were coming to the Exchange.

"I will ask, I will ask, but I promise nothing, no, no?"

"Of course, if you can't find out, it doesn't matter . . ."

"Give me one day, yes, yes?"

As Diêm walked away, Étienne called after him.

"You know, I'm not a tourist . . ."

Diêm tilted his head, the crest of hair rose and fell. Having overheard Diêm's conversation with the porters earlier, Étienne had noticed a certain tone and intonation and thought it best to set the record straight.

"I am grateful to you for showing me a little local colour," Étienne smiled. "It was very kind, but you don't need to put on a Vietnamese accent with me. You can dispense with all the yes, yes, no, no . . ."

Diêm smiled and nodded.

✳

Although he suspected that Diêm was paid handsomely for his various services, Étienne was reluctant to be indebted to the man until he knew who he was.

"Diêm does all sorts," said Gaston. "He takes whatever work

he can get. The thing is, what with ... eight children ... not to mention his parents, and in-laws living with him, that's a lot of mouths to feed!"

Gaston toyed with his signet ring, as though to emphasise the disparity in his circumstances and those of Diêm.

"Obviously, he always has his eye on transfers ... But it's penny-ante stuff. Small deals, minor contracts. Diêm just dabbles. Nothing like the big companies, you might call him a journeyman trader. Strictly bush league ..." He twisted his face into a condescending smile; a very different face from the one he used to greet customers.

Gaston's desk was only metres from Étienne's, and there, at forty-five-minute intervals, he welcomed a motley procession of applicants ranging from Vietnamese businessmen dressed in European suits, patent-leather shoes, gold bracelets and tortoiseshell glasses to planters' wives and members of the Expeditionary Force.

Étienne spent the afternoon reviewing the suspect files he had set aside that morning.

In the absence of detailed instructions from the director, and in an attempt to make sense of his work, he picked out the highest transfer request, a $150,000 piastre order placed by a company called Leroux Frères for school books, intended, according to the justification, to further the "development of French culture, language and literacy among the indigenous populations of Indochina". Étienne headed up to the archives on the top floor where old Annie, silent and wizened as ever, greeted him without a word. She disappeared into the grey aisles overflowing with boxes and bulging leather binders.

"Leroux Frères, there it is."

He signed the permission slip and went back to his desk to read the file.

Over the previous four years, Leroux Frères, an import-export company with headquarters on 12, rue Filippini, had made a dozen transfer applications for a wide variety of imports: hairdressing equipment (scissors, razors, hairdryers and curling tongs), agricultural tools (ploughs, ploughshares, picks and rakes), even outboard motors "to power the junks shipping rice to the various ports of Indochina". The French company had invoiced astronomical sums for the outboard engines, listing them as RN-P1 prototypes. Étienne could not understand why junks carrying rice would need prototype engines, still less why more than sixty were imported. Sixty engines smacked of industrial production ...

The total transfers granted to Leroux Frères totalled more than two million piastres worth seventeen million francs in Saigon ... which ballooned to thirty-four million when it reached France.

"I apologise for interrupting you ..." Étienne stepped into Monsieur Jeantet's office. "Do you have a moment? The thing is ..."

Étienne fervently hoped that he would finally be told what was expected of him, but Jeantet merely nodded to a man in his fifties on the far side of the counter, who gave the director a little wave, as though the two men shared some secret arrangement.

"That is Monsieur Michoux. He was here yesterday, and he has come back today ... The clerks at the counter are overwhelmed, but Monsieur Michoux absolutely must have his appointment today since his ship sails tomorrow."

Étienne looked completely bewildered, which served only to irritate Monsieur Jeantet.

"Any citizen permanently leaving Indochina has the right to repatriate all his goods and chattels to France," he explained peremptorily. "Surely that much is obvious?"

His voice softened and he carried on in a casual tone intended to underscore the routine nature of the situation.

"Assuming his application is in order, you need simply authorise the transfer ..."

With a wave, he beckoned the man called Michoux as he walked away. Then he retraced his steps.

"Ah yes, Le Métropole, the place is an institution, you have to visit. Come have an aperitif with me, we'll talk about Beirut. Besides, the work here is so boring, we could do with a distraction ... Seven o'clock sharp, all right? Because later on ... well ..."

He passed the approaching Monsieur Michoux, who slumped into the chair facing Étienne with a sigh of relief.

Jeantet went back to his office; the case no longer interested him.

Monsieur Michoux dabbed his brow with a large checked handkerchief.

"I never did get used to the climate," he said, holding out a thick dossier dark with sweaty fingermarks.

Étienne began the slow process of inspecting the documents.

"Is it because of the weather that you're leaving?" he asked as he checked off the documents one by one.

"Mostly, yes. It's too much for me. The humidity, the heat, to say nothing of the torrential rains that go on for weeks. It's a shit country! The thing is, I'm from Longué-Jumelles, you understand . . .?"

"No, not really."

"'The balmy spring of Anjou' – does that ring a bell?"

Monsieur Michoux had spent his entire time in Saigon working for Marton & Xavier. He was leaving Indochina with a fortune amounting to more than a million piastres.

"I see that you were earning about two thousand piastres per month, is that right?"

"Yes, why?"

"Because even if you managed to save your whole salary over a period of ten years, that would be less than a quarter of what you have . . ."

"Yes, but I don't see . . ."

"Well, I was just wondering where the balance came from."

Monsieur Michoux looked pained.

"From my wife, if you must know."

Then, seeing that Étienne was still waiting for an explanation: "She gambles."

Having admitted to this loathsome vice, Monsieur Michoux's face brightened.

"Thankfully, she is very lucky."

"So I see . . ."

Monsieur Michoux was leaving Indochina with four times what he had earned in a decade. His eight million francs that would become sixteen as soon as he disembarked in Marseille.

Basically, he was a frontman.

He was leaving with money entrusted to him by others on which he obviously took a generous commission. But since Monsieur Michoux was permanently leaving the country, Étienne could see no reason to reject his application. He stamped the transfer authorisation. Monsieur Michoux looked extremely relieved to be going home.

✳

Étienne left the Exchange early, on the pretext that he was moving in to his new apartment, and took a cycle rickshaw to Norodom Palace. Close up, the vast building was even more impressive than it had appeared the previous night. He climbed the sweeping stone steps and explained the purpose of his visit to the man on the reception desk. From here he was pushed from pillar to post until he finally arrived at the office of a caporal-chef with an inflated sense of rank who quickly corrected Étienne when he addressed him as "Monsieur".

"Many soldiers don't bother to write home," he said when Étienne had summarised the situation.

"But some write home regularly. Raymond did. That's why . . ."

The caporal-chef settled back in his chair and hunched his shoulders, as though preparing to hibernate.

"You haven't been here long, have you?"

It did not sound like a question.

"A few days . . ."

The caporal-chef clicked his tongue; he was not surprised.

"Here, it's routine for soldiers to be out on mission for a month."

"Without reporting back?"

"There are few postboxes out in the paddy fields."

"Are you saying that units don't have radios? That their leaders don't report their position?"

"What exactly is going on?"

Étienne wheeled around.

A confident, imposing man in his fifties wearing the uniform of the Foreign Legion was standing in the doorway.

"This gentleman is enquiring after his cousin," stammered the caporal-chef. "Legionnaire First Class Meulen."

"Van Meulen, Raymond," Étienne corrected him.

The officer stared at Étienne for a long moment.

"A cousin ... You say he's your *cousin*?"

Étienne knew the tone only too well, the phrase dripping with innuendo. He said nothing, but held the officer's gaze.

"3rd Foreign Infantry Regiment, sir," said the caporal-chef. "2nd company."

At this, the officer raised an eyebrow and turned back to Étienne.

"We cannot discuss the movements of operational units, I'm sure you understand, Monsieur ..."

"... Pelletier."

The colonel nodded – I see, I see, a cousin ...

"The Việt Minh have spies everywhere, Monsieur Pelletier, they are constantly looking for information about our movements. The slightest leak can put whole squadrons at risk."

"The gentleman has only been in Saigon a few days, sir," said the caporal-chef, as though this explained everything.

"In his last letter, my cousin mentioned a mission in Hiến Giang," Étienne said.

"There are no troop movements near Hiến Giang," snapped the officer, who was at least a head taller than Étienne.

"But ..."

"Had anything happened," the colonel ploughed on, irritated by this interruption, "the family would have been notified. And since you are family ..."

He turned on his heel and strode off down the corridor.

"Caporal-chef," he growled as he walked away, "please accompany Monsieur to the exit."

This did not prove necessary, as Étienne had already left the office. As he reached the stairs, he saw the senior officer enter an office marked LIEUTENANT-COLONEL BIRARD.

Étienne left the Norodom Palace disheartened: if the military were this tight-lipped about information, he had little chance of finding out the truth.

"The slightest leak could put an entire squadron at risk," the colonel had said. What was Hiến Giang? A village? A military base? As he considered these possibilities, he realised that he was on rue Filippini.

Out of sheer curiosity, he walked to number 12, headquarters of Leroux Frères, a company that imported one hundred and fifty thousand piastres' worth of school books. It was a Corsican bar called A Volta.

*

Le Métropole was a vast two-storey building on the corner of the rue Catinat and the place du Théâtre, with high windows, with a third-floor mansard on the roof terrace. From a distance, the building looked as though it was lit up like a Christmas tree. This was *l'heure de l'apéritif*, the holy hour when anyone who was anyone in Saigon congregated at Le Métropole for cocktails, generating a cacophony that even the live orchestra could not drown out, their voices echoing in unintelligible waves when, by the purest chance, there was a lull in the proceedings. Finding Monsieur Jeantet proved quite an undertaking. Étienne weaved his way between tables, ignoring the stares of the booming men and giggling women, dodging waiters in white jackets carrying huge trays laden with brightly coloured sodas in tall frosted glasses, red and gold bottles immersed in buckets of ice and tinkling champagne flutes. Whenever a tray was dropped, roars of laughter would spread from one table to the next, as though this were a birthday party.

He found Jeantet at the far end of the terrace, standing with his back to a tall green plant with large leaves. When he saw Étienne, he looked surprised, as though he had completely forgotten his invitation. Then he gestured irritably to a rattan chair.

"Sit down, for God's sake, everyone is looking at you."

"I hardly think these people are interested in me," said Étienne, glancing back at the large, busy terrace.

"Don't you believe it. You work for the Exchange, it's very

important here. In a few days, perhaps in a few hours, everyone here will know who you are. If they don't know already."

He had, it seemed, the utmost contempt for the raucous crowd around them.

"We call this place Radio Catinat. This terrace is a hothouse. Here, everything grows and flourishes, rumours, secrets, threats, negotiations, everything. To say nothing of the poisonous plants. This is where women choose their lovers and men flaunt their mistresses. In Saigon, everybody sleeps with everybody."

Étienne immediately realised that their aperitif had not been arranged to talk about Beirut and the idyllic day and a half that Jeantet had spent there, or even to explain the nature of his job at the Exchange. The director was simply a depressive in need of company. Gaston had talked about the director's beautiful wife, his children, but Maurice Jeantet needed something more, he needed an audience; today, it was Étienne, tomorrow, someone else.

From time to time, Jeantet would wave his hand or nod at someone, but these distant desultory greetings were like concessions he regretted having to make. Imperiously, he ordered two glasses of calvados and a bottle of soda water. Étienne, who was unaccustomed to hard liquor, quickly felt the effects. But he was not alone in feeling tipsy. This cheerful, boisterous crowd looked nothing like a people at war. Even Lieutenant-Colonel Birard in his freshly pressed uniform with a woman on his arm did not look like an officer on the field of battle.

"Here, we don't say 'war', we say 'peacekeeping', there's a subtle difference!"

Jeantet gave a short, dry chuckle. When he spoke, he stressed certain syllables, giving his statements a jerky, unpredictable quality, where his tone seemed to contradict his words.

"The French government has given up on trying to exterminate the Việt Minh. Good thing too, because it's impossible. Communists are like crab lice, you think you've got rid of them, but there are always just enough left to start a new infestation. So, the new government plan is to isolate them. That would suit everyone: the Việt Minh would have their territory, France would have the rest.

There would still be occasional tensions and skirmishes, because it's in everyone's interest to keep this going for as long as possible. This war is much too important to allow it to end."

"Surely peace is better than war . . ."

"It depends. Because there's war and then there's *war*. Back in France, for example, no one gives a damn what happens here, because we're all professional soldiers. As far as they are concerned, so long as young men are not being called up to die in the paddy fields, peace and war amount to the same thing, since it makes no difference to their daily lives."

As Jeantet rambled on about the military situation, Étienne, whose thoughts never strayed far from Raymond, decided to try his luck.

"The military, I mean the legionnaires . . . What exactly do they do?"

"Operations. The Việt Minh throw grenades on café terraces, the legionnaires burn their villages – when they can find them. It's a kind of exchange of goodwill. The Expeditionary Force wages a traditional campaign, the Việt Minh wage guerrilla warfare and here in Saigon we stuff our faces."

He downed his drink in a gulp.

"Saigon is a world apart."

Étienne remembered the explosion he had heard late that day, which he had assumed was a blown tyre. Had it been a grenade?

"Of course, I'm not saying there are no risks here," Jeantet said.

He glanced around the terrace.

"But look at them . . . They don't look like people living in fear, do they? And do you know why? Do you?"

Étienne shook his head.

"Because the game is worth the candle, that's why."

Étienne seized the opportunity.

"You're right, the people here don't seem worried. I'm planning to use my free time to explore the countryside. I was thinking of going to Hiến Giang . . ."

Jeantet squeezed his eyes shut like a schoolmaster dismayed by a pupil's mediocrity.

"You want to explore, to do the tourist sights, here in Indochina?"

"Actually, I have a cousin who . . ."

"You clearly don't understand where you are."

Jeantet looked at his watch and gave a little sigh to underscore his weariness. He hesitated for a moment, then suddenly made up his mind.

"Come on, I'll show you something . . ."

Jeantet was already on his feet. As he strode across the long terrace, Étienne saw him responding to the greetings of everyone he passed with a grumpy, evasive shrug that bordered on boorishness. Without slowing his pace, he handed a few crumpled notes to a waiter.

They headed down the rue Catinat, a street lined with ice-cream parlours and opulent cafés, a bustling, hectic thoroughfare thronging with Europeans going to ballrooms, hawkers selling char sui pork, soldiers, slender Vietnamese women with a feline grace who walked arm in arm. Jeantet moved with a dyspeptic gait, shooing away begging children and stallholders offering street food.

They came to the quai de Belgique. On the corner stood the imposing Crystal Palace Hotel, a building like a wedding cake whose soft, languid curves made it seem as though the windows and terraces might spill out onto the pavement.

Jeantet did not break his stride, but marched into a lobby so full of plants it looked like a tropical hothouse, headed straight for the lift where a Vietnamese bellhop, dressed like a pageboy from Chez Maxim, did not even trouble to ask where they were going, but took them up to the fifth-floor terrace. Here, beneath a great glass canopy, American women clutching glasses of champagne idly gossiped, while German, French and English men in evening suits or dinner jackets smoked cigarettes and chewed the fat.

Night had fallen and the illuminated terrace looked like an ocean liner adrift on a dark ocean.

Jeantet grabbed a glass of champagne from a tray without thinking to offer one to Étienne, then, perching his buttocks on the edge of a ceramic planter containing a huge banana tree, he jerked his chin towards the motley crowd.

"Everyone who is anyone can be found on the terraces of Le

Métropole and the Crystal Palace. Ageing diplomats, mercenaries, philanderers, corrupt bankers, alcoholic journalists, prostitutes and demi-mondaines, French aristocrats, crypto-communists, wealthy planters – you'll find them all here. It's a mistake to think of Saigon as a city. It is a world of its own. Corruption, gambling, sex, booze, power – here, every vice is given free rein, under the aegis of the great goddess they all worship, Our Lady of the Piastre!"

With a flick of his wrist, Jeantet emptied his glass into the planter and strode through the crowd. Étienne followed him to the dimly lit edge of the terrace where the director stopped and laid his large hands on the parapet.

Étienne stared out into the night and felt a curious emotion as he saw the darkness pierced by the countless lights of ships at anchor.

"Can you smell it?" said Jeantet. "The river . . ."

The babble of the English conversations faded and died, as though a movie had just ended, and gave way to the deep, oppressive silence that shrouded the banks of this unsettling ink-black river, and, as their eyes became accustomed to the gloom, they could dimly make out what looked like the tall grasses of swamps or paddy fields.

"The Việt Minh are over on the far bank," Jeantet said. "They're surrounding the city."

He turned back to the small crowd laughing at each other's jokes.

"What you see here is all that remains of French Indochina. Truth be told, Saigon is little more than a besieged fortress."

They turned back to the river.

"Out there in the jungle, France has built hundreds of small garrisons that are utterly useless. The Expeditionary Force struggles to defend them. Where possible, it even tries to gain a little ground, occupying villages like Hiến Giang, for example, but seen from the sky, those hundreds of forts are nothing more than besieged outposts. Or will be by tomorrow . . ."

Étienne suddenly felt a wave of vertigo. Raymond and his comrades were out there in that thrumming, sweltering black hole; Raymond, whose physical presence he could feel in that instant, like his warm, familiar breath.

"Exploring the country, as you put it, would be suicide. You wouldn't get two kilometres. The only way to leave the city is under armed escort and, even then, you never know whether you will reach your destination . . . Saigon has become an island."

There was something different about Jeantet's voice, it had dropped to a whisper, a new thought slowly unfurled, pervasive and sinuous as seaweed.

"When it comes down to it, the piastre is Saigon's last link with the rest of the world."

This word seemed to rouse him. He turned to Étienne.

"Even the wealth here is artificial. It exists only by fiat. The Việt Minh are gradually taking over the rice fields, the plantations and the suburbs. They can persuade and they can sow terror, but taking Saigon is a very different matter. Because" – he jabbed an angry forefinger at the heavens – "here in Saigon we have the piastre . . ."

Suddenly, the conversation was interrupted by a distant explosion. On the far side of the river, a bright glare blossomed some kilometres away, followed by the red glow of a raging fire.

"It's one of the French outposts defending itself," Jeantet said coolly. "The Việt Minh usually attack at night. If the fort can hold out until morning, it might have another few weeks. If not, the Expeditionary Force will build another a few kilometres away."

Étienne's mind instantly imagined Raymond again, blockaded inside a bamboo tower, with Việt Minh soldiers attacking from all sides, emerging out of the thick darkness only when they were right in front of you.

"It seems endless," Jeantet said, "and yet the end will come. This is a war that cannot be won. The government knows that, everyone knows. But in the meantime, we pretend."

He turned back to the terrace.

"Look at them . . ."

The fleeting shock triggered by the explosion had already faded. The jaunty conversations had resumed.

Jeantet looked at Étienne and laid a hand on his shoulder.

"Welcome aboard the *Titanic*."

84

5

You can tell at a glance what kind of man he is …

Hélène did not hate her parents, but she had felt so lonely since Étienne's departure that she mustered all her rage and took it out on them. Hers was a strong personality, loath to make concessions, willing to provoke. Whenever she felt lost or unsure of herself, being a contrarian offered her a logic. Moral anarchy was something she used to resolve her uncertain conflicting desires. This was how she had come to sleep with her maths teacher, Xavier Lhomond. One day she had asked Étienne:

"What do you think of forty-year-old men?"

"I think they're twenty years older than you."

Étienne, a past master in doomed love affairs, did not approve of his sister's choice, but had been unable to dissuade her from pursuing a relationship from which she expected nothing and which would inevitably make her deeply unhappy. Étienne, who had so many objective reasons for his suffering, could not see the point of his sister suffering needlessly.

Lhomond was the very epitome of an ageing beau: he had a stature that made him an ideal tennis partner and a shock of white hair that he combed back from his rugged face. And pale blue eyes … His every gesture and inflection exuded smug self-satisfaction. His sanguine outlook on life together with his many conquests had convinced him that he was invincible. Being impervious to self-doubt, he aggressively pursued almost every woman he met. His successes, though notable, were purely statistical.

He had been quick to spot Hélène, easily one of the most beautiful students in the school. She felt more flattered than seduced, but took a certain dizzy pleasure in evading the attentions of a man almost as old as her father – though decidedly more handsome.

The affair had not been as easy as she had hoped. Hélène had only the vaguest notion of what a man and a woman actually did in bed, and what she had glimpsed of her brothers' anatomy when she accidentally walked in on them made the idea more worrying than reassuring.

Her mother, who regularly railed against girls who 'lost their virginity', without ever explaining what this entailed, was of little help. Hélène was prepared to do things with her teacher that she would never have done with a boy her own age, because the very nature of their sin reeked of fire and brimstone, something in which a mature man would be well versed. And Lhomond was able to allay the fears of pregnancy that troubled all girls, even virgins. He had managed to acquire American condoms, he confided to her in a low voice, as though he belonged to a brotherhood that was at once powerful, mysterious and reviled.

Despite her misgivings, Hélène had entered into this relationship with a knot in her stomach, much to Lhomond's joy. He was the sort of man who took pleasure in hurting women, but did so psychologically rather than physically.

Their early sexual encounters felt to Hélène like a variant of hazing reserved for girls, and she decided that sex was something to which a person had to consent to be considered normal.

She and Lhomond had sex every Monday morning, because classes did not start until 3 p.m. Lhomond claimed that Monday was a good day because "it set him up for the week".

Keenly aware that having a female student regularly visit his home might be compromising, Lhomond rented a suite at the new Hôtel Kassar, whose owner, a friend who shared his moral turpitude, offered him a discounted rate. For Hélène, the delicious thrill of forbidden love was joined by the trappings of luxury: a bathroom as large as a bedroom, a bedroom as large as a living room, a living room that looked out onto the sea with a complimentary bowl of fruit and terry cloth bath towels. To give a fuller picture, it should be said that Hélène was in the throes of discovering sexual pleasure, no small thing in itself. And that she suspected, from Lhomond's various memory lapses and his apologies, that she was not his only lover. She would have been furious if he had taken another pupil as his lover; this was her one stipulation, the one area where she demanded exclusivity. Lhomond, never sparing in his promises, was happy to swear as much.

Lhomond's ploy for approaching his female students was the "photography club". It was a genuine extracurricular activity, though the club – a handful of students to whom he taught the basics of photography and the secrets of the darkroom – now met only sporadically.

Madame Pelletier sometimes confided her doubts about the teacher to her husband. As a woman with a keen knowledge of men, she considered Xavier Lhomond overweening, conceited and smug, or, in her words, "You can tell at a glance what kind of man he is . . ."

When she warned her daughter, Hélène said: "Let him try, I'll give him what for," enjoying the double entendre.

As for Monsieur Pelletier, he merely laughed. "Angèle, they're scientists! They study photography the way I study soap, it's something they're passionate about, and you can hardly complain about her getting an education!" Hélène gave a sardonic smile and said: "No, there's nothing wrong with learning new things . . ."

For a decade now, Louis Pelletier had been president of the private school attended by his children. As such, he knew all the teachers and staff members, and he reassured his wife about Lhomond, believing that the anxiety was bad for her health.

This was a special year for Louis, the last of his presidency. He had donated twenty thousand francs to the school without consulting his wife. When the headmaster protested that this was too much, *far* too much, Louis said: "It's my last child's last year at the school, it's the least I can do!" The money was intended for the communal cash reserves used to finance pupils' trips abroad, end-of-year events, etc. In mid-March, Monsieur Pelletier decided to check the communal funds – an unusual event, since accounts were usually audited at the end of the school year, so his decision to do so two months in advance came as a surprise to everyone. Not least the school bursar, Monsieur Chakir, a diligent, vigilant, rather fretful Indian man in his fifties, who was so formal and punctilious it was almost embarrassing. He immediately took President Pelletier's request as a sign of mistrust. Louis was forced to lavish him with compliments, and swear on the lives of his children that he was not motivated by suspicion in order to convince Monsieur Chakir that the audit was merely a duty under the school's statutes.

"I just want it over and done with, you understand?" Louis said.

To allay any misgivings, he invited Monsieur Chakir to lunch at the new Hôtel Kassar.

"How about next Monday? I'm told the food is excellent. It's been a year since it opened, and I haven't had the chance to visit yet . . ."

Louis suggested that the bursar meet him there in the morning, and together they could work in one of the small lounges available to hotel guests, then, when they had dealt with the red tape, they could have lunch in the restaurant overlooking the sea. A glance at the overweight bursar was enough to know that an invitation to lunch would seal the deal. Monsieur Chakir accepted on condition that he paid his share; he did not want anyone to think that . . .

"Very well," Louis said, "I shall see you there on Monday."

Only an innocent would consider it a coincidence that the Hôtel Kassar was about to welcome a father in its restaurant and his daughter in the bridal suite on the same day, at the same time.

6

The girl on the bridge was already a distant memory

For a long time, Bouboule had been waiting for the day when he might view the world with something other than bitterness. A fortnight earlier, he had thought the moment had finally come. The deadline was today. But the hours passed and nothing came.

Forty-five minutes had elapsed since he arrived at the restaurant at precisely 6.30 p.m. He had telephoned on three separate occasions; he could not bring himself to do so again. Monsieur Couderc would be furious. And soon it would be too late, the offices would be closed.

A waitress appeared and set down the poireaux vinaigrette in front of him. She was a girl of about twenty, her sullen face was speckled like a turkey egg with freckles, but she had full, round breasts. Jean loved women's breasts. Except Geneviève's, which now sagged quite a bit, but these were something else ...

My God, what a life!

It was a provincial restaurant, Jean could not even remember the name of the town – it was somewhere in the Loiret, or Eure-et-Loir, or perhaps Loir-et-Cher. The telephone obstinately refused to ring. Had he given the correct number? He could hardly call the office to check that the number they were not trying to call him on was the correct one ...

What a life!

As he stared at the three leeks lying limply on the plate, he wondered whether this was rock bottom. Or whether there was another flight of steps leading down. He felt miserable, not that anyone could tell. Only someone who knew Bouboule could guess what storm was raging in the mind of this supposedly apathetic man.

He glanced at his watch. 7.30 p.m.

"Don't you fancy it?"

The waitress was not trying to be friendly. Customers were as scarce as the food on offer; things would improve when ration cards were replaced by shops filled with food. Jean pushed away the plate – no. With an affected sigh, the girl picked it up; his loss was someone's gain; the leeks would not go to waste.

Minutes passed, but because of the rationing, Bouboule hoarded his carafe of wine.

If this did not work out, what would become of him?

Jean had only just arrived back from Beirut. The mere thought of the journey and the time he spent there made him edgy. Geneviève had clung to his father's arm, heaping him with compliments that underscored the yawning gap between father and son. "Your father's so daring!" she exclaimed. There was not a word about her father-in-law she could not turn into an aphorism. Whenever Bouboule tucked into his dinner or helped himself to more meat and vegetables, Geneviève would grumble: "You'll get fat if you're not careful, Jean!"

As if it were not enough that the outward journey had been an ordeal and the stay in Beirut a constant humiliation, the return journey had been torture. Monsieur Pelletier had not been able to book berths for both his sons on the same ship. This was Bouboule's only consolation: there had been no one to witness his humiliation. Having learned the customs and conventions of sea travel on the outward journey, Geneviève imperiously strode to her cabin as soon as they boarded. It was as though she owned the ship. Within a day, she was the darling of every officer and the scourge of every chambermaid. Bouboule could feel the other passengers' pitying stares; they talked about him as though he were an invalid. Geneviève, on the other hand, had never been so happy. Though it was difficult to say quite how she spent her days.

Jean was only just recovering from the painful ordeal when he heard that Monsieur Couderc was looking to hire a sales representative to deal exclusively with Paris and the suburbs. This would mean he could be home every night. Not that Bouboule particularly enjoyed spending time at home; the joy of being reunited with Geneviève had long since faded. What appealed was the prospect of no longer having to spend his life in hotel rooms. He found the endless treks through the provinces depressing, it was the kind of tedium that sapped your whole life. It might be different if business was good, but everyone seemed to be struggling. Anything and everything was available on the black market for those who could afford it, which made it impossible for legitimate companies to do business . . . Jean represented six different companies, which meant lugging around six catalogues for cleaning products, household equipment and fancy goods. Worse still, he had to cart around a trunk filled with kitchen utensils (a select group of items that Monsieur Couderc expected to sell well – not that anyone gave a damn) and he had to keep a detailed list of every hardware shop, grocers and ironmongers that bought six dozen candles, four mops, two ladles or a single bucket. Jean earned his living piecemeal.

Jean loathed provincial hotels – the blistered wallpaper, the chipped washbasins, the snoring neighbours, the damp sheets, the threadbare carpets. So, when he heard that there was an opening for a Paris rep, he raced round to Monsieur Couderc's office. "I'll give it some thought, Jean . . ." – which could mean yes or no. Jean racked his brains but could think of no reason for Monsieur Couderc to favour any of the other sales reps over him. His earnings were not much lower than theirs, and then there was his father, who was a personal friend of Monsieur Couderc, which was how Jean had come to be hired in the first place. If his father's connections were enough to get him hired, thought Jean, they should be enough to get him promoted. He tended to forget that the brand-new Renault 4CV paid for by his parents had played a crucial role in his candidacy.

The blanquette de veau arrived, two slices of overcooked veal in a tasteless sauce. Jean began to eat. Being made exclusive Paris sales representative would put an end to the long string of failures that haunted him. Today was Tuesday. In two days, he would be back in Paris, then, on Sunday, an interminable lunch with François (who would probably arrive with a girl on his arm, possibly the girl he had brought last time, a brunette with small breasts). Geneviève was in favour of this Sunday tradition. "Family is sacred," she would say, as though she cared a jot about her own family. François found the lunches boring, but could not always come up with an excuse to wriggle out. No one enjoyed the occasions, but nonetheless they made the effort. For Geneviève, Sunday lunch was a precious moment, since François and his girlfriend were a captive audience who would listen to her talk about her life and, more especially, her husband. She never sounded as though she were complaining, she talked about her hardships in an almost desultory tone, but in the end it all came down to money, or the lack of it, which made Jean responsible for the mediocrity of their existence.

Geneviève's pleasure at having François to lunch in their apartment was inversely proportionate to the space available for entertaining.

Their dining room also served as a bedroom: one wardrobe doubled as a kitchen with a sink and a small bench had a two-ring hob connected to a gas cylinder. The porcelain bowl that served as a toilet was out on the landing. Dinner for four involved pushing every stick of furniture out of the way; the dining chairs bumped against the bed frame. Jean argued that they were fortunate, given that more than half a million Parisians lived in cramped hotel rooms, but Geneviève was not persuaded. She would sigh deeply, close her eyes and say plaintively to François: "Yes, it's a little cramped. When Jean gets a better job, we'll move, but for now . . ." Thus, the precarity of their circumstances was blamed not on the housing crisis, but on the fact that Jean did not earn enough.

In fact, the tiny kitchen might just as well have been reconverted into a wardrobe since Geneviève never cooked. She had an arrangement with Madame Faure, their next-door neighbour, to prepare meals three times a week. Geneviève did the grocery shopping because Madame Faure had difficulty getting around, and they lived on the fourth floor with no lift. In exchange, Madame Faure, who was an exceptional cook, created meals of uncommon brilliance from the miscellaneous foodstuffs Geneviève managed to glean from shops, where nothing was available, and the black market, where everything was too expensive.

On days when François came to lunch, especially if he was bringing company, Geneviève always found some way of arranging for Madame Faure to serve the meal. It was heart-breaking to see this stalwart woman tiptoeing around the space, clutching her serving dish and weaving between the chairs.

"It looks delicious!" exclaimed Geneviève. "Would you care to serve, Madame Faure?"

Accordingly, in an apartment with no space to receive guests and little food to feed them, Geneviève managed to have herself waited on hand and foot, as though she had a maidservant and the concomitant means.

"When Jean finds a better job," she would say, "we'll get someone in to do the housework, I can't manage by myself . . ."

François, who had once staunchly defended his brother, now scarcely bothered. Jean attributed this change of heart to their recent trip to Beirut, to the moment when François had come to find him on deck and patted his shoulder, as though offering his condolences. Things were bad enough, but now it seemed he was an object of pity.

Jean had dreaded their return to the little apartment near Porte de la Villette after such a luxurious crossing. But, in fact, Geneviève was not given to reproaches; her mother tongue was mockery.

Although she was utterly bored, and Paris life had failed to live up to her expectations, Geneviève would never openly criticise her husband. Her weapons were insinuation, allusion, intimation, which were all the more laden with reproach for being delivered with a smile, as though they were only minor details. "I must look a fright – I didn't go to the hair salon this week, but what can you do, prices are going up all the time!" Jean even managed to remain silent when she said with a dry little laugh: "I think I'll pour myself another little glass of wine, it's not every day we get the opportunity."

The prospect of a job based in Paris was exactly the opportunity Jean had been waiting for. It might open the door to a better future and allow him to get his life back on track. Geneviève was also on tenterhooks. "It's about time they gave you some real responsibility." Jean didn't dare imagine what lunch with François would be like if, by some misfortune ... He was already depressed at the thought of Sunday lunch, since they would also have to talk about the situation with Hélène. She had written to both her brothers to say she was thinking of moving to Paris. "Life here is absolutely unbearable ..."

"And I suppose you think it's not unbearable here," thought Jean.

He drained the carafe of wine. Without even noticing, he had eaten dessert (some kind of pastry, it was hard to tell). It was only 8.25 p.m. but already the restaurant was deserted. The waitress behind the counter yawned. Jean would have to leave soon.

He had been there for more than two hours.

At this sudden, overwhelming realisation, his blood ran cold. He got up from the table, marched over to the telephone like a grenadier, picked up the receiver and asked the operator to put a call through to Paris. The waitress made the most of this opportunity to clear his table and wipe it down, making it crystal clear that they were waiting for him to leave so they could close up for the night.

Monsieur Couderc took the call.

"Ah, it's you, Jean!"

"I'm calling about ..."

He somehow could not frame the question.

"About the Paris job, am I right?"

There was a note of regret in Monsieur Couderc's voice. He was a kind man, he could be a little hot-headed, but he had a good heart.

"Listen, Jean, I'll be honest."

It was over.

Jean could have hung up straight away, but he didn't.

"I've decided to employ an external candidate, I hope you understand. I've got nothing against you, far from it. I just think it's best to ... how shall I put it ... to bring young blood into the company."

He was saying this to someone who had not yet turned thirty.

"But we'll talk about your prospects soon, all right?"

"I resign."

Jean was surprised to hear himself say the words.

There was a silence.

"Don't be hasty, Jean . . . Let's talk about it when you get back, what do you say?"

"I resign," Jean repeated.

Then he hung up. His hands shaking, he seized the bill and paid it.

He took the receipt, carefully folded it and slipped it into his wallet as always, mumbled goodnight, pulled on his coat and left the restaurant.

Half an hour later, he watched from his car as the waitress emerged and headed down the main street towards the bridge. He drove past her, pulled up a short distance ahead, got out of the car and walked towards her.

The little town was shrouded in sleep. It had rained earlier in the evening and the pavements glistened. Jean was worried that the woman would turn right, but she carried on walking towards him. She recognised his face as she passed and frowned. Jean looked blankly at her. A moment later, he felt her eyes on him as she glanced behind her. He waited until he was certain that she had walked on before he turned, retraced his steps, and using both hands and all his might, hit her on the back of the head with the wheel crank he had hidden under his raincoat. She fell to the ground. The blow had been so swift, so brutal that she probably had not suffered. She was dead the moment the iron bar split her skull and crushed her brain. He stepped over her body and walked back to his car, put down the iron bar on which a small tuft of her hair had snagged, and drove away.

To return to his hotel, he had to drive over the bridge where the girl's body lay slumped on the deserted pavement. The pool of blood made a black stain on the road. The town was appallingly deserted. About ten kilometres later he came to another bridge where the road spanned another bend of the river. It was here that he tossed the wheel crank over the parapet.

He spent the night tossing and turning about his resignation.

What would he do now? How would he tell Geneviève? What would his brothers, his father think? These thoughts played on his mind until dawn.

The girl on the bridge was already a distant memory.

She was the second woman he had killed since he arrived in France.

And then there was the girl in Beirut.

7

It's cruel to mock the afflicted

"Ah, so you work at the Exchange?"

The craggy-faced French official with the bulbous purple nose, who had thus far shown little interest in Étienne, suddenly emerged from his torpor. Not so much because he hoped to use him as a contact to apply for a "transfer to France" (though never say never), but out of respect for a colleague whose bribes doubtless dwarfed his own.

"You were saying . . ."

"Raymond Van Meulen, 3rd Foreign Infantry Regiment."

"I'm making a note."

His handwriting was such a scrawl it was a wonder he could read what he had written. On his desk, for the benefit of visitors, a small sign read: GEORGES VAILLANT, PRIVATE, SECOND CLASS.

The French High Commission in Indochina was reminiscent of both an embassy and a police station in that it combined the flaws of both. Here, one was not passed from pillar to post, the bureaucratic procedures were clear and seamless, they simply led nowhere. "This is a matter for the Expeditionary Force!" exclaimed the alcoholic when he finally understood Étienne's request.

"Yes, but the military refuse to provide any information."

"I'm sure they have their reasons . . ."

"And what are your reasons?"

It had been at this point that the clerk discovered that Étienne worked at the Indochinese Currency Exchange.

He leaned towards Étienne (his breath was potent, he clearly lived on Pernod).

"To be honest with you, they don't tell us anything either. Everything is top secret. But . . ."

He glanced around to make sure that no one could overhear. "I'll make enquiries."

He stood up with a beaming smile; he had been fiercely efficient, he was proud of himself.

"Make enquiries? When? Where?"

Until now, the clerk had been considerate, even resourceful, but the young man was beginning to annoy him.

"Point one, I shall enquire with the powers that be, point two, I shall do so as quickly as possible. You should allow at least a week, nothing will happen before then."

As he left the High Commission, Étienne's heart hammered in his chest.

He felt an urge to break everything in his path.

His questions to the Expeditionary Force had been met with silence; here they were met with incompetence. There was nowhere left to turn.

Étienne had been in Saigon for four days now, and had made absolutely no progress. His anxiety had gradually given way to guilt, as though this were a race against time, that he alone could ensure Raymond came back safe and sound, and then only if he acted quickly.

Diêm had promised to get information. Diêm was Étienne's last hope.

But Diêm had disappeared. He had said it would take a day for him to find out, but Étienne had not seen him since.

That evening, when Étienne left the Exchange, he took a taxi to the canal. "He lives somewhere near the car ferry," Gaston had said in a scornful tone that Étienne understood only when he arrived. Here, where the diversionary canal met the River Saigon, the middle-class houses with their little gardens and verandas had given way to patched-up makeshift huts with yards that spilled into each other where children waded through the mud among chickens and pigs. The place bustled with activity: over here, women were weaving, cooking, sewing, darning and making rattan baskets, while over there men in vests were repairing engines, motorbikes, sewing machines.

Étienne's arrival caused a stir among the children to whom he gave loose change – a fatal mistake, as the crowd swelled to three times its size. As he emptied his pockets, Étienne repeatedly asked for "Monsieur Duong Khắc", then tried "Khắc Diêm", and finally "Monsieur Duong", the last possible permutation. The swarm of children made it difficult to advance. Étienne turned this way and that, not knowing what to do, since all the houses looked alike. He was about to give up when he saw an old man with a goatee perched on a tyre in the shade of a wizened tree checking through pieces of paper. As Étienne walked over, the children hung back, perhaps fearful of the old man. When he reached the man, he saw that the pieces of paper were actually lottery tickets sold all over Saigon for a game called "Thirty-Six Beasts and Four Geniuses".

The man spoke French.

"Yes, I *think* I know where Diêm lives."

His message was clear. Étienne took a banknote from his pocket, then another. The old man stared at him evenly as he dug out another bill. When he thought he had paid enough, Étienne simply shook his head. The old man stoically pocketed his takings, struggled to his feet, walked across the large yard and past a row of houses, then pointed to the back of a hut that looked as though it had been patched up after a hurricane.

News clearly travelled fast – much faster than Étienne – because when he reached the shack, Diêm was standing in the doorway, his hair like an exclamation mark pointing at the heavens. "Ah, Monsieur Étienne," he said, but he did not step outside, as though he was trying to block his visitor's view.

Behind him, several children and two elderly women stood watching the Frenchman warily.

Étienne stepped forward.

"Monsieur Étienne ..." Diêm said again.

"It's about my cousin, you said you could get information. But when you didn't come back, I took the liberty ..."

It was hard to tell which of the men was more embarrassed. Diêm, who had been dreading this question, held out his chubby hand and Étienne shook it.

"It's just that ... I did not find out anything, yes, yes ..."

Then, remembering Étienne's previous comment, he gave an awkward smile and carried on in a low voice, now almost devoid of accent:

"There has been no information about troop movements."

"I didn't need you to tell me that, it's what everyone has been saying."

Diêm smiled and bit his lip, shaking his head so that the crest of hair rippled.

"I'm so sorry ..."

It was then that Étienne realised Diêm was lying. And with that lie, this man he barely knew, whose sole responsibility had been to find him an apartment, had destroyed his last hope of finding Raymond.

Diêm was silent not because he had found out nothing, but because he had been ordered, perhaps even threatened.

What about Raymond's mission was so classified that a man like Diêm would keep silent rather than take a hundred piastres for passing on the information?

Étienne had endured four days of anguish and futile attempts, four days haunted by the thought that the man he loved might be dead, the man for whom he had travelled half the world, for whom he would do anything, absolutely anything ... Étienne burst into tears.

It made for a curious sight, this young European man sobbing in a dirt courtyard before a Vietnamese family circumspect to the point of mistrust.

Diêm was still smiling, but it was a cheerless, affected smile, even his unruly tuft of hair had flattened. Behind him, no one moved. What was happening was unprecedented. Étienne turned around and fumbled for a handkerchief, determined not to make a spectacle of himself, but the wave of anxiety that had swelled since his arrival, the feeling that he was going round in circles, the loss of confidence, the black thoughts, the prospect of failure, all these things now poured forth in this sudden, unexpected sadness. He heard Diêm's voice, suddenly shrill and commanding, issuing orders in Vietnamese, then felt a hand on his shoulder.

"Come, Monsieur Étienne, you cannot stand here ..." said Diêm and led him to the door.

"I look like a man in mourning," Étienne thought and, prompted by his innate superstition, summoned all his strength to shake off this impression.

They stepped into a large room where burlap sacks pinned over every window made the darkness seem even blacker than it was outside and lent the faces of the old men and the children sitting there the mysterious air of conspirators or celebrants gathered for some clandestine mass. On the long table in the centre of the room was an empty tray that looked as though it had just been cleared, though it was covered with a fine layer of black which an elderly woman was brushing off with a straw brush.

"Come in, Monsieur Étienne, sit down . . ."

Diêm issued a series of orders. One of the children got up and fetched a glass of water, a woman appeared with a basket of fruit. The smell of the room was difficult to define, a mixture of incense, fermented fish and something acrid, bitter that Étienne did not recognise. As his eyes adjusted to the gloom, he was surprised to see a great number of small painted figurines on the shelves that lined the walls. There were more plaster figurines on the floor, and in straw-filled boxes, ready to be shipped. There was a pile of crates that had already been sealed; the room looked more like a warehouse than a living room.

Étienne took a seat, watched by this silent group whom Diêm did not trouble to introduce. The silence made the situation more uncomfortable, and Diêm seemed to sense this, because he immediately began to speak quickly, and a little too loudly.

"We paint statues used to honour the dead, yes, yes. This is Confucius, this is the Buddha."

Étienne was startled to realise that there were, in fact, only two different figures. Where were the paints, rags and brushes?

"It is the family business, small business, small profit," said Diêm, as though apologising for the humble task.

Suddenly, Étienne needed air. He got up to leave. He had not touched his glass of water.

"Thank you," he said, although to whom was unclear.

He turned to the door, took a step, slipped on some fallen straw and gripped a shelf to steady himself. One of the figurines crashed to the floor, eliciting a scream from those present. From the broken remains of Confucius, a roll of paper unspooled and came to rest next to Étienne's shoe; inside was a small cylindrical package containing a glossy, brownish, somewhat viscous substance . . .

No one moved. Étienne stared at his feet; he had no idea what the substance might be, but he knew it was not prescribed by the Faculty of Medicine.

At length, an old woman stepped forward and swept away the remains of Confucius.

Diêm picked up the little package and held it in his hand, as though about to offer it to his guest.

"It is a small business, you understand? It makes little money, but the family is big."

Étienne stopped him with a wave.

"It's none of my business, Diêm . . ."

Almost reluctantly, he looked around at the sea of faces, most of them were children ranging in age from four to fifteen. Now he understood the reason for the burlap sacks over the windows. What lay in wait for the family, if they were caught, was prison.

"What is it?" he said, out of curiosity. "Opium?"

Diêm laughed cheerfully.

"Oh no, no, Monsieur Étienne! Opium is for people who are rich. This is dross, it is what is left when the opium has been smoked. Very bad. Only for poor people. Very bad."

Étienne glanced at the shelves, at the dozens of frozen figurines.

"We only do the packing. We put a stick of dross up the arse of the great Confucius, and when a crate is full, it is shipped somewhere else in the country."

He grabbed a Buddha statue and handed it to Étienne.

"Here you are, Monsieur Étienne, a souvenir of your visit. That one is empty, you understand?"

Étienne took it with a smile.

"We used to do only Confucius," said Diêm, "but then we changed. The Buddha is better."

"Really?"

"Yes, the Buddha, he has a bigger arse than Confucius, it is more practical."

Diêm walked Étienne out to the yard.

"I can ask a neighbour to take you to the station on his bike."

"No, thanks, I'll walk."

"It is a long way ..."

Étienne nodded to the Buddha he was holding.

"He and I can have a chat ..."

He was about to leave when Diêm tugged at his sleeve.

"Monsieur Étienne ..."

The crest of hair now stood up straight, swaying wildly each time Diêm jerked his head.

"Life is hard, you understand, with the war, and the Việt Minh who extort us, and the French who exploit us. I'm always looking for a good business. I have many ideas, but in the end, I take what I get ..."

He nodded to the house, the yard.

"All this is not good for the children. But this is all I could find. This year is harder than last year ... To stop with the Buddhas, I would need to earn money, for the children, for the family. I have an application ..."

"For a transfer?"

"Yes, very small, very small transfer, if you could ..."

"How much?"

"Oh, only fifty thousand piastres."

"I can't promise anything, Diêm ... I don't know."

In the distance, two of the youngest children had crept out of the house and were watching the two men curiously.

"Bring me your application and we'll see."

*

He headed back, feeling quite shaken. He had no faith in the clerk at the High Commission who had offered to "make enquiries", and he felt heartsick at the thought of Diêm's young children forced to be part of this wretched traffic in drugs.

At the Exchange, he was met by a pile of pending applications that reeked of business scams.

The Exchange received about sixty applications a day. They dealt only with sizeable applications because the most modest transfers, from civil servants sending part of their salary to France, or parents sending money to children studying back in France, were sent directly by money order.

The pile on his desk comprised thousands of piastres of imports that represented millions of francs in France. And still no one had told him what he was supposed to do.

He decided to take the bull by the horns and knocked on the door of Monsieur Jeantet's office.

"I need instructions."

Jeantet looked up and said: "Have you seen this?" as though he had not heard the question.

He folded the newspaper, took off his glasses and rubbed his eyelids for a minute.

"I swear they're obsessed with pieces . . ."

Étienne was already inured. He knew there was no point trying to interrupt the director, the only thing to do was wait in silence, try to work out what he was thinking and then look for a window of opportunity to reel him in like a large fish that has to be brought to shore with the utmost care in case the line should snap.

"The Việt Minh . . . Up near Nam Khái . . . That's up north, near RC 4 . . . They hacked four French gendarmes to death with a machete, the pieces were found piled up by the roadside with the four heads placed on top of a jumbled mass of arms and legs. No one could work out which limbs went with which head . . ."

Étienne felt the blood drain from his face. Were the dead men definitely gendarmes, could they have been legionnaires?

"The gooks are like that," said Jeantet, "they hack things up, they can't help it. Even their food comes in little chunks! It's an obsession, they can't kill someone without grinding him into mincemeat. It must be in their blood . . ."

He got up, walked around his desk and picked up a small black leather photograph frame.

"Did I show you this? That's my dog ..."

Without waiting for Étienne's reaction, he set it down.

"The way the French military work is more psychological. One time, when we were trying to get the Việt Minh to reveal information, we took them up in a plane. We tossed three of them out in mid-air. Let me tell you, the ones that were left told us everything they knew. There's a certain elegance to the approach, don't you think? Have I shocked you?"

Étienne was white as a sheet. He was still thinking of the roadside where the remains of the four gendarmes had been found in piles. Was this what would happen to Raymond?

"Oh, well, I suppose war is war ... Anyway, you were saying you needed instructions ...?"

He was staring at a point somewhere above Étienne's head.

"Yes, well, I expected as much ..." he said dreamily. "Instructions ..."

Étienne needed to focus on something – anything – other than that road in the jungle. He launched into his speech.

"I have been checking dossiers ever since I got here, and now I am supposed to meet with the applicants in person. Some of the applications being submitted are suspicious."

"Suspicious ...?"

"Overcharges, over-invoicing ..."

Étienne did not have time to finish his sentence before Jeantet strode over as though about to smash his face.

"But I know all this, Monsieur Pelletier! Did you honestly imagine that *you* had uncovered the trafficking of the piastre? Just who do you think you are, my young friend?"

His fury abated as quickly as it had flared. Jeantet went back, sat at his desk and ran his hands over his face. He was so weary ...

He reached out, picked up a photograph and turned it so that Étienne could see.

"My first wife. Miriam. A bitch like you cannot imagine ..."

He set it down again.

"There's nothing we can do about it," he whimpered, "you understand? There's nothing we can do ..."

"But, if we're the ones who issue the authorisations, why—"

"They don't need authorisations!"

Étienne waited.

Jeantet, who had hoped the conversation was at an end, was exasperated that he still needed to explain.

"The piastre is part of the French franc zone. If people want to transfer piastres to France, we have no right to object! In theory, they don't even need to ask for an authorisation."

"So, what exactly are we here for?"

"We're playing for time."

Jeantet had finally hit rock bottom. He gestured to the chair reserved for visitors and Étienne sat down.

"The parity between the Indochinese piastre and the French franc is automatic. Notionally, there are no conditions to be fulfilled in order to transfer money. Our job at the Exchange is to put obstacles in their way, nothing more. Because" – it was clear from his expression how shocked he was by the magnitude of the disaster – "this business has already cost France one hundred and eighty billion francs, do you understand?"

Étienne tried to take in this astronomical figure.

"If we don't put obstacles in their way, within a few more years Indochina will be able to buy France with its own money."

"And there's nothing we can do about it?"

"There is. We act like civil servants: we irritate people. We quibble, we cavil, we equivocate, we nit-pick. As I told you: we're playing for time."

"By what right?"

"We have no right. In fact, in the end, we have to sign off on the transfers. But filing an application has become so infuriating that it makes for something of a deterrent."

Étienne still did not see how he should go about his work. In concrete terms.

"We leave it up to the imagination of the individual. Some clerks just demand larger and larger bribes in return for stamping an authorisation, that's their look-out. The rest . . ."

Jeantet gave an equivocal shrug, the rest . . .

*

Étienne's first weekend in Saigon came all too soon. Time was, he had looked forward to his first weekend, now it seemed like a flat boundless desert marked only by the bouts of panic that would suddenly overwhelm him. A dozen times, he thought about renting a car to go to Hiến Giang, only to remember Jeantet's words: "You won't get far without an armed escort."

Every night he brought home fresh fish for Joseph, who had filled out a little since his arrival and now camped at the foot of Étienne's bed when not lying on the windowsill like a sphinx watching the world go by.

On Saturday morning, Étienne was woken by a thudding on the stairs that sounded like the men delivering his trunk some days earlier.

"You said you were too hot, yes?"

Diêm shook his crest of hair and beamed, then pointed to two men setting a battered fridge the size of a wardrobe on the landing.

"American!"

This, apparently, said it all.

Étienne attempted to refuse, but before he could the contraption had already been pushed into the tiny apartment. Diêm had no doubt that his initiative would be appreciated. Étienne took a step back. Now he saw it against the wall, the fridge took up a third of the room. Diêm plugged it in.

"Does it run on diesel?" asked Étienne.

"Yes, it can be a bit noisy at first, but it quickly settles down, you'll see. It's a bargain. For seven hundred piastres, it's a bargain."

Étienne's mouth dropped open.

"But for four hundred piastres, Monsieur Étienne, it's almost a miracle ..."

The fridge was grotesque, overpriced and utterly ridiculous ... He could almost hear Raymond howl with laughter. "Ah," he'd say, "I see you live with your fridge?"

Joseph warily padded up to inspect the beast, then bounded on top and calmly settled himself.

"All right," said Étienne and took out a hundred and fifty piastres.

Diêm briefly frowned, but his expression quickly resumed its usual cheery obsequiousness.

Étienne assumed that Diêm would want to talk to him about the transfer application again, but this did not happen.

"Enjoy your Sunday! You'll probably want to visit the city . . ."

Diêm was always looking to turn a little profit and Étienne was afraid he would offer to be his guide; he wanted to be alone.

"I'll probably wander around, but mostly I'm going to rest. I'm exhausted after my first few days in Saigon."

"I understand . . ."

The fridge did not "settle down". It would be silent for an hour or two, then suddenly judder, let out a hoarse yelp, and begin whistling like a steam engine trying to pick up speed, and when it did, the noise became a dull rumble like a sleeping snorer. Étienne grew to like it. Raymond also snored. Surprisingly, Joseph was not remotely disturbed by the rattling and clank of the appliance where he now spent much of his day, curled up next to the painted Buddha from Diêm.

Étienne spent his Sunday drinking beer on café terraces, sampling char sui pork and fresh pineapple from various stalls, and browsing shops selling bicycles, radios, kitchen utensils, second-hand books, household equipment and tools, all stacked vertiginously high. There was nothing in the world that could not be bought on the streets of Saigon, where expressionless shopkeepers stood in doorways, picked their teeth, used long poles to take down items beyond arm's reach, and proved fearsome hagglers when it came to prices. Standing in front of an electronics shop, Étienne suddenly felt the urge to buy a camera so he could capture these images, keep a record of them for Raymond, for Hélène. At first, he found the idea amusing. Whenever he had borrowed the camera Hélène used in her school photography club, the results had been disastrous. He was incapable of framing a shot, the subject invariably ended up on the edge of the picture, or cut in two. When his mother and Hélène laughed at his attempts, Étienne would pretend to be offended: "I have a slight strabismus in my right eye, it's cruel to mock the afflicted."

True to his impulsive character, which regularly led him to make unhelpful, eccentric or dangerous decisions, he bought a Leica, which the dealer had to show him how to use, and which he advised Étienne to wear around his neck to avoid it being snatched.

Late in the afternoon, he went down to the docks and photographed coolies, scrawny, nimble, expressionless men who unloaded bags of rice that were heavier than they were, while their foremen blew whistles.

The whole harbour teemed with trucks, with sampans pulling in to the wharves of the Messageries Maritimes, everywhere he looked there were bags of rice, rubber, products grown on the plantations, untreated timber, rubber plants, while dockers weaved their way between the cars of owners who had come to supervise the unloading, secretaries bent double so that bills of lading could be signed on their backs, money was passed from hand to hand, and the clamour of voices was drowned out by the querulous sirens of ships seeking a path. Somewhat dazed, Étienne wandered off past the arcades of the General Stores. He had bought some mangoes and, looking around for somewhere to sit, spotted a vacant lot with a cement pillar where he could perch. The sky over Saigon was uniformly white. He had written a brief letter to his parents and a longer one to Hélène. To his mother he wrote that he had not yet found Raymond, but presented it as a normal, predictable delay. To Hélène he had told the truth: "Everywhere I turn, the authorities refuse to tell me anything . . ." If he could not find Raymond, what should he do? Should he stay or go back to Beirut? He remembered Hélène's last letter, the bitter complaints about having to live with their parents. He understood her grievances, in fact he shared them. But now that he had left, Beirut was in the past; whatever happened, his life was forever changed. With or without Raymond.

The very thought made his heart ache.

He got to his feet and, before leaving, turned and surveyed the patch of waste ground which he now realised was a dump. There were crates and sacks, all manner of appliances, even the shell of a burned-out car. His attention was caught by a number of pallets stacked with broken engines, rusty outdated models, many of them stripped, probably for spare parts. He walked over and, on the crankcase of one engine, he read: RN-P1.

These were the famous "prototype outboard motors" imported only months earlier by Leroux Frères to power the junks that plied the river.

The discovery felt like a personal wound. The currency trafficking in the piastre was what sustained and encouraged this futile war in which Raymond had, for the moment, disappeared.

He felt an insidious fury well up inside.

He set off for home, taking a tortuous route that even he did not understand. But everything became clear when he realised that his feet had led him to a seedy neighbourhood, a street lined with bars, where prostitutes touted for trade and Vietnamese men with waxen faces silently smoked cigarettes while scrutinising passers-by with professional attention. But this street was not his final destination. After many twists and turns through the tiny neighbourhood, his intuition led him exactly to a bar with a small terrace. All the customers were packed inside the bar, which was raucous, cheerful, lively, filled with voices and braying laughter. This was Le Camerone, the watering hole favoured by the legionnaires.

Étienne slowed his pace.

Three men in uniform came out and sat at one of the many tables crowded onto the pavement. They glared at him. There was something unsettling, even hostile in their amused silence, in the way they raised their beers as though toasting him.

Étienne took fright and walked away as fast as he could.

He could still hear them laughing when he finally found a taxi.

*

Fuelled by his anger and despair, when Étienne arrived at the Exchange on Friday, he was irritable, short-tempered and driven by a destructive rage. As he scanned the first applications, the Exchange's dubious financial practice appeared to him as a personal insult. The very administration that refused to give him any information about what had become of Raymond was demanding that he rubber-stamp fraudulent applications all day long, that he play a role in fostering this war.

Some superstitious notion urged him to kick over the traces; this was his way of fighting back, of nurturing hope.

He set down the pile of applications next to his desk; he would deal with them later.

He needed to get to the heart of the matter. He walked up to the main counter and offered to see any waiting customers.

The first was a Chinese comprador whose facial features all seemed to be flowing inexorably downwards, as though he were made of wax.

"I see, building work on a country house ..." said Étienne, consulting the dossier, ". . . in Rambouillet."

The comprador's snub nose and thin lips made him look like a turtle. He moved with languid gestures and spoke in a schoolboy French that was punctilious, pedantic and smug.

Monsieur Qiao: Étienne had seen his name on a number of dossiers.

He was acting on behalf of an official at the High Commission.

"Yes, Rambouillet, it's near ..."

"Thank you, I know where it is. And the transfer would be for four hundred thousand francs ...?"

"That's correct."

Étienne leafed through the dossier. The official was using money from Indochina to pay for repairs to his second home. There were estimates from roofers, builders, carpenters, none of which could be verified unless you were in France. The four hundred thousand piastres sent to France would become a million francs the moment Étienne stamped the authorisation.

"Something seems to be missing ..."

"What might that be?"

"The photographs of the house."

"It's a works file, I don't see—"

"Or should I say photographs of the ruin, because for that much money, your client would be better off buying a new house, right?"

He closed the dossier and handed it to the comprador.

"Copies of the entry from the land registry, deed of purchase, history of the property, architects' reports justifying the work required, permission or a notice of exemption from National Heritage, and, for each estimate, a photo of the current state of repair so that we can decide whether it is necessary, and a scale drawing of the expected result."

Monsieur Qiao set his lips, stood up and made to leave, then retraced his steps and bent down.

"Ten thousand francs," he said.

Étienne peered at him.

"In the currency of your choice."

The man placed the file back on his desk.

Étienne picked it up and handed it back.

"For ten thousand francs, you can probably get aerial photographs."

8

The flames of desire

Geneviève sat enthroned in their apartment like an empress. Jean, having spent his days looking for a new job, would come home late in the afternoon to find her in precisely the same position, sitting at the end of the table in the cramped dining room, her back to the window, smiling, useless, and dressed to the nines. Did she adopt this pose when she heard his footsteps on the stairs? It looked as though she had been sitting there all the time, ready to greet her husband as a petitioner whose grievances she was prepared to address with kindness and understanding. When she was not smoking, she kept her hands serenely folded on the table, her pudgy fingers entwined, her nails immaculate.

To Jean, Geneviève's life was a mystery.

What did she do all day? She told him very little. "I went shopping," she would say abstractedly. With what money, Jean wondered, they had so little. But to ask that question would be a slippery slope, so he never ventured.

"Did it go well?" she would say.

Every time Jean came home from an interview, she asked the same question. And Jean always gave the same answer.

"Not very . . ."

This time it had been a job as a sales representative for tools. The applicant was expected to be familiar with pipe spanners, pliers and drills, so the interview had not taken very long.

"Next!"

He had queued for almost three hours for an interview that lasted less than five minutes.

Every morning, Jean would go downstairs, buy a newspaper and go through the classified ads, just as he had done with the evening paper the day before. He would carefully cut out job advertisements and paste them in a notebook, together with the dates, he would write letters, telephone if there was a number, or leave the apartment to go to interviews or to queue with the other unemployed men when the advertisement said: "Apply in person to . . .", followed by an address and times of opening. Despite his great advantage in owning a car, Jean was hampered by a lack of serious, verifiable references. He applied for all manner of jobs in sales (the only field in which he could claim some experience), but there was mass unemployment, the job market was tight, and there was always someone who had an inside track.

Geneviève, perhaps out of kindness, never asked for details of these interviews, she simply recorded the facts: Bouboule had once again come home empty-handed.

"What about you?" he had said the previous day in a sudden fit of anger.

Geneviève raised an interrogative eyebrow.

"Well, it's not as though you have a job either!"

"I," she said in the tone of someone confident of her position, "I am a civil servant!"

Jean had never really understood the whole business about her transfer. Geneviève's father was poised and self-assured: arranging the transfer would surely be a formality. There was a direct link between the Ministère des Postes in France and the Lebanese postal service, and Geneviève's father had insisted he could use his connections to get her into the French civil service. To Jean, the whole affair was utterly mysterious; almost no one in France could find a job, so it was hard to imagine Geneviève would be offered a post without so much as lifting a finger. Although the couple's finances were at their lowest ebb, Jean secretly hoped that his wife would not get a job before he did. The prospect of enduring Geneviève's condescending look was more than he could bear.

The table was laid for a "family lunch", meaning they would be joined by François (who said he was coming alone). The sight of the costly porcelain plates and linen napkins in their tiny apartment was heart-wrenching. Geneviève had insisted on buying a silver planter and a dinner service of Limoges porcelain as a wedding gift to herself. "That's simply the way these things are done," she had decreed. And although most of their possessions were back in Beirut until they could afford a house large enough to accommodate everything, Geneviève had brought with her the planter, the china and the table linen (as well as two sets of bedclothes, including those with which they had dressed the nuptial bed on their ghastly wedding night, which they now slept on every other month). The impeccably laid table was a middle-class island that clashed with their lowly surroundings and, to Jean, it embodied his wife's towering contempt for the pauper's life to which he had condemned her.

The delicious aromas of the meal Madame Faure had prepared for the occasion wafted in from the landing.

François appeared at the door carrying a bunch of carnations, which sent Geneviève into raptures.

"I asked Madame Faure to make us coq au vin," said Geneviève, though she had given no specific instructions.

"Wonderful," said François, who had never liked coq au vin.

The two brothers sat facing each other with Geneviève at the head of the table. She looked as though she was about to ring a bell to summon a butler.

"So," she said, "is it all over with darling little Mathilde?"

Mathilde, Jean remembered, that's right. Mathilde with the small breasts who was shockingly sexy. Out of common decency, François could not tell them that their previous (and only) lunch with Geneviève and Jean had been more than enough for Mathilde. "Your sister-in-law is completely crazy, darling, and your brother is a milksop. Just having to sit and watch them is excruciating, so I think I'll pass."

François tried to think of something to say.

"I've got a post as a reporter on *Le Journal du soir* ..."

The words came before he could stop them. Though he had promised himself not to mention the new job. Not to throw his sister-in-law more red meat she could use to humiliate Bouboule.

But the past two weeks had been a thrilling adventure that rivalled the thrill of shaking hands with Général Legentilhomme in May 1941. For François, being at *Le Journal* was like being in love.

There was another, more obscure and embarrassing reason for his confession. Now that Geneviève and Jean were living in Paris, François could not keep up the lie that he was studying at the École Normale Supérieure, as his parents still believed. Sharing his secret with Bouboule did not worry him, but he had the vague feeling that Geneviève might try to use it to her advantage, which was why he was determined to make a success of his career as soon as possible, to defuse the explosive power his secret might have on the family.

It was a hackneyed subject, but one that François could never quite put out of his mind. Bouboule, the eldest son, had proved he was not up to the task of running the family business, but at least he had been given the opportunity. Needless to say, François would not have agreed to take up the torch after his brother's disastrous experience, but he was hurt that his father had not asked, thereby depriving him of the pleasure of refusing. Nobody ever asked François for anything. He had always been a brilliant student, but although everyone applauded his results they were not interested in his studies. They had admired his bravery in 1941, but there had been no glory and no medal at his homecoming, his wartime accomplishments were relegated to the rank of anecdotes and mentioned only as a historical curiosity. Then, one day, his parents had simply moved on, transferring their interest and concern from Bouboule to Hélène, completely bypassing François ... Oh, they had loved him, François knew that, but deep down he had been deprived of something vital. So, although he regretted announcing his new job at *Le Journal*, it had been a Freudian slip, he simply could not help himself.

Fortunately, his news was overshadowed by the appearance of Madame Faure, straining under the weight of coq au vin with steamed potatoes, which she would have surely dropped had not François rushed to help her. Geneviève's satisfaction as she watched this little scene made her cheeks flush.

François's reprieve was short-lived, for as soon as Madame Faure had served the meal and retired to her own apartment, Geneviève resurrected the subject.

"So, tell us about this new job at *Le Journal*! I want to know everything."

Geneviève seemed to hang on her brother-in-law's every word with the same passionate enthusiasm, thought Jean, that she had shown in Beirut when listening to Monsieur Pelletier talk about perfumed soaps.

Jean did not resent his brother for wanting to do well in his new job. François, after all, was the model son that he had singularly failed to be. He would have been happy to announce that he had found a job too. Nor did he resent his wife, this was who she was, who she would always be. Jean was not jealous by nature.

"I'm working in the news department," said François, trying to stick to the essentials.

"How exciting!" exclaimed Geneviève, a trickle of wine sauce at the corner of her mouth.

François could not resist embroidering his new responsibilities a little, and claiming credit for some of the articles that had appeared in *Le Journal*.

In fact, Malevitz, the editor-in-chief, gave him the chilly welcome he reserved for someone who had been forced on him. He was a newspaperman of the old school, he believed no one should get a free pass, and that reporters should spend a long time paying their dues before being given responsibility. So he had sent François to do the rounds of police stations and local hospitals. François spent his days poring over mundane police reports – the endless domestic disputes, the countless drinking binges and street brawls – desperately looking for some hook, some angle that would catch the reader's attention to justify his writing an eleven-line article.

Although his job was less than enthralling, François found the daily routine of *Le Journal* intoxicating; to him, there could be no more addictive drug. He never missed an opportunity to go down to the presses, to savour the electrifying moment when the paper was put to bed, the chorus of people shouting, the chattering of Linotype type followed by the hum of the rotary presses. He would discreetly pop his head around the door of the Copyediting Room where men huddled around a vast table, proofreading and correcting articles in the glare of the crisscrossing spotlights, amid clouds of cigarette smoke and overflowing ashtrays.

Wherever he went, François found himself bumping into Denissov, driven and focused, tirelessly reading and rereading proofs and final proofs ... François longed for the day when he would take his place at an editorial meeting ... Though that day was a long way off.

As he prattled on, François glanced at his brother, who was bent over his plate and did not seem to be listening. Bouboule, he sensed, was a man at the end of his tether, worn down by the thousand little defeats he had already endured.

"Can you believe it, Bouboule?" Geneviève said at every opportunity.

Bouboule could easily believe it.

"We need to talk about Hélène," he said suddenly.

All three fell silent as they marshalled their strength to deal with a situation that was deeply problematic. François and Jean knew from Hélène's brief missives that she found life in Beirut impossible now that Étienne had left.

Étienne and Hélène were known as "the twins". Although he never said it, Jean thought of them as "the girls". He meant no harm by the nickname, but, when he imagined Étienne in the throes ... Jean, who had no sexual drive whatever was a little disgusted by his brother's.

Since Étienne's departure, Hélène had been like an orphan. Or a widow.

Étienne rarely wrote to François or Bouboule. They imagined that he and his legionnaire were spinning out love's sweet dream and François had better things to do than write letters. Jean pictured Étienne's friend, a tall man, almost disconcertingly masculine ... He dismissed the image from his mind.

In her most recent letter, Hélène had asked whether one of them might take her in.

"That girl will be the death of your mother!" said Geneviève with an impenetrable smile.

For François, who could think of nothing but his new job, and Jean, who could think of nothing but his lack of a job, the request had come at an awkward moment.

"We can easily have your sister to stay with us," said Geneviève, beaming. "We can just replace the table with a bed. There won't be any space to eat, so we'll dine in bed, like the sultans of the Orient!"

She was proud of the image she had evoked.

"What better way to foster conjugal intimacy!"

Geneviève often referred to "conjugal intimacy", a curious concept that simultaneously referred to her desire for peace and quiet, her taste for idleness and the right conferred on her by marriage to be spiteful to her husband and deprive him of conjugal relations. To François, the mention of "intimacy" sparked memories of their crossing aboard the *Jean-Bart II*, so he quietly finished his potatoes.

"You're right," said Jean. "This place is much too small."

"I have the same problem," said François, who had never invited Jean and Geneviève to visit.

"Surely it can't be that small?" said Geneviève. "Besides, now you have your new job, you're surely planning to move?"

"I'm on a reporter's salary, I can't afford to be extravagant."

In her letter, Hélène had said that she wanted to come to Paris to study.

"To study what?"

No one knew. Hélène made no mention of a subject, as though all options were open to her, so it hardly mattered. Jean, always a diligent worker, considered it obscene for someone to have so many talents and yet do nothing with them.

"Living with your parents in Beirut hardly constitutes an ordeal ..."

The moment the words were out, Jean regretted them. He more than anyone could understand why Hélène would find it difficult to be dependent on their parents.

"Anyway, I wrote back to Hélène and told her we couldn't take her in," Jean lied, vowing to do so the following day.

"So did I," said François, folding his napkin.

The matter was closed, but both brothers had a vague inkling that it might not remain so.

"I hope you don't mind," said François, "but I'll have to get going ..."

"A romantic tryst ..." Geneviève whispered in a tone she hoped was suggestive.

"Not really," François laughed. "*The Flames of Desire* is playing at the Régent cinema, the screening starts at four o'clock ..."

As if under a sudden electrical impulse, Geneviève sat up quickly.

"I'd love to see *The Flames of Desire* ..."

François bit his lip – how could he have been so careless?

"Darling, wouldn't you like to see *The Flames of Desire*?"

While Jean was struggling to come up with an answer, she got to her feet (like fat people who turn out to be brilliant dancers, Geneviève moved with the verve and elan of a svelte woman).

"You don't mind if we join you, do you?"

No, no, it didn't bother François "in the least".

It was agreed that Geneviève would need a moment to "put on her face".

"We'll see you at the Régent!"

"The screening is at four o'clock," said François, looking at his watch. "We don't have much time."

"We'll be quick!"

The brothers exchanged an awkward look. Both were horrified by the prospect, but could think of no way to get out of it. It was too late.

François gave a little wave and left.

"See you soon," he muttered, but no one heard.

9

Nothing and no one could have stopped him

The fridge gave a long, guttural roar, followed by a gasp, a rattle. The Buddha slowly juddered as though burping in slow motion. Joseph solemnly raised his head.

Étienne woke.

Sunday morning, nine o'clock, he had slept like a stone. He wanted to get up, but did not have the strength. The noise from the street meant he had not got to sleep until two or three in the morning. My God, but Saigon was noisy . . .

He hated this city, he hated this country, he hated this war, he wanted only one thing: to find Raymond and plead with him to move somewhere, anywhere else. Surely there were more salubrious countries on earth than Indochina? He could not understand why Raymond had fallen in love with it . . . The words hurt him.

The fridge bellowed more hoarsely. Étienne forced himself to get out of bed and open the door of the fridge. It uttered a long groan that Étienne cut short by kicking the metal side, which was usually enough to silence it. As it did now. Unsettled by the sudden blow, Joseph gave a reproachful whimper, then curled up and went back to sleep. As did Étienne.

What a week . . .

Things at the Exchange had quickly become strained.

Opening one of his files, he had found an envelope containing two thousand dollars.

"You forgot this," Étienne said without even looking at the client. "When plain brown envelopes are a required part of a dossier, you will be the first to be informed."

In his first three days, Étienne had rejected half his applications

– a staggering percentage – and word had quickly spread through the departments. "I hear the new guy is blocking transfers."

It was not easy to block transfers. Jeantet had said as much to Étienne, and several well-informed compradors had not failed to remind him.

"There is no crime in requesting a transfer," growled a bald Frenchman with huge sideburns that covered fully half his face, who had submitted a request to import stationery, eighty thousand piastres' worth of notebooks, paper, pens, etc.

"Who said anything about a crime?"

"Well, if there is no crime, just stamp the form right here and authorise the transfer."

"There is no crime, but there is a quota."

The client looked dumbfounded; this was something he had never heard of.

"For certain kinds of transfer," said Étienne, handing back the dossier, "we have a maximum quarterly quota. We reached the quota this morning. It's ridiculous, I know, if you had only come yesterday . . ."

Étienne was not very popular with his colleagues. "What do you mean, he's blocking transfers?" they muttered in the hallways.

"The date of the commission has not yet been fixed . . ." Étienne said to the manager of Kaler & Valesco, an import-export company applying to import Limoges porcelain to the value of 190,000 piastres or a million and a half francs, which, when it reached France, would instantly become three million francs.

"What commission?"

"The quality control commission. New orders from the Ministry of Finance. We are required to set up a commission to review certain dossiers before authorising transfers."

The client was thunderstruck.

"Certain dossiers? Which dossiers?"

"It depends on the product being imported. In this case, Limoges porcelain. If you were importing Baccarat crystal, the authorisation would have gone through without a hitch, but porcelain . . ."

"Hold on, hold on! Can we see the ministerial directive and a list of the products in question?"

"The ministry is a slow-moving beast. We should have it within two or three months, you know how it is. In the meantime, it's our job to enforce it."

On Wednesday morning, Gaston had come to see him.

"You are ruining my job, Pelletier . . ."

"And what exactly is your job? Upgrading your ring twice a year?"

Étienne's tone, like his expression, was brusque and chilly; this was a man who had been seething since he first arrived in Saigon. Gaston pretended that he suddenly understood Étienne's mistake.

"Oh, I see. You think that money transfers to France are immoral, don't you?"

"Soldiers are being slaughtered out here so that some shyster businessmen can make a fortune on the back of France's treasury . . ."

"Not at all, not at all, my friend! The French economy *needs* this war! The war is bringing in three times what it's costing. The piastre is a weapon. It is thanks to the piastre that we manage to persuade certain people who might otherwise side with the communists."

"You don't persuade them, you buy them off."

"All right, then, so we buy them off, would you rather we killed them?"

Gaston put a friendly arm around Étienne's shoulder.

"Hey, relax, Pelly! In this business, everyone's a winner. Now . . . you don't *have* to get in on the scam, but just think about your co-workers . . ."

And indeed, Étienne's co-workers were quick to hammer home the point.

Their complaints reached Jeantet, who had summoned Étienne to his office on Thursday.

"If you order me to sign all transfers, Monsieur le Directeur, then, of course, I will . . ."

"Not all of them, you fool, quite the opposite! Some agents are prepared to accept what others will reject, that is the glorious uncertainty of bureaucracy."

Étienne stood before Jeantet's impressive collection of photographs.

"Just keep doing what you're doing."

Jeantet stood up from the desk and approached Étienne. In passing, he grabbed a small leather-lined photograph frame.

"Did I ever show you this? My first wife, Miriam ... You can't imagine ..."

Étienne closed his eyes. His stupefaction bordered on admiration.

"So," Jeantet said abruptly, "it is my job to call you in and let you know that people have been complaining, so I'm telling you: people are complaining. That's it. People are complaining ..."

"And ...?"

"No one can accuse the Exchange of being too easy-going! The proof is that some applications are rejected. So, reject them, my friend, reject them!"

Needless to say, this meant that Diêm's application came at precisely the wrong moment.

Étienne happened on him standing outside the Exchange. His demeanour was so self-effacing he looked as though he was trying to blend in with the wall.

He held out his dossier. Étienne did not need to open it to know it was a spurious request.

"What is the purpose of the import application, Diêm?"

"Rice."

"Rice? Really? You want to import rice ... to Indochina?"

Diêm pulled a face; this was all he had been able to come up with.

"Not just any rice, Monsieur Étienne, Camargue rice! In Indochina, we don't have Camargue rice, so we have to import it."

They were walking towards the harbour. Étienne wondered whether he could reasonably authorise rice imports.

He let out a long sigh. It was not so much the request that he found intriguing but the process.

"Tell me, Diêm ... There's something I don't understand. You send piastres to a French company that is supposed to ship rice to you. In actual fact, eight months from now, three sacks of mouldy rice will be shipped here and the dossier will be closed. What fascinates me is the francs ..."

"What francs?"

"Well, when the piastres arrive in France, you will convert them into French francs, no?"

"That is the plan, Monsieur Étienne, absolutely."

"What can you do with French francs given that you live here in Saigon?"

Having reached the quays, they stepped to one side so they did not get in the way of disembarking passengers.

Diêm looked embarrassed.

"With the French francs we buy gold, Monsieur Étienne, then we ship the gold back here, convert it into piastres and apply for another transfer."

Étienne was struggling to assess the consequences of this currency trafficking. Diêm understood his bewilderment.

"That's how it works here, Monsieur Étienne, the piastre is sent to France, sent back here, then sent back again ... When it comes to finance, Indochina has invented perpetual motion."

"And how is the gold shipped here?"

Diêm looked towards the liner and all the smiling passengers coming down the gangway, suitcases in hand.

Étienne followed his gaze. Diêm's crest undulated left to right as he watched the machinations of customs officers as they stopped certain passengers and checked their suitcases while waving others through. Clearly the customs officials were showered with bribes, just like the clerks at the Exchange. The trade in piastres was a cottage industry on an industrial scale.

"I'll look at the dossier, Diêm, but I'll be honest, I don't want to give you much hope ..."

It broke his heart to refuse. He could still picture Diêm's children standing in the yard, staring at him; the same children who would spend their nights stuffing drugs up the Buddha's backside.

But how could he reject so many applications only to authorise one that bordered on the ludicrous?

*

On Étienne's second visit to the High Commission on Saturday morning, the alcoholic official who had promised to "make enquiries" about Private Van Meulen no longer regarded him admiringly as a colleague at the Indochinese Currency Exchange. The vast quantities of Pernod he had imbibed since daybreak made it impossible for him to indulge in verbal jousting, so he elected to state the bald facts.

"The French authorities have provided no information."

"Which authorities?"

"The French authorities, as I just said."

"All right, but which French authorities?"

Under normal circumstances, the official would not have deigned to reply, but Étienne's question bordered on insubordination.

"You know what an authority is?"

"I have some idea, but it's your interpretation that interests me. Because, when French soldiers disappear, I'd like to know which 'authority' can make a decision to provide no information to their families."

And so they argued, rage against Pernod, an argument that quickly got out of hand, there was mention of a "pisshead" and a "queer".

A security officer intervened, he grabbed Étienne by the arm and forced him downstairs to the exit. Ironically, Étienne was the alcoholic, being thrown out of the High Commission like a drunk being thrown out of a bar.

*

His second Sunday in Saigon got off to an even more depressing start.

He spent much of the morning lying in bed, reading Raymond's letters. "It was so good to be able to see you . . ." he had written the day after he sailed. Raymond had always preferred to make light of his heartache and to mock his misfortunes, and Étienne had often found himself reproaching his lover's levity. At school, it had been called glibness, François called it flippancy, Bouboule called it superficiality. Other than Hélène (and she did not count), Raymond was the only person to tell Étienne that what he called "his tenderness" made him feel lighter. "I am heavy by nature," he wrote, "your gentleness makes me calm, makes me feel lighter." What was this cross that Raymond had to bear? Would Étienne ever find out?

From the top of his fridge, Joseph shot Étienne a reproachful look. You're not planning on spending all day moping, are you?

Étienne got up, got dressed and went out.

He headed away from the city centre, towards Chinatown, a disreputable district the locals said was "night and day in Saigon". Though quiet, humdrum, almost innocuous by day, it was volcanic, disturbing, sensual and dangerous after nightfall. Étienne walked for a long time along the rue des Marins with its stalls selling grilled food, and shops selling spices, flowers, birdcages, baskets, even hats, while the trams weaved their way through the street. Everyone here ate out in the street, at ramshackle stalls where sweaty cooks worked tirelessly behind the veil of steam that rose from the pots of rice, the smoking grills. Étienne felt terrifyingly alone, not because he was the lone European in the crowd, but because he was unhappy and could see no end to his misery.

In the early afternoon, he headed back to the city centre, to his own neighbourhood, the beating heart of Saigon pulsing with power and money, with pretty women, fat wealthy Chinese men and high officials, the sort of people who had an iced drink at the Pagoda every afternoon, an aperitif at Le Métropole in the evening, and would later be seen in the gaming rooms, on the floating terraces, with Martinis and brandies and soda flowing through their veins, and strings of coloured lights lending a decadent lustre to dinner jackets and a Parisian veneer to the colonial chatter of the regulars.

Although Étienne had headed towards the rue Catinat, his feet refused to obey.

He found himself again outside the terrace of Le Camerone. The legionnaires glowered at him; with thin-lipped smiles, they sized him up, tried him and found him wanting. But Étienne stepped forward; nothing and no one could have stopped him.

He paused next to a table where three soldiers were sipping beers.

"Hello, I'm looking for one of your comrades, Raymond Van Meulen. 3rd Foreign Infantry Regiment, 2nd Company. We've had no news from him since 22 February. Neither HQ nor the High Commission are prepared to give out any information . . ."

His voice trailed off.

As he had expected, as he had feared, nothing happened. After a long silence, one of the soldiers got up and went into the bar. Étienne could hear him talking loudly, his accent was from somewhere in northern France. The other legionnaires were no longer glaring, they had turned away and were staring at the street, at their drinks; a pall fell over the terrace, an ominous silence that seemed to portend tragedy.

It appeared in the form of a man in his fifties. Though considerably shorter than his comrades, he had a handsome square-jawed face and pale eyes. He donned his white képi as he approached Étienne.

"Who are you?"

His tone was not aggressive, nor even suspicious; it was a simple question and he waited for an answer.

"My name is Étienne Pelletier."

But, rather than explaining further, he found himself saying:

"I've come from Beirut to find him."

"Are you a relative?"

The question had none of the sordid innuendo of Lieutenant-Colonel Birard.

"No."

The veteran soldier calmly studied Étienne as he weighed his decision; no one said a word.

"Come with me."

They walked a little way along the pavement. The soldier stopped and turned to Étienne.

By the time Étienne realised who he was, it was too late.

This was the messenger he had dreamed about so often.

In the harsh sunlight, he was a hazy figure whose features Étienne could barely make out; a dark silhouette framed against a deep blue that made him seem ghostly.

"Raymond Van Meulen is dead," he said calmly. "I'm so sorry."

Soon there will only be the bad seats

The Régent cinema was only a few minutes' ride on the métro, but Geneviève, on one of her characteristic whims, decided that they should walk. "The film starts at four o'clock," Jean pleaded, but it was futile. "We've got time. Besides, the walk will do you good. You don't get enough exercise." As though Geneviève hadn't deserved the same reproach, but let's move on.

Having spared herself the crowded métro where a quarrel would have been embarrassing, Geneviève made the most of this forced march to give free rein to her fury. Jean, who had expected some unpleasant remark on the subject of his unemployment, was surprised by her change of tack.

"You know, your parents could do a little more to help us," she said.

Jean stood open-mouthed and watched as Geneviève casually carried on walking with small, determined steps. Monsieur and Madame Pelletier had been very supportive: it was they who had bought the Renault 4CV to make finding a job easier, it was they who had interceded to persuade Monsieur Couderc to hire Jean and it was they who, every month, sent the funds without which the couple could never have made ends meet.

"The pittance they send is just their way of humiliating us. They want to make it crystal clear that *they* have money and *we* don't."

His wife's accusations, as ignoble as they were unjustified, left Jean stunned, but what stopped him from retorting was the fact that this was something new.

Never before had Geneviève allowed herself such a direct assault. He rose to her level.

"Your parents could help out too," he said.

With the courage of a coward, Jean did not defend himself, but went on the attack. Instantly, he realised his mistake. Geneviève, who was smiling at every passer-by as though she knew them personally, did not even look at Jean.

"My parents think I am free of financial concerns. They think I married the eldest son of the Pelletier family."

It was difficult enough for Jean, this life marked by a string of failures, a lack of money, the need to live off his parents, not to mention his gruelling marriage to a woman who did not love him any more than he loved her, this paltry existence that offered him no future, no pleasure, no sex, no joy, no love, no appreciation, but he was so choked by the injustice of it all that he could not say a word.

He walked two steps behind Geneviève, trailing in her wake, his silence tantamount to agreement.

Geneviève continued to flash her puerile, perfunctory smile at shop windows and passing children.

"At a time of national crisis, my husband had the bright idea to quit his job with Couderc."

Geneviève often talked about Jean in the third person, as though he were not there, as though she were confiding in a friend. Indeed, she adopted a tone of amused irony, of complicity, of feigned enthusiasm; these were one-act plays in which Jean was the only audience, the sole dedicatee, played out with all the emotional distance required by a live performance. There was an invisible wall between them that prevented Jean from speaking, from responding, one that rendered him powerless. Powerless – the very word was excruciating.

"You'll see, in a month's time, my husband will have to sell our car just to survive. Life is bad enough already, without having to . . ."

Jean thought he might be dying.

He opened his mouth to speak only to realise that they had arrived at the cinema. Hardly had he uttered a syllable than Geneviève, seeing François pacing nervously, shouted: "We're here!"

"Get a move on," she said, turning to Jean. "Stop dawdling, the film is about to start!"

François gritted his teeth. Aside from the fact that he had never intended to invite them, the cinema was now almost full. Twice the usherette had come to say: "You really should go in, monsieur, soon the only seats left will be bad ones." As the cinema-goers streamed in, François had stared at the métro, only to see Jean and Geneviève appear, on foot, still some distance away, Geneviève leading the way with her sprightly little step and Bouboule, two paces behind, always trailing behind; it was unbearable, they were spoiling everything.

"I bought the tickets," he said, as they headed inside.

"How much do we owe you?" said Geneviève, opening her handbag.

"We'll sort it out later."

François knew she would never offer to pay him back, but all he cared about was not missing the start of the film.

Jean followed the crowd, but his mind was elsewhere.

Geneviève's accusations had been vile, cruel, intended to hurt, and they had succeeded.

There was rampant unemployment, but to listen to Geneviève tell it, Jean was the only man unable to find a job.

True, his parents helped out, but it was never enough.

The house lights were being dimmed as they entered the cinema.

"I'm sorry, I don't have three seats together any more," whispered the usherette.

"It doesn't matter," said François.

Geneviève and Jean found seats at the back, near the aisle, while François followed the beam of the torch to the front row; he was the only one to tip the usherette.

Jean found stepping into the rustling darkness an overwhelming experience. No sooner had he sat down than he was gasping for air and squirming in his seat.

"Sit still, Jean, people will notice . . ."

This was Geneviève's constant concern, what people would think, what the neighbours would think. When they bought curtains for the dining room window, she chose a pair they could ill afford, saying: "They look expensive."

The movie began, the audience gave a collective "aah". Geneviève unfolded her arms, leaned towards the screen. From the opening bars, the theme music swept her away, from her blissful smile it was clear she had entered a different dimension, one filled with romance, with passion; already she could feel *The Flames of Desire* burning within her.

Afraid that he might faint, Jean got up and walked down the aisle to where a small green light indicated the toilets. There were two doors, Gents on the right, Ladies on the left. He pushed past a woman rushing back inside; the movie had started and no one wanted to miss a moment. As he stepped into the toilets, he had to squint against the harsh light. He walked over to the urinal. He had no need to urinate, but his heart was hammering, his hands were shaking, he was convinced he would collapse here, his back to the half-open doors of the foul-smelling stalls, he felt as though he was dying.

Suddenly, he raised his head.

As though propelled by some new, unexpected source of energy, he left the toilets, walked along the narrow corridor and went into the Ladies. It looked empty, but Jean's instincts had not failed him: the door to one stall was closed; there was someone inside.

Jean was completely lucid, his mind registering every detail, every sound, his brain storing every sensation the moment had to offer. Without a second thought, but with calm determination, he stood in front of the closed door, which opened almost immediately. The young woman was staggeringly beautiful; Jean was lost for words. She gave a surprised little "oh", but it was too late. Jean had already grabbed her by the hair and she was on her knees, arms stretched out to the ceiling. He gripped her head with both hands and smashed her skull against the toilet bowl, but she turned her face at the last moment and he succeeded only in breaking her nose and slashing her cheek. She was bleeding heavily. He stepped back to avoid the spray of blood and, grabbing her head again, pounded it against the porcelain toilet and then against the wall. The woman crumpled in a heap, blood pouring from her. Jean stepped out, closed the cabin door and washed his hands in the basin without looking at himself in the mirror.

Moments later, back in the cinema, he peered into the darkness as he groped his way to where Geneviève was sitting and sat down.

His wife did not notice his return any more than she had his departure.

Jean stared at the flickering images, but nothing stuck in his mind, he was completely drained, he could have fallen asleep.

On the screen, a man was talking to a girl. He was saying something, she listened, she understood, then she spoke to him; they clearly felt a connection because now their lips were pressed together. To Geneviève, the scene was much more real than life, or more real than her life. It was at that moment that the whole cinema was frozen by a shrill scream: "Help! Help! A woman has been murdered! Help!"

There came the sound of hurried footsteps, shouts, everyone in the cinema turned towards the toilets. The projector juddered to a halt. "Help!" shrieked a panicked voice. "Murder!"

The house lights came up. There was a stampede. It was as though fire had broken out in the projection booth and was threatening to spread. Everyone was on their feet and scrabbling to get out; in an instant the seats were empty. Geneviève was pushing her way through the crowd. Jean took her by the arm and they headed for the exit. The audience was pushing and shoving, panic had begun to spread, a man appeared – probably the cinema manager – he tried to say something but no one listened and he was swept along by the crowd as they poured out of the building and across the street. Once there, they stopped and fear gave way to morbid curiosity and they turned as one and stared back at the building.

François, for his part, had elbowed his way into the toilets. He had been first to jump to his feet and had run towards the corridor leading to the toilets. He had almost reached the source of the screams, but could move no further. Despite the desperate crowd attempting to leave, a small group had gathered near the toilets, and everyone was craning their necks trying to catch a glimpse of something.

"Out of the way!" said François.

"Police," he roared, when no one moved. "Out of my way!"

This was the magic word. The crowd parted. A few people were standing in the doorway of the Ladies, but no one had dared go inside. The usherette was leaning against a washbasin, hands covering her face, shaking convulsively.

Opposite her, one of the stall doors was ajar; a pool of blood was spreading across the floor and trickling between the shock of blond hair spread out on the tiles.

François swore under his breath – why hadn't he brought his camera with him?

He stepped forward, slowly pushed open the door to the stall and saw the woman sprawled on the floor.

He knelt down, suppressing the urge to retch, then reached out and touched the woman's shoulder. He glanced behind him. There was no one. He reached out his other hand. Slowly the corpse rolled onto its back, revealing the victim's shattered face. Hearing a sound behind him, François turned. The usherette was vomiting into the sink.

He turned back to the body on the ground and took out his notepad.

*

Jean and Geneviève had joined the group on the opposite pavement. Had someone called the police?

"Did you see anything?" asked a woman, her voice trembling with fear.

"A dead woman! In the toilets!"

The versions varied from one spectator to another, but all seemed to agree.

"She was murdered right there in the toilets!"

"Strangled," said one.

"Stabbed," said someone else.

The crowed parted slightly as an elderly woman on Geneviève's right was taken ill. Her face was frozen, white as a funeral shroud, her lips moved soundlessly as though she were praying.

Geneviève helped her sit down on the pavement.

"Is she the one who found the body?"

"No," said her husband, almost apologetically, "but she did see it, she said it was gruesome."

"Her head . . ." the woman whispered. "It was like it had been slammed against the floor!"

There came a chorus of "oohs" and "aahs" as this nugget of information spread.

Geneviève put an arm around the woman's shoulders.

"The top of her skull," the woman said. "Crushed. It was terrible, terrible . . ."

*

François had struggled not to throw up at the sight of the unfortunate victim. Now, the stench of vomit rising from the washbasin mingled with the smell of fresh blood made his stomach lurch into his throat. But he managed to keep a grip on himself. Hurry up, he said to himself, just hurry up. He held his breath and tried not to look at the flecks of brain matter stuck to the wall. He took out his handkerchief, wrapped it around his hand and picked up the victim's handbag, a pearl bag with a gold clasp. He got to his feet, gripped his notebook between his teeth and stepped out of the stall so he would have more light.

Now that there was a police officer present, the gaggle of onlookers became bolder, poking their heads around the door. The officer seemed preoccupied with examining the contents of the victim's handbag, so they crept further, and one by one, as at a freakshow exhibit, they came upon the gruesome scene, quickly clapped a hand over their mouths to stifle their screams. They filed past, horrified and thrilled by these shocking images they could relay to others, some of which had already reached the crowd across the road where Geneviève was still cradling the distraught woman on the pavement.

All the while, François was working frantically.

He turned away from the body, the face had now turned purple, opened the handbag and found an identity card.

My God . . .

Mary Lampson!

*

Outside the cinema, the police had arrived. One of the officers bent down next to the woman who had had a funny turn. "It's all right, madame, we'll take care of you . . ." Then, turning to the others, he growled: "The rest of you, stand aside!"

The woman got to her feet, clutching her husband's arm, and stumbled away. The crowd had also begun to get bored. Now the police were here . . .

Geneviève stepped back and glanced at Jean, who was looking a little unwell.

"Let's go," she said.

They walked towards the métro. Then, suddenly, Jean stopped dead.

"We haven't seen François . . ."

"What do you expect, with all those people running around all over the place . . ."

She was not particularly eager to see François just now; perhaps she should have reimbursed him for the tickets. She carried on walking and Jean trailed after her.

"It's unbelievable, isn't it? Right in the middle of a movie!"

Geneviève did not sound shocked, merely amazed that such a crime could be committed in a crowded cinema. She shook her head, as if to say: "He must have some nerve . . ."

"And after all that, and they didn't even refund our tickets."

As the métro stops flashed by, Geneviève gave Jean a sidelong glance.

When they got back to the apartment, it was not yet six o'clock.

Half-heartedly, Geneviève set about clearing the table, which still bore the remains of lunch; the room was as cheerless as a wet weekend.

"You don't look too good."

"I'm fine, I'm fine."

They hung their coats up by the bed as usual.

"What's this?"

Geneviève was studying Jean's jacket, screwing up her eyes.

Jean said nothing.

She touched the stain with her forefinger. Almost brought it to her lips . . .

"Is it . . . blood?"

She turned to face him.

He stammered something incomprehensible, then, suddenly beaten, he slumped into the armchair, his knees spread.

Geneviève went over to him, her voice was grave. It was not the tone of the angry schoolmistress she sometimes used with him.

"You need to be careful, Jean, you know that, don't you?"

He nodded, yes, be careful . . .

She stared at her crimson forefinger as she rubbed it against her thumb. She smiled absently, as though at some ancient memory.

"The problem is . . . it stains . . ."

She said it as a simple fact.

Jean was deathly pale.

She ran her splayed fingers through her hair.

"You're a little shaken, my little Bouboule, but that's all right . . ."

She took his head in her hands and held it against her belly.

"Everything is going to be all right," she crooned. "It's nothing, don't worry . . ."

For a long time they did not move.

Then Geneviève knelt between Jean's legs.

She smiled as she grabbed his belt and unbuckled it with a single movement.

11

I've checked, there's not a centime missing

Although Monsieur Pelletier would never have admitted it, he had been more affected by Étienne's departure than he let on. He secretly shared Hélène's sorrow; he too missed his youngest son's dry wit, his hard-won *joie de vivre*. At home, it felt as though something was missing. The feeling was more acute than it had been when Bouboule and François left. His eldest son's departure had been an escape, almost a relief. With the younger, it had felt like victory, the prospect of success at the École Normale Supérieure: François would be someone. When he thought about his sons, he could not but feel sorry for Jean who, Monsieur Pelletier had to admit, had no aptitude for anything, he hadn't even married well; Jean was languishing and his future looked no brighter than his angst-ridden unexceptional youth. Monsieur Pelletier had not known what to do with Jean, and did not realise until it was too late. Bouboule had deserved a better father. The failures of the son were visited on the father; it was heart-breaking.

Louis Pelletier even reproached himself for the joy he felt at François's effortless success – it was too easy ... He admired François. At eighteen, the boy had signed up to fight in a war that seemed lost and which he had helped to win, one that had brought him nothing, not even the respect of his country. Monsieur Pelletier felt this ingratitude as keenly as if he had been the victim. To see the success he had made of his studies was truly something.

And then there was Étienne ... Monsieur Pelletier, who never let his innate sentimentality cross the threshold of the soap factory, felt guilty that he had not told Étienne how much he loved him before he left.

Now, they had only Hélène, and she wanted to leave too, you

had only to look at her to know that she was just waiting for something, for some door to open. She was too young, too immature, she needed to be steered from the paths where her fiery temperament might lead her, to be protected from the temptations of her age ... While Angèle was relieved to see Étienne fending for himself, Louis was grateful that François (who was studying at a prestigious university) and Jean (who could not shake his rotten luck) still needed his financial support. "At least we're still of some use!" he would say proudly and Angèle, glancing at Hélène, would mutter that she was not so sure.

This was what Louis was thinking about when Monsieur Chakir stepped into the lobby of the Hôtel Kassar in a suit two sizes too small, clutching an outsize briefcase like a leash.

It was 11 a.m. and Monsieur Pelletier reluctantly turned away from the Mediterranean, which in late morning was a reddish purple; the "wine-dark sea", thought Hélène, who had read Homer and was standing in front of the picture window of a room three floors up, gazing at the horizon while, behind her, Xavier Lhomond was thrusting away, whispering lewd insults that left her bored. She had never understood this aspect of his sexuality. She had ceded to his every whim, but some, like this, bordered on the ludicrous; it was not worth it. She felt him stiffen, he let out a moan. She had enjoyed beautiful moments with him and with others ... In the beginning it had been exhilarating. Lhomond photographed her, found her beautiful, his caresses were divine, but, as the months passed, his imagination, his passion and his admiration had palled. She had confessed her disenchantment.

"If all you want is to fuck me once a week, just say so, it'll make things easier."

Lhomond had slapped her. Hélène could not believe it. Even her father had never raised a hand to her.

"Does that make things clearer?" he said.

He had undressed her while she was still in shock. When he climbed on top of her she started to sob and this seemed to arouse him greatly; he licked away her tears saying: "Go on, cry, cry, you look so beautiful when you cry." Her sobbing redoubled and when it was over she did not know what to do. Now, he often slapped her, he had developed a taste for it and she no longer knew what she wanted. It was at that point that he started talking dirty, which quickly turned to him insulting her, and Hélène accepted it because Lhomond could be unpredictable. When she said she might stop seeing him, he would fly into a rage, and she instinctively brought her hands up to shield her face, then he would take her in his arms – this was the moment she loved – and he would stroke her hair, her neck, her back . . .

*

Monsieur Pelletier counted the banknotes and handed them to Monsieur Chakir, who, in his beautiful, cursive handwriting, wrote out a "receipt for donation". It was really a huge sum, one of the largest the school had ever been given.

"This is a historic moment," said Monsieur Chakir.

"It's only money," Louis said.

They spent an hour going over the school's accounts, checking the calculations. Chakir's bookkeeping had a meticulous, detailed precision that Louis found unnecessary and tedious. By now, he was eager for lunch.

As they headed to the dining room, they checked their briefcases into the cloakroom.

"Will they be safe here?" said Monsieur Chakir.

"In a hotel of this stature? Come, come . . ."

As they arrived at their lunch table, Louis suddenly slapped his forehead.

"I forgot to call my wife! Do you mind?"

Monsieur Chakir gave a little wave – not at all, go ahead.

Louis went back to the cloakroom and, having checked that Monsieur Chakir was admiring the views of the wine-dark sea, opened the school treasurer's briefcase, took out the wad of cash and slipped it into his own case.

Over lunch, Louis was not particularly talkative. But Monsieur Chakir needed no encouragement to prattle on, so Louis simply smiled and nodded. Étienne's first letter from Saigon had recently arrived and Louis had found it deeply concerning. There had been none of the joy that everyone expected, and nothing, of course, about being reunited with Raymond since Étienne had not yet tracked him down. "He's probably out on a mission somewhere, he'll be back in a few days," was what Étienne had written. Then came the incident that Louis tried to dismiss from his mind, but which continued to haunt him ... Angèle, who was convinced that Étienne was more forthcoming with his sister than with his parents, had ... rifled through her daughter's private papers. The very thought made Louis queasy. Such things were simply not done. But the results of Angèle's search made him still more uneasy for, in the letter his wife discovered, Étienne had written: "There is no sign of Raymond! Everywhere I turn, the authorities refuse to tell me anything ... I can't get a wink of sleep. I fear the worst. What if Raymond is dead?" Oh, he had included a few typical witticisms (he told Hélène that Joseph was now homosexual, he related an anecdote his parents did not understand about seeing Joseph screwing the Buddha on top of a fridge, which was probably a euphemism for something else that Louis didn't understand ...), but you could tell that his heart wasn't in it. Étienne was worried, Raymond had disappeared. He had said nothing about his job at the Indochinese Currency Exchange. Louis flinched when he remembered raising a toast to the whole family: "To Saigon!"

In retrospect, he felt ridiculous.

*

"Stop!"

Hélène laid an imperious hand on Lhomond's chest that stopped him in his tracks.

"Over there, the table on the right, it's my father ..."

They were at the far end of the corridor that led out to the terrace, the only possible exit. Lhomond warily peered around the corner. Hélène was right, that old fool Pelletier was having lunch with the school treasurer, the fat Indian, Chapir, Chamir, something like that, Lhomond couldn't remember, Indians all looked the same to him.

"Shit ..."

Lhomond glanced at his watch. They were already running late.

"Have they nearly finished?" he asked.

Hélène peered again.

"I think they're on the coffee, but they could be awhile yet, you never know."

Lhomond turned to her, annoyed.

"If you'd just shifted your arse a bit ..."

This was unfair. Hélène's father and Monsieur Chakir had clearly been here for an hour or two. What Lhomond should have done was not come here today, go somewhere else, but ...

"Stupid bitch!"

He looked at his watch again.

"Damn it, I can't afford to be late!"

He was tapping his foot; Hélène had ceased to exist.

"I can't stand around here, I have to get home, pick up my lesson plans ..."

He was muttering to himself.

There was another way out, but that entailed walking the length of the terrace, which would make him even more noticeable. Hélène could feel him steeling himself.

"Shit, shit, shit," he muttered through clenched teeth.

He made up his mind.

"I'll walk quickly, I'll duck behind them and keep to the right. With a bit of luck ..."

"What about me?"

"You stay right here, got it?"

He was livid.

"If you skip school, who's going to care? You wait here until they leave, however long it takes, is that clear?"

But for the fact it would attract attention, Lhomond would have slapped her; that would have made him feel better.

He set off.

Louis looked up just as Lhomond was passing and brushed against their table.

"Well, well," he exclaimed, "isn't that Monsieur Lhomond, the maths teacher?"

"Indeed it is!" said Monsieur Chakir, delighted at this chance encounter. "Monsieur Lhomond! Hey! Monsieur Lhomond!"

Everyone in the room turned, except for the fugitive who put his head down and looked as though he planned to raze everything in his path.

"That's very strange," Louis said.

Monsieur Chakir could not believe his eyes.

But the treasurer's troubles were far from over because, after the president had paid the bill and they returned to the cloakroom, Monsieur Chakir's briefcase felt surprisingly light. Puzzled, he opened it. The large leather wallet containing the school funds was missing. This would have been a bitter blow to anyone.

For Monsieur Chakir, it was a catastrophe. Had he been Japanese, he would have committed seppuku on the spot.

"Well, I never . . ." Louis Pelletier said over and over.

Then, coming to his senses, he strode over to the reception desk to explain what had happened, and Hélène took this opportunity to creep out.

The maître d'hôtel appeared, a search was conducted, a call was put through to the manager at his home, the whole thing seemed impossible – how much money was in it? You don't just leave a briefcase like that in the cloakroom, ventured a member of staff. Louis saddled his high horse. How were we to know that this hotel is a den of thieves? The argument was becoming heated. Then a cry from Monsieur Chakir silenced everyone.

"Monsieur Lhomond!"

"What about Monsieur Lhomond?" said Louis.

Trembling and white as a sheet, the poor treasurer was clearly racked with guilt. It took some minutes for the other to work out his train of thought: Monsieur Lhomond had obviously passed the cloakroom where the briefcase was stowed; it was odd for the maths teacher to be here at the hotel, since he lived in the city centre; almost everyone in the school had been aware that he and Monsieur Pelletier were meeting at the restaurant to go over the accounts, Monsieur Lhomond had deliberately pretended not to hear when Monsieur Chakir called his name; he had absconded . . . like a thief!

Now that he had the bit between his teeth, there was nothing anyone could do. Louis said it sounded a little far-fetched, but when Monsieur Chakir refused to budge, he made a conciliatory suggestion.

"Why don't we go and have a polite chat with him? And if intuition proves incorrect, as I think it will, we'll simply report the theft to the police. Besides, money isn't everything, I'll cover the loss . . ."

"Impossible!" said Monsieur Chakir.

His very life was at stake.

They caught a taxi outside the hotel and headed for the rue du Commandant-Deligeard. The mailbox in the hallway indicated Lhomond's apartment was on the second floor, they raced up the stairs as fast as their respective weights allowed and Monsieur Chakir hammered on the door while Louis said repeatedly: "Come now, Monsieur Chakir, you're overcome, you need to calm down . . ." But the treasurer was not listening. "Monsieur Lhomond, open this door!" Neighbours popped their heads out; Louis gave an apologetic shrug.

The door opened.

The teacher looked nervous; he had his lesson plans under his arm. He tried to walk past them, but Monsieur Chakir grabbed him by the sleeve and before Lhomond had time to close the door behind him, Monsieur Chakir had pushed it open and stepped inside.

What ensued was very strange indeed.

Lhomond, deathly pale, stood frozen, staring at Monsieur Pelletier, his lips parted on a word that did not come. Without taking his eyes off the teacher, Louis stepped around him and entered the apartment.

Monsieur Chakir, now completely calm, had taken barely three steps into the room. Rooted to the spot, he stared helplessly around the living room.

Two of the walls were covered from floor to ceiling with large photographs.

The photographs were of young girls, all naked, some in languid or lascivious poses, but most were seductive, showing off their bottoms, their vulvas, always staring straight into the lens. What was most shocking was the contrast between the extraordinary youth and innocence of the models and the lewdness of their poses; the incongruity was heart-breaking.

There were more than fifty photographs.

Including dozens of pupils from the school.

Louis recognised faces of former pupils, now married with children, and more recent photographs: over there was Monsieur Chakir's daughter, and next to her Hélène ...

Monsieur Chakir stood paralysed in front of the wall of images.

As for Louis, he turned and left, walked back across the landing and down the stairs while Monsieur Lhomond, in a toneless voice, pleaded, "I'll resign, I'll do it today ..."

Louis walked home, and from there went straight to the factory where he locked himself in his office.

It had been a bitter victory ...

His suspicions had been aroused when he first met the teacher at the beginning of the school year, when Hélène joined his class. Lhomond was simply not the kind of man he felt he could trust with his daughter. His suspicions had been reinforced when Hélène signed up for Lhomond's after-school photography workshop. Teaching maths was one thing, but extra-curricular activities ... Seeing that Angèle was concerned, Louis had tried to reassure her: there was no point in both of them worrying. "It's a very good school, Angèle!" At a meeting with the school board, he had taken the opportunity to consult the teacher's schedule and compare it with Hélène's timetable. When he discovered that Hélène was setting off to school on mornings when she had no lessons and when Lhomond was coincidentally not teaching, Louis took his bicycle and rode around the city. It was ridiculous, but Louis could not see what else to do. Ridiculous but productive, since by bicycle he could cover much of the city in a morning. It took only three such mornings to find what he was looking for: the teacher's car parked in front of a new hotel in the west of the city.

Shortly after noon, he saw his Hélène emerge and, ten minutes later, that bastard Lhomond, who sat in his car for a long time, gazing at himself in the rear-view mirror and running a comb through his hair before driving off. Louis's first instinct was to smash the man's face, but that risked making the teacher into a martyr in Hélène's eyes, and that was not his aim. So, Monsieur Pelletier had come up with a more convoluted and, ultimately, unnecessary plan. His idea of asking to go over the school accounts and inviting the treasurer to the Hôtel Kassar had been for nothing. In the end, he had not needed to steal Monsieur Chakir's wallet, hide it in Lhomond's apartment and pretend to find it.

After a fashion, discovering Lhomond's collection of photographs had pulled the rug out from under his feet.

Louis Pelletier slipped the treasurer's wallet into a large brown paper envelope with a note to Monsieur Chakir. "The staff at the hotel found your wallet. I've checked, there's not a centime missing! Yours faithfully, Louis Pelletier."

He asked one of the young factory workers to deliver the package, which arrived just as Monsieur Chakir got home.

Louis sat brooding for a long moment; he remembered seeing Hélène creeping through the restaurant, hoping that no one would notice her.

Louis was in great pain.

First Étienne, now Hélène . . . What was wrong with this family? Had he failed them somehow?

That evening, he was silent, almost morose.

"Is there something wrong at the factory?"

"No, no . . . Everything is fine," he said with a smile.

Hélène thought back to the moment when she had spotted him on the restaurant terrace; he looked like a different man now.

"What about you, darling," said Angèle. "Everything all right?"

"Yes, fine. Monsieur Lhomond resigned this afternoon. He was offered a job in Tripoli, he had to start right away, so he didn't come back to school."

She had been told the news when she arrived at school to find there was no class.

She felt both a strange relief and a dull ache; something had been stolen from her, but she could not say what.

"It's for the best," said Angèle. "I never did care for that man."

"There was nothing wrong with him," her husband said indulgently. "He was a very devoted teacher . . ."

Hélène looked at her parents; they looked old.

It was then that she realised that she too would soon be leaving home.

12

When a life is permanently turned upside down

Étienne spent the afternoon in his room, his face buried in his pillows.

Ever since his arrival in Saigon, he had felt deep down that he would never see Raymond again. How else to explain the prolonged silence? He had hoped that perhaps Raymond had been wounded, perhaps even captured, but he was dead.

Life now looked like a barren wasteland.

He became aware, in sudden flashes, that he would never see him again.

The legionnaire had said little, sticking to the bald facts: the remains of Private First Class Van Meulen and a number of his comrades had been found by a search patrol.

How had he died? Had he suffered? Where was he buried? Had his family been contacted?

When Étienne pressed him, the soldier had responded with vague nods. How much did he truly know? Impossible to tell. He had passed on the news out of sympathy for the young man, and in solidarity with his fallen comrade, but would go no further. When Étienne bombarded him with questions in a faltering voice that betrayed his distress, the soldier simply said:

"Mission reports aren't shared with regular soldiers, you understand? We only know what the top brass choose to tell us ... We have honoured our comrades. They have been avenged, take my word for it ..."

He made to salute, but, fearing it might seem pompous, gave up and went back into the café.

When not plunged into a bottomless void at the thought of never seeing Raymond again, an exhausted Étienne heard this sentence running through his head, haunting and mysterious: "Mission reports aren't shared with regular soldiers." Had Raymond been shot? Had he been stabbed? Was he really dead?

The leader of the search party that found Raymond and his comrades had written a report, which was probably buried in the archives of the Expeditionary Force. Étienne remembered Lieutenant-Colonel Birard, ramrod straight in his uniform, staring straight ahead, peremptorily announcing: "There are no troop movements reported near Hiền Giang." The only thing that still connected Étienne to Raymond was this "mission report"; Birard had probably read it, perhaps even had a copy.

Étienne wanted to kill him.

But this was not why he took a cold shower, dressed and headed down to Le Métropole. He was unarmed, and he was not fool enough to grab the officer by the throat. He simply wanted . . . the truth.

He intended to cause a scene.

No one could stop him.

The Sunday crowd was no different from those who came during the week, though now they gorged on idleness and pleasure. The wives and daughters of senior civil servants had spent the day bathing in the swimming pools of the plateau residences, and now sipped cocktails, while the men treated themselves to cigars.

Lieutenant-Colonel Birard had not yet arrived, but Monsieur Jeantet was seated at his usual table. When he saw Étienne, he beckoned him over. Then he noticed his underling's disconsolate expression.

"What's the matter with you?"

"I'm just feeling a little off colour, it's nothing serious."

Étienne scanned the crowd on the large terrace constantly. Jeantet stared at him.

"You seem in a strange mood this evening . . . Are you looking for someone?"

"No, I'm sorry . . ."

But his search had not been fruitless.

"Shit . . ."

"What is it?"

"Over there . . . isn't that Monsieur Michoux?"

Jeantet looked embarrassed, he turned away and heaved a sigh.

"I thought he had left the country permanently," Étienne said. "He transferred all his worldly goods back to France!"

"And then he came back, I know . . . It's the third time he has done it, he leaves every two years. After a while, he claims to feel 'homesick', so he comes back and takes up his old job at Marton & Xavier."

Michoux, who was drinking with friends, looked happy as a newlywed.

"You could have told me," Étienne said.

"If I'd told you, it would have put you in an impossible situation, given that he had actually sold all his possessions and handed in his resignation. We had no grounds to refuse his application, that's just the way it works, it's the law . . ."

But Étienne was no longer listening.

Monsieur Qiao, the turtle-headed comprador, had suddenly appeared before them wearing an elegant suit. He bent down and solemnly greeted Monsieur Jeantet, then nodded to the two empty chairs.

"Do you mind?"

Étienne had a lump in his throat, he wanted to kill the man standing in front of him. If he had had a gun, he would have put a bullet through his head.

Because Monsieur Qiao was not alone.

"May I introduce Vĩnh, one of my nephews?"

A slim, graceful boy took the seat next to Étienne. Very handsome.

"Vĩnh is nineteen, he is studying hotel management."

Étienne, stunned by the circumstances, could not take his eyes off the boy now smiling awkwardly at him, who was not a day over sixteen.

"I've taken the liberty of briefly interrupting you to talk about my client's application. You remember, the building work on his house in Rambouillet?"

"No one tells me anything . . ." said Jeantet, who could not have cared less. "What is this about?"

While Monsieur Qiao restated the reasons for his client's application, Étienne tried to catch his breath.

In exchange for his authorisation on the transfer request, Monsieur Qiao had come to . . . offer him a boy. It was very simple.

What followed was a single glance, but it would be etched on Étienne's memory as one of those rare moments when the course of a life is forever changed.

It was not the look of the boy sitting next to him, available and willing, but that of Lieutenant-Colonel Birard, who had arrived without Étienne noticing.

He was sitting four tables away, looking from Étienne to the young Vietnamese boy next to him, a look that was at once prurient, triumphant, disdainful, mocking.

Humiliating.

Appearances were against him. Étienne could have laughed it off, after all he had a clear conscience, but the news of Raymond's death had left him shattered, he had no fight left in him, so he abruptly got to his feet.

Monsieur Qiao trailed off, nonplussed. Étienne turned to the director.

"See you tomorrow."

Then, without a word, he left Le Métropole, took a taxi to the canal near the car ferry, paid four times the fare, said: "Wait here," strode across the dirt yard, shooing chickens from his path, threw open the door to the shack and, seeing Diêm sitting at the table flinch and the faces of everyone else turn as one with a look of fear and terror, walked over and said:

"Diêm, I am going to authorise your request for a transfer."

"Oh, monsieur . . ."

"In fact, I will even make it for ten times the amount."

"Excuse me?"

"Find a pro-forma invoice for five hundred thousand piastres for something, anything, and I will authorise it as soon as I receive it."

"But . . ."

"In exchange, I need you to do something for me."

This time, Diêm made no attempt to interrupt, he simply waited, his face tense.

"I need you to get me a copy of a report from the Expeditionary Force Headquarters. Do you think that's possible?"

Diêm closed his eyes for an instant.

Then, calmly, as if against his better judgement, he simply nodded: yes, it was possible.

13

Don't do anything without talking to me

Mary Lampson.

My God ...

François turned back towards the toilet stall.

The long, slim body. The blond hair.

He tilted his head to see whether he could make out her face, but the shattered skull, the black blood made it impossible. The stench of blood and vomit was getting to him.

He looked down at the identity card.

Nationality: French
Address: 12, rue Général-Lenizewski, Neuilly-sur-Seine
Height: 1 metre 70. Weight: 53 kilos

Hurry up.

François feverishly kept taking notes. To avoid leaving finger-prints, he carefully used his handkerchief when picking up objects.

Hurry up.

Her wallet contained several hundred-franc notes, the cards of various shops in Paris, and a handwritten note: "My darling, don't do anything without talking to me. Let's make the decisions together. I love you." It was signed: "M."

A makeup bag. Some chewing gum. A bunch of keys.

Hurry up.

He could hear voices in the corridor. "Stand aside, stand aside, ladies and gentlemen, please ..."

François stood up, stepped over the corpse, put the handbag back where he had found it, stuffed his handkerchief in his pocket and bumped into the policemen as he walked out.

Turning back, he noticed that the onlookers had traipsed through her blood, there were crimson footprints all over the tiles.

The usherette was sitting next to the aisle. The cinema was now almost deserted; the only sound, the voices of the policemen in the toilets.

Sitting next to the usherette, the projectionist was patting her hand, saying, "Ginette . . . Ginette . . ."

François knelt in front of her and took out his notepad.

"You were the one who discovered the body . . ."

Ginette's face was pale and streaked with tears. Next to her, the projectionist looked little better. Over and over, he mumbled: "It's unbelievable, unbelievable . . ."

"I'm from *Le Journal du soir*," François said.

The usherette stared at him blankly. François turned to her friend.

"Ginette," said the projectionist, "he's with *Le Journal* . . ."

The usherette brought her hands up to fix her hair. "I must look a fright . . ."

"What's your name?" said François.

*

"Rue Quincampoix, and step on it."

François was in a state of excitement verging on panic. He reread his notes, checked his watch, it was not yet six o'clock, they would be putting the second edition to bed. It was feasible; only just, but it was feasible.

How long would the story run? The murderer might be arrested within a couple of days. With what he had discovered in the victim's handbag, François was sure he had material enough for several articles . . . assuming he was allowed to write them.

He took a deep breath, jotted down a number of ideas, scratched them out nervously, and stopped on a formula . . .

He raced up to the editorial department, taking the stairs four at a time.

There are some days when everything goes like a dream. The

young woman who was murdered at the Régent cinema would scarcely have agreed, but for François what happened was all but a miracle. Malevitz, the general news editor, who usually took barely three days' holiday a year, was at his daughter's wedding, and the editor-in-chief was not at his desk.

So François approached Denissov directly.

"A murder in a cinema . . ."

"Page four, two column inches," said Denissov, without looking up from the proofs strewn all over his desk.

"The victim is a young woman of twenty-six, her skull was smashed against the toilet bowl."

"Page two, one column."

"She's a famous movie star."

Denissov's head jerked up; a perfect demonstration of the reflex arc.

"Who?"

François vacillated, it was difficult for him to keep quiet, but announcing the name of the victim was like a haemorrhage: you never knew how serious it would be.

"Mary Lampson."

"My God! Front page. Malevitz isn't here today, give it to Chaussard and be quick about it."

"I want it . . ."

Denissov grinned.

"You'll get your turn . . ."

"It's going to be huge, chief, it'll run for at least three days, and we're the only paper to have it tonight."

"All the more reason not to ruin things. Give it to Chaussard."

"I am an eyewitness, I was in the cinema. I'm not suggesting an article, I'm offering a witness statement."

He stepped forward and handed his notebook to Denissov, who took it and gave it back almost immediately.

"I want the piece on my desk in twenty minutes. If I don't think it's up to scratch, you give all your notes to Chaussard."

At 7.30 p.m. the second edition of *Le Journal du soir* was very different from every other newspaper. While *L'Intransigeant* led with "TERRIBLE MURDER AT RÉGENT CINEMA" and *L'Aurore* with "TRAGIC DEATH OF ACTRESS MARY LAMPSON", *Le Journal* ran a two-column headline:

STAR ACTRESS MARY LAMPSON BRUTALLY MURDERED IN PARIS CINEMA

Our reporter was at the scene when the murder was committed
"It was horrifying . . . !"

14

Waiting for something to happen

Étienne naively assumed that Diêm would be able to get hold of the mission report straight away.

"That's not how things work, Monsieur Étienne," Diêm whispered when they met.

The crest of hair was fluttering frantically.

"I need to make the right contacts, track down the right people, work out how much the bribes will be, then find a way to make a copy of the report without attracting attention, it's quite a job . . ."

That day he had been waiting for Étienne on the pavement, both hands gripping a huge iron frame.

"What's that?"

"A bicycle, Monsieur Étienne. A Dutch bicycle, yes, yes . . ."

He clicked his tongue, angry that he had forgotten Étienne's instructions about his verbal tics.

Now that Diêm had pointed it out, Étienne could see that it was indeed a bicycle, but one so huge it took him a moment to register what it was. The handlebars and saddle were dizzyingly high. The wheels were twice the normal size, as though every Dutchman was two metres tall. There were no brake levers; to slow down or stop the rider had to backpedal.

"It's for you, Monsieur Étienne."

"Good grief."

"While you are waiting . . ."

"So, are you going to be able to get me that report?"

"I am hopeful, yes . . . In a few days."

In the meantime, Étienne cycled around Saigon. It was an unusual experience, being so high above the road. He was not a skilled cyclist and took a few nasty tumbles. He almost ran over a young man who suddenly stepped into the street. Étienne recognised him as the boy that Monsieur Qiao had introduced to him (or, rather, had offered him) some nights before at Le Métropole. They boy recognised him too, but Étienne rode on without a word.

At the Exchange, he decided to relax his usual attitude. If Diêm managed to get him the report about Raymond's death, he would have to authorise a rather large transfer. The best way not to draw attention to this fact was to approve a flood of others so Diêm's would go unnoticed.

So, Étienne, like his colleagues, started authorising transfers.

"Good work, old man!" said Gaston. "You're doing the right thing."

Étienne felt like slapping him, but instead flashed him a smile.

He spent his evenings curled up with Joseph, who responded to his affection.

Raymond's death still seemed utterly unreal. He had only the words of a legionnaire, and one who had not even been at the scene, so could know nothing about it. Étienne took heart in this. But soon it occurred to him that the legionnaire had no reason to lie. The soldier had sworn that Raymond and his comrades had been avenged. So Raymond must be dead. Joseph nestled closer to him. They spent whole nights huddled together.

Étienne got a letter from Hélène. "Given the time that has passed, I'm sure by now you and Raymond have been reunited." She described at length the horrors of living with "Mama and Papa Pelletier". "You can't imagine how bored I am . . ."

Actually, Étienne could easily imagine, it was something he had experienced, the tedium of living with people you love but cannot abide any longer. "I'm even bored with Lhomond," she wrote, "he can be cruel to me sometimes, but the boys at my school are all dumb, so what can I do?" Étienne remembered the mathematics teacher who ran the photography club and taught chess, preferably to young girls, out of school hours. He felt guilty that he had not persuaded Hélène to break off the relationship before he left. Now he was on the far side of the world . . . Deep down, he knew,

Hélène was doing exactly what he was doing, moping around and waiting for something to happen.

"It's taking a long time," he chided Diêm.

"It's coming, it's coming," said Diêm, conscious that he was trying Étienne's patience and eager to be helpful. "Is there anything else you need, Monsieur Étienne?"

"I have an American fridge and a Dutch bicycle, so I'm all right, thank you."

The one bright spot in this moribund period through which he drifted came one morning when he found Jeantet's door open and his office empty. Although it was not really in his nature, the sudden opportunity to satisfy his curiosity prompted him to step inside and wander around. There, before him, was Jeantet's complete collection of photographs.

There were only two subjects. Itsou, the beloved German shepherd that had died the previous year, and his ex-wife, Myriam, whom he referred to as a terrible slut. The photos of the dog were on the left, the ex-wife on the right. There were about thirty in all. All the pictures looked alike. Whether of his German shepherd or his ex-wife, all the photographs had been taken on holiday, in the mountains, by the sea, on a café terrace, on the street, although there were a few highly posed portraits whose artistic aspirations had yielded terrifyingly mediocre results.

Had Étienne not been so anxious and so impatient, he might have wondered at the psychological mindset of a man who collects only pictures of his former wife and his dead dog.

15

They won't catch the Big Bad Wolf anytime soon

"He's amazing!" said Geneviève. "Don't you agree, Jean?"

Jean said nothing, Geneviève's enthusiasm made him uncomfortable. She had *Le Journal du soir* open on the dining room table.

"Whenever Mary Lampson had a new film out," she explained to Jean, who had not asked, "she would go to the cinema incognito to watch the audience's reactions. She would wear dark glasses and lock herself in the toilets until the film started to make sure she wasn't recognised."

She was reading aloud François's article about the young actress (interspersed with personal comments).

> Needless to say, the public have been utterly devastated by news of the tragedy.

"Well, yes, obviously, it's a terrible tragedy!"

> Marie Legrand, who was born into a humble working-class family and chose the stage name Mary Lampson, was not only one of the most ravishingly beautiful young starlets . . .

"I suppose she was pretty . . ."

> . . . she had an irresistible charisma that captured the hearts of many cinema-goers, both male and female.

"Very true . . ."

She possessed a courage matched only by her profound humility. Indeed, Mary Lampson never publicly talked about the fact that – at the tender age of nineteen – she enlisted in the Allied forces where she served as a military nurse from 1941.

"Can you believe that? The woman was a heroine, that's what I say."

It was only when a journalist discovered her service record that she addressed the issue, remarking with disarming simplicity: "I did only what so many others did . . . And I deserve much less credit than many of them!"

"So unaffected . . ."

It was her steadfast character allied to an extraordinary emotional maturity that catapulted Mary Lampson to stardom in 1946 with her very first film, *One Hour of Glory* . . .

"Oh, I *adored* that film . . ."

. . . the poignant tale of a blind woman who travelled halfway across the world to search for her lost brother. The French public was held spellbound by the fairytale romance between Mary Lampson and her dashing co-star Marcel Servières, from their magical engagement through their lavish wedding.

"Oh, I remember the photographs, all those famous people!"

Unsurprisingly, the news of Mary Lampson's sudden tragic and mysterious death, snuffing out the brilliant glow to this shooting star, has left the general public shocked and appalled.

"Your brother is a wonderful writer, don't you think, Jean?" Jean said nothing.

Without pausing to catch her breath, Geneviève rushed downstairs to the newsstand on the avenue Jean-Jaurès to buy the late edition. Jean had never seen his wife so excited. When she came back, she was wound up like a spring.

"Guess what?"

Jean could not guess.

"Apparently Mary Lampson was filing for a divorce ... There have been rumours ... Well, let me tell you something ... Are you listening?"

"Oh, yes, yes," stammered Jean.

"You don't seem particularly interested!"

"I am interested, but the thing is, I ..."

"Here, look at this ..."

She tossed the late edition of *Le Journal* onto the table. François had made the most of his fortuitous head start.

As soon as he had finished writing his first article – and while the police were still locked in discussions with Juge Lenoir, the examining magistrate leading the investigation, about whether to impose a media blackout on the case – François requested a photographer and rushed to the home of Marcel Servières to inform him of his wife's death.

The man's attractiveness was a mystery. You could study him at length without finding a single remarkable feature. But as soon as he was in the spotlight, he had a magnetic charm that was all but irresistible.

The photographer managed to capture the moment when Servières, who had buried his face in his hands, looked up as if to say: "Can this be true?"

François had come up with the headline.

"WHAT KIND OF MONSTER COULD DO SUCH A THING?"

*A devastated Marcel Servières howled when he learned
from our reporter that his wife, the actress Mary Lampson,
had been savagely murdered hours earlier at the Régent cinema*

The entertainment department at *Le Journal* had provided François with the necessary biographical details and mentioned the divorce rumours that had been circulating in the business, and which François, in his article, treated with great circumspection.

"Well?" asked Geneviève.

Jean did not know what was meant by this question.

"Look!" insisted Geneviève, jabbing her forefinger at the picture of Marcel Servières.

Still, Jean did not understand.

"Well, personally, I think there is something shady about this guy. He's a complete hypocrite, can't you see it?"

Jean was struggling to work out what his wife was trying to say.

"He's a B-list actor," she went on. "Servières owes his whole career to his wife. So, if the rumours were true, and Mary *was* going to divorce him, that would explain a lot . . ."

Frustrated at her husband's puzzled expression, she rested her case:

"Don't you think that's a good motive for murder? She decides to leave him, he kills her!"

Jean looked shattered.

"B-but, Geneviève . . ." he stammered, "h-he . . . d-didn't k-kil . . ."

"Poppycock! Nobody knows who killed her!"

She beamed at him, and she seemed so happy, so self-possessed, that Jean was shaken and perplexed.

Was it possible that Geneviève had forgotten what had actually happened to Mary Lampson?

If she believed what she was saying, then Geneviève was beginning to lose touch with reality.

If she did not believe it, then she was profoundly evil.

"Oh dear, oh dear . . ."

Jean came to himself. Geneviève had just finished François's article.

"A post-mortem! Can you imagine what they'll do? Such a pretty little thing, and they are going to cut her up, and for what? I ask you! Dear me, no . . ."

Shaking her head sadly, she folded the newspaper. She looked devastated.

"I read somewhere that they cut off the top of the skull with a saw so they can take out the brain. To weigh it! Did you know that?"

She placed a finger at the base of her throat and another at the base of her abdomen.

"And they slice you up from here to here and take out everything – everything, the guts, the organs, everything!"

Jean was beginning to feel ill.

"They'll analyse the contents of her stomach to find out what she ate. Well, I think it's disgusting. I mean, what business is it of theirs? Are you feeling all right, Jean?"

He had slumped into an armchair.

Geneviève stood in front of him, took his hands in hers and said in a dreamy voice:

"They won't catch the Big Bad Wolf anytime soon, will they, Bouboule?"

*

For the first time in his career, Juge Lenoir was being courted by the media and his elation brought a blissful smile to his face utterly at odds with his words. The press conference took place two days after the murder, when the magistrate insisted on personally announcing the results of the autopsy on Mary Lampson. He talked about "detailed internal examinations", "extensive and traumatic injuries" and "frenzied violence" with an eagerness that bordered on delectation.

Like his colleagues at other newspapers, François was looking forward to the post-mortem, though he had one more reason than they.

The other reporters rushed back to their newsrooms to report that Mary Lampson was two months pregnant at the time of her death.

François alone did not.

Instead, he went straight to the home of Marcel Servières.

Servières's agent, Michel Bourdet, a man of about forty who dressed with understated British elegance, politely declined François's request.

"I'm sorry, there can be no interviews. Marcel is exhausted, as I'm sure you can understand . . ."

"Tell him that among the effects in his wife's handbag there was a somewhat compromising letter."

The change of heart was swift and urgent.

Marcel Servières came downstairs. He looked pale and haggard, his voice had the gravelly hoarseness of a man who had been chain-smoking for days. He looked ten years older.

When he reported back to the news desk, Malevitz and Denissov agreed that François had played his cards extremely well. *Le Journal* still had a scoop on every other paper.

That evening, he penned the headline:

LETTER IN MARY LAMPSON'S HANDBAG: "DARLING, DON'T DO ANYTHING WITHOUT TALKING TO ME. I LOVE YOU"

Husband Marcel Servières says: "I had no idea Mary was pregnant. I suspected she had a lover."

"I assure you I did not write that message," Servières had insisted. So, François withheld the fact that it had been signed "M."; he could use it for his next article.

Juge Lenoir had not been expecting this. The day after the murder, in the greatest secrecy, he had commissioned a graphologist to compare the message with a sample of Servières's handwriting. Seeing the information in the public arena sent him into a towering rage. Lenoir was only in his thirties with little experience of criminal cases, but found himself thrust into the spotlight when, by a complicated causal nexus involving case conferences, duty rosters, staff shortages and lack of resources, he found he was the only magistrate in the public prosecutor's office on the Sunday when the tragedy occurred. His demeanour, a curious mixture of dread and exhilaration, reflected his love–hate relationship with the media. Thus, although he despised journalists, he loved François because he was also a witness in the case. Twice, the two men had shared their impressions. François was the only reporter whom Juge Lenoir did not feel was overrated. Now, feeling betrayed, he picked up the phone and called Denissov.

"Your reporter has . . ."

"Journalist, not reporter."

"As you wish . . . Your journalist has published confidential information relevant to this investigation in a clear contempt of court! I cannot let this stand!"

François, who was quietly sitting in the chair on the other side of the editor's desk, was lapping it up.

"You are absolutely right, Monsieur le Juge, it is intolerable," said Denissov. "In fact, I plan to commission an article about this very point for our next edition."

"What do you mean, an article? What article?"

"An investigation into the fact that police officers, bailiffs and members of the public prosecutor's office routinely provide classified information to the media in direct breach of the secrecy of judicial inquiries. And that they are discreetly but handsomely remunerated for doing so. There will be blood on the parquet, let me tell you!"

"Hold on, hold on!"

"We intend to name names! And the sums involved! We plan to trace the practice back as far as we can, because these officers of the court are a disgrace to the Republic and . . ."

"Hold on a minute!"

Denissov observed a brief silence.

"Monsieur le Juge, this is what I propose. I will have the article written up and wait for you to call me back. If I don't hear from you, I'll toss the article into the wastebasket, what do you say?"

16

Give your brother a little wave

"Hurry up, Jean, we can't be late."

"What? Where are we going?"

It was an unvarying feature of Jean's life that he always trailed after his wife.

"To Mary Lampson's funeral ... Where do you think?"

Jean stared at his wife, wide-eyed.

"Why on earth would we go to her funeral?"

He was aghast.

"Oh, come now, Jean! Don't you know ...?"

Geneviève was so indignant she was temporarily lost for words.

"If we didn't go to the funeral, what would people think?"

Jean was bewildered, he had no idea to which "people" Geneviève was referring, nor why they mattered.

"Do I have to spell it out for you, Jean? We were witnesses and, as such, we have a duty to the unfortunate victim!"

This was a new tic: whenever Geneviève mentioned Mary Lampson, she would close her eyes and make the sign of the cross, a brief interlude before she resumed the conversation.

"What duty?"

"Compassion, Jean, we have a duty of compassion!"

Jean could not remember his wife ever using this word.

"To all intents and purposes, we were with her on her deathbed. The least we can do is attend her funeral," said Geneviève. "Now, come on. Hurry up. I've laid out your dark blue suit, it's the most appropriate for a funeral."

Reluctantly, Jean donned the suit while, out on the landing, Geneviève chatted to Madame Faure.

"We have to go, I'm sure you understand. It's with a heavy heart, but we feel it's our duty . . ."

Jean felt sick to his stomach. Were they walking into the lion's den? Geneviève seemed to have no idea of the risks she was running. On the day after the murder, she had been keen for the two of them to respond to the police appeal for witnesses.

Jean had demurred.

"But François knows we were at the cinema, after all we went there with him. How would we explain not giving statements?"

Then, with a disarming smile, she added:

"Besides, we've got nothing to hide, nothing to be ashamed of."

Geneviève was the picture of elegance when they visited the police station.

"It was horrifying," she said to the detectives, her clenched fist pressed against her lips, her eyes bulging. "Simply horrifying . . ."

Jean was startled by her words, by her whole attitude. As far as he knew, Geneviève had seen nothing; like everyone else, she had rushed to the exit without so much as glancing at the toilets . . .

"I stayed next to my wife," Jean said.

He was particularly proud that he had the presence of mind to add: "She was terribly frightened, you know."

The implication being that he had not personally seen anything, being too busy protecting his wife from this grisly spectacle.

Based on these tenuous circumstances, Geneviève considered herself a witness to the crime and, as such, a person of some importance. To her mind, it logically followed that she should attend Mary Lampson's funeral.

As they neared the Église Saint-Germain-des-Prés, they discovered all the streets were cordoned off – the boulevard Saint-Germain, the rue de Seine, the rue des Saints-Pères, the rue Bonaparte. Wherever they turned there were barricades manned by uniformed police officers, hundreds of people thronged the square outside the church.

The huge crowd had been drawn as much by the young starlet's fame as by the whiff of scandal generated by Marcel Servières's allusion to his wife's infidelity. Rumours spread like wildfire. The starlet's parents had been hounded by journalists for their reaction.

The working-class couple were too overwhelmed by what was happening to respond. In the impromptu interview broadcast on the radio, all that could be heard was Monsieur Legrand's faint, almost inaudible voice as the reporter answered the question for him.

As this family tragedy played out, the real shock had come from Mary's younger sister, Lola, a tall, slender girl of eighteen with blazing eyes, who stubbornly sided with Marcel Servières against her parents. The public eagerly awaited the reaction of Michel Bourdet, wondering whose side he would take, given that he had been the agent of both Mary and her husband.

Geneviève moved like a steamroller through the milling crowd on the rue Bonaparte, and by dint of much jostling, elbowing and swearing managed to reach the barrier, trailing her husband in her wake.

The cordon was manned by a young officer and his older colleague, who had disappeared for a moment to summon reinforcements, since the crowd was getting too big.

"Let us through, please," said Geneviève in a peremptory tone.

The young officer studied this short, plump, single-minded woman whose haughty demeanour brooked no argument.

"I'm sorry, madame, I'm afraid we cannot ..."

"We are the witnesses, monsieur!"

Wedding ceremonies required witnesses, thought the policeman, perhaps they were also required at funerals.

He was visibly ill at ease.

Geneviève chose this particular moment to proclaim:

"If you do not allow the witnesses through, you will find yourself demoted, my young friend! Demoted!"

The crowd further along the barrier were beginning to push, and the young officer did not know where to turn. Paralysed by doubt and persuaded by Geneviève's overweening arrogance, he capitulated.

"Go through," he said.

Just as Jean slipped through the barrier after his wife, the crowd began to shout, reinforcements arrived, there was almost a riot, but Geneviève strode on.

"What a crowd! Now, hurry up, Jean, we'll be late."

François, who had been refused entrance to the church with his photographer from *Le Journal*, stared in amazement as they passed.

"Give your brother a little wave, Jean . . ."

But Jean had something else in mind; the two brothers stared at each other for a long moment until the surging crowd swept the couple into the nave.

So it was that Geneviève Pelletier and her husband came to be sitting in the fourth pew at Mary Lampson's funeral, directly behind the family, among the relatives and friends in showbusiness.

"There's Bachelin," Geneviève whispered to her husband, nodding discreetly at the actor. "And there, at the back, isn't that Minister Le Pommeret?"

The bitter divide was visible from the seating of the congregation.

To the right of the aisle sat Mary Lampson's parents. Her father, in his Sunday best, stared intently at the floor as he offered support to his grief-stricken wife. To the left, the recently bereaved husband, who was half a head taller than everyone else, was flanked by Lola, her eyes still blazing with silent fury, and by his agent, Michel Bourdet, with his British stiff upper lip.

Regardless of which camp they had chosen, all those present were profoundly affected by the loss. "To lose a child is a terrible tragedy under any circumstance," François had written in his article the night before. "But while we can reconcile ourselves to a death due to illness or accident, we cannot accept it when it is the work of a cold-blooded murderer." The description of the crime scene was still fresh in the minds of every reader. By shattering Mary Lampson's skull and mutilating her, her killer had not simply murdered a dazzling young woman, he had committed a crime against beauty.

"See him over there?" Geneviève whispered to Jean, nodding towards Marcel Servières. "He even looks like a murderer."

The funeral proved to be such an ordeal for Jean that he began to wish for a miscarriage of justice. Let someone be arrested for her murder, he thought, anyone, so long as it is not me.

"Pretty soon, they'll get the results of the handwriting analysis," Geneviève went on, while the mourners next to her fumed that she should be whispering at such a time. "When they do, I bet you he'll be in a prison cell."

The requiem mass dragged on and on. For Geneviève, it was one of the greatest moments of her life.

She sobbed so loudly that a neighbour, seeing the depth of her grief, put a consoling arm around her shoulders. Geneviève pressed her handkerchief to her lips. For his part, Jean flushed crimson and began to tremble. When the organist played Bach's "Prelude and Fugue in F minor", it pierced his very soul. He felt as though he stood accused by the stained-glass windows and the statues; he feared the vaulted roof would collapse and bury him.

Next to him, Geneviève blew her nose loudly and muttered: "Poor little thing, my God, poor little thing . . ."

Jean lost two kilos during the mass.

As the congregation was filing out of the church, there came a sudden scream. "Mary!" Adrienne Legrand, the starlet's mother, stood, wringing her hands, calling to her daughter, she would have hurled herself onto the coffin but her husband restrained her. Her screams chilled the blood of everyone. Marcel Servières was deathly pale. Eventually, the grieving woman was led away.

The mourners struggled to regain their composure; the incident had upset them all.

"I thought it was terribly moving," said Geneviève.

Cameras flashed and by the late evening editions, the photograph of Mary's sister Lola being comforted by Marcel Servières was on every front page.

Outside the church, Geneviève and Jean encountered François while they waited for the pallbearers to carry out the coffin. François was astonished to see his sister-in-law sobbing as though she were family. His press pass had proved useless at getting through the police cordon, and he could not help but wonder who had intervened to allow his brother and sister-in-law to attend the mass. He was annoyed at this, and was about to ask Jean, but seeing that he too was distraught he began to wonder whether he was missing something. Had they been personally acquainted with Mary Lampson?

"I have to say," Geneviève said, replacing her handkerchief in her handbag, her eyes now dry, "Servières's funeral wreath looks tawdry and cheap. Don't you think so, Bouboule?"

17

The letters of Étienne would be found . . .

When Étienne returned to his flat on Friday, he found a package
and a brown paper envelope on his doormat.

The package contained the letters he had written to Raymond
after he left, which Diêm had managed to retrieve. Étienne burst
into tears. As for the envelope, he could not bring himself to open
it, he simply did not have the strength, he stumbled around the
room, pounding on the fridge door, which accepted the blows
without protest, then collapsed in a heap on his bed.

Joseph jumped down from the fridge and curled up next to it.
The cat was not purring, it was staring at the envelope.

"All right," said Étienne at length.

```
From Lieutenant Falcone
1st Parachute Regiment
to
Monsieur le Commandant Lachaume
1st Parachute Regiment
Mission Report

The unit it is my honour to lead took off the moment
we received intelligence, i.e. on Tuesday 9 March 1948
at 14:55 hours. We arrived at the target zone at 15.34
hours. I issued the order for the paratroopers to jump
at 15:40 hours over the clearing designated "the Valley
of the Rushes".
[...]
The Việt Minh had clearly waited to be spotted by a
French reconnaissance plane before putting their plan
```

```
into action and leaving the area.
The French soldiers who were killed had all been
previously tortured, each in a different manner:
Caporal-chef Vertbois had had his ...
```

The advancing water buffalo were heavy, sluggish animals. As they plodded, their heads swayed to and fro, and their bells tinkled. The width of the yoke meant that the great beasts passed either side of the buried legionnaires, their hooves almost brushing their heads, dragging behind them the harrow whose broad blades turned the soil, tracing four deep furrows of muddy earth. Raymond was seized by a blind panic.

```
[. . .]
The "staging" of the execution should be seen as a Việt
Minh reprisal for the incident of ...
```

Like his comrades, Raymond struggled with all his strength to free himself.

Then suddenly he thought of the letters he had left back at camp. He would die, Étienne's letters would be found, everyone would know that ...

It was a foolish thought; what did it matter now?

The blades caught his first comrade under the throat, the harrow slowed for a brief instant, the water buffalo were whipped, they bowed their backs and strained at the yoke. When the head was finally ripped from the torso, it rolled to one side, and Raymond saw the eyelids flutter, the mouth grow wide, the severed head screaming silently.

By now, he could feel the thud of the buffaloes' hooves against the ground. Sometimes their horns pointed towards the heavens, at other times they were pointed at the pale, tense faces, as though marking them out for death.

The comrade just in front of him let out a hoarse, guttural howl. This time Raymond could clearly hear the harrow's curved tines as they pierced the base of his comrade's chest and scraped against the vertebrae, ripping away the head, which somehow remained attached to the harrow like a wide-eyed balloon.

Raymond watched as the buffaloes' flared nostrils snuffled along the ground, he felt the shock of their heavy hooves in the pit of his stomach, heard the ploughshares slice through the heavy soil.

The sky went dark.

Raymond lost consciousness and never woke again.

II
Saigon, September 1948

18

Imported from Denmark

How long had Vĩnh been gently shaking him by the shoulder?

"It's three o'clock ..."

Étienne tried to sit up, failed, and collapsed onto his back.

He was struggling to breathe, his mouth was dry, his tongue furred. The headache that would stay with him for much of the morning had already begun its slow vice-like grip of his temples and his forehead; this piercing, merciless migraine was the worst.

For a long moment, Étienne stared at the loose ceiling slats, which, in the darkness, had taken on shapes he could not quite remember, birds perhaps ...

"Wild cranes ..."

"It's three o'clock," Vĩnh said again.

"Fuck off!"

He immediately regretted this flare-up.

"Sorry ... Just give me a minute ..."

He tried to marshal his strength.

Vĩnh waited patiently, patting his hand to ensure he did not drift off again. Étienne turned to look at the young man next to him. The graceful eyebrows and glittering eyes were set in a serious face that sometimes had the stillness of a Venetian mask. It seemed ageless. In fact, some months earlier, Vĩnh had reappeared in his life as though he had fallen from heaven.

Two weeks after learning of Raymond's death, Étienne author-ised the transfer for renovations on the Rambouillet house, rubber-stamping the shrewd application submitted by Monsieur Qiao, the turtle-headed comprador.

In losing himself in opium, Étienne became addicted to the piastre; he desperately needed money.

Monsieur Qiao had brought the promised ten thousand francs but Étienne handed back the bribe: he would not sign the authorisation for less than fifteen thousand ... The following day it was young Vĩnh who brought the money from the comprador to his apartment. The young man handed Étienne the thick brown envelope, then simply stood on the threshold, prepared to do his duty. Étienne took the envelope, smiled and made to close the door.

"You're very sweet, but that's not necessary."

Vĩnh slid one foot forward, his face a mask of panic. If he went back without completing his mission, things would not go well.

"All right, come in," Étienne said wearily. "Do you at least know how to make tea?"

Vĩnh knew how to make tea. They had talked for a long time. Vĩnh admitted to being eighteen – who knew? He had come to Saigon on his own and was earning a living as best he could.

But what about the hotel management course?

"I wash dishes at the Dragon Rouge . . ."

He smiled as Joseph padded towards him.

"He is a dragon also?"

Vĩnh spoke passably good French, but was reluctant to speak in long sentences, though he was also laconic by temperament.

They talked about Saigon for some hours and discovered their shared hatred of the Việt Minh. The young Vietnamese man, who hailed from the northern region of Tuyen Quang, told Étienne that the communists had been extorting his village for years and had killed several members of his family whom they accused – without evidence – of passing information to the French.

Joseph kept his distance, dispassionately observing the scene.

When it came time for Étienne to head off to Le Grand Monde – the Great World – where he would spend half his week's commission losing at knucklebones and tai xiu before going to the opium den to squander the other half, Vĩnh left with him. Out on the pavement, they shook hands.

But Vĩnh came back. Étienne had no idea whether he had been sent by Monsieur Qiao and did not ask. Vĩnh made tea and tidied the apartment, not because he was a servant, but because he was bothered by the chaotic mess; Étienne could tell he would have done the same thing at home. From atop the juddering fridge next to the Buddha, Joseph watched the young man warily.

That evening as they stood in the kitchen, Vĩnh glanced at Étienne with a hint of worry in his eyes. Étienne said nothing, he simply walked out, closing the door behind him.

At the time, he was a regular at a luxurious establishment frequented by the elite, which had alcoves piled with blankets and cushions, low tables and large, ornate daybeds. There, one of a bevy of silent, skilled young women would gesture for him to lie down, place a cushion under his head, gently take his ankles and move his legs into the perfect position; they would deftly prepare the opium pipe that filled him with a boundless sense of wellbeing. Étienne was still a novice, so it took him seven or eight draws to finish a pipe. But before long, with the help of the girls' practised preparation, he learned to smoke a pipe in three deep lungfuls, which allowed him to reach a universe of tranquil quietude where he seemed to float above the world.

When he left the smokehouse sometime around midnight, he found Vĩnh waiting for him. The young man hailed a cycle rickshaw, took the unsteady Étienne home, helped him to undress and put him to bed. From the fridge, Joseph watched the scene play out. He saw Vĩnh sit next to the bed and wait until Étienne was soundly asleep.

The cat peered at Vĩnh.

At about three o'clock in the morning, Joseph got up and stretched, leaped down from the refrigerator, crept towards the second bedroom and sat on the threshold.

"All right," said Vĩnh as he, too, got to his feet, unrolled a straw mat and went to sleep.

Some time had passed since those first days. Over the course of six months, many things had changed.

First and foremost, Étienne was fast gaining a reputation as the most extortionate clerk working for the Exchange. This was how he was known to regulars at Le Métropole. "There's a man who can get blood from a stone", or "He's a dab hand for other people's pockets". The opium cost less now, since Étienne had tired of opulent smokehouses and now hung out in squalid dives peopled by living skeletons with sunken eyes and jutting bones. Most of his money was spent on gambling at Le Grand Monde. Vĩnh said nothing, he simply watched and worried. The gaming rooms reeked of penury and ruin, the smokehouses of decay and death. Was this what Étienne was looking for?

One night, after he had brought Étienne home, Vĩnh lay down next to him and stayed there. Étienne found himself clinging to the young man. In his sleep, he would hug him like a bolster. From time to time, Vĩnh offered ethereal caresses that seemed to come from nowhere. It was a subject they never broached. Vĩnh's silken warmth, his discreet, endearing presence, had the same balmy effect as the tropical climate, enfolding and exhausting.

There was a tacit agreement between them. Vĩnh took care of the apartment and did the shopping. He fed Joseph fish and prawns, and they became good friends. Étienne paid for everything and ensured that Vĩnh wanted for nothing. At night, they would lie next to each other and an exhausted Étienne would quickly drift off into restless dreams.

When Vĩnh came to the smokehouse to help him to his feet and out into the street, Étienne wished that he could show his gratitude, but he was so drained that words failed him. Such a beautiful face, he thought . . . How he wished he could fall in love with him.

His every joint ached.

That night, as he usually did, Vĩnh had slipped an arm around Étienne and supported him for the first faltering steps. After that, he could walk unaided and, by the time they had negotiated the labyrinthine corridors, weaving their way between the bunks where emaciated bodies lay slumped, passed the grimy table where the Chinese owner counted and recounted the sticky, crumpled banknotes that were the night's takings, and reached the exit, Étienne, though exhausted, was himself again. Except for the blinding headache . . .

"How much?" he asked as Vĩnh hailed a cycle rickshaw.

The night was hot and sultry. The rainy season was late this year, but already the air was so muggy with the promise of torrential rain that it was difficult to know whether to hope for a cloudburst or not. To avoid answering Étienne's question, Vĩnh pretended to be focused on the arriving rickshaw. Étienne, whose legs were still trembling, was like a molten weight around his shoulders.

"Well, how much?"

Étienne spoke in the imperious tone of an old man.

"Fifty-six," said Vĩnh.

Though impatient to ask the question, Étienne had already lost interest. He was gazing in astonishment at the Siêu Linh banners that fluttered listlessly above the street.

Vĩnh helped him into the back of the rickshaw and squeezed in next to him. Étienne's head slumped onto the chest of the young man, who stared out at the street. He had not had time to get comfortable, the seat was digging into his back, but it would be a short journey. At this hour, the streets of Saigon were deserted but for a few soldiers on leave, a handful of prostitutes, and a few drunken Europeans. The men emerging from bars and gaming rooms concluded their whispered conversations, one eye on the street, the other on their cars. But they, too, found their gaze drawn to the fluttering red banners emblazoned with a blue horizontal line surmounted by a sunburst of golden rays. This was the symbol of the Siêu Linh, a sect much talked about in recent weeks, whose procession the following Sunday would conclude with the inauguration of their cathedral. Devotees of the sect had spent the week roaming the city with ladders, hanging banners, pennants and flags above the streets, draping windows and even rooftops; whole streets were blanketed with this blue horizon from which the suns of the Supreme Soul shone.

"I'm curious to see what they're like," said Étienne.

When the rickshaw dropped them off, he had to steady himself for fear of falling. Fifty-six opium pipes in a single night. Almost seventy, if he included those he had smoked at home. Étienne had lost a lot of weight. Vĩnh did everything he could to get him to eat something nourishing, but Étienne had no appetite. In the morning, he left for the Exchange on an empty stomach, and at lunch could think of nothing better than to go home and smoke a few pipes.

He had moved into a new apartment, one situated much closer to the Exchange. He had taken it on a whim. The exorbitant rent was vastly more than his monthly salary, but Étienne, striding like a conquering hero through the vast rooms and out onto a terrace that overlooked the whole city, had said:

"I'll take it!"

He had nodded to the agent, a Vietnamese man in a threadbare three-piece suit with a crimson flower as large as a soup bowl in his buttonhole.

"My good Vĩnh, tell the man I'll take it! Get him to drop the rent thirty per cent and we'll move in tonight!"

After half an hour of haggling, with the rent reduced by only fifteen per cent, an exasperated Étienne took a wad of crumpled piastres from his pocket, pressed them into the agent's hands and muttered: "Go on, buzz off . . ."

No sooner had he moved in than he lost all interest in the apartment.

He and Vĩnh occupied only three of the five vast rooms; the place felt like a deserted train station. Joseph resumed his place atop the convulsive refrigerator next to the Buddha. When the cat was curled up next to the figurine, it was difficult to tell which was the more philosophical.

Étienne took down the portrait of Raymond. The photograph, taken in the mountains, showed him smiling and stripped to the waist, glistening with manly sweat, standing next to a woodpile with an axe at his feet. Raymond would have been in his twenties at the time, but Étienne could no longer remember the photograph being taken. He had other, more recent, photographs, two of which were framed. But, haunted by the depressing spectacle of the frames on Jeantet's desk, Étienne had decided to put his in a drawer.

Raymond appeared in his dreams, he was in terrible agony, and yet it was Raymond, exactly as he had known him, as though it were a living photograph . . . He lived in dread of these nightmares. It was always the same scene, Raymond captured by Việt Minh soldiers who inflicted unspeakable atrocities on him. By morning, a blood-smeared Étienne would be slaughtering dozens of Việt Minh with a machete.

184

It was 8.30 a.m.

Vĩnh had already made tea and peeled the fruit he had bought from a street hawker that morning, together with fresh fish for Joseph, while Étienne, sweating and gasping, was still lying in bed, trying to shake off the gruesome images that had made him weep until he was utterly drained.

Just as a functioning alcoholic can look fresh and well rested after a night of heavy drinking, so Étienne, who rarely got to sleep before dawn, was surprisingly punctual at the Exchange. He would arrive a minute or two before nine o'clock, saunter past the empty office of Gaston, whose timekeeping was patchy, say good morning to Belloir, then knock on the door of the director, who spent his mornings drinking green tea behind his serried ranks of photo frames. When Jeantet got up to shake Étienne's hand, he would sometimes make as though to pick up a frame and proffer it, mechanically extending his arm, opening his hand with a brooding expression, only to give up with a disappointed shake of the head.

"Still no news?" Étienne said.

"Alas, no," said Jeantet, with a hangdog look.

Two days after Étienne had authorised Diêm's ludicrous transfer to import five hundred thousand piastres' worth of Camargue rice, the man had disappeared. They had agreed to meet the following day, but Diêm did not appear. It was not until a week later that Étienne became concerned when, on his way to the rue Catinat, he heard a woman scream and saw a motorbike roar past in a cloud of white smoke.

On the pavement, a man lay in a pool of blood, his throat cut from ear to ear. Étienne immediately recognised the thickset Vietnamese man in his sixties as a comprador he had often seen doing business with Gaston.

His first thought was of Diêm's strange disappearance. Was this how some deals worked out?

Étienne stifled the urge to retch as he saw blood spurt from the man's carotid artery, but the other passers-by seemed unruffled, they stepped around the body, no one wanted to get involved.

"So, you've never seen that happen before?" Jeantet said, with a faint air of surprise, smiling benignly, as though Étienne had just discovered a Vietnamese tradition.

"Every group in Saigon has its hired killers – the Chinese bankers, the compradors, the import-export companies, the Việt Minh, the religious sects, the traffickers, everyone." Jeantet offered this explanation in a tone of mingled joviality and pity for these gooks with their strange habits.

"Here in Indochina, such killings are a way of sending messages. The groups here communicate in a language no one else understands, and murder is simply part of the grammar."

Jeantet was happy with this turn of phrase. He put an almost fatherly arm around Étienne's shoulder.

"Diêm is of no importance to anyone, my friend . . . Don't worry, he's a nobody, who on earth would want to kill him?"

Jeantet's intention was to reassure, but Étienne could not help but think of the shelves lined with figurines of Buddha and Confucius, their arses stuffed with opium residue, and the dubious dealings they entailed. And he felt terribly guilty because, ordinarily, it took weeks, even months, to set up a five hundred thousand piastre deal of the kind he had persuaded Diêm to accept. It took time to assemble the necessary accomplices, frontmen, documents, addresses, invoices – it was a whole industry. By increasing Diêm's original transfer request tenfold, Étienne had forced him to seek out collaborators. The eventual application had been submitted on behalf of a company Étienne had never heard of called Peeters & Renaud. Diêm had found himself negotiating a huge transfer that would have whetted many an appetite.

"As to his application . . ." said Jeantet, as if he had been thinking the same thing. "Perhaps his eyes were bigger than his stomach."

That night, Étienne had gone to visit Diêm's home.

There was no one, the house was deserted. On the shelves once groaning with statues, two clucking chickens now perched. Étienne had asked the neighbours, but they knew nothing, or would say nothing.

At the "headquarters" of Peeters & Renaud on the rue d'Ayot,

Étienne found no office, not even a nameplate, no one in the building had ever heard of the company.

The following night, he had gone back to Diêm's house and, standing in the yard facing the abandoned house, he showered everyone – neighbours, old men and children – with a wad of piastres in small denominations, promising a reward to anyone who could provide him with information. The people in the yard took the money, but no one said anything. The old man who had first guided him to Diêm's house was not sitting on his tyre. Étienne remembered seeing him thumbing through lottery tickets for the Game of Thirty-Six Beasts. He set off for Le Grand Monde where the draw was held.

It was a huge edifice on the rue des Marins, in the Chinese district called Cholon. The place was a sort of caravanserai housing gaming rooms, theatres, restaurants, bars and shops, and it was here that after dark all the gamblers, night owls, whores, gangsters, bourgeois, farmers and coolies came to lose in a few short hours all the money they had earned during the day, while clerks and civil servants spent what little money they had not managed to transfer to France. At the gaming tables, Étienne would sometimes run into Gaston, who polished his signet ring for luck before rolling the dice. He would also encounter Georges Vaillant, the civil servant from the High Commission, wandering around clutching a glass of anisette between trembling fingers.

All day, touts would roam the city selling tickets for the Game of Thirty-Six Beasts in which each player, having read a riddle that referred to the legends of the Middle Kingdom, had to name the Beast or Genie involved. Every evening, a huge crowd would cluster around the stage on which the box containing the solution ("And the answer is . . . the toad!") was opened, resulting in a handful of winners and a multitude of losers.

Étienne looked around for the old man with the beard, but he was only too aware that the chances of finding him were one in a hundred. But just as the crowd dispersed, and the losers drifted off to the gaming tables to squander what little money they had left,

Étienne spotted him, poring over his tickets, flicking through them again and again, hoping he had missed the one depicting the toad.

The information cost Étienne forty piastres.

"They left in the middle of the night, about a week ago," said the old man. "The whole family . . . They didn't take a thing with them."

Quickly realising that the family would not be returning anytime soon, the neighbours began to help themselves. After the first pieces of furniture were taken away, everything quickly disappeared, and within two days, the house was bare. As to the reason for their departure, Étienne learned only that "Diêm seemed like he was in a big hurry . . ."

All around them, the milling crowds whispered and jostled.

"They just climbed into a truck, with the whole family in the trailer . . ."

The family's sudden flight took on a curious significance for Étienne. He had been troubled when he discovered the sordid trafficking into which Diêm, his family and even his children had been forced. Moreover, he owed Diêm a debt of gratitude, since he had managed to unearth the report into Raymond's death which finally provided answers to the agonising questions that had haunted Étienne since his arrival. Had this been the cause of Diêm's troubles? Who had he approached to get the report? What price had he had to pay?

Spring was long forgotten, summer had passed, now it was September, Diêm had disappeared into the vast morass of Indochina, as had Étienne after a fashion.

He felt terribly alone.

"Come home . . ." his mother had concluded one of the eight-page letters she sent every week detailing daily life in Beirut as viewed from the avenue des Français. And, as if Étienne did not spend enough time torturing himself, Madame Pelletier kept questioning him about Raymond's death, clearly believing that what little her son had told her ("he died fighting in northern Indochina, they said he was killed instantly, that he didn't suffer") masked something much more painful. Étienne's loneliness stemmed from the fact that he had no one to talk to. Hélène was too young to be burdened with the monstrous truth. Étienne might have opened up to his father, but he could not bring himself to write, he simply did not have the strength. As for François and Jean, they were in Paris and probably had enough on their plates. Étienne sent them brief banal notes from time to time and received guarded, self-conscious replies. "I hope you're getting over your friend's passing," Jean wrote in his assiduous, schoolboy hand. "Have you been able to find out exactly how Raymond died?" wrote François, who was probably top of his class at the École Normale Supérieure.

The thought of going back to Beirut, back to his parents, was unbearable ... So much so that Étienne had panicked when his mother suggested they might come to Indochina for Raymond's funeral. The tone of her telegram asking for the date of the funeral suggested she was already packing their suitcases. Étienne had immediately sent a wire: "MILITARY FUNERAL ALREADY PERFORMED – STOP – BROUGHT FLOWERS TO MILITARY CEMETERY ON YOUR BEHALF – STOP – LOVE.

He continued to write to Hélène, but the distance between them, the time it took for letters to arrive and the struggle to find words made it feel like an artificial exercise. They wrote to say how much they loved each other; this was the one thing they could still share. Despite her youth, Hélène could tell from his letters that Étienne was no longer the passionate, optimistic young man she had watched leave for Saigon.

Meanwhile, at the Exchange, Jeantet had not failed to notice that his once rigid, moral, incorruptible junior clerk had, almost overnight, become the most unprincipled man in the establishment. But the director took a particular delight in the way he did things. Étienne demanded extravagant bribes with a broad smile, he authorised the most eccentric applications, favouring those importing musical biographies in Hebrew that would be of no use to engineers applying to import machine parts.

Étienne did not hesitate to make the most outlandish suggestions to compradors, who would give him a sidelong glance, wondering if this was a trap or if perhaps the clerk was completely insane.

Whenever he got his way, Étienne would race into Jeantet's office waving a dossier.

"Guess what it is this time?" he would giggle.

Jeantet would settle back in his chair, close his eyes and, with a weary sigh, say: "Go on then, tell me everything."

"A snowplough! Three hundred thousand piastres! Imported from Denmark."

"Great . . ."

A fortnight later, it would be brine vats for making sauerkraut, or ice picks. Étienne would howl with laughter and pound his fist on his desk while his colleagues watched him suspiciously. Étienne was also capable of vanishing mid-afternoon and not reappearing until the next morning, ashen, his eyes glazed. It was not unusual to find him slumped on a pile of mail sacks in a corridor.

Finally, it came: the day of the Siêu Linh procession that had all of Saigon in a state of consternation.

Étienne was amused to note that Vĩnh seemed excited by the much-anticipated event. The sect seemed to exert a curious fascination on him, though the whole city seemed intrigued to some degree. At Le Métropole, no one talked of anything else. The leader of the Siêu Linh, a man named Loan, was reputed to be a shrewd, suspicious man. He was said to be authoritarian, Machiavellian. While living as a hermit in northern Indochina, Loan had had a vision. The Supreme Soul had appeared to him in the form of a bright sun on a blue horizon, and commanded that he surrender himself, body and soul, to the glory of the Supreme Soul. Loan had immediately set out across the country, and finally settled some forty kilometres north of Saigon. There, he had cured three children of fever by having them drink water from his cupped hands; disciples rushed to him, trumpeted his miracles. In order that the sect could protect itself from bandits, from the Việt Minh, from gangsters and from the French military, the sect had marshalled an efficient army. People said that, during his great march to Saigon, Loan had gathered hundreds of disciples; the army reported that a stream of followers, including entire families, travelled in his wake. Ten days before his arrival, they had overrun the streets of Saigon and festooned them with flags and banners.

"He has come to dedicate his church," said Vĩnh.

The "church" was a large dockside warehouse recently purchased by the sect, where Loan's army of followers had been working tirelessly, replacing ordinary windows with stained glass, exchanging rusty steel gates for intricately carved porticos. None but the faithful working there were allowed to enter. When the procession finally arrived, there would be a grand ceremony to welcome all those (like Vĩnh) who were curious about the sect, but only the faithful would be permitted to attend the mass itself. (Étienne could but wonder how the sorting would be done.)

The Supreme Soul, in His munificence, had ensured clement weather for Sunday's procession. From early morning, the streets of Saigon were thronged with onlookers, people sitting on their porches, old women perched on stools, boisterous children trying to catch the strings of the banners. By noon, the café terraces were filled to capacity.

"So, you've come to watch?" Jeantet said, when he spotted Étienne approaching the terrace on rue Catinat with a camera slung over his shoulder.

Gaston was also there. Étienne nodded to the crowds and the bunting.

"Looks like a stage of the Tour de France, doesn't it?"

He took several photographs of the procession as it moved through the cathedral square. First came the stately bass tattoo of a hundred drums, then a blaze of fabrics in green and gold that the wind lifted above the first vehicles, which were drawn by disciples in white robes who moved with grave solemnity. The procession was still some distance away but, instead of the shouts and whoops Étienne had expected, the moment was shrouded in a tense silence. There was something extraordinary about the incessant beat of the drums, the slow grandeur of the procession, and as the number of acolytes grew and swelled, it triggered a sort of paralysis in the onlookers, as though a sea had opened up before them and would not close again. Something about the white robes of the faithful, the eerie silence of this presence, the perfect synchronicity of their movements, made it seem as though they were twice, three times, ten times more numerous than the onlookers. On either side, the procession was flanked by lithe, muscular men, raised machetes resting on their shoulders, marching in step ... The procession was a boundless, inexorable tide of identical disciples, a single, fluid, homogeneous unit; it was one person, one spirit, one body. Then, suddenly, the figure of Loan appeared, standing on a chariot drawn by dozens of his disciples, he looked as though he were riding this immense human serpent. If onlookers had expected a giant, what they saw was a rather short man, robed in a long red and gold chasuble and an improbable headdress from which hung golden tassels that jangled when he moved his head. With his ebony sceptre topped by a yellow sun, he blessed the crowd with simple, sweeping gestures.

Unsure what to do, some of the onlookers made an oriental bow. Others followed suit. Vĩnh was about to do the same but, seeing Étienne laughing, he held back.

"Oh, my good God!" Jeantet said.

"I don't believe it!" said a thunderstruck Gaston.

Étienne, who was staring through his camera lens, suddenly erupted in a gale of laughter.

As his chariot drew alongside them, the high priest of the Siêu Linh had ceremoniously turned and now gazed at them with open arms.

"Hahaha!" roared Étienne.

It was Diêm.

19

The time has come to reap the rewards

All the way across Paris just to attend a dinner ... Geneviève had suggested taking a taxi but Jean pretended not to hear – their funds were at their lowest. She held up her hands in submission: fine, have it your way, we'll take the métro ... For the past two days, Jean had been tetchy and short-tempered. Coming back from a two-week trip to find a summons to appear before the examining magistrate made him very nervous.

A day earlier, he had arrived home to find his wife sitting at the table, smoking, as usual; she was impeccably made-up and looked radiant. When he came in, she had not moved but simply watched as he unpacked his suitcase and put his things away.

"Did it go well?"

Every time he came home, it was the same question. And since Jean simply moved his head in a gesture that was not easily interpreted, she added:

"What I mean is ... nothing particularly untoward?"

Jean had grunted, a barely audible "no". How long had she been asking him this question? What was she implying? Jean could easily have answered her questions, but he preferred to treat them as another mystery in this creature he did not understand.

His wife was increasingly mysterious. Her mother had died suddenly in early September, and Jean had had to scrape together the funds so that she could go home to attend the funeral. When she left Paris, she had been like a grieving war widow with a brood of hungry children, sobbing her way through so many handkerchiefs he had felt like handing her a bath towel. But she had returned from Beirut strangely calm. Jean found her ... "fresh" was the word that sprung to mind. This strange change of attitude, he discovered shortly afterwards, stemmed from the fact that when Geneviève had seen her three sisters in mourning black they had seemed more beautiful than ever, and next to them, sullen in her charmless dress wearing a hat that verged on the ridiculous, she had felt ugly when she was merely plain. In that moment, Geneviève had not hated her sisters (she hated them already), but her mother, who, in dying, had forced her to make this mortifying comparison. Geneviève had dried her tears before she even entered the church, had excused herself from the graveside, explaining that she had to visit her in-laws and had spent her second day in Beirut touring the soap factory, and stuffing her face with pastries.

Jean was always worried by Geneviève's sudden changes of heart. Was he worried that one day he too would be cut loose? After all, Geneviève fell out with almost everyone . . .

But, just now, Jean was not thinking about this doubtful prospect, but about a much more worrying circumstance. This summons to appear before the examining magistrate . . .

Were it not for Geneviève's morbid fascination, Jean might have forgotten the long-drawn-out "Mary Lampson case", just as he had forgotten the girl he had "known" in Beirut (this was the word that came to mind when he thought about his victims, being unaware of the biblical sense . . .) or the waitress in the provincial town whose name he could not remember. But now, six months after the death of the young starlet, the examining magistrate had decided to stage a reconstruction of the crime, and, to this end, had summoned all the witnesses who had come forward. Was this a set-up? Was he walking into a trap hatched by the magistrate and set up by the police?

"It must be terribly fascinating, a crime reconstruction, don't you think?" said a delighted Geneviève.

She had treated this summons like an invitation to a wedding or to a masked ball; it was thrilling and exciting.

Just as she had been charmed by the unexpected invitation from Georges Guénot.

For the four months that Jean had been working for him (leaving twice a month for a ten-day tour, lugging a suitcase filled with panties, petticoats, brassieres, etc.), Monsieur Guénot had taken little interest in his new sales rep. So, when he invited Jean to dinner ("with your good lady, of course"), it had come as a surprise. To Geneviève, this meant a meal in a fancy restaurant, something she would never turn down.

Jean had been in a tearing hurry, worried that they might be late. He had glanced at the clock, and it was at this point that Geneviève had suggested the taxi.

Everything seemed to worry Jean. Hardly an hour passed when he was not utterly overwhelmed, when he did not feel the urge to open the window so that he could breathe . . . or throw himself out.

Geneviève made no attempt to quicken her pace; hurrying was beneath her.

Seeing them arrive, Monsieur Georges – as he insisted on being addressed – eyed them a little scornfully, then got to his feet and proffered his hand, which Jean and Geneviève politely shook, unaware of the imperial aspect of the gesture.

Monsieur Georges was in his forties, his hair grey, his features drawn back as though he had just weathered a storm; his eyes constantly watered and he dabbed them with a handkerchief he kept in the palm of his hand. A prudent, fretful man, he cast upon the world a cold, mistrustful eye that could not fail to impress.

Having little imagination, and no facility for small talk, Jean launched into an account of his latest sales trip as soon as they sat down to eat. His fondness for minutiae about the orders, the distance covered and the clients quickly became boring and repetitive. Monsieur Georges let him enumerate the tedious list of appointments, delays and excuses and simply nodded; a half-smile that was difficult to interpret played on his lips. Geneviève, for her part, had her nose in her plate and was eating enough for four.

Without troubling to comment on Jean's lengthy account, Monsieur Georges abruptly turned and began to ask Geneviève about her childhood, her family, her career – everything about her seemed to fascinate him. Geneviève beamed at him; she was in seventh heaven. Given that her position in the postal service had not yet been confirmed, Monsieur Georges mused, might she be interested in a job? Geneviève gave a little laugh, and thanked Monsieur Georges with a wave, no, no, *so* kind of him to offer, but Jean earned enough to support them both! She was drinking quite heavily, she had a taste for white wine; Monsieur Georges ordered a second bottle.

Jean was reassured to note that his boss was more interested in his wife than him; he felt safe. Now that he had given a laboured report of his business trip and Monsieur Georges was cupping his chin and gazing doe-eyed at Geneviève, Jean's more pressing concern resurfaced: the police summons, the reconstruction of the crime – what was it hiding?

It was scheduled to take place at the Régent the following morning at ten o'clock. The prospect made him feel distinctly uneasy. Especially since François and Geneviève never shut up about it, as though it were "their case", the greatest, most exciting thing that had ever happened in their lives. At every Sunday lunch, François would bang on about the examining magistrate, the grisly nature of the crime, the family of the victim, despite the fact that they knew all the details from his articles in *Le Journal*. If that were not bad enough, Geneviève encouraged François, listening to him spellbound and prompting him whenever he fell silent. She could cup her chin in her hand and gaze at him exactly the way Monsieur Georges was doing this evening, while Geneviève prattled on about the "friends" in Beirut she "missed so terribly". Jean had no idea who she meant, probably the dozens of boys she used to suck off in the woods. Jean poured himself some more wine; there was never any at home.

He looked at Geneviève, flushed pink, her eyes shining, her voice a note higher than usual. He still found her puzzling, he had no idea what she thought of life or, indeed, what went on inside her head. Every evening, she would slip on one of the short nightdresses he peddled all over France and climb into bed; she never read, she would simply turn out the light, lie on her back with her arms by her side, fall asleep in an instant and not move again all night. Like her daily vigils at the dining room table, she would wake up exactly as she had fallen asleep. Sometimes, Jean would watch her while she slept. Her silence and her utter lack of movement awed him; she looked like a corpse. Since the pathetic failure that had been their sex life when they first married, Jean had never made advances to his wife – not that she would have let him – but even if he had wanted to, he could not have brought himself to touch her, there was something terrifying about her stony sleep . . .

"What do you think, darling?"

Geneviève was staring at him with a passion that owed a considerable debt to the white wine. Jean was completely at sea. Monsieur Georges tactfully rephrased.

"Would you be tempted by the opportunity to run a shop selling household linens . . .?"

Without waiting for Jean's reaction, Geneviève clapped her hands like a little girl on Christmas morning. She had always dreamed of being a shopkeeper. Jean was more circumspect. The proposal had come out of the blue and he always needed time to process new ideas. Where would the money come from, he wondered. And where would they acquire their stock?

"I have endless amounts of fabric," Monsieur Georges was saying. "These days, labour is cheap. It would cost very little to run up sheets, pillowcases, tablecloths and towels. I'd supply the materials at cost price. You take care of the workmanship and the shop. I'd match your investment and double it, but I'd only take fifty per cent of the profit."

By now, Geneviève had seized Jean's arm and was clutching it in a childish manner, but Jean paid her no heed, he was thinking through the terms of the deal. They would buy "at cost price", but Monsieur Georges could name a figure, it would be impossible to tell whether he was making a mark-up. On the other hand, Jean could fiddle the figure and thereby even the score. They would rip each other off; it was a sound commercial prospect.

Monsieur Georges had come well prepared: he reeled off the average rental price for a shop in a working-class area of Paris, the attendant fees and charges, he had even drawn up a quarterly sales forecast. After he had taken his share of the profits, Jean and Geneviève would be left with four hundred thousand francs.

"What sort of fabrics do you have?" asked Geneviève excitedly.

Monsieur Georges had everything: ticking, cambric, cretonne, various weights of cotton, but also satin, poplin, terry cloth, felt, even elastic and fleece. The more the list went on, the more tightly Geneviève gripped Jean's arm.

"And we're talking about old stock?"

"It's all pre-war. But in excellent condition, I've made sure of that!"

Geneviève gazed at Monsieur Georges as he launched into an explanation about buying stock from Le Sentier, storage costs, how ruinous the war had been for small businesses, to say nothing of the clothes rationing.

While Jean focused on practical questions and talked about deadlines, Geneviève flitted from one subject to the next with no order or method – it was quite infuriating.

They would need money ... But, even if Jean could get his hands on the funds, was this what he wanted to do? Then again, Jean had never known what it was he wanted to do. A joyous, tipsy Geneviève was continuing to drain her glass at an alarming rate. Monsieur Georges was suddenly the most fascinating man on earth, and Jean could not help but wonder if his wife were not about to crawl under the table. It was time to get her home.

"I'll give it some thought," Jean said soberly.

Monsieur Georges dabbed his eyes and explained that he had considered other candidates, but wanted to work with them. "Such an *admirable* young couple ..." he said. Jean could not see quite what there was to admire.

Out on the street, Geneviève took Monsieur Georges's hand in hers. A passer-by might have wondered whether she was going home with her husband or with his boss.

They caught the métro home. This time Geneviève offered no objection.

It was almost eleven o'clock, there were few trains running. Geneviève seemed suddenly serious; her smile no more than a tic. She stared abstractedly, without a word, at the posters, the passengers, at the stations flashing past. Jean did not dare say anything.

Was she disappointed that he had been less enthusiastic than her? As so often, each retreated into their own thoughts. Geneviève was probably dreaming of being the owner of a boutique; tomorrow it would all be forgotten.

When they reached Porte de la Villette, they walked the rest of the way. They had not exchanged a word since leaving the restaurant, though this was not unusual.

They climbed the four flights of stairs, Geneviève hung up her coat.

"For this shop . . ." she said, turning to face Jean.

She glared at him.

"Are you going to ask your parents for the money?"

It was the question he had been dreading, but though he had known it was coming, he had not thought of an answer.

"The thing is . . ."

She interrupted him by squeezing his arm.

"It could be a gold mine, my love . . ."

"My love." This was a first. Even when they were courting, she had never used the words.

"Don't you realise what that was all about?"

"Well, uh . . . opening a shop . . .?"

"No, no, Jean, I mean what it was *really* about . . ."

He had no idea what she was getting at.

Geneviève began to undress. She slipped on a nightdress.

"I've rather taken to Monsieur Guénot, he makes me laugh! Imagine calling yourself 'Monsieur Georges', as though you were running a bordello . . ."

She turned and stared at Jean for a long moment.

"And he thinks he can take us for fools . . ."

Jean was surprised; he did not understand what she meant. Geneviève set a pan of water on the stove for her intimate *toilette*. At such moments, it was customary for Jean to turn away and busy himself with something else so as not to disturb her.

"Monsieur Georges bought up stock," she said as Jean undressed and stared out the window. "But he didn't buy it before the war. He bought it *during* the war. That vile bastard bought up stock from the Jewish merchants in the Marais who were forced to sell everything so they could flee. And he didn't pay much for it, let me tell you. He kept the stock all through the war, maybe even sold some to the Nazis. And now that things are getting back to normal, it's time to rake in the profits. Get out the fabric, sell it on, you don't just triple your money, you make twenty, thirty times what you paid, and you generously offer twenty per cent of the profits to a couple of suckers who are prepared to get into debt to rent a shop and pay to run up tablecloths and sheets."

Hearing Geneviève empty the water from her basin, Jean turned back to look at her.

"And that's precisely what we're going to do, Jean."

"But . . ."

Geneviève walked past him, lay down on her side of the bed and patted the space next to her, beckoning Jean to join her, which he did as warily as if he were about to lie down with a savage beast. They lay stiffly side by side without touching, both staring up at the ceiling.

"We are going to fleece him, Jean."

Geneviève's voice was dreamy.

"We are going to take back what he stole, we are going to take back every *sou* from that *cunt*."

The vicious insult echoed around the room and inside Jean's head for a long moment. When he finally turned to look at her Geneviève was already fast asleep.

20

I was expecting something different

They were allowed to take a taxi. Like everything else at *Le Journal*, expenses adapted to the news cycle and François had carte blanche because Denissov was happy with the circulation figures. "A good crime is a crime that appeals to readers," he said. This was a particularly good one. There was a young, pretty victim, a thrilling dash of horror, an unusual crime scene and a perfect suspect in the person of the husband (who was probably having an illicit affair with Lola, the victim's younger sister – though no one had any evidence to support this). Most of all, the whole affair was bathed in the dazzling, toxic glow of the silver screen . . .

As he headed towards the Régent cinema, François considered just how far he had come.

He had made a dazzling first impression at the news desk to which Denissov had propelled him. It was something he was genuinely good at. He had a flair for a splash headline, a feel for the interests and appetites of the reading public and a taste for the dramatic – in less than three weeks, a number of his stories had made the front page. The Lampson case had been a godsend. It had given François the front-page column inches that would otherwise have been out of reach for months, perhaps even years.

Malevitz, the chief news editor, judged writers by their results and readily agreed this new recruit had talent.

In the meantime, François's salary had been bumped up by a third, which, though hardly cause for celebration, made the prospect of repaying his parents seem possible. And yet, his career path had not quite taken the turn he had anticipated, for while he would have felt confident telling his parents that he had abandoned his studies at the École Normale Sup to become a distinguished leader writer, he was reluctant to admit that he spent his days writing about murders, crimes of passion, tragic disputes over wills, bank raids and black-market racketeering. François had always dreamed of writing investigative pieces on burning social issues, or working as a foreign correspondent, so he was less than fulfilled by the relentless drip of mundane stories that required him to find some hook, some angle that would appeal to the readers. He could not help but wonder whether this was a dead-end job, and whether his flair for lurid stories would doom him to stay on the news desk.

The only one of these stories he still wanted to pursue was the Lampson case, since it had given him a fast track to success and remained his mascot.

But six months after Mary Lampson's murder, little headway had been made in the investigation.

Handwriting analysis of the note that had been signed simply "M." had given rise to a battle royal between experts and graphologists that the public found fascinating. Juge Lenoir was forced to concede that the author of the letter had not been Lampson's husband, Marcel Servières. Servières's lawyer used this admission to shout from the rooftops that Mary had been cheating on his client with whoever had penned the famous note, the man who had doubtless got her pregnant and probably killed her.

The lawyer representing Mary Lampson's parents immediately insisted on a second opinion by a new graphologist, who concluded that Servières "might" have written the note.

As for the examining magistrate, he was drunk on power and, for the first time in his career, felt entitled to indulge the "feeling in his bones" that told him that Marcel Servières was guilty. To the magistrate, the man's alleged relationship with his wife's younger sister Lola was beyond belief; it marked Servières out as a pervert who would be capable of anything, even murder. So the magistrate had been bitterly disappointed that handwriting experts had robbed him of a spectacular arrest.

François felt that the investigation was getting bogged down and that Juge Lenoir was overwhelmed not merely by events themselves, but by the unprecedented public interest in the crime. Senior figures in the public prosecutor's office were doubtless hounding him, willing him to fail . . .

François brooded about these things in the taxi taking him to the Régent.

Sitting next to him, a young photographer with a camera wedged between his knees, was reading his latest article.

POLICE RECONSTRUCTION:
WILL MARY LAMPSON'S MURDERER BE THERE?

This morning at the Régent cinema there will be a reconstruction of the tragic events that led to Mary Lampson's murder, in the presence of all the witnesses who came forward. This marks a decisive turning point in the investigation

Who stood to benefit by the young starlet's death? Why was the murder so brutal and savage? These are the questions that trouble the examining magistrate, Juge Lenoir.

Will one of the witnesses remember some detail that might shed light on this extraordinary case?

It is possible that the murderer is one of the three witnesses who did not come forward to help with police enquiries. Then again, it is well known that murderers are obsessed with their misdeeds and often feel compelled to return to the scene of their crime . . . If the murderer is among the 226 witnesses present, will he finally speak out?

In an attempt to resolve some of these questions, Juge Lenoir has summoned all those who were present on the day of the tragedy, that is to say, the entire audience that attended the fateful screening at Le Régent of 28 March 1948. Of the 230 people who had bought a ticket to see the movie (excluding Mary Lampson herself), 195 came forward in response to an appeal by police. This left thirty-four witnesses whom the police have spent several months tracking down. Leading the investigation, Commissaire Templier made use of every tactic at his disposal: police interviews, enquiries with relatives, calls to informants, and this strategy paid off, with a further thirty-one witnesses traced. Why had they not responded to the police appeal? Among their number were recently released convicts, petty crooks planning a heist, public figures concerned about their privacy: all had their reasons.

Even today, there remain three witnesses who have not been traced by the police ... whose inquiries are far from over.

A cordon had been set up around the entrance to the cinema to corral the crowd of rubberneckers and to isolate the witnesses, who blushed at questions shouted by the journalists while preening like local heroes.

Juge Lenoir, accompanied by the commissaire de police, stepped towards the group. Since the magistrate was a rather short man, a dais had been set up, but the effect was the opposite of what had been intended. Perched above the crowd, he looked even more diminutive.

Commissaire Templier, who was not much older than the magistrate, had a calmer, more measured temperament. In contrast to his appearance – the square face, the taut, shiny skin, the coarse features, the short slicked-back hair – his voice was surprisingly soft and melodious, almost feminine, which gave the uneasy impression of a badly dubbed actor.

As the magistrate struggled to mount the dais, beneath the mocking eye of the commissaire, François walked over to Geneviève and Jean. Given the circumstances, there were no fond embraces, but the two brothers shook hands. Jean was pale and wringing his hands together. Geneviève was trembling with excitement.

"Are they going to re-enact the murder when we're in the cinema?" she asked. "Will there be screams and everything? Will they have a stand-in playing the murdered girl?"

François recognised the look in her eyes as the one he had seen when they first stepped aboard the *Jean-Bart II*.

Jean was even paler than usual and seemed feverish.

"He's a sensitive soul," Geneviève said. "Having to go back in there knowing what happened, well, it upsets him ..."

She shot her husband a poignant, protective glance, even going to far as to stroke his cheek.

"You are a sensitive soul, aren't you, Bouboule?"

Jean did not move, he stared blankly at the doorway to the cinema.

"So, how exactly do these things work?" said Geneviève again.

"I would like to thank you all for coming!"

François was spared having to answer as everyone turned to the dais where Juge Lenoir was holding a megaphone so large it hid most of his face. To those witnesses unfamiliar with him, the examining magistrate looked like a loud-hailer on squat, spindly legs.

"The purpose of this re-enactment is to allow each of you to refresh your memories of the film screening ... the, um, film screening, and at the end ... I mean, after this reconstruction ... any of you who have remembered something ... that is, something new ... should come to me and make a further statement. For the moment, all I ask is that you ... that you retrace your steps, and ... I mean, that you do exactly as you did last time."

He turned anxiously to the commissaire with a look that said: "Was I clear enough?" The commissaire replied with an ambiguous gesture, reached out, took the megaphone and stowed it away. The crowd set off.

Lined up behind the barriers, uniformed police officers advised the witnesses to take up their positions in the queue. There was a lot of barracking, *I was standing here, oh no, you were over there, really, are you sure?* Jean and Geneviève, who had arrived last, took up their place at the back of the queue. The audience trooped past the usherette and into the cinema where the same scene was played out again, *I was sitting here, no, sorry, I was the one sitting here, I remember because that tall man there was blocking my view so I must have been sitting behind him!*

François and his photographer quickly made their way along the queue, hoping to overhear the conversations of the witnesses, or even the magistrate. At the head of the line, François was required to produce his ID card and his summons. The photographer, who was not among those requested to attend, headed back, while François rummaged through his pockets to find the summons.

"Hang on!" François shouted after him.

As the photographer retraced his steps, François whispered: "First street on the left! And make sure you're ready!"

A police officer was blocking François's path, since he had not yet found his summons. The magistrate sidled over, all smiles, and said to the officer:

"The gentleman is with the press. You can let him in ... but only as a witness!"

It was unclear what such a distinction meant.

*

"We were sitting here!" said Geneviève smugly, as though proud of the location.

Jean was staring at the door that led to the toilets.

Three times, the house lights were switched off, the film began and the usherette had to scream: "Help!", and then: "Murder!" At the first attempt, she was so choked up that the words caught in her throat. From the theatre, Geneviève yelled: "Louder, we can't hear a thing!", and seeing a couple of people take offence at her intervention, added: "Well, we can't, can we? And if there's no scream, it's not the same ..."

The reconstruction dragged on for an hour and a half.

When everyone was seated, Juge Lenoir and Commissaire Templier saw that there were two empty seats in the middle of the centre row. These were two of the witnesses who had not come forward. But given where they had been sitting, it was unlikely that they had anything to do with a crime that had taken place on the far side of the cinema. If they had left or returned to their seats, they would have forced half the row to get up after the movie had started. Theories were becoming increasingly rare.

Those sitting on either side of the empty seats were questioned, but could remember very little. "There was a stout little woman, I think," said one. "No, no, no, it was a young, thin girl in a grey coat," said another. "Besides," said a third person, "who looks at their neighbour when they're chatting to their friend and waiting for the movie to start?"

The third empty seat was on the other side of the theatre, at the end of a row. But the magistrate's questions elicited no more information. "I'm not sure," said the person sitting next to the empty seat. "I don't know if there was anyone sitting here when the film started . . ."

François made the most of his time to go up to the booth and talk to the projectionist, who, since Le Régent was a small establishment, was also the owner. And the cashier. He had a wide face with enormous cheeks and a horizontal mouth so large one wondered how many teeth he had. A white-haired man in his fifties, it was he who had first persuaded the usherette, Ginette, to talk to the reporter from *Le Journal*. François's interest was purely practical. He wanted to know how much of the theatre was visible from the small projection window. The answer: almost none. It would mean craning one's neck to get past the bulky lens.

"Even then, you may be able to see something when the house lights are up . . ." said the projectionist, all teeth, "but when they're down . . ."

Looking around the booth, François could see how someone could be passionate about this job. The projector, which was as tall as a man, looked like the sort of machine you could talk to. There was a bench where strips of film could be repaired, and all around were piles of metal cases housing reels of film. It was a mysterious grotto, at once comfortable and intimate.

"It's all I've ever wanted to do since I was fourteen years old," said the projectionist.

François noticed the man wore no wedding ring. He was married to Le Régent.

"And your name . . .?" François ventured.

The man held out his hand.

"Lenfant," he said. "Désiré Lenfant."

The booth was accessed via a spiral staircase; it was almost like being in a submarine. Footsteps echoed on the wrought-iron steps, making the banister shake. François stood aside to let a boy pass.

"Hi," said the boy as he reached the top.

"This is my nephew, Roland," came the projectionist's voice and François turned back to him. "He's another one that's got the bug . . ." said Lenfant. "Isn't that right, Roland, you've got the movie bug?"

The boy blushed. François smiled: the cinema was a whole world unto itself.

"Well, he's only eleven, so he's not allowed to see all the films yet, but he helps out in his spare time, don't you, Roland?"

Having experienced similar scenes with his father, François remembered how paralysing it was for a boy to be held up as a shining example; it was like emotional blackmail. His own father had often spoken on behalf of his children . . .

During the reconstruction of the crime, four witnesses raised their hands to say they wanted to add to their initial statements.

As the magistrate thanked the other members of the audience and told them that they could leave, François ran to the emergency exit. The handle almost came off in his hand. The fire door, which served little purpose beyond decoration, was already ajar. François pushed it open and quietly ushered his photographer in, whispering: "When I give the word, you'll have exactly one second to take a flash shot, all right? You won't get a second chance before we get thrown out on our ears!"

The examining magistrate and the four witnesses were in a corner, near the screen, surrounded by the commissaire and a few hangers-on still reluctant to leave. A uniformed officer muttered quietly: "Move on now, ladies and gentlemen, leave the magistrate to get on with his work . . ." Nobody moved.

One of the witnesses said that he was not sure he had been sitting in the same seat. "Is that all?" the magistrate said, baffled. It was all.

A second witness disputed whether the usherette had screamed: "Murder!", arguing that what she had said was "Murderer!"

The magistrate, by now confused, had already turned to the third witness, who could no longer remember why he had raised his hand.

François, who was as disappointed as the magistrate, glanced at the commissaire, who was watching the scene with a vague smile laden with ulterior motives.

"I was in the toilets when it happened," said the fourth witness, Marthe Soubirot, a woman in her fifties who had made herself beautiful for the occasion. "When the house lights went down, I was coming back from the bathroom and a man pushed past me just as I came back into the cinema . . ."

"Just a moment, just a moment," interrupted the magistrate, flabbergasted at this new revelation. "A man . . . And you only thought to mention this now?"

Overcome by guilt, the woman clammed up.

"Perhaps it slipped your mind . . ." suggested the commissaire.

The officer's soft, gentle, feminine voice was reassuring; Marthe Soubirot turned to him and said:

"I remembered going . . . going to the loo, I mean. I just didn't remember when exactly, because I didn't want to miss the start of the film, you know?"

She turned and gazed at a dark spot somewhere in the theatre.

"It was my husband who reminded me. 'That's when you went to the loo,' he said. And that's when it all came back to me. The man pushing past me, and the film was just starting, so you can imagine that I wasn't about to stop and argue!"

"What do you mean, 'the man'?" said the magistrate. "What man? What did he look like?"

Madame Soubirot eyed the magistrate worriedly; he seemed in a feverish state.

"What Monsieur le Juge is asking," said the commissaire coolly, "is whether you think you would recognise the man again . . ."

"Maybe," the lady said. "I'm not sure, but, well, maybe, I don't know . . ."

"Now!" François hissed to his photographer.

There was a blinding flash, everyone turned, the magistrate opened his mouth to remonstrate but it was too late. François had already raised his hands in the air: all right, all right, we're leaving.

"Did you get it?" he said as they walked towards the exit.

"Oh, yes!"

Outside, only Geneviève and Jean were still standing around.

"I thought it was very disappointing," Geneviève said. "I was expecting something different . . ."

But François was already hailing a taxi.

"Sorry, I have to go . . ."

He spent the trip back to the newsroom feverishly making notes and trying to come up with a headline. When they arrived at the rue Quincampoix, he sent the photographer off to develop the film.

"Bring me the picture as soon as you have it!"

He raced upstairs to Denissov's office and handed him his notebook:

"I THINK I'D RECOGNISE MARY LAMPSON'S KILLER," SAYS SURPRISE WITNESS

Stunning new revelation may force the police to arrange a series of line-ups in an attempt to flush out the murderer

"And I got a photo of the witness," said François. "We are the only ones!"

Denissov gave a little grunt that meant "Well done!"

It had been an exhausting day for François. One that he thought was over when he finally filed the finished, proofread article and left the offices of *Le Journal*; but he was mistaken, because outside on the pavement Hélène was waiting for him carrying her little suitcase.

21

I am but a humble servant

For several minutes, the city of Saigon seemed stunned, as after a heavy cloudburst. The procession of the faithful had ended with marshalled ranks of drums, cymbals and rattles, and soon all that remained was the distant fluttering of colourful tunics through the haze of heat. Those who had followed the Siêu Linh procession to the end had seen hundreds of followers pour into the vast hangar that had become the sect's new cathedral, which was emblazoned with symbols of superhuman size that gazed down on the bustling coolies, groaning under the weight of cargo, as they loaded and unloaded the ships in the port.

On the streets of the city centre normal activity resumed, and there was much comment about the spectacle provided by the Siêu Linh. Étienne was still laughing at the sight of Diêm as a guru. Gaston was lost for words. Monsieur Jeantet offered to buy all three a drink and they were now sitting on a café terrace.

"Good old Diêm . . ." muttered Jeantet, who was never surprised by anything.

"Did he make a killing on the piastre?" asked Gaston, who equated all important events in Saigon to the activities of the Exchange, which was never far from the truth.

"Thanks to our friend here" – Jeantet bowed to Étienne – "Diêm made a transfer of half a million piastres."

It was difficult to tell whether the remark was intended as caustic or complimentary.

"More than enough to buy a warehouse on the docks and convert it into a cathedral," he added.

Gaston, an expert in such matters, nodded sagely at this stunning coup.

Behind his beaming smile, Étienne was beset with questions. He had been stunned by the stature of the Siêu Linh guru. It was so completely at odds with Diêm's unassuming persona. Why had Diêm abruptly left Saigon several months earlier? How had he persuaded his followers that he could cure children of fever? Had he lived as a hermit and been visited by divine revelation? What was Diêm's real plan? Was all this simply about the money?

It was at this point in his deliberations that Vĩnh appeared.

Even those who preferred women were not impervious to the young man's grace. His handsome looks sent even the most jaded souls into a kind of fluster – even Gaston, as Étienne noted with amusement.

Vĩnh was invariably serene, almost detached. He leaned close to Étienne.

"The Pope requests a few moments of your time . . ."

"The Pope . . ." Étienne burst out laughing; this was definitely a day of surprises. Vĩnh was offended, as was clear from the almost imperceptible shadow that flickered over his face. He had said "the Pope" with great solemnity, and was hurt by Étienne's mockery.

"Gentlemen!" announced Étienne, rising to his feet. "Duty calls. I must leave you for a brief moment to commune with our new messiah."

He drained his glass in a single draught.

"Wait for me. I shall glorify, I shall genuflect, I shall beseech absolution and then I shall come back and get roaring drunk."

Without looking at Étienne, Jeantet raised his glass above his head.

"Bring back a few crumbs of sanctitude and I will buy the next round."

*

Étienne had expected a cathedral thronged with the faithful, but the hangar was almost empty. He stood in the doorway for a long moment, amazed by the immensity of the space and the opulent decor. To either side of a wide central aisle, tall painted screens created niches, each housing a figure of an animal, real or mythic – Étienne recognised the Bee, the Peacock, the Vulture, the Prawn – and an altar bearing the emblem of the Siêu Linh on which sat an oil lamp. Thousands of incense sticks burned next to ornate bowls containing offerings. The warehouse skylights, four or five metres above, were now transformed into stained-glass windows depicting allegorical scenes, though these were barely visible through the dense cloud of heady smoke that floated below the ceiling, giving the cathedral the air of a vast ghost ship. But what was most startling were the imposing full-length portraits that adorned the vast painted screens, each depicting a figure Étienne was surprised to recognise. Marie Curie holding a microscope towards the viewer; Victor Hugo in a scholar's robe with a luxuriant beard, as ramrod straight as Justice; Alexandre Dumas with a shock of curls, penning *The Three Musketeers* with a goose quill. Further off, there was Einstein, his head ringed by a crown of planets, there was Saint Theresa, shrouded in sheets, birthing a child or in the throes of orgasm, depending on one's view; close by, Louis Pasteur was raising a syringe to the heavens. Jesus on the Cross was flanked by Abraham Lincoln and Joan of Arc, and next to them came Mohammed and Leo Tolstoy ... All of these public figures – so unexpected in a church – were painted against the same background: a blue horizon surmounted by a dazzling sunburst.

The vast, empty space served only to heighten the sense of majesty.

Once Étienne had recovered from his initial shock, he wondered aloud:

"Where have those bastards gone?"

He cupped his hands around his mouth.

"Diiiii-êêêêm!"

"Hee, hee, hee ..."

Étienne turned around to find Diêm, beaming broadly, still wearing a long red toga and sporting a crimson mitre that looked like a dessert mould with small tassels that looked like curtain ties. The curious headgear reminded Étienne of the red felt tarbooshes common in Beirut in his childhood. The mitre was surprisingly tall – presumably so as not to flatten Diêm's unruly crest of hair. The young man's face seemed somehow different from what Étienne remembered. He still had the same prominent, burnished cheekbones, the same twinkling eyes, but there was something new about him, something stiff and reserved, a humility that seemed at once modest and self-satisfied.

"Monsieur Étienne . . ."

"Well, well, my good Diêm, I . . ."

Diêm interrupted with a wave of his hand.

"The name is Loan, if you don't mind . . ."

"Loan it is, then . . ."

The Pope of the Siêu Linh leaned close and whispered:

"The name means 'phoenix', he who rises from the ashes . . . hee, hee . . . Come with me, Monsieur Étienne."

No sooner had they set off down the central aisle carpeted in gold and green, than Étienne noticed that the cathedral, which he had thought deserted, was filled with people in white robes who now emerged from the countless niches and bowed low as their Pope passed. Loan moved with an artless, affable majesty. It was a surprisingly slow gait, as though every step was the result of prayer and reflection. Étienne looked back. Vĩnh was standing in the doorway, his head bowed.

As they reached the chancel, Étienne saw gigantic banners representing Earth, Air, Fire and Water spilling down from the rafters.

At length they came to the rear of the building, climbed three steps and stepped into a large room furnished with brocade armchairs, vibrant silk cushions, carved beds with exquisitely carved headboards, coffee tables inlaid with ivory, all redolent of a mixture of incense, tea, pepper and . . . opium. It was a smell Étienne was not likely to mistake.

Four elderly dignitaries approached, their pointed goatees and wrinkled faces half hidden by their blue-tasselled caps, their hands and arms invisible beneath their white robes. The four men bowed low and then left the room, passing four worshippers in blue robes who silently brought tea and an oil lamp that gave off acrid smoke.

"The lamp," asked Étienne. "Is it really necessary?"

"This is the lamp of knowledge, Monsieur Étienne."

"Perhaps that's just as well, my dear Di ... my dear Loan, because there are a number of things I am keen to learn!"

Loan gestured for Étienne to sit, while he settled himself in an armchair placed on a low platform, which, despite its height, towered over the room like a throne. The tassels on his cap twirled for a moment, then stopped.

A disciple silently appeared, stood behind the Pope and, using both hands, solemnly removed the mitre to reveal the unruly crest of hair proudly raised to the sky. Having reverently placed the tasselled cap on a high table, the disciple disappeared.

Étienne gave a thumbs-up and looked around as though admiring a new apartment.

"There I was thinking you were importing fridges. My God! Pardon the pun – you really have come up in the world!"

"Hee, hee," Loan giggled into his cupped hand.

"I see you're doing the 'hee, hee, hee,' again ... If it's for my benefit, there's no need."

Loan looked at him with twinkling eyes, but said nothing.

"The last I heard, you'd disappeared faster than a fart in a gale! I went looking for you, the house was empty, you'd left in a blind panic ..."

"Oh no, Monsieur Étienne, there was no panic ..."

Loan gestured, two disciples appeared and with grave, ceremonial gestures, served the tea.

"You see," said the Pope when they had left, "when you authorised the transfer for me (ah, Monsieur Étienne, I did not have time to express my gratitude as I should have), well, to cut a long story short, if I did not want my ... associates ... to help themselves to the lion's share, I thought it best not to hang around, you understand?"

Étienne remembered the import-export company Peeters & Renaud with its ghostly headquarters on the rue d'Ayot.

"Some partners can prove very acquisitive; you never can tell. Now I can confidently return, fearing nothing and no one. I am the messenger of the Supreme Soul, you understand?"

As Étienne looked at Diêm, whose every movement caused the coxcomb of hair to quiver, he felt the urge to giggle.

"And . . . how exactly did this manifest itself?"

"A revelation, yes, yes. The Supreme Soul appeared and said to me, 'Cease your dabbling in trifling matters and proclaim the Truth.' Hence the name of our church. Siêu Linh means 'Supreme Soul'."

"And, tell me, did this happen before or after I authorised the transfer?"

"Just after. The Supreme Soul had long since chosen me, but waited until I had the means to carry His word."

"Very wise of Him . . ."

Loan sipped his tea, smiling blissfully and contentedly at Étienne over the rim of his cup.

"Tell me again Di . . . uh . . . Loan. You set up this business . . ."

"My church!"

"Your church, sorry . . . You set it up within a few short weeks, it all happened very quickly."

Loan set down his cup and leaned towards Étienne with the beatific smile of a man happy and relieved to be able to confide his heart and soul.

"Very quickly, Monsieur Étienne, and do you know why?"

With a flicker of his eyelashes, Étienne said: "No."

"Our success was instantaneous because we created a high-quality religion. It really is first-rate, Monsieur Étienne, you would be hard pressed to find better. Through me" – he placed his hand on his heart – "the Supreme Soul explained that, throughout history, He had sent many messiahs and now the time had come for Him to reign. In person, so to speak."

"Ah, yes, the portraits of Victor Hugo, Lincoln . . ."

"Even Jesus! All were messengers sent by the Supreme Soul. All have benefited humanity, according to His instructions. And now . . ."

"Now it is your turn to be the messiah?"

"Monsieur Étienne, you are mocking me . . . True, I have been appointed Pope of the Siêu Linh, nevertheless I am but a humble servant of the Supreme Soul, I am merely His messenger. I am in contact with the Supreme Soul, and I relay messages to the faithful, nothing more. Siêu Linh is the natural outcome of all other religions, if you like. A unifying church! Believers in all messiahs can find a place here, yes, yes."

"I'm told you have performed spectacular miracles, that children have been cured of fever by the laying on of hands?"

Loan looked down coyly.

"The Supreme Soul allowed me to put a little quinine in the hollow of my hands . . ."

"It was a means to an end . . ." Étienne could not help but smile.

"Exactly," said Loan, "a means to help me to persuade others. But that is no longer necessary now, the faithful encourage the faithful . . ."

Étienne was convinced that a delicate hint of opium floated in the air. To an outsider, their conversation, punctuated by long silences, was like a game of chess, with each player taking time to deliberate.

"And the Supreme Soul visits you, the Pope. In dreams, I expect . . ."

"No, no, Monsieur Étienne, the Supreme Soul writes to me."

"By the Indochina Postal Service?"

"Tut, tut, tut . . ."

Loan reached out to a low table with the carved feet of a griffin.

"This is the basket of Truth . . . The Supreme Soul writes commandments with the pen attached, I read them and relay the messages to the faithful. In this way, we cannot stray, since His word comes to us directly."

Étienne pointed to the table.

"May I?"

Loan, delighted, gestured to indicate that Étienne was free to approach the table. On it was a small, oblong wicker basket of the kind found everywhere in Indochina. A ballpoint pen had been attached to the handle. Étienne glanced at the Pope, who closed his eyes in agreement. Étienne gently picked up the pen: engraved on it was the name of the Indochinese Currency Exchange. It was one of the pens used by clients to sign documents when requesting a transfer.

"Remarkable," said Étienne, returning to his seat. "And so the Supreme Soul writes to you in French? Can I see one of her messages?"

Loan reached into the drawer of the tiny lacquered console to his right and reverently took out a piece of paper. Étienne held it tenderly, as though it were a relic, and read, "Form an allyence with the French."

"Well, isn't that something? The Sovereign Soul may not be very good at spelling, but . . ."

"Supreme!"

"Excuse me! I would love to witness the moment when the Superior Soul writes to you . . ."

"Supreme, Monsieur Étienne, the Supreme Soul! But such a moment of truth is reserved for Great Initiates."

"I see, and . . . are there many Great Initiates?"

"At the present time, there is my brother, my wife and an elderly neighbour who is very devout, yes, yes, one of the first disciples. It is the Supreme Soul who designates the Great Initiates."

Étienne suddenly got to his feet and Loan briefly flinched, but the young man simply leaned close and whispered:

"Tell me, is that opium I can smell?"

"The burdens of the church are onerous, Monsieur Étienne, so the Supreme Soul allows me moments of repose. On condition that I do not abuse it."

"And I don't suppose now would be a moment of repose?" Étienne whispered.

"Alas no, Monsieur Étienne, I must shortly preside over the Ceremony of the Word . . ."

Étienne's eyes widened.

"The Supreme Soul cannot be left without the means of communication, so, in a great ceremony before the faithful, I change the ink cartridge in the pen so that the messages can arrive unhindered."

"That is very sensible of you, very wise." Étienne jabbed a forefinger at the heavens. "A pity the Supreme Soul does not have a telephone, don't you agree?"

"You mock me, Monsieur Étienne . . ."

"No, no, not at all! Not at all! I've heard that you have a private army too?"

"A modest group and not strictly speaking an army. Merely a few of the faithful who ensure the safety of their brothers and sisters."

"A few?"

"Just over four hundred."

Étienne's jaw dropped.

"I am sorry, Monsieur Étienne, but the ceremony is about to begin, I must go and prepare myself."

A disciple appeared and solemnly replaced the tasselled cap on the Pope's head.

Loan stood up, stepped down from the dais and he and Étienne headed for the door.

"One more thing, if I may," said Étienne. "Do your followers believe all this? I mean, *really* believe?"

Loan stopped and allowed his eyes to wander for a moment.

"The success of the church came as a surprise to me too, Monsieur Étienne, I make no secret of that. But I have come to understand that the Supreme Soul chose the perfect moment. France no longer offers a solution for Indochina (though France alone seems not to realise this fact). With the Việt Minh threatening to impose communism, what else is left? Religion. Our church offers protection to the faithful. In South-East Asia, no man can live in isolation, we gather together in order to survive. The Supreme Soul opens its arms and protects the faithful, that is what our followers have realised."

Étienne had a fleeting memory of the men armed with machetes who had marched through the streets of Saigon flanking the procession. And he remembered Belloir's explanation: "Between the colonialism of the French and the terrorism of the Việt Minh, the sects are the only way to get a bit of peace."

"So, tell me, Loan, where have you been all this time?"

"I have been in Hiến Giang. It is a few hours north-west of Saigon."

Loan smiled, but seeing Étienne's face crumple, he held out a hand.

"Are you all right, Monsieur Étienne?"

He seemed genuinely concerned.

"Yes, yes, I'm fine, it's probably just the heat."

Was Loan deliberately tormenting him? Étienne wanted to know for sure.

"It was where ... You know ... where my ... cousin. The legionnaire."

"I'm so sorry!" said Loan, clapping his hand over his mouth. "I'm so sorry, I forgot ..."

"In the Valley of the Rushes."

"Oh yes, the plain north of Hiển Giang."

As he tried to compose himself, Étienne asked:

"What brought you there?"

Loan spread his hands wide.

"It was there that I was led by the Supreme Soul. Life there has been made difficult by the presence of the Việt Minh."

"And ...?"

"And those who live there want only one thing: to be rid of the communists who rob and terrorise and murder them! This is why our church is well established in the area. We offer a more reliable solution than the Expeditionary Force ..."

Étienne saw through Loan's manoeuvre.

"So, you're offering your services to France."

Loan let out his little giggle only to be interrupted by a wave of Étienne's hand. The Pope of the Siêu Linh did not take offence, but adopted his most paternalistic tone.

"The administrative governor is very happy with our presence."

Clearly, the French government's representative in the region was prepared to help Loan's sect become established.

"And you would like the High Commission and the Expeditionary Force to ratify your agreements ..."

"Exactly."

"You are proposing a sort of franchise, right?"

"A franchise ... that sounds a little frivolous, Monsieur Étienne, but ... there is something to it ... We set up local churches and, with France's help, run the Việt Minh out of the area. It is in everyone's best interests. As a religion, we remain independent, and, rid of the thorn in its side, the flag of France continues to fly."

Étienne now clearly understood the reason for this procession through the streets of Saigon.

"And you have come here, in all humility, with a few thousand disciples, to prove to the High Commission that you have the necessary forces to make such a commitment."

Loan clapped silently.

"The Supreme Soul that guides me is wise and prescient, yes, yes."

As he said this, the tassels of his cap jiggled and twined happily.

"And surprisingly tactical!"

"The legacy of a thousand years' experience, Monsieur Étienne."

As the door swung open, Étienne was struck by the vast crowd that had swelled and now filled the whole warehouse. Loan tugged Étienne's sleeve.

"Monsieur Étienne, I asked to see you because I wanted to make a request ..."

As the cathedral echoed to the sound of gongs and rattles, and the voices of the congregation drifted on the air, Étienne took his leave and headed back to the café terrace, where Jeantet and Gaston were becoming impatient.

"We were just about to leave, old man, this has been a long-drawn-out ..."

Seeing Étienne, he stopped in his tracks, his last word dropping like a stone.

"... business."

"It may have been long-drawn-out, but it was worth it," said Étienne, now sporting a blue cap which he tilted from side to side, shaking the tassels.

Gaston warily handed him his cocktail and Étienne raised the glass towards Jeantet and Gaston.

"Gentlemen, feel free to congratulate me. I have just been appointed Papal Nuncio."

I demand compensation

"You're saying this is worth sixty thousand francs?"

Jean was devastated. The shop was hideous. Ramshackle, filthy and hideous.

"No," replied Geneviève, "I'm saying we're going to ask your parents for sixty thousand francs."

"Impossible!"

Geneviève's concept of the marriage was akin to a war of occupation. It was not enough to quash any attempt at independence; the very idea of mutiny had to be pre-emptively crushed.

"What do you mean, impossible?"

It was a word Jean often used in response to Geneviève's demands, and he had rarely prevailed, but this time he felt resolute. Firstly, the project had never appealed to him; secondly, the shop was a dive, and lastly, since they had helped find him his first job in Paris and given him the money to buy a car, he simply *could not* go cap in hand to his parents again (he too emphasised certain words to underline his thought, it was a family trait they inherited from their mother).

"Impossible," Jean said again.

"Oh, there he is!" cried Geneviève as though she had not heard.

The estate agent was an elderly man, bent double by camptocormia so severe he had to tilt his head to one side to look ahead, and spent the rest of the time staring at his shoes. It was impossible not to wonder how he managed to get around. For Jean, it was a painful sight.

"I've got the key somewhere," he said, rummaging in his pockets.

"Come on, hurry up," said Geneviève, "we haven't got all night!"

"I'm coming, I'm coming . . ."

Finally, he fished out a large key, but the door still had to be unlocked, a difficult manoeuvre given his stance.

"Let me," said Jean.

Geneviève made a little pout; she did not believe it was the client's place to do such things.

The frosted glass door creaked on its hinges, releasing a blast of stale air, dust, mould, oil, caustic soda and wax. The smell of washing powder was overwhelming.

"The previous tenant was an ironmonger," said the agent.

"Impossible . . ." muttered Jean.

The shop, which was about forty square metres, was paved with yellowed concrete tiles. The shelves, as though exhausted by long neglect, had collapsed on top of each other and drew jagged lines across the walls. Pushing by Jean, Geneviève muttered to herself:

"It's perfect . . ."

Then, out loud:

"My husband is right, it's impossible."

"What sort of shop are you planning to open?" asked the estate agent.

"Household linens. How much is the monthly rent?"

"Thirty thousand francs . . ."

"No, no, the place needs *far* too much work. Well, thank you, goodbye." She was already walking away with a spring to her step.

"Wait a minute!"

The agent struggled to meet her eye while Geneviève drew herself up to her full height, as though determined to gain a few more centimetres.

Indifferent to the negotiations, Jean went around the counter and into the back room where two desks had once been used for paperwork. It was dreary. Through the skylight, it was possible to glimpse a little of the neighbourhood: a section of wall, a triangle of sky above and, if you craned your neck, the pavement of the next street. "The 18th arrondissement is perfect," Geneviève had decided. "Working class, just as it should be."

Geneviève despised the working classes, but she believed that there was nothing better for trade.

"Impossible," Jean was still muttering to himself when he came back to find that Geneviève had forced the estate agent to pace up and down the shop, and was commenting: "Come over here, look, the window is broken! And over here, this one's broken, too. And that's nothing, come with me . . ."

She seemed to be deliberately forcing him to look at details at the top of the walls. "And just look at that ceiling." The agent craned his neck to try to see what she was talking about, but by then she was already complaining about the mouldings and the beams . . .

A few short minutes later, Jean and Geneviève were walking back down the boulevard.

"Forty thousand francs for two months," said Geneviève, "and we will be reimbursed for half of the cost of renovation up to a maximum of fifteen thousand francs."

Jean had said nothing. The agent had shaken their hands and they watched as he shuffled away like a twisted vine, with feeble, staggering steps.

"And the neighbourhood . . . Perfect!"

Geneviève gazed at the surroundings as though she had just inherited the place.

"We couldn't have found better."

Still, Jean said nothing.

"It's just as I predicted," she added. "Forty thousand for the rent, fifteen thousand for the renovations, that's sixty thousand, exactly."

"It's fifty-five thousand . . ."

Jean instantly regretted the comment. Geneviève had managed to bring him out of his self-imposed silence. They came to the métro station.

"A letter will take much too long," Geneviève said. "You'd be better off telephoning your father."

"As I said already, it's out of the question! My parents have already helped us a lot, I can't ask them for another sixty thousand francs."

Geneviève stopped in her tracks.

"Not sixty thousand, three hundred thousand!"

Jean was panic-stricken.

"Sixty thousand francs to get the shop up and running, and two hundred thousand to pay for the manufacturing work."

"That makes two hundred and sixty thousand," said Jean.

His voice was meek. He had conceded on the principle, soon he would concede on the amount.

"Two hundred and sixty, three hundred thousand," said Geneviève, "it hardly makes a difference, and this way we'll have a little put by."

"I can't ask my parents for that much money, it's impossible."

"Well then, I'll do it."

"You'll do what?"

"I'll phone your father. I demand compensation."

Jean did not understand.

"For our marriage. False promises were made. I was told I was marrying the heir to Maison Pelletier, and I find myself hitched to a second-rate sales rep who earns next to nothing. I was told I'd have a wonderful life in Beirut, with lots of children, and what happens? I have to make do with a slum apartment on the outskirts of Paris with an impotent husband. I'm going to demand compensation. One hundred thousand francs. I'm going to sue your parents!"

As she announced this decision, she arrived at the steps that led down to the métro station.

Jean stared at her head. Geneviève's arms were too stubby to reach the back, where poor combing revealed the grey roots of her hair. This was the spot he would hit if one day he decided to murder his wife.

23

What am I going to do with her?

As they walked down the street, François and his sister looked like an old married couple about to come to blows. Passers-by turned to stare.

Squeezed into the short coat that was so fashionable in Beirut, Hélène looked a little ridiculous in Paris. She looked like a farmer's daughter. I shall spare the reader the howls of "You're completely out of your mind!" and "Do you realise what you're asking?" from François which had already been answered.

"What do you expect me to do with you?"

"I'm not asking you to *do* anything with me!"

She emphasised the word unduly. François was about to tell her she sounded just like their mother, but Hélène drowned him out.

"All I'm asking is for you to put me up for the night. One night! Is that too much to ask?"

He had left her to carry her own suitcase, like a cuckolded husband.

"Well, now that you mention it, yes! I have a life too!"

"Yes, I can see that ..."

She turned back to the offices of *Le Journal*, where some of François's colleagues were standing in the doorway watching and laughing. Above them, the newspaper's black and red logo covered most of the facade.

"Is this the new headquarters of the École Normale Supérieure?"

"Oh, don't you start!"

François strode towards the métro, and Hélène scurried after him like a mouse. He turned back to her.

"And how exactly did you track me down?"

226

Each phrase was intended as a slap in the face, but more than half missed their target.

"It wasn't difficult! Even your concierge knows more about your life than your family!"

François was almost ashamed of his stupidity. Léontine Moreau had never been able to hold her tongue, she was an inveterate gossip.

"Oh, dammit all ... If you won't help me, I'll find some other way!"

She turned on her heel. With an angry sigh, François went after her and caught her by the elbow. It was their third U-turn.

In front of the offices of *Le Journal*, François's friends stood smoking cigarettes, staring at the couple and making whispered bets.

"Ten to one they do another U-turn ..."

"Put me down for a hundred francs."

"Deal!"

"And what about our parents?" shrieked François. "What did you tell them about going away?"

"I told them I'd be staying with you, but don't worry, I'll set them straight! I'll write and tell them that you kicked me out!"

This seemed to herald another volte-face, but just at that moment Hélène stopped, as though about to set down her suitcase. In the doorway of *Le Journal*, everyone held their breath. "Come on, come on, turn around, little girl," one of them said under his breath. "Keep walking, keep walking ..." hissed another.

"I'm not kicking you out, I don't have room for you."

"It amounts to the same thing ..."

"Come on, Hélène, you can't up and leave home just like that!"

Hélène dropped her suitcase with a dull thud.

"You're saying that in 1941 you didn't leave home 'just like that'?"

She had her arms folded like a stern schoolmistress.

"I was going off to war, you silly dope!"

"All right, then, I'm a dope ..."

She picked up her suitcase.

227

"Well, goodbye and thanks for everything."

"We have a winner!" shouted one of François's friends from *Le Journal*.

And while his comrade fished out his wallet, François turned around and headed in the opposite direction, following in his sister's footsteps.

"And how exactly did you break the news to our parents?"

"I sent a telegram from the airport."

François stopped dead.

"A telegram? The sort of thing you send when someone's dead?"

*

"GOING TO PARIS – STOP – STAYING WITH FRANÇOIS – STOP – EVERYTHING FINE – STOP – WILL WRITE – STOP – HÉLÈNE."

Having been alerted by his night operator when the telegram arrived, Monsieur Cholet, the postmaster, had raced over to the avenue des Français. Monsieur and Madame Pelletier had not even noticed that Hélène was not in her bedroom, she was constantly coming and going, so they never really knew where in the house she was, and on days when she did not have permission to go out, she was in bed by midnight.

Louis had read the telegram aloud and instantly dropped it so he could support his wife, who was swaying and gripping the back of a chair.

"Could you go and fetch Doctor Doueiri?" he said to Monsieur Cholet.

Not that the doctor could do anything, but Monsieur Pelletier was anxious to be rid of the postmaster who, since his daughter's marriage to Bouboule – which he considered a fiasco – was visibly delighted by every misfortune that befell the Pelletier family. Ever since Jean and Geneviève's departure for Paris ("the escape", as he called it), he had refused to partner Louis in games of belote, forcing him to partner with the moronic Doctor Doueiri, making Wednesdays a weekly ordeal.

While he waited for the doctor to arrive, Louis Pelletier allowed himself to sink into one of those silent meditations he once performed while watching, hypnotised, the soap bubbles in the factory vats. He patted Angèle's hand and suggested she lie down. Neither of them said a word, each was thinking about the novelty of this situation which, although inevitable, had caught them off guard. Had all the children left? Was there nothing left but to grow old? What kind of wife would Angèle be now? And what kind of elderly husband would he be? What would their marriage be like now, wondered Angèle.

Before long, Doctor Doueiri arrived with that worried little step and the bustling demeanour he adopted when he sensed that things might get out of hand. He felt Angèle's pulse, something Louis had already done, looked deep into her eyes, something Louis had already done, and recommended she rest, as Louis had already suggested. He left at once, he had many patients.

"What did Doctor Doueiri say?" asked Angèle after he had left.

"He thinks it's just a hot flush."

Angèle closed her eyes, distraught.

For almost an hour, Louis sat on the bed, one hand holding his wife's, leafing through *L'Orient*. He was about to head off to the soap factory when Madame Pelletier, feeling his hand slip from hers, gripped it tightly.

A worried Louis paused a long moment, like a child caught doing something naughty. Angèle murmured something he could not quite hear. He leaned closer.

"Louis," she whispered.

She opened her eyes. It was a look he immediately recognised, one that conjured the young woman he had fallen in love with, the woman he had married in Beirut twenty-five years before, a woman he understood without the need for words.

Then he leaned over, brushed his lips against hers and said simply: "It's all right, my darling, don't worry. I agree."

*

Hélène had spent her childhood watching her father order Cinzano. François almost told her she was not old enough, but checked himself in time.

They were sitting in Le Petit Albert, a café near his apartment. Hélène had put her suitcase down next to her, and suddenly she looked like a young girl who was overwhelmed by emotions. François thought she looked like a child, though her posture was surprisingly adult.

"You have it," she said, sliding her glass over to her brother.

She didn't like the taste, but she did not want to order anything else. A simple gesture: no, thanks. François downed the Cinzano in one gulp, though he also hated it. His hand was trembling, he broke two matches before managing to light his Gauloise. Pale and seething with rage, he stared from beneath lowering brows, unable to get past a single idea: having to take care of his younger sister, to live with her, to be responsible for her – it was beyond him. He loved her, of course he did, but he was too young to be a father, and that was the role he would have to play. She had to go home, he had to persuade her, but now that she was here …

He did not seem to be looking at her, though in fact he was watching her reflection in the terrace window. She was undeniably pretty. Had she ever been with a man? The shudder that ran through him at the thought was proof that he was not ready to confront the issue. She had to go home. While there was still time.

Hélène stared at the glass of Cinzano her brother had just quaffed. She began to sob quietly, as though the disappointment of her choice of aperitif mirrored her situation. She did not regret leaving Beirut, no, it was the choice of Paris that troubled her. She should have gone to Saigon, should have found Étienne. He would have understood her, whereas here … She had thought and thought for a long time, but what would she have done in Saigon? Here, in Paris, she could think about studying literature. Or attending the École des Beaux-Arts. But she knew she was thinking of these choices simply because she had to think about something. The truth was that she had chosen Paris over Saigon because she had been afraid of being consumed by Étienne's grief.

Despite his attempts to hide it, despite the reassuring things he wrote, she knew her brother well enough to know he was utterly wretched. Three times in his letters he had said he took comfort in knowing that Raymond had not suffered, which was two times too many. While their parents might be taken in, Hélène was not. Étienne made no mention of the war in his letters either, despite the fact that in the six months he had been there, Hélène had read countless news stories in *L'Orient,* articles about Việt Minh ambushes in which French soldiers were killed, negotiations suspended following attacks on some town whose name she could not pronounce, reports on the Expeditionary Force struggling to defend a road in the north against savage Chinese communists said to be on the verge of invading the country ... In his letters, Étienne had said that he planned to stay in Indochina for as long as he was in mourning. Hélène had been too afraid to join him.

Now, she had only to look at François's stubborn expression to realise that the prospects offered by Paris were not much brighter ...

Her fear, her cowardice, her indecision, her helplessness ... at the thought of these, she sobbed harder.

A bewildered François stubbed out his cigarette, reluctantly got to his feet, went around the table and tried to hug his sister; it was a clumsy hug, he simply did not know how.

He babbled stupid things, like a lover apologising for a break-up.

"We need to let Bouboule know you're here," he said finally, adding inanity to clumsiness.

Hélène looked up. At the sheer absurdity of François's suggestion, they laughed, a ragged, uncertain laugh, and realised that they barely knew each other.

What little they did know dated back to their childhood, a period marked by the seven years that separated them, and by Hélène's exclusive, intensely close relationship with Étienne. Hélène looked at her brother with fresh eyes. The man whose heroic feats, as recounted by their father (she was heartily sick of hearing about his role in war, his success at university), had loomed over her childhood as a role model and a threat, was not the same François she saw now, laughing and confused; this was a different man, a stranger with a familiar voice, a familiar face. She was also aware that his life was based on a lie; the myth of the École Normale Sup ... She felt oddly relieved. Which was worse: to run away from her parents' home, or to lie to them for two years?

As for François, he sensed that their relationship had only just begun.

"I can't take care of you," he said.

"I'm not asking you to. I need a bed for tonight, that's all."

"And what about tomorrow night, where will you sleep?"

"I'll work something out ..."

My God ...

"How much money have you got?"

Hélène felt foolish. She had spent everything she had on her plane ticket.

"At least tell me that you've eaten something?"

François gestured to the waiter.

"Jean-Claude!"

He was an elderly man, with bowed legs and strands of white hair combed across his balding pate. His face was haggard, his eyelids drooped.

"And obviously you haven't got any ration coupons," said François, looking at his sister.

Hélène looked down, fumbled for a handkerchief. The waiter stood next to the table.

"It's all right, I don't want anything, I'm not hungry."

François kneaded his temples with both hands as though seized by a sudden migraine.

"Listen," he said at length. "You wait here, I'll be right back."

Hélène suspected that François had a woman in his life. He hadn't mentioned a woman in his letters home, or when Hélène had asked if she could stay, so the notion was no more than a vague fear. Rather than going up to his apartment, François had insisted on coming to this café a stone's throw from his home, and now here he was saying: "I'll be right back."

"He's actually going to ask this woman whether he can let his own sister stay the night!" she thought. "What a pathetic coward!"

She felt a surge of black fury.

And this was the man she had thought she could count on?

Meanwhile, François was racing up the stairs.

It was Monday, so Mathilde would not be working at La Belle Jardinière. She did not have the key to his apartment, but Léontine, the concierge, was authorised to let her in, and in exchange she would bend Mathilde's ear for twenty minutes in the stairwell. So, François could sometimes come home in the evening to find Mathilde sitting at the kitchen table, listening to the radio and eating a can of sardines. Or mackerel in white wine. Mathilde was constantly eating, she would eat anything, at any hour, and she never gained a gram. She was a strange girl. There was nothing remarkable about her appearance, not her nose, or her mouth, or her eyes, but for some reason she was incredibly alluring. Not at first sight, perhaps, but look at her for a moment and it was impossible not to find her attractive. She said very little, she listened without appearing to. Until she spoke, François never knew what she was thinking.

There was no sign of Mathilde. She was very unpredictable. François was relieved, it gave him time to think about how to break his news, which would have serious implications for their relationship. Mathilde lived with her brother Gilbert. If they could no longer meet at François's apartment, where would they go? He pictured them renting a room by the hour in a seedy hotel ... Furiously, he kicked the door.

He took the stairs four at a time, and strode angrily into the café. But Hélène was no longer there.

"She left just after you did," said the waiter. "She left you the bill. That'll be eight francs fifty."

24

I have a life too

When she reached the Gare Saint-Lazare at 9 p.m., Hélène was exhausted, drained by the series of bad decisions she had made in a single day. As soon as François had left, she had stood up and grabbed her suitcase; so angry was she that when the bow-legged waiter tried to charge her for the drinks, she snapped: "Take it up with my brother." She said it with such cold fury and seemed so determined that the waiter hesitated to go after her, by which time it was too late, she was already far down the street and running into the métro station.

This was one of a series of unfortunate ideas, the first of which was to go seek out her brother Jean.

When Geneviève had spotted her outside the building, she welcomed her with open arms, warmly kissing her on both cheeks, but alarm bells went off in Hélène's head when her sister-in-law smiled and said:

"It's so nice of you to drop by and see us!" and, as though Hélène had protested that she could not stay, she added, "I'm sure you can make time for coffee with us, come on, I won't take no for an answer."

Bouboule hugged his little sister, clearly shocked.

"What are you doing here? Do the parents know you're here?" This was all he could think to say.

"They're aware."

Like François an hour earlier, Bouboule did not even think to offer to carry Hélène's suitcase. All three used the time it took to climb four flights of stairs to consider their next move, so when they arrived at the apartment, all three spoke at once, a brief cacophony that trailed off into silence.

"Can I use the toilet?" said Hélène.

The apartment seemed dreadfully small. The bed took up much of the space. Hélène realised that Geneviève's frequent complaints about her living conditions were well founded.

"It's just down here, my dear ..."

Geneviève stepped out onto the landing and pointed to the door with a ceremonious gesture. Her tone, like that of a maid in a grand hotel, clearly said: "See the hovel I'm forced to live in."

Hélène wriggled inside and shot the bolt. When she sat down, her knees almost touched the door. Outside, Bouboule and Geneviève were whispering. Hélène caught only brief snatches, but they were clearly arguing. Had Bouboule suggested that they let her stay?

Simply by turning up, she had triggered a futile domestic dispute, since the apartment was obviously too small to accommodate her even for one night.

When Hélène reappeared, Geneviève made to go to the kitchen but paused.

"So, you've run away from home too? Your mother must be in a state ..."

She said it with relish, as though recounting an amusing anecdote.

"Maman is very well, thank you, it's so nice of you to be concerned."

"I'm glad to hear it," said Geneviève. "She's had trouble enough from her sons ... Hasn't she, Bouboule?"

When she used his nickname, it was often with a hint of irony that Jean pretended not to notice.

"I was on my way to François's place," Hélène said.

"You won't stay for a coffee?" said Geneviève.

Bouboule looked relieved.

"François's place," he said a little too eagerly. "That's a good idea ..."

And, since a solution had been found, he relaxed, and for the first time he smiled at his sister.

"So, what are you planning to do in Paris?"

"I'm moving here."

"Yes, but what are you going to do with yourself?" said Geneviève.

"Study at the Beaux-Arts."

This off-the-cuff statement surprised even Hélène. With her father, it had been a justification, with Geneviève, it was intended as a slap in the face, but it had never been a serious plan.

As so often, Hélène expressed her doubts in the form of a provocation.

Geneviève, who had instantly forgotten her offer to make coffee, had taken up her usual seat at the far end of the table and was staring at Hélène as though she were her own daughter.

"And what, when all's said and done, is the purpose of the Beaux-Arts?"

"When all's said and done, to create art."

"No, I mean, can you make a living from art?"

"You have a better chance of earning a living than if you stay at home."

They stared at each other in silence.

Jean desperately tried to change the subject.

"So, what about this coffee?"

"No, thank you."

Hélène had already picked up her suitcase and was opening the door.

"Come back anytime!" called Geneviève.

Jean ran out onto the landing.

"As you can see, it's very small, we don't have room . . ."

Hélène was already two steps below him. Jean was wringing his hands. "A bag of nerves, that's what he looks like," thought Hélène. The idea shocked her. For as long as she had known her elder brother, he had been unhappy, clumsy, sweaty, but now she felt a surge of pity. She retraced her steps, dropped the suitcase and took him in her arms. He melted into her and she tried to comfort him.

"Are you all right, Bouboule?"

He nodded; no words would come.

Hélène saw that the apartment door was ajar; she knew that Geneviève would be behind it, all ears.

"I have to go," she said.

She kissed her brother's cheek. It was slick with sweat.

It was half past three. Hélène had arrived in Paris at noon and already she had exhausted the two possible places where she had hoped to stay.

She walked to the Porte de la Villette and took the métro to the Grands Boulevards. She had heard the words a thousand times from her mother's lips. "Les Grands Boulevards," she would say with a mixture of envy and nostalgia, a place that promised untold pleasures that, if her mother was to be believed, could be found nowhere else on earth. What Hélène found was simply a wide thoroughfare filled with rumbling cars, trucks and motorbikes, crowds of people racing to catch the métro, hopping on buses as they passed. A young paperboy was calling: "Get *Le Journal du soir*. Surprise witness in Mary Lampson case to attend a line-up tomorrow! Get *Le Journal du soir*!" Passers-by tossed coins which the boy snatched from the air. The papers sold like hot cakes.

Hélène stopped. Mary Lampson, the shocking murder case that François and Jean had been indirectly caught up in. Geneviève had mentioned the case in a letter to the family in March. Most of their news about the brothers came from Geneviève. Hélène could understand why François did not write much to their parents, after all he was supposedly a student, so writing would mean piling one lie upon another. As for Jean, he had simply scrawled "love, Jean" at the bottom of the letter Geneviève sent to her in-laws in which she described in lurid detail their visit to the cinema where, by dazzling coincidence, the young starlet had been brutally murdered.

Hélène still remembered the sense of shock she had felt when she heard about the actress's death. She had first seen Mary Lampson in a movie some months earlier and thought she was wonderful. The notion that Geneviève and her brothers were somehow connected to the tragic event – however remotely – had left a big impression on her. Paris was a city where such things happened. On the front page of *Le Journal du soir* she saw the photograph of a woman in her fifties, wearing a hat. The surprise witness. She looked utterly unremarkable. Hélène wanted to buy a copy, but only men bought newspapers, and besides there was the question of money. She had no idea how much such things cost in Paris, and now that she would have to fend for herself . . .

She remembered that she was hungry.

She passed an elegant brasserie in which she saw a number of couples, unlike the bars where there were only men. She went in, set down her suitcase, ordered a glass of mineral water and a sandwich of ham and cornichons, which she devoured greedily. With the pleasure of eating came a flicker of hope. She needed to find a hotel room for a few days until her parents could send her money. Her earlier assertion that she would study at the Beaux-Arts now filled her with enthusiasm. The decision was made. She would find a job to pay her rent. She was pretty enough to get work as a life model for art students. Suddenly Paris seemed beautiful. The warm hubbub of the brasserie filled her with a sense of wellbeing, as did the ever-changing spectacle of the Grands Boulevards, which she watched through the window. She had finally arrived. Beirut was behind her, childhood was behind her, Hélène had finally plunged into the wide world.

*

François hailed a taxi – heedless of the fare – and headed for Bouboule's. It was the only place where Hélène could be. "Fucking moron!" he muttered to himself – how could he have let her wander off in a city she didn't know? And with hardly a penny to her name. Thinking that he would find her at Bouboule's reassured him. Knowing that it was the last place on earth she would want to be, terrified him. With Hélène, as with Étienne, there was no middle ground, no moderation, they made a good pair . . .

François suddenly had a vision of two people on the road to ruin.

Étienne had written to him only once or twice; most of what he knew came from their mother. He had decided to stay on in Saigon, despite the raging war. No one really knew how Raymond had died, but he was dead, so what was Étienne hoping for in a ravaged country that was severing its few remaining ties with

France by the month? And now Hélène had shown up in Paris unannounced. Their behaviour was incomprehensible, illogical . . .

Just pray that she's at Bouboule's. François urged the driver to put his foot down; he had the money out of his pocket as the taxi slowed and, as soon as it stopped, he leaped out. But François did not need to climb the stairs. When he pushed the door open, he found Bouboule slumped in the small passageway that led to the courtyard where a few people parked their cars. He was shaking his head, distraught.

"But she came here?" François said.

"She left fifteen minutes ago . . ."

"Where did she go?"

"Your place."

"No, she'd just come from my place."

"Shit . . ."

François slumped down next to his brother. Their shoulders touched.

They sat in silence, contemplating the disaster of their own making. Just like when, as boys, they had done something wrong and were waiting for their parents to come home and punish them.

But this was not a broken window, it was Hélène, an eighteen year old left to wander the streets of Paris because neither of her brothers had been prepared to take her in.

*

The waiter casually dropped the bill onto her table as he passed. Hélène picked it up. She was shocked by the total. One hundred and twenty francs! She glanced around, noticed the large pot plants, the stained-glass lampshades hanging from the ceiling. No wonder she had been seduced; a cursory look at the other customers made it clear that this was a very chic brasserie. Seeing the women in elegant dresses, the gentlemen in suits, Hélène felt ashamed. In her Beirut outfit with her little suitcase, she probably looked like a maid . . . One hundred and twenty francs. She was determined not to make a spectacle of herself by laying her money on the table and counting it. From memory, she had about six hundred francs left after the cost of her ticket . . . How much would a hotel room cost? The day had flown past, it was already late afternoon. She quickly paid, left the brasserie, spotted a sign for Saint-Lazare train station and headed off on foot – the expense of a bus ticket seemed excessive. She felt a creeping panic. She arrived at the station in a sweat, looked for a left-luggage counter.

Twenty-five francs.

Now what?

The most urgent thing was to find a hotel. The suitcase was heavy, she would check it in to the left luggage office, and leave her money in it for safekeeping. Discreetly, she counted her fortune. She opened the suitcase and, before handing it over to the clerk, slipped four hundred francs between her clothes and pocketed the remaining fifty francs.

She started by investigating the hotels nearest the station, avoiding those where liveried porters were opening car doors and carrying trunks. After twenty minutes' walk, she found rather more modest establishments. Even here, the first prices she saw on the signs affixed next to the front doors ran to 800 francs a night; the cheapest were 600 francs. Panic mounted that she would not find a room, that she would have to sleep on the streets like a tramp. She carried on searching, systematically opting for less attractive streets. She saw many hotels, but none with rooms for less than five hundred francs. She could barely afford a single night. Fleetingly, she thought about going back to François's place, but ruled it out. The prospect of going back to François or to Jean was unbearable.

It was dark now.

At around eight o'clock, she finally found a hotel offering rooms for 350 francs. She crossed the street to take in the facade. Paint was peeling from the building and a faint yellow glow came from behind the faded curtains on the windows. She saw a woman enter, followed by a man in an overcoat. The reception desk was visible, and Hélène watched the man take money from his wallet while the woman stood to one side. He must be requesting a room. Clearly there were vacancies. Having to pay 350 francs for the night would leave Hélène with very little money, but tomorrow was another day.

She noted the address: Hôtel Hekla, rue de la Jonquière. It took her more than three-quarters of an hour to walk back to the Gare Saint-Lazare, she didn't want to take the métro, a second-class ticket to see Bouboule had cost her ten francs.

Hélène retrieved her suitcase. She felt vaguely relieved. It was late, but she had found a hotel within her price range. It would not be very luxurious, but at least she could sleep and . . . It occurred to her that she should have asked if there were rooms available. She had seen a man pay at the reception desk, but that did not mean there were other rooms free. Perhaps he had taken the last one. The prospect that she might have to start over was devastating. She dropped her suitcase. Suddenly she felt herself violently jostled, she almost fell, "Excuse me, mademoiselle," came a voice, but by the time she had turned around a man had grabbed her suitcase and raced off. She shouted: "Hey, you there!" then: "Stop, thief!" A few passengers turned to looked, a woman shot her a concerned look, but walked on. The station concourse was surprisingly empty.

Hélène stood, frozen.

Everything she possessed had been in the suitcase, four hundred francs, her clothes, there would be no hotel room; she felt tears welling.

Determined not to make a spectacle of herself, she set off on foot, left the station, blew her nose.

The station clock read 9 p.m.

There was nothing left to do but go back to François. Or to Jean. Perhaps it was a quirk of character, but she immediately knew that this was something she would *never* do. She would die before going back to them.

Paris had begun to come alive. Couples and groups were streaming into theatres, restaurants and cinemas. Hélène wandered without thinking, senselessly muttering: "Never, never." She found herself back at the rue de la Jonquière, as though she hoped her suitcase and her money might be there . . . Where could she sleep? She thought of going back to the station, there were benches in the waiting room. But having had her suitcase stolen, she knew she would not spend the night there unmolested ... "Never," she muttered again. Then, the idea occurred to her.

Find a man for the night.

The solution was at once terrifying and obvious. How did you go about finding a man for the night? How should she go about it? She had no idea what she should agree to. Would it be as it was with Lhomond? Would some man pay her to slap her and then brutally take her against the wall? Would she even get a good night's sleep? She mentally pictured the scenario, a series of flickering images based on what little she knew of women selling their bodies for the night. In her mind, the imaginary client was never more than a looming, menacing shadow, a heavy weight pressing on her; she shuddered at the thought. Finally, she arrived in front of the Hekla Hotel. Only then did she realise how events had conspired to bring her to this moment. There was the woman she had seen earlier, this time followed by a man in a white mackintosh who was different, but performed precisely the same gestures, stopping at the reception desk, taking out his wallet, while the woman, leaning on the banister, one foot already on the first stair, observed him ... Seeing the two of them, she realised that this thing she had been dreaming about, this frustrating, exciting, pragmatic, shocking act, was something she could not bring herself to do. She stood on the opposite pavement; the couple had gone upstairs. She wondered how long it took, turning a trick in a hotel room. Whatever it was, it had nothing to do with somewhere to sleep.

The tears that spilled down her cheeks owed as much to despair as to exhaustion.

She had to face the unthinkable, go back to François's place, knock on the door, tell him: "Someone stole my suitcase." Would there be someone in his bed?

At the métro station, she stared at the network map, trying to figure out the way back to François's arrondissement when her eye fell on a station named Europe – place de l'Europe. The Hôtel de l'Europe. Madame Ducrau. "Your father's mistress ..."

Monsieur Pelletier was well known there; they would let her stay one night on credit. Perhaps even two nights!

She still had her papers, she could prove that she was Mademoiselle Pelletier, they even had her Beirut address. This was her last chance. If they refused to take her, she would ring the doorbell at François's place, and if there was a girl in his bed, she would personally throw her out – Hélène had as much right as any woman to sleep at her brother's house!

It was 10 p.m.

The Hôtel de l'Europe was immaculate, nothing at all like the Hôtel Hekla. A young bellboy in a red suit and a little cap gave Hélène a puzzled look; travellers with no suitcases were clearly rare. Given she had only a handbag, maybe she looked like a whore.

"Can I help you?"

Hélène turned, the boy was very young, no more than fifteen.

"I'll deal with it, Gabriel!"

It was a woman's voice. She was standing behind the reception desk. Madame Ducrau, probably, though she did not look like her father's mistress, she looked positively ancient, but she was cheerful, dressed to the nines and heavily made-up despite the lateness of the hour.

"You must be Hélène? Come on, come in!"

When she heard her name echoing around the foyer of a hotel where she had never set foot, Hélène was terrified; she turned to run, but heard the manageress saying:

"Your daughter has arrived, Monsieur Pelletier!"

From the adjoining salon that Hélène had not even noticed, her father appeared, wearing the blue suit he donned for business trips and funerals.

"Just as well I reserved the table for eleven o'clock, isn't it?" he said with a smile.

25

Diplomatic bag, natürlich!

By truck, it was – theoretically – a five-hour journey during which all sorts of things could and usually did happen. Saigon had had a number of dry days, but now the rainy season had suddenly decided to make up for lost time. By the time the small convoy of seven vehicles set off, the water rushing through the streets had risen to halfway up the wheels. Heralded by a blast of cold wind, each cloudburst lasted for an hour or two, rarely more, giving way to bright, clear, muggy periods when all the city's bustling activity was done.

But at dawn, the rain was coming down so hard visibility was less than a few metres, it required headlights to see even the rear of the next vehicle, and they had to travel nose to tail.

"Why didn't we just wait for the rain to stop?" Étienne asked naively.

Capitaine Moinard, a man with a frighteningly banal face and the moustache of a gendarme, had insisted on leaving in the early hours.

"Even if we make slow progress, we'll make some headway."

He had the logic of a gendarme, too.

"Move it!" he urged as the convoy rolled at walking speed through the torrential downpours and wheels spun in mud that came up to your calves when you had to get out because the vehicle was stuck.

"Stop!" he barked suddenly, although the road ahead looked clear for five or six hundred metres.

He ordered the convoy to stop, sent out four scouts equipped with grenades and explosives, and instructions they didn't need, since – being Việt Minh prisoners – their one job was to clear the route at the risk of their lives.

Rolling far enough behind to give them time to act in the event of an ambush came a ragtag collection: soldiers from Morocco and Chad, Vietnamese auxiliaries (recognisable by their tattered clothes and worn-out shoes) and a gleaming platoon of soldiers loyal to the Siêu Linh: in all, some thirty men in seven French armoured cars. To Étienne, this disparity symbolised a war in which France had tried almost everything, succeeded in doing nothing, and was now doomed to constantly improvise against a political tide as changeable as the raging river, using the only means it could find to hand in often illegal and always tortuous circumstances.

The bright young things in the convoy were the Siêu Linh soldiers, who made up fully half the troops. Pope Loan had insisted they be provided with new, tailored uniforms, proper shoes and fully operational weapons – three things rarely available to troops supporting the Expeditionary Force, as auxiliaries hired on an ad hoc basis knew from bitter experience.

"You will be escorted by an elite unit, Monsieur Étienne," Loan had assured, making the tassels on his cap dance.

Loan had asked for help in authorising new transfers of piastres for the sect, which made Étienne an important guest.

"Very well," said Étienne, "but I want a hat with tassels. Like theirs."

He had nodded to the silver-haired, bearded dignitaries in white robes crowned with magnificent blue felt caps in the form of jelly moulds.

"Alas, Monsieur Étienne, such vestments are reserved for senior church dignitaries ..."

"Then make me a dignitary."

"Oh, Monsieur Étienne, you are putting me in a difficult position! Come on, I am asking for your help in the fight against the Việt Minh, surely a noble cause?"

"The noblest, Holy Father, I despise them, they are murderers."

"Well then? You already have your reward, Monsieur Étienne – you are fighting a holy war!"

"I agree, but if I'm fighting a holy cause, I'm entitled to some sacred headgear."

"With all due respect, Monsieur Étienne, it would be unseemly to raise a Frenchman to the rank of Cardinal of the Siêu Linh. The faithful would not understand."

"I fully understand – but what can I say, Holy Father? I have a hankering for a blue hat."

Loan, as the reader will know, was nothing if not pragmatic.

"I may have a solution," he announced, humbly yet triumphantly.

And so, in exchange for a tasselled cap he pledged never to wear in public, Étienne was appointed secret Papal Nuncio to the Siêu Linh.

"Secret, covert and clandestine, Most Holy Father," said Étienne. "You have my word of honour. I won't spit on my hand, but I cross my heart."

He had sported the holy headgear to dazzle Jeantet and Gaston, but after that he wore it only in his apartment, under the amused eye of Joseph and the reproachful glare of Vĩnh, who considered it blasphemy.

And although Étienne joked about it, he considered that there was nothing immoral in authorising transfers to help the Siêu Linh, since it amounted to fighting the Việt Minh. Like many of his colleagues at the Exchange, he had come to believe in the peace-making properties of currency transfers, even if they were a serious drain on France's treasury.

When it came time for Loan and his cohort of followers to leave for Hiến Giang, with assurances from the High Commission that the French administration would help establish the church there, Étienne had champed at the bit.

"The Papal Nuncio must know the terrain," he said. "We feel it right and fitting that we visit the area."

Ever since his appointment, Étienne had begun to refer to himself by the *pluralis majestatis*.

"It is a very dangerous undertaking, Monsieur Étienne."

"We are cognisant of the fact. Nonetheless, we have so decreed. No Hiến Giang, no rubber stamp."

Loan was intractable.

"The risks are too great, Monsieur Étienne, I'm sorry. If anything should happen to you, I would never forgive myself."

"Well, then, we shall write to the Supreme Soul."

"Excuse me?"

"Since the Supreme Soul writes to you, it stands to reason we can write to it?"

Loan stared at him intently, with deep furrows between his brows.

"What do you intend?"

"A mass, Most Holy Father. I shall don my blue headdress, shake the tassels, call upon the faithful to petition the Superior Soul . . ."

"Supreme!"

"Exactly. Then I shall request a letter confirming that yours truly is indeed prohibited from apostolic tourism, and bow my head in prayer."

Loan let out a long sigh, clearly close to giving in. Étienne found the whole thing amusing, but even as he prevailed, he felt a pang of grief, for if his manner had been playful, the subject was serious.

"You know that that's where my cousin died, Loan. In Hiến Giang."

There was a quaver in his voice, a barely suppressed sob.

"Without the benefit of your protection, I will never be able to go there," Étienne explained.

"But . . . what do you expect to find?"

Étienne did not quite know, but he felt he could not truly mourn until he saw the place where Raymond had died.

"I have no grave where I can go to grieve . . ."

Loan closed his eyes, as though beseeching the Supreme Soul to forgive him for the evil he was about to do.

So it was that, three weeks after the sect departed for Hiến Giang, having requested a week's leave from the Exchange, and flanked by an elite escort of Siêu Linh under the command of Capitaine Moinard, Étienne undertook the journey that was part pilgrimage, part desire for revenge. If both these motives were laughable, the latter proved less so, since the journey only served to deepen the hatred Étienne nurtured for this army of shadows who thought nothing of flaying soldiers alive and then beheading them with ploughshares.

While the foot soldiers of the Siêu Linh had returned to Hiến Giang in trucks and on foot, Loan had made the journey by plane. The sect had bought an ancient decommissioned Lockheed Vega and repainted it in the colours of the Siêu Linh. It was the Pope's pride and joy. He had christened it Chim Ưng.

"It means Eagle," he said proudly.

To Étienne, the comparison between a decommissioned Lockheed Vega and an eagle was sheer poetry.

Loan did not care, he travelled by plane whenever possible. Disciples rolled a royal blue carpet to the steps leading to the papal plane, it was a splendid sight. Loan had insisted on making the trip to Hiến Giang in full pomp and ceremony, which meant by air, shrugging off the argument that the nearest landing strip was six hours' drive from Hiến Giang, so travelling by plane would take longer than travelling by truck.

Some weeks earlier, Étienne had attended the ceremonial launch of the august aircraft, and had been aboard the inaugural flight, piloted by an ex-Lufthansa captain fired for drinking on the job and hired by Loan for chicken feed and two crates of gin. While the two dignitaries accompanying him trembled from head to foot, Étienne had roared with joy as the wind pouring through cracks in the fuselage whipped his face and the engines stuttered alarmingly.

Much as he had enjoyed his baptism by air, Étienne was happy to be making the trip to Hiến Giang by truck. The rainstorm that accompanied their departure had petered out within twenty minutes, but although Capitaine Moinard had been right to give the signal for departure, he did not seem smug. He was merely doing his job.

The sun made a dazzling reappearance, and even the most jaded travellers were stunned by the beauty of the landscape. With dark dense jungles, boundless paddy fields and rolling blue mountains, this was a country that teetered on the border of heaven and hell. As Étienne gazed in awe at the rushing rivers flecked with foam that snaked between green fields, he understood why people were prepared to fight for this country, even if this was not their primary motivation.

An hour later, the trucks began to struggle. The deep potholes forced drivers to make awkward manoeuvres, and each time the convoy slowed there came the fear of an ambush. Was this a natural rut? Did those potholes seem freshly dug? Had the tree half blocking the road fallen of its own accord? Capitaine Moinard quietly chewed on his moustache, and from time to time, as though emerging from deep meditation, would order the convoy to stop, climb down and study the surroundings, talk to the Vietnamese auxiliaries familiar with the area and, if circumstances required, order them to get out and survey the terrain, or tell scouts to march ahead while the vehicles sat, engines idling, machine guns trained on the four cardinal points.

The trucks regularly became mired in thick mud churned up by the torrential rains, sometimes forcing the convoy to stop for an hour or more.

Étienne soon managed to discourage any attempts at conversation by Capitaine Moinard, who was merely trying to be civilised but much preferred silence. Étienne, too, favoured silence because, as the convoy plunged deeper into the jungle, through swamps, along furious, rain-swollen riverbeds and overflowing paddy fields, he felt that he was experiencing something of what Raymond had experienced. He could hear the rain rattling on the truck roof, just as Raymond had; he trudged through mud, as Raymond had, when he had to get out to lighten the load of the truck. He almost hoped that there would be a Việt Minh ambush, that he would be taken prisoner, tortured, then skinned alive ... Étienne suffered twice over, from the grief he still felt, and from his facile attempts to fashion a novel from his lover's death.

Although it had set off before dawn, the convoy did not reach Hiến Giang until late in the day.

"Without the need to fire a single shot," said Capitaine Moinard gravely, as he saluted Colonel Philippe de Lacroix-Gibet, who had come to welcome the guests from Saigon.

Flanking the colonel were Loan, in freshly pressed robes, looking pious and devout, rubbing his little hands as though washing them, and the sort of civil servant who always insists on being addressed as Monsieur So-and-So, as a mark of respect for his person and his office.

"Monsieur Claude Grandvalet, of the High Commission."

He proffered a lean, pale hand that was suspiciously clean and looked as though it was freshly manicured every morning. Everyone seemed to be sending a message with their hands. Loan's handwringing simpered, "Thank you, gentlemen, for coming here at my invitation," the colonel's brusque handshake with Étienne growled, "So this is the arsehole who's going to pester me all week," while the civil servant's pampered paws announced, "I represent the law and order; feel free to spread the word."

It was clear that the colonel despised the civil servant, who cordially returned the favour, and that neither would have lifted a finger had Loan fallen under the wheels of a passing truck. This febrile atmosphere instantly appealed to Étienne, who said, as he shook their hands:

"Thank you for your welcome, gentlemen, I don't suppose you have any opium going begging?"

The men pretended to be shocked. They laughed it off rather than taking offence. Étienne's position at the Exchange in Saigon made him the object of naked greed. Every man present seemed to have a transfer request behind his back, poised to receive the divine rubber stamp.

Loan approached Étienne and, clasping his hands over his chest, gave a deep bow.

"Monsieur Étienne, I shall leave you with your hosts. Might I expect your noble presence at mass the day after tomorrow?"

"Ah, Sunday mass, just like with the Catholics? It's a little un-original, isn't it? Surely the Superior Soul is above such things?"

"The *Supreme* Soul ... Siêu Linh is a syncretic religion, Monsieur Étienne, we adopt the best of all that has gone before us ... and all that is to come."

Étienne whispered into Loan's ear:

"Can I wear my bobble hat or would you rather . . . ?"

Seeing Loan's grimace, Étienne closed his eyes and nodded. "All right, all right, I'll come incognito."

Then, making the most of their aside, he said:

"Holy Father, would it be unseemly to ask you for a little . . . ?"

He replaced the last word with a wink.

Loan was already nodding.

"Everything is prepared, Monsieur Étienne, you will want for nothing."

The Expeditionary Force had their barracks in a ramshackle fort. These were soldiers from various different units, as resolute in their actions as they were lax in their dress code. The barracks presented a curious spectacle of bare chests, tattoos, blue eyes, olive complexions, faded uniforms, laundry strung from lengths of rope, arm wrestling on wooden crates, oiled rifle stocks, tarpaulins stretched between tent poles where men squatted to play cards, and – most surprisingly – a priest who calmly strolled through the chaos. With his beard as long as a sapper's apron, he would have been mistaken for a legionnaire, but for the huge gold crucifix over his chest like the number on a cyclist's jersey that marked him out as an army chaplain.

Étienne paused for a second.

He recognised the short, broad-shouldered, square-jawed, clear-eyed legionnaire who had just turned his back as the officer who had informed him of Raymond's death on the terrace of the Café Camerone in Saigon.

Étienne was convinced the soldier had recognised him and turned away.

Subconsciously, what had brought Étienne to this place was the hope that he might encounter this man, who could show him the spot where Raymond and his comrades had been found, the small Valley of Rushes mentioned in the military report. It would be impossible for Étienne to ask Colonel Lacroix-Gibet or the civil servant, since he was not supposed to have read the report. This evasive soldier was his only hope. But Étienne quickly learned from other officers that this unit of the Legion had completed its tour of Hiến Giang and would be leaving for Saigon within hours. Not only had the veteran soldier been evasive, now he was leaving just as Étienne arrived.

He had made the journey for nothing.

Rain had flooded the yard hours earlier, but with the tropical heat, the clay had partly dried, leaving vast muddy puddles people had to skirt around, such that the parade ground looked like a chain of floating islands between which officers zigzagged, leaped, slalomed and swore.

At one end of the enclosure was a large wooden building that downstairs housed the military administration and upstairs the colonel's spacious apartments, where Étienne was to stay. Led by a caporal, he weaved his way through the muggy maze of corridors and upstairs to the quarters reserved for the occasional guests: a large room equipped with a ceiling fan, plunged into semi-darkness by shutters intended to keep out the torrid heat which, even at this late hour, with the rains now long forgotten, was still stifling.

"Colonel Lacroix-Gibet would be honoured if you would dine with him. Dinner is at twenty hundred hours."

It was less an invitation than an order. The caporal did not wait for an answer but took his leave. As soon as Étienne was alone, he stripped and, using the hand pump, showered in lukewarm water. Then, exhausted, he sprawled naked on a bed that sagged in the middle and sank into a late afternoon nap, from which he was eventually woken by the dull thunder of the rain on the roof. Peering through the window, Étienne saw the flooded parade ground, churned up by heavy vertical sheets of rain.

Dinner would begin in a few minutes. Étienne hurriedly dressed and left his room. He was completely disoriented. Had he been this way? He walked a few metres, thought he recognised where he was, then retraced his steps. There was no one about. Then he heard voices, spotted an open door. To his relief, it was the caporal who had shown him to his quarters, now sitting chatting with a colleague. He was seated behind a small desk papered with maps studded with coloured pins.

"I got a little lost . . ."

"Don't worry, it happens to everyone. Everyone gets lost the first time. I'll show you . . ."

"Is that real?" said Étienne flippantly nodding to a little skull being used as a paperweight which looked like a nod to Shakespeare in this bureaucratic setting.

"Absolutely! A gook last year, I personally cut his head off, didn't I, Jeannot?"

"Affirmative."

Étienne watched as the two men exchanged a smile, as though recalling a colourful anecdote from the past that had become poignant with time.

"Jesus, the little fucker could really scream, do you remember?"

The caporal raised his forefinger.

"The thing is, in movies, they swing their sword and – bam! – the head comes right off, just like the guillotine. In real life, it's very different, let me tell you. You hit the vertebrae, you try a little higher, a little lower, first one then the other, it's complete carnage and it takes forever."

Étienne looked from the caporal back to the skull; a queasy feeling stole over him.

"And that's not the worst of it! To get a nice clean skull, you have to get all the flesh off. I had to boil it for four hours solid, can you imagine? Even that wasn't enough, I had to scrape off the last bits with a knife."

"You're going to make monsieur late," said the other man.

As though from far away, or through a partition wall, Étienne heard his own voice say:

"You cut his head off . . . while he was alive?"

Everything sounded more and more dreamlike. Étienne could clearly see, but sounds came only as a muffled echo.

"Well . . . somewhere between the two . . . the generator there had worn the gook down a bit . . ."

He nodded to a dynamo in the corner of the room, a small rectangular box mounted with pedals, like a bicycle.

"We attached the electrodes to his balls, he was dead beat, he couldn't talk any more, so what were we supposed to do? He'd told us everything he knew. Hadn't he, Jeannot?"

"You're going to make monsieur late," said the other man again.

"All right, all right ..."

Étienne could no longer remember what he was doing here; the image of the skull bubbling in a pan made his stomach turn.

"I'll show you the way," said the corporal.

It took several minutes for Étienne to recover, during which time they walked towards the colonel's apartments.

"Ah, I see you have met Caporal Couchet!"

The caporal was standing to attention, but the colonel had already turned away and, taking Étienne by the shoulder, was guiding him into the dining room.

"It's going to be 'potluck', as they say. My wife is in France for the month with the children, so I'm afraid when it comes to cooking and serving, things aren't quite what they should be ..."

Present were Monsieur Claude Grandvalet, the civil servant, and a commandant whose name and rank Étienne forgot, being still in shock.

Colonel Lacroix-Gibet was a tall, whip-thin man with curly red hair and the feigned bonhomie of a landowner, an aristocrat who cultivated a certain boorishness to please the rabble. He was one of those men who, having never failed, never doubted themselves. Though he affected to be good-natured, in reality he was terribly pretentious. One could easily imagine him on horseback, at a steeplechase, part Pukka Saab, part thoroughbred. He poured whisky without asking who wanted it, and gestured to seats at the table. From the moment you entered, you were under his authority.

A uniformed batman wearing an apron served chilled fish with mayonnaise and, despite having the hands of a boxer, tried to make his gestures seem elegant and refined. Out of context, it might have seemed funny, this ceremony devoid of women, like a drag act at a cabaret club.

"So, Monsieur Pelletier, how are things in Saigon?"

The wine flowed, as did the conversation. After the chilled fish, there was hot fish, and conversation revolved around the metropolis, a terrain inhabited by fools and incompetents. The waiter dropped some cutlery, picked it up with a gesture he hoped was sophisticated, and placed it back on the table.

Having now regained his composure, Étienne answered the questions perfunctorily, struggling to seem interested. He ate and drank. Conversation had somehow drifted back to the caporal.

"Ah, Corporal Couchet!" chortled the colonel. "I don't know what we would do without him, don't you agree, Grandvalet?"

"Indeed, indeed."

"What exactly does he do? I mean, what are his duties?" Étienne said.

"He works in intelligence. He's a past master at extracting information . . ."

"Yes, I saw that . . . Tell me, does he lop heads off with a sword or a machete?"

"Ah yes, his skull – he's very proud of that . . ."

The colonel replied as though he had not noticed Étienne's withering sarcasm.

"With a machete, I expect," he said, with sudden concern. "We don't have any swords in the barracks . . ."

The commandant nodded, yes, definitely a machete. The civil servant masticated his fish and nodded solemnly. It took a few seconds for Étienne to realise what was intended as irony had been treated as technical curiosity. These people were proud of what they were doing.

"There are those who criticise the army," said the colonel, "there are even those who mock it, oh yes! But this conflict has demonstrated our extraordinary capacity to adapt. You have to understand, Monsieur Pelletier, we were expecting a war. A traditional war, with front lines and hand-to-hand combat! Man to man, if I may put it thus. It demonstrated a serious misunderstanding of the Yellow Man. They are a deceitful race by nature. The gooks are not brave, but they are tenacious. So, they invented a form of war that replaces traditional combat with terrorism. Guerrilla warfare. Our enemies wear no uniforms; I'd almost go so far as to say they have no army. Our enemies are everywhere, they blend into the population like fish in water. They appear out of the blue, ten or fifteen of them, launch an attack, cut off heads and vanish as swiftly as they appeared. We're not talking about an army of soldiers but a gang of thugs and murderers. So, what did we do? We adapted. We met their revolutionary war with a counter-revolutionary war! Haha!"

"Does that involve sticking electrodes on their balls and cutting their heads off with a machete?"

"Among other tactics. When fighting murderers, by which I mean terrorists, the only real weapon is information. When we catch one, we don't treat him as an enemy combatant, we treat him as a criminal, which rather changes the dynamic . . ."

Either the colonel was a formidable debater capable of completely ignoring the tone of a question to focus only on the content, or he was so convinced of his own rectitude that he heard only his own thoughts. It was difficult to tell.

"And it doesn't bother you," said Étienne, pouring himself some more wine, "that you are turning your soldiers into torturers?"

At this, the delegate from the High Commission flinched and looked up, outraged. The commandant dropped his fork, which clattered on the porcelain plate. Once again, Colonel Lacroix-Gibet demonstrated his innate sangfroid.

"It is a tactical decision, Monsieur Pelletier, no more, no less. We are merely adopting the methods of our enemies. First we hire informants in the markets and the shops, then we choose our scouts and interpreters from among the gooks. Divide and conquer! And, yes, we use their techniques against them! From the outside, it might look a little grisly, but when you've been here a while, you'll understand. A few months ago – it was the end of February, am I right?"

The commandant, who had not opened his mouth, nodded sagely.

"A few months ago, a unit of the Expeditionary Force was taken hostage in an ambush here in Hiến Giang. A handful of valiant legionnaires."

Étienne had been deliberately provoking the colonel; now the trap was sprung.

"The Việt Minh tortured them for almost ten days and in the end, do you know what they did?"

Étienne wanted to roar: "Yes!" but he had neither the time nor the willpower.

"When they were found, one of the soldiers had had his hands cut off, another had had every joint broken, a third had been flayed, his body was red raw, he had only a few shreds of skin left, all the rest had been peeled off probably with a razor, and the . . ."

Étienne banged his fist on the table, causing the cutlery to rattle, and an empty bottle to topple, dragging a glass with it . . .

The colonel was smiling deferentially.

"Of course, of course, you're right, the Việt Minh are a vicious and cruel enemy . . ."

He turned to his batman.

"Could you have coffee and liqueurs served in my office, please?"

He got to his feet.

"Gentlemen, I don't like to boast, but I think I can offer the best Havana cigars in Indochina. My brother-in-law gets them for me. Diplomatic bag, *natürlich*!

For the remainder of his stay, Étienne never managed to return to reality, to himself, never managed even to think straight. He listened, only half-conscious, to the smoke-filled conversations in the colonel's office, then went back to his room and sprawled on the bed without troubling to undress, and lay there, with no thought of what he was doing, waiting for some cloudburst to bring down the roof and the ceiling and drown him in his grief.

He loathed this war with every fibre of his being. And yet, without knowing why, he did not decide to leave, as though he were waiting for something – but what?

Next to his bed, Étienne had found a long pipe carved with the emblem of the Siêu Linh; in this, the Holy Father had kept his promise: the opium was of rare quality and considerable quantity.

Late in the night, Étienne sank into a dreamless sleep, but woke the following morning exhausted and anxious, as though somewhere in his dulled mind there lurked a gruesome memory that his mind refused to grasp.

Out on the parade ground, an impeccably equipped company of the Siêu Linh army was preparing to leave on a mission with a unit from the Expeditionary Force. Since the triumphant procession through the streets of Saigon and the subsequent announcement that French forces were prepared to help the Siêu Linh recapture the region, many local villages had approached the sect, which now had a promising network. Through judicious use of informants, spies and others, the army had succeeded in cutting off the Việt Minh's boltholes and gradually forced them back to the border of the region. Then, in a ploy that was part colonial conquest and part mafia takeover, the Siêu Linh introduced a patriotic tax intended to pay for the security of the villages within its ambit.

Étienne went down to the parade ground. The early sun was already melting away the large puddles that had formed during the night; white whorls of gauzy mist rose and melted into the air. Heading for the entrance, Étienne took a winding route, past a makeshift grille and a series of locked outbuildings with closed doors. Suddenly he felt a hand grab his elbow; before he had time to react, there were two hands, then four, and he was dragged into a room that smelled powerfully of spices and dried fish. The room was so dark, he could see nothing. There were two or three men. The first one punched him hard in the stomach, Étienne fell to his knees, then the second man held his arms while the third kicked him in the ribs.

It was a brief, terrifyingly effective attack.

Seconds later, gasping for breath, Étienne was spewing his guts onto the dirt floor. When he looked up, the squat, lantern-jawed, blue-eyed legionnaire was standing in the doorway.

"I took a risk in Saigon when I passed on confidential information about Raymond Van Meulen. It's a direct breach of orders to pass on sensitive information, and I'm not one to question orders. But I told you what I did because Raymond was . . . he was a good man. Don't make me regret it."

Étienne was still panting.

"I just wanted to make sure you understood . . ."

As Étienne tried to raise himself onto his elbow, the legionnaire calmly left and closed the door behind him.

Étienne spent a good hour writhing in agony on his bed before the pain subsided. He was left with purple bruises from the steel toecaps, and a sense of humiliation that quickly turned to fury.

Abruptly, he got up.

The penny had dropped.

This country was not for him; he had to go. But go where? He did not stop to wonder.

He had to leave.

Right now.

He was packing his belongings when the bedroom door burst open.

It was the colonel, suited, booted and beaming broadly.

"You need to understand ... My apologies, I should have knocked ..."

Then, without pausing, he said: "Come with me!"

His broad smile was that of a man accustomed to being obeyed.

"I'm heading back to Saigon," said Étienne, as he continued to pack his case.

"What? Already? I see ..."

The colonel seemed disconcerted, disappointed even. But from Étienne's blank expression and the fact that he was bent almost double, the colonel realised that something had happened that he did not want to know about.

"Right, well, we'll sort that out for you. It's too late to leave today, but I'll arrange an escort for you tomorrow, if that's all right."

He was about to leave, then turned back.

"This isn't about our little dinner party last night, is it ...?"

"No, absolutely not," Étienne said coldly. "On the contrary, everyone was ... quite civilised."

The colonel, who was no fool, studied Étienne for a long moment.

"Good. You leave tomorrow."

It was no longer an offer but an order.

"In the meantime, I came to show you something, a curiosity . . . We've spotted a Việt Minh installation about fifty kilometres north of here."

"Maybe some other time . . ."

"We leave for the Valley of the Rushes in twenty minutes, if you are interested . . ."

Étienne had suddenly straightened up.

The Valley of the Rushes. Where Raymond had died.

And so, moments after deciding to leave the country, Étienne found himself in a jeep leading a column of five heavily armed trucks and soldiers in camouflage dress.

An hour and a half later, they came to the banks of a canal where scouts had prepared sampans loaded with weapons and boxes of ammunition. The atmosphere was tense and silent, as though the troops feared they might wake the jungle, which became thick and tangled as the boats set off on the slow journey north. On either side, they were flanked by walls of dark, dripping vegetation. The air was so humid it was almost impossible to breathe. The water was thick with rushes and lotus, the banks crumbled to swampland, and the stench of rotting food was overpowering. For an hour, no one smoked, no one said a word. Étienne felt the jungle closing behind him, he felt as though he were crossing the River Styx, then suddenly, at some silent signal, the sampans stopped. Everyone was on tenterhooks. Étienne could not work out what they were looking at, what they were expecting, nothing had changed. The boats set off again, more slowly now, as a mountain rose above the canopy to their right. Then came the alarm, the wail of some sort of foghorn, and a kilometre or so behind the screen of trees, there was a thunderous commotion, and soon after the roar of exploding shells and fighting.

"It's all over," the colonel said philosophically. "We've been spotted. We'll keep going, but it's too late."

The sampans had already pulled in to the bank and the soldiers were hurriedly unloading the weapons and ammunition. For three-quarters of an hour, the column marched through swampland, sinking up to their ankles on the muddy paths.

The colonel seemed highly amused. Pointing to the fiery glow, he said:

"They burn whatever they can't take with them, but everything they build is based around the fact that at any moment they can be forced to relocate. A Việt Minh factory can be dismantled in an hour. You'll see, by the time we get there, there'll be nothing there." Then, pensively, "But I'm betting there won't be no one there . . ."

At length, they came to a place where the straw huts were burning. There were deep ruts in the earth that led down to a hidden tributary: the machinery and equipment had been dragged onto boats. All that remained was lumps of useless metal, dismantled parts, broken and upturned jars of chemicals, and stocks of food that had been doused with petrol and torched, which now gave off thick, acrid smoke. Strewn here and there were random tools and empty crates.

Around them the swampland stretched as far as the eye could see, stands of rushes and gnarled trees whose roots seemed to float on the water's edge. Weapons in hand, the soldiers warily searched what was left of the Việt Minh factory.

"They didn't all make it out," said the colonel. "Equipment first, men second, that's the Việt Minh motto."

"What was this place?"

"A munitions factory. Machine tools, lathes and generators for making homemade grenades that they set off in village markets, toss into the premises of uncooperative shopkeepers, landmines they bury along the roads as we pass."

He gazed out over the swamp, smiling.

"There are dozens of Việt Minh soldiers right in front of you. You can't see them, they hide under the water, they can stay there for hours on end. Stay long enough and you'll be able to shoot them, one by one, as they come up for air. Like a rifle range at a funfair."

He looked around.

"But we can't afford to hang around. Before we knew it, we'd be surrounded and attacked by hordes of Việt Minh. It would be a bloodbath . . . This is the third time we've tried to take them by surprise. We'll try again, that's all."

Étienne wandered over to one of the few straw huts that had not been burned, probably because it contained nothing of importance. He saw a jumble of shoes, tattered rags, shoelaces, bottles, it looked like a rubbish tip. He kicked aside some rusty kitchen utensils and was about to walk away when he spotted a scrap of paper, the tiny fragment of a label sticking out of an empty ammunition crate. He picked it up and read it.

KALER & VALESCO, IMPORT-EXPORT CO.

The name rang a bell; Étienne racked his brains for a minute.

Then it came to him. The transfer request for importing Limoges porcelain. More than a million francs sent, almost three million when it arrived in France.

What was the label doing there . . .?

"We're about to set off, my friend . . ."

Colonel Lacroix-Gibet had come to fetch him.

Étienne stuffed the label into his pocket.

"What's wrong? Not feeling sick, are you?"

"No, no, I'm fine," muttered Étienne as he turned to follow the officer. But what he was really following was a train of thought. As they walked back towards the trucks, he followed the thread to its logical conclusion and realised the consequences of his discovery.

If the label was there, that meant the goods that had been imported had wound up in the hands of the Việt Minh.

And the import had been authorised by the Exchange.

One of the side effects of the war was the traffic in piastres. French companies and local businessmen exploited this to make themselves rich, but there was something worse.

The Việt Minh had managed to gain access to the system.

To traffic in piastres in order to arm themselves.

This meant only one thing, one terrible, tragic thing.

Even as it waged war on the enemy, France was unwittingly financing the Việt Minh.

26

If I were you, I'd go and see

A taxi dropped Hélène and her father in front of Le Grand Café Capucines, which was quickly filling up with theatregoers who had just come from the nearby theatres.

The place was rowdy, boisterous and beautiful. Hélène followed the waiter across the tiled terrace – her father had requested that they be seated in the adjoining room – through the orange glow cast by the glass art deco ceiling. When the waiter pulled out the table, she sat on the red velvet banquette. Even in the pale glow of the sconces with their vermilion shades, her beautiful face showed the ravages of the day.

In the taxi, her father had explained that he had taken a flight from Beirut only six hours after hers.

"You took the midnight plane," he said. "I took the next flight out."

He had gone straight to François's place, but had found no one except the concierge – "Call me Léontine" – who would happily have kept him talking all day.

Next, he went to Bouboule's apartment.

Hélène could not work out whether her father had eventually managed to track down François or Bouboule. She was so angry with her brothers that she did not ask.

"Things didn't exactly work out with them, then?"

"Not exactly, no," said Hélène, pretending to read the menu. "I'm tempted to have oysters to start, what do you think?"

"Let's have oysters!"

Once the order was placed, Louis slipped his glasses back in his breast pocket. Hélène was curious to know by what miracle they had found each other.

"Oh, there was no miracle! You left with very little money, so I thought, if she doesn't end up staying with one of her brothers, she'll go to the Hôtel de l'Europe."

To complement the seafood platter, Louis had ordered a bottle of Muscadet, which arrived in an ice bucket.

As he tasted the wine under the patient and confident eye of the sommelier, Hélène felt as though she were seeing the man her father had been in his youth, and thought him not handsome, but better: she thought him a gentleman. She had the fleeting, painful yet reassuring feeling that as long as her father was around, nothing bad would happen to her. By the time he set down his glass and said, "It's fine," he was her father once more.

"So, Maman asked you to come and take me home ..."

Her tone was sharp and aggressive, but Louis pretended not to notice.

"No, she did no such thing."

He nodded to the oysters.

"Good, aren't they?"

"Maman is ..."

"You know what she's like ... Aren't you eating?"

"I am, I am! So, if you're not here to take me back ..."

Louis clicked his tongue as he sipped his white wine.

"Excellent, excellent ... Well, your mother knows what she's dealing with. When a child leaves home, they never come back. She's been through it three times."

"Yes, but they were sons ..."

"Indeed. That's why I'm here."

Hélène had no idea what her father expected to say to her. Louis set down his cutlery and looked at her.

"Your mother and I wanted to make sure that your situation is ... stable ... and that you're safe."

"In concrete terms?"

"In concrete terms, I don't know. But I'm sure you can grasp the principle."

"It sounds a little abstract."

"That's the problem with principles, they are abstract. So, tell me, what are you planning to do here?"

For his main course, Louis ordered kidneys in a wine sauce, saying, by way of apology, "Your mother never makes them!" Hélène opted for the duck breast. The restaurant was filled with the aroma of grilled meat, seafood and freshly uncorked wine mingled with cigarette smoke. The clamour of conversation, in the midst of the last service of the evening, grew louder, and bursts of laughter came in sudden waves. Hélène's mind was humming with the art deco brasserie, the frantic day and her father's face smiling gently, to say nothing of the Muscadet. She felt very emotional. As did Louis. Never before had he had dinner with his daughter tête-à-tête. She was, he decided, extraordinarily beautiful. Something that hurt all the more since he had seen her naked on the wall of Xavier Lhomond's apartment, and felt sullied by the image. Not because she had been seduced by his sordid games, nor because her pose was provocative to the point of being indecent, not even because he had seen her naked body, but because Hélène was now an adult, a woman who, unbeknownst to him, had been with men, because she was no longer his little girl – and the young woman his daughter had become was a person he did not know.

"What were you saying?"

"I was asking what you planned to do in Paris?"

"I thought I might study at the Beaux-Arts . . ."

Louis nodded. If Hélène had expected him to disapprove, she was disappointed.

"It's a little late to enrol this year, no?"

Hélène was dumbfounded.

"Is that all you have to say?"

Louis peered at her for a moment.

"Oh yes, I'm sorry, darling! I meant to say: 'Study at the Beaux-Arts?! Over my dead body! You'll marry a pharmacist or I will cut you off without a penny!' I'm not on form this evening."

Hélène could not help but smile.

"And Maman . . .?"

"She will make her peace with it. We cannot expect our children

265

to be like us – just look at Bouboule. I pushed him to be like me and look what happened."

From her father's tone, Hélène could tell that the memory was still painful. She felt an urge to hold his hand. Louis Pelletier was a chameleon, she thought. Moments ago, she had thought him a dapper gentleman, now he was a tender, elderly patriarch.

Louis was silently brooding, and it took him a second to come back to the subject of the École des Beaux-Arts.

"If I were you, I'd go and ask. Some people may have dropped out, you never know . . ."

"Papa! You have to pass an examination to get in!"

"Then show them what you're capable of . . ."

Hélène was astonished at his naivety. Right now he seemed positively antediluvian. Especially when he added:

"Do it for me, please . . . Go there tomorrow and ask if they have a place. If you want to win, you have to play!"

Monsieur Pelletier had come to Paris to help his daughter; he had appeared like a Messiah. He had booked her into an opulent suite ("The biggest you have, Madame Ducrau, it's for my daughter!"). On hearing that her suitcase had been stolen, the manageress had provided a bag of toiletries. "Tomorrow," her father had said, "you can go to La Samaritaine and buy everything you need!" He had done everything that was humanly possible.

Hélène did not have the heart to refuse him this.

"All right, Papa, I'll go to the Beaux-Arts and ask if they have a place," she said reluctantly, though she knew she would do no such thing – she didn't want to look a fool.

Louis ordered the profiteroles because "your mother never makes them". The excitement, the dinner, the wine . . . already Hélène could feel her head begin to droop. Only the cigar smoke from the man at the next table was keeping her awake.

In the taxi, she dozed against her father's shoulder. He half carried her to her room, laid her on the bed and slipped off her shoes. She would shake off her drowsiness just long enough to undress. But before she did, she beckoned to her father as he soundlessly tried to creep away.

"What is it?"

"I love you, Papa."

"I love you too, poppet."

It was completely unexpected. This was what he used to call her long ago, when she was a little girl.

27

Everyone here knows what I am talking about ...

Jean was relieved, a great weight had been lifted, the horizon seemed clear, the storm clouds were dispersing. François's article in *Le Journal* clearly stated that a series of line-ups would be conducted at the commissariat on Friday at 6 p.m. Sixty-four men had been summoned to appear. It was there in black and white: "under subpoena to appear".

But Jean had received no subpoena.

It was now Thursday, the postman had come and gone. Nothing.

He felt the same surge of relief he had felt when his father had said: "I don't think you're cut out for the soap factory."

Although he generally did not discuss the case with Geneviève, he was so elated that he could not help but say something.

"I haven't been summoned."

"I know," she said.

Something about her tone, her look, filled Jean with such dread he had to steady himself against the doorframe. He knew the pose so well: chin high, eyes wide, on her lips a brittle, mocking smile. It inevitably heralded one of those disasters only Geneviève could trigger; there had never been an exception.

She, too, had been waiting for the postman. Then Jean had watched as she dressed, stood at the mirror to adjust her hat, and went out without a word, throwing him into a blind panic.

She had gone straight to the Palais de Justice and demanded to speak to Juge Lenoir. That was impossible, the magistrate was a very busy man, they would find someone else to speak to her.

"You will most certainly not! Tell the magistrate it is vitally important, it's about the Mary Lampson case. I am a witness."

Geneviève stood stock-still in the middle of the corridor. The magistrate appeared, but he failed to recognise her.

"Madame . . .?"

"Pelletier. I am the wife of Monsieur Jean Pelletier and I demand to know why my husband has not been called in for the line-up!"

This was quite surprising. The magistrate wondered whether he had heard her correctly.

"I mean to say," Geneviève continued, "as a citizen of the Republic, he is entitled to serve the justice of his country!"

Juge Lenoir had cracked many hard nuts in his time, but Madame Pelletier, he sensed, was in a class of her own.

"He is not on the list, madame."

For the magistrate, bureaucracy prevailed over all else, it was an unerring weapon, one he had used many times.

"What list?"

"The list of men subpoenaed to attend."

"I see. And who drew up this list?"

"I did."

"Then perhaps you can explain why my husband is not included."

They were back to square one, so he tried a change of tack.

"He does not meet the criteria. And now, madame, I'm afraid I must leave you."

Lenoir took a step to the right, Geneviève a step to the left.

"Madame, you are obstructing justice!"

"So be it! I will go and explain myself to the minister in person!"

Suspects, co-conspirators and mule-headed citizens threatening to go "over his head" were an occupational hazard in the judiciary. But this woman's fury reminded Lenoir of the slow, inexorable advance of a steamroller. The magistrate was alarmed. Such situations could easily spin out of control.

"And then I shall go to the press!" snapped Geneviève. "I may be the wife of Monsieur Jean Pelletier, but I'll have you know that I am also the sister-in-law of François Pelletier, a senior reporter at *Le Journal du soir*. I'll tell him how you've bungled this investigation. You may have your lists and your criteria, monsieur, but I have justice on my side! And let me tell you . . ."

"It is a question of weight."

Now that the magistrate had resorted to justifications, Geneviève knew she would prevail. But she trod carefully.

"What exactly does that mean?"

"The witness is positive that the man who jostled her in the doorway of the toilets was slim."

"Are you calling my husband fat?"

She had won. Juge Lenoir knew it.

"Very well, this is completely futile, but if you insist . . ."

"Oh yes, we insist!"

Lenoir felt a great weariness.

"In that case, I shall issue a subpoena for your husband."

*

When Jean heard the news, he went ashen.

"I took that magistrate down a peg or too, I can tell you . . ." said Geneviève as she took off her hat.

"But, Geneviève," Jean spluttered. "You know perfectly well that—"

"What? What do I know?"

She planted herself in front of him, arms folded, chin high.

"You know . . . that night, I . . ."

Jean felt a wave of doubt.

Had they been talking at cross-purposes all this time?

Did Geneviève really not understand what had happened?

The sheer scale of her misapprehension made it difficult to think.

"Geneviève, I was the one who . . ."

He was cut short by the bell. Geneviève went and opened the door. Jean almost fainted: it was a uniformed police officer.

He had only come to deliver the summons.

"About time, too!" said Geneviève snatching the piece of paper.

She signed on behalf of her husband; the policeman did not dare object.

She closed the door and turned to find Jean slumped in a chair. She set the summons down on the table and went over to him. He looked up. He was bathed in sweat; fat drops trickled from his hair-line down his temples and hung, suspended, from the tip of his chin.

She knelt down in front of him and gave him a conspiratorial smile. With one hand, she stroked his cheek, as she might a child she was reproaching. She laid her other hand on his crotch.

"You're worrying about nothing ... If the police were going to find that vicious murderer, they'd have tracked him down already, wouldn't they, my little Bouboule?"

*

Just as Monsieur Pelletier insisted there was no better hotel in Paris than Madame Ducrau's, so he believed that the only place to shop was La Samaritaine. Hélène, however, opted to go to La Belle Jardinière. Her father had given her ten thousand francs. She had thought him generous, but once again she had failed to allow for the cost of living in Paris. A simple pair of stockings cost two hundred and fifty francs. Simply buying the essentials (toiletries, underwear, skirts, blouses, etc.) would require her to be careful, thrifty. Living in Paris would be a struggle.

When she joined her father at the end of the afternoon, he noticed that her bags were inscribed with the logo of La Belle Jar-dinière, but elected to say nothing. Madame Ducrau had reserved a table for them by the window, "the lovers' corner", as she called it.

"Do you know what's really going on with Étienne?"

The abruptness with which Monsieur Pelletier posed this ques-tion (Hélène had just finished recounting her day) was enough to make it clear that it had been on his mind for some time. And he was staring at her intently, as though primed to uncover the lies she told him, the things she chose not to say.

Hélène finished her piece of cake and poured herself another cup of tea.

"He doesn't want to come back."

"I know that, he wrote to us, no, what worries me is ... the life he is living."

Back on the avenue des Français, things might have been

different. But here, in this place that belonged only to her father, Hélène did not have the courage to lie.

"All I know, Papa, is that he's not telling the truth to anyone. Not even me. The things he wrote about Raymond's death were too pat, they didn't ring true. I don't know how he is dealing with his grief – you know what Étienne is like, with him it's all or nothing . . ."

"Do you think we should have gone out to Saigon when Raymond died . . .?"

"No, it wouldn't have made any difference, Étienne would have put on a brave face, just like he used to at home."

Louis wanted to be a good father, but he knew simply raising four children was not enough to warrant the title. He had been partly responsible for ruining Bouboule's life, and perhaps he had never understood Étienne. He was afraid that the future would show him that he had not done enough. He was terrified that time would show he had done no better with François. That left only Hélène.

"Perhaps I wasn't meant to have children . . ."

He mumbled the words into his coffee cup.

"Oh, Papa . . ." said Hélène.

Seeing her father light up a cigarette, she took out the pack of American cigarettes she had bought. Louis, who had never seen his daughter smoke, said nothing but reached across the table and lit hers.

He glanced at his watch.

"I've booked a taxi for seven. Geneviève suggested that we meet them there, though I don't know if it's a good idea . . ."

"How long do you think this thing will last?"

They talked about the identity parade as though it were a movie or a play.

They arrived to find an excitable Geneviève in the café next to the Palais de Justice.

"That's it," she announced, "it's time!"

She gestured to the clock on the wall.

"If they're running according to schedule, it should just have started . . . Oh, how I'd love to be a fly on the wall."

Suddenly, she stared at Monsieur Pelletier. He saw her mentally change subject.

"Come sit with me, Papa. Since we have a little time . . ."

Louis went and sat next to her.

"I need to talk to you about a matter that concerns your beloved son."

*

The police had divided the men into groups of six. Jean was in the fourth group. François had managed to be in the first, thereby allowing him to observe the other line-ups as a journalist. Juge Lenoir hoped the article would be flattering.

"Dear God," thought François, looking at his brother's haggard face, "Geneviève was right, he's very emotional . . ."

For several months, the efforts of Commissaire Templier's team to track down the thirty-one witnesses who had not responded to the police appeal had provided material for a series of articles as thrilling as any serial drama. Each new witness offered a new story, a new potential suspect. Denissov had been gleefully rubbing his hands for half a year. "I hope the last one they find is the killer," he would say at the editorial meetings that François was now routinely asked to join.

It had been his idea to refer to the witnesses that the police had failed to find as "The Three", a clever moniker that other newspapers swiftly adopted.

So far, all the evidence suggested that the murderer was one of The Three, but if not, he might be among the men summoned to appear today, and the woman he had jostled in the cinema might unmask him.

Juge Lenoir had explained how the process worked, but, since he had done so in his own inimitable fashion, Commissaire Templier summed up the instructions for each new group. Although none of the witnesses had anything to hide, an eerie silence hung over the room where they were gathered.

The fear of mistaken identity hovered over the proceedings; the witness, Marthe Soubirot, looked nervous, she might pick the wrong man, any one of them could end up in a prison cell by nightfall ... The first groups trooped in and re-emerged looking as though they had just stepped off a rollercoaster and were feeling distinctly queasy.

When his turn came, Jean, who was sweating under his clothes and discreetly dabbing his forehead with his sleeve, stepped forward with five other men. After stating his name and showing his ID card, he took up his position, second from the right. They stood facing a line of police officers behind the lone chair in which the witness, wearing a hat, was biting her nails. The magistrate was talking to her in low, urgent tones. The harsh light half blinded the men on the low platform. They had to turn right, then left, then back to face the witness and wait for the commissaire to say: "Thank you, gentlemen, you may go."

But no one was allowed to leave. Everyone had to wait until the bitter end.

What had started as a tiresome but necessary process was becoming ominous.

There were whispers that the witness had voiced suspicions about one of the men.

"She's not certain it's him, but maybe ..." François hissed when Jean came to ask about the rumours.

"Maybe what?"

"Maybe she's right, maybe it's him, we're not sure."

The door opened and the last group filed out. There was a further wait of twenty minutes.

It was difficult to breathe, what with the heat of the seventy men holed together, the cigarette smoke and the palpable tension. Someone asked if the windows could be opened, the commissaire refused for security reasons, then changed his mind when a man stumbled forward, on the point of collapse. It was Jean. Someone brought a glass of water and a policeman slapped his cheek.

The little magistrate appeared clutching a piece of paper.

"Messrs Klein, Nalliers, Jeunet, Nagéar, Pelletier and Cageot ..."

There was something of a commotion as some of the others stood aside, looking relieved.

"What is the meaning of this?" said a man in his fifties. "Why has my name been called?"

Jean rocked in his chair, he felt he might cry.

"We're just double-checking, gentlemen," said Commissaire Templier. "One more line-up and you can all go home."

This time, three officers joined the commissaire in checking the papers and the position of everyone in the line. Once again, Jean was second from the right. They stood staring at the witness for much longer than they had the first time. The woman in the chair squirmed as though she urgently needed the toilet. At the officer's command, they made their quarter turns. When the order came for them to turn and face the witness, it hit Jean like a thunderbolt, he felt his legs give out under him, he squeezed his eyes shut and almost laid a hand on his neighbour's shoulder for support.

"Open your eyes, please, Monsieur Pelletier," said the commissaire, who was all but invisible in the harsh glare.

They stood for a long time. Jean was muttering to himself, "I can't take it any more," he felt every muscle relax, felt his bladder about to empty.

"Thank you, gentlemen, we're done," said the commissaire.

Jean would never know how he managed to step down from the dais and go back to the adjoining room. All the other men had been allowed to go. There was François, with a dozen uniformed officers, taking notes as the last men filed out. Juge Lenoir appeared in the doorway looking grave.

"Monsieur Klein, thank you for your time ..."

The man walked out. Jean stared as the magistrate pointed to him.

"Monsieur Pelletier, thank you ..."

"Am I free to go?" he asked.

"Yes, you're done here," said Lenoir.

François had stayed behind, but he was not looking at his brother, he was in whispered conclave with Commissaire Templier.

*

It was some sort of ectoplasm that drifted across the boulevard, in a screech of brakes and car horns, and floated into the brasserie.

"Ah!" said Geneviève. "There's Bouboule!"

Jean saw his father and Hélène were sitting at a table.

"You're sweating like a horse," said Hélène, kissing him on the cheek.

Monsieur Pelletier said nothing.

Jean felt as though he had arrived at the wrong moment, that he had interrupted a private conversation between his wife and his father. But already Geneviève was demanding that he tell them what had happened, bombarding him with questions, pressing him for details. As she listened to Jean's jerky account, she turned to Hélène and to her father-in-law as if to say: "Isn't this thrilling?" Had anyone been arrested? "No," Jean said, "I don't think so."

"So, it was all for nothing?" said Geneviève, disappointed. She ran her hand over Jean's sweaty cheek and added: "Well, maybe next time."

"Is François not with you?" said Monsieur Pelletier, who was worried about their restaurant reservation.

"He said he'll join us later," said Jean, who had already drained his glass of beer.

*

"I'm sorry," said François.

"We started without you!"

This was not the same man Jean had seen at the préfecture, he was flushed and cheerful, and talking very loudly.

"I'll have what she's having," he said to the waiter, nodding at his sister's plate.

Monsieur Pelletier poured François a glass of wine, then raised his own. Everyone did likewise.

They all felt ill at ease. Hélène, because she was the runaway, and they would doubtless discuss "her situation" (and she was not about to let anyone, even her father, make decisions without her being present), her two brothers, because they had failed their younger sister, Geneviève because her father-in-law had been evasive when she had asked for money for the shop.

"It's not every day that I buy a round in Paris," said Louis. "A toast – to Étienne, whom we dearly miss. We are all very sad about what he has been going through."

Such bromides threatened to cast a pall over the evening, but everyone raised their glasses, Geneviève a little less enthusiastically than the others.

"It's possible to grieve without neglecting one's responsibilities to the rest of the family," she said crisply.

Then, faced with bemused looks from the rest of the family, she added:

"He barely writes to Jean. And Bouboule is his elder brother!"

Oh, they thought, is that all? Even Jean felt relieved: Geneviève's moods were like ripples in a millpond. The aperitif and the first bottle of claret would quickly pass over.

On the subject of family, Monsieur Pelletier told them he had sent Angèle a telegram to reassure her.

"Maman sends her love," he said.

Then came the meal. Between courses, there were cigarettes and another bottle was ordered. The person who spoke least was Geneviève. Jean looked at her surreptitiously. He already knew what she would say as soon as they got home: "They make me feel like I'm a spare part . . ."

Jean drank thirstily. He felt at peace. Twice he had thought this case was closed; this had been the third time, but it was finally over. He was helping himself, and it was Hélène who gently laid a hand on his when he reached for the bottle again. Monsieur Pelletier was saying to François: "You really must tell me how things are going at the Grande École . . ." and François blushed as he picked up his glass, tried to look composed as he said: "Yes, yes, we do need to talk . . ." then changed the subject.

"Are you planning to stay in Paris for a while, Papa?"

"No! I don't like to leave your mother on her own for too long. I'll use the opportunity to make a few visits on behalf of the association" – it took François a moment to realise that his father was talking about the Federation of Overseas War Veterans – "and then I'll head back. I've booked a flight for the day after tomorrow."

By common consent, they ordered the Baked Alaska suggested by Monsieur Pelletier ("Your mother never makes it"). There were cheers as it was flambéed at the table. Louis made the most of the ensuing silence to announce:

"So, our little Hélène has decided to stay in Paris to study, isn't that right, darling?"

Hélène silently nodded.

"But Paris is a big city and Hélène here is only eighteen."

"I'm nineteen, Papa."

"Almost nineteen, but that doesn't matter. Maman and I don't want to have to worry about you, we just need to know you're safe, protected . . . Everyone here knows what I'm talking about."

Jean and François could guess where this was headed. Since he could hardly ask either of them to take Hélène in, he would ask that they "look out for her". It was the old story. In fact, both were more than happy to "look out for her", take an interest in her life, offer brotherly advice. But this was not what their father had in mind.

"Since Hélène cannot live with a young married couple, I propose that she move in with François . . ."

"Wait a minute!" An indignant François dropped his spoon.

But Monsieur Pelletier wagged an imperious index finger at his son, something he did not usually do, and carried on as if he had not been interrupted.

"And since this would be impossible in the cramped apartment you currently rent, I spent the afternoon looking around and I've found just what you need. A three-room apartment, so you can all have your own room and . . ."

"But how much does that cost?" said François, in a panic.

"It's not cheap, but I've paid the first year in full, so you won't have to worry about the rent and you can concentrate on your little sister. And where is this apartment? Can you guess?"

François felt the blow coming. He didn't believe it, but he felt it. He closed his eyes, his father gave a conspiratorial chuckle . . .

"Rue des Arquebusiers, near the offices of *Le Journal du soir*. That will be handy for work, won't it?"

François was incandescent. If his father knew about this job, then someone must have said something. Hélène? Jean? Geneviève? Monsieur Pelletier had only arrived in Paris the previous day, there were no articles by François in today's edition and *Le Journal* was not distributed abroad.

"If you agree," said Louis, "we'll keep this little matter to ourselves, son, and wait a while before we tell your mother. She's a little fragile at the moment."

François agreed. He nodded vehemently, he agreed to everything.

He felt embarrassed, but also relieved. His father had not taken the news badly, in time he would tell their mother and everything would be sorted. And a bigger apartment meant he could still be with Mathilde, they would simply need to juggle things to fit in with Hélène's timetable. He smiled at his sister. No, he thought to himself, she would never have betrayed him. He turned to Jean, just as their father was turning to his elder son.

"Of course, Jean will have to do his bit too. And you, Geneviève. I want Hélène to be able to count on you."

"Er . . . what exactly would that mean?" said Jean, his voice a little slurred.

"It means she should be able to come to you for help and advice."

"Oh, really?" Geneviève said pointedly. "So, you're asking us to be responsible for your daughter's moral welfare, Papa?"

"Yes, Geneviève, that sums it up rather well. And I'm sure you'll do so with wisdom and compassion."

Geneviève was livid, she was about to leap to her feet, she had a few home truths to tell this old fool, she would make him sorry he had come . . . But, in his softest voice, Monsieur Pelletier carried on.

"And as to your request, my dear Geneviève, of course we will lend you the money you need to set up your little shop, that goes without saying."

Monsieur Pelletier then turned to his daughter, who was clearly trying to envisage her new life. But the harshest words were yet to be said, so he forged on:

"As for you, Hélène, I want you to do as your brothers tell you. They are older, they know more about life, more about Paris. If you need anything, you go to them, and you listen to them."

Hélène's expression hardened; she was about to explode. Then Monsieur Pelletier drove home the final nail.

"If the three of you can make this work, you can finish your studies here and choose your own career, no one will force you to do anything. If not, you will immediately come back to Beirut and we will discuss the matter there."

Monsieur Pelletier had said what he had to say, but he did not want it to seem like a public dressing-down. He leaned towards his daughter and whispered:

"I love you."

Hélène looked at him, tears in her eyes, and threw her arms around his neck. Suddenly she was afraid at the thought that he was leaving, that he would no longer be there for her. She inhaled the smell of cigarettes and soap in his clothes. She was determined not to cry in front of her brothers. She sat back and stared at them. I won't give them the satisfaction.

"Shall we go?" she suggested cheerfully.

Jean was not yet out of the woods. It had been a gruelling day, but it was not quite over.

As Monsieur Pelletier asked for the coats, François announced:

"Oh, the reason I was late was because I was writing up my article. The witness, Marthe Soubirot, formally identified a suspect. A man named Germain Cageot. He murdered Mary Lampson."

Everyone was stunned.

So that was it, it was over, the case had been solved.

"Why did he kill her?" said Hélène.

"No one knows yet."

Monsieur Pelletier was helping Geneviève on with her jacket.

"Thank you, Papa," she said with a smile and Louis thought: "Silly little bitch . . ."

"Has he confessed?" he asked as he headed towards the door.

"Not yet," said François, "but I don't think he'll hold out long."

Jean's pallid complexion was put down to too much alcohol.

Geneviève turned to him, smiling like a newlywed.

"It's been a perfect day, hasn't it, Bouboule?"

28

It's what the public want

The 9.30 a.m. editorial meeting at *Le Journal* followed a precise ritual. The seven heads of department sat in seven chairs facing Denissov's desk while he stood with his back to the window, framed against the light.

Stan Malevitz, the head of news, took the chair on the left of the semicircle while his nemesis, Arthur Baron, head of politics and diplomacy, sat on the far right.

It was surprising that the two men so cordially loathed each other, since physically they looked like two knaves in a pack of cards. Malevitz had white hair and black eyebrows; Baron was the mirror image, with black hair, white eyebrows and a white beard. But for that, both were the same height, both had the same paunch, the same hairstyle, the same expressive lips. At editorial meetings, Malevitz, who boasted that he was a former cyclist (twenty years earlier, he had taken part in the six-day event at the Vél' d'Hiver, and lasted less than four hours), spoke in vernacular and frequently used slang. Out of sheer spite, Baron adopted an exaggeratedly rarefied French. In the hallways and in their departments, the two men spoke in the same, simple style. Nothing offered a clearer illustration of Denissov's leadership; these two heads of department were his left and right hands, and their mutual antipathy made it easy to manipulate them. The editor of *Le Journal*, who was locked in a ruthless war with the other Paris newspapers, had fostered rivalries in the offices on the rue Quincampoix; he called it competitive spirit, and it was a powerful means of control.

The question this particular Saturday morning was the relative merit of the announcement of a miners' strike in northern France and the surprise arrest of Germain Cageot, which meant François had been invited to the meeting to support Malevitz.

"This strike could lead to civil war tomorrow," said Baron.

"Why not a world war, while you're about it!"

Denissov sat in silence. Both articles would be on the front page, but only one would have the banner headline, the screamer roared out by newspaper sellers on street corners. The headline could mean success or failure for this issue. It was a war of attrition that ended each night with the last edition, only to start over, the next day, with the first.

Baron gave a heavy sigh. He was tired of having to explain things that should be self-evident.

"The Communist Party and the CGT have mobilised everyone: the Secours Populaire to tend to the wounded, the Union des Femmes to provide food for protestors. A whole series of walk-outs and picket lines has been agreed. *L'Humanité* has called for a class struggle."

"That doesn't make it a civil war," said Malevitz. "It makes for protests and a few scuffles; we've seen it all before."

"Meanwhile, the government, which has been anticipating this for months, is purging security forces of left-leaning members, has abolished the right to industrial action for police officers and has sent hundreds of officers north to administer beatings."

François had been following the social unrest. It stemmed from the strikes a year earlier in which a number of workers had been killed. Slashed wages and piecework payments had drastically reduced miners' standard of living, and forcing those suffering from silicosis to return to work had been seen as a deliberate provocation.

"Didn't you predict all this last year?" said Malevitz. "We've been flogging the same story for twelve months. I don't see the point of doing it again."

Baron gave him the superior, vaguely contemptuous look he reserved for the news desk as a whole.

"I think you are not truly cognisant of what is happening ... This is not a clash between the government and unions. It is the communist party storming the citadel of the French Republic, it is nothing less than an uprising. If they succeed, we will be under the communist boot, like the Czechoslovakians . . ."

"I am perfectly cognisant – it's the same old government propaganda that gets trotted out every day. But we are not the official organ of the government. *Le Journal du soir* is not *Le Journal officiel.*"

The argument had quickly drifted from the subject. Denissov, a keen fan of bullfighting, watched eagerly. In a minute or two, he would blow the whistle and the game would be over. Baron and Malevitz knew this.

"Are you saying you have a better story?" said Baron.

"Germain Cageot! I think readers are more interested in Mary Lampson than in Maurice Thorez."

He turned to François: right, you're up!

"Cageot is a violent man," François said. "He has a record: four arrests for assault, always on women. He was picked out of an identity parade by a witness who saw him coming out of the toilets where Mary Lampson was murdered."

"It's a sordid vignette," said Baron, "not a social phenomenon."

"It's what the public want."

"All right, Stan, that's enough . . ." said Denissov wearily.

The argument had been running for as long as *Le Journal.*

Denissov turned to François.

"What do you think?"

The editor had a knack for asking awkward questions; the thorny issue in this case was that François did not agree with the head of his department.

François felt that the miners, who had been lionised by the government when they were needed to fight the "battle for coal" between 1945 and 1947, and commended as the "hardest workers in France", were now roundly despised.

The humiliation he had experienced after fighting in Syria had made François very suspicious of the cynical ingratitude of people in power. But he could not, in all decency, agree with Arthur Baron.

With a heavy heart, he said:

"I think the strike is important, but it doesn't start until Monday. If we write about it now, we'll be accused of fanning the flames – and anyway, what can we say that we haven't already said? Our readers are gripped by the Mary Lampson case. The arrest of a suspect . . ."

"A suspect or the guilty party?" Baron interrupted.

"A suspect who has been arrested because the magistrate believes he is guilty."

"What have we got?" asked Denissov.

"A mugshot taken yesterday during the line-up. His criminal record. And an interview with Mary Lampson's parents, who I'm meeting in an hour. I'm planning to ask their reaction to the arrest."

There was silence.

"Sold," said Denissov, and adjourned the meeting.

François stared at Baron.

He had made an enemy to be reckoned with.

29

It's not good to meddle with these things . . .

"Leaving already, my friend?"

Loan had come as soon as he heard the news. Étienne was pacing around his room, his body bent. The pain in his gut from the legionnaires' boots had come back. He had finished packing his case. Through the open window, he could hear the trucks idling. The escort organised by Colonel Lacroix-Gibet was waiting for him on the parade ground.

"It's Sunday . . ." said the Pope.

His tone was pitched somewhere between concern and disappointment.

Since the early hours, Étienne had been consumed by a sense of dread he could not contain. The chance discovery of a label from a Saigon import-export company pointed to a possibility that beggared belief, one whose consequences he could not fully fathom. He had mulled it over all night, determined to be logical, to be rigorous; was this a foolish mistake on his part? Still, everything pointed to the same terrifying conclusion. If the Việt Minh had found a way to profit from the traffic in piastres, it was forcing the French government to finance its guerrilla war against France. If true, this was a bombshell.

"Sunday or not, I'm going back to Saigon."

"Monsieur Étienne, if there is anything I can do . . ."

As he reached for his suitcase, Étienne stared at Loan for a moment, then sat down on his bed.

"Yes, there is something you can do. You can give me your honest opinion."

"Oh, Monsieur Étienne, who am I to offer an opin—?"

"No bullshit, just answer me: is it possible that the Việt Minh have found a way to traffic in piastres?"

Loan's mouth fell open. He pressed a finger to his upper lip.

"What the . . .? It seems highly unlikely . . ."

"Why?"

Loan sat on the bed and looked pensive.

"The thing is, currency transfers are the epitome of the very capitalism that communists despise. The Việt Minh have a very strict moral code, it's what has made them powerful. It's impossible to shake their convictions, to challenge their dialectic. They're not interested in the piastre."

"So, they're not pragmatic?"

"Oh, they are!"

Loan let out a high giggle and his tassels danced.

"Extremely pragmatic, I would say. But first and foremost, they are ideologues. And the piastre doesn't fit into their frame of reference."

✳

"So, you've cut short your leave?" said Jeantet when Étienne appeared on Monday.

"I missed you too much, Monsieur le Directeur."

"Huh, huh, huh!"

This was Jeantet's laugh, a sort of muffled bellow.

"With all this rain, there was no point, really," said Étienne. "I may as well save my holiday for a proper trip."

It was not yet 10 a.m., but Jeantet, who had just arrived, was already leaving. To go home? Somewhere else? His working practices were a mystery.

"There are days," he said, closing his office and nodding to the public waiting rooms, "when they bore me to tears, you know what I mean?"

Some conversations with Jeantet bordered on the cryptic.

Without waiting for an answer, he strode past the rows of desks and disappeared.

"What brings you here, old man?"

Gaston Paumelle was surprised to see Étienne, who blamed his sudden return on the weather.

"Oh yes, the bloody rainy season . . ."

Gaston thought he was right to come back to the Exchange; he himself never took time off.

Étienne spent his day among the archives.

The elderly Vietnamese woman, whom he had not seen for months, did not look a day older; then again, it was difficult to know how she could. The only change was that her visor was now bottle-green.

"Very fetching," said Étienne.

The woman's face remained inscrutable. Étienne set down a list of his requests, she read it slowly, then set off through the warren of files.

Étienne asked for dossiers, drew up lists, requested more files, sent some back, asked for new ones. The old woman calmly did as he asked without a word. This carried on all morning.

He discovered very little about the Kaler & Valesco Import-Export Company; certainly not enough to trigger an investigation, or even further digging. Over the past months, the company had requested a number of small transfers for various materials, but nothing that looked as though it would be of use to the Việt Minh. He made up a long list, but there was nothing here that he had feared or expected.

At lunch, Gaston patted him on the shoulder.

"So? I hear you have a little crush on Annie."

Étienne feigned surprise. Gaston rubbed his fingers together and grinned lasciviously.

"Well, spending all day upstairs with her looks a little suspicious . . ."

He nudged Étienne in the ribs.

"Make the most of it, she'll be pensioned off before long!"

Étienne realised that his investigations were likely to pique the curiosity of all and sundry. Even if the archivist had not asked what he was doing, sooner or later his superiors would want an explanation.

Nonetheless, he spent the early afternoon continuing his research. More dossiers, more files, more lists, all as unpromising as the ones he had consulted earlier.

"Tea?"

The elderly archivist was holding a red cast-iron teapot and proffering one of the small tea bowls that burned the drinker's fingers. She was not smiling; she never did. It was almost four o'clock.

"What are you doing?" she asked as she poured the tea.

Her voice was surprisingly young, and she had almost no accent.

"Statistics. Monsieur Jeantet wants figures, statistics, graphs, percentages. For the ministry."

"And lists," she said coolly, nodding to the papers strewn over the desk.

"That's where the work starts . . ."

Étienne decided it was time to leave. Quickly, he gathered up the scattered dossiers.

"Have some more . . ." said the archivist, setting the teapot in front of him.

"That's all right, thank you, I—"

"Have some more."

Her tone brooked no refusal. She had wandered off. Étienne was anxious to be gone. He folded his lists and stuffed them into his pockets, but just as he was reaching for the doorknob, the archivist appeared behind him. She was carrying three fat dossiers tied up with string.

"Heurtin Frères," she said.

Étienne hesitated.

"It is a subsidiary of Kaler & Valesco."

He reached out to take them.

"Dossiers cannot be taken out of the archives," said Annie. "It is against the rules."

Then, having reminded him of the protocol, she glanced at the clock on the wall.

"I'm sorry, but it's time to close up."

She had handed the files to Étienne and was ushering him

towards the door. He did not have time to say a word before he found himself in the hallway and heard the key turning in the lock.

That evening, Joseph was surprisingly restless. Descending from his refrigerated throne, he nervously circled the bed where Étienne was dictating lists of dates, amounts and imported products to Vĩnh. Finally, he curled up and watched as the two men worked feverishly, sometimes glancing at the window or the door before turning back to the bed.

"What's wrong, Joseph?" asked Étienne.

The cat did not answer but stood, watching them, silent and sphinx-like.

Heurtin Frères had requested numerous sizeable transfers. Among invoices for kitchen equipment, there were suddenly batches for hiking boots. An order for nine hundred flashlights and two-way radios imported from France was buried in an invoice for toys and board games; there were orders for bandages, tents and spare parts for electric generators. Documents proved that all the goods had been shipped to Saigon, where importers were supposed to distribute them to shops, but it was more than likely that the materials had gone to Việt "factories" like the one Colonel Lacroix-Gibet had spent months trying to find.

To Étienne, the most important revelation was that the majority of the transfers had been rubber-stamped by Gaston Paumelle.

That evening he did not go to Le Grand Monde, or to the opium den. Vĩnh prepared his opium pipes. Étienne slipped away, but instead of sinking into blissful peace, he felt a fury thrumming inside him that the opium did nothing to allay.

The following morning, he went back to the archives, concerned that he had misinterpreted Annie's intentions. But the archivist did not ask about the Heurtin Frères dossiers. As far as she was concerned, they had disappeared.

"Tell me, Annie, is there any way to search for transfers by the clerk who authorised them?"

"It should be possible," she muttered.

And so, in the late afternoon, he crept back to the archives, and left with two boxes which he slipped into his travel bag.

He spent the evening leafing through files authorised by Gaston without finding anything suspicious.

There were only the transfer requests he had found the previous day. Had he been mistaken?

Night had fallen, and with it the rain. Vĩnh began to prepare the opium pipes. Étienne lay on his side and listened to the opium crackle beneath the flame. His body was already anticipating the sense of calm the first puff would bring when, all of a sudden, he sat up and grabbed Gaston's dossiers, which were scattered over the bed.

If the Việt Minh were trafficking in piastres to import weapons for their guerrilla war, they would not stop at that.

They would want money.

To buy weapons.

He began searching for transfers that were not related to the import of goods, but simple requests to send piastres to France, which, when they arrived in France, would be doubled and converted into French francs and could then be used to buy weapons.

Viewed in this light, Gaston's dossiers proved very revealing.

A whole section of the traffic in piastres was based on the claims for "war reparations".

Companies presented reports from the police, the gendarmerie, even the army, alleging damage to rubber and cotton plantations, to silkworm crops, building sites, shops – damages caused by the actions of the Việt Minh. The losses calculated by insurance experts were reimbursed in full by the French government. Some claims were for damages caused during the Japanese occupation between 1940 and 1945, which the insurance experts agreed were difficult to assess, though they nonetheless approved them ...

Étienne did the sums. Gaston's files included claims for war reparations amounting to more than one hundred and twenty million piastres.

Two billion French francs that had disappeared into thin air, no one knew where they had gone ...

Étienne was exhilarated by his discovery, though he realised that it would serve no purpose. The damages might be real and, even if they were fictitious, there was no proof that any monies had been passed to the Việt Minh.

The following morning, Étienne bumped into Gaston. He was no longer wearing only the signet ring whose bloodstone grew according to the backhanders he received; he now had a second ring.

"Is that new?" said Étienne.

"Yes."

He smiled ingenuously.

"The ring trick is pretty good, but it has its limitations. I can hardly walk around with a diamond that weighs two kilos! So, I've decided to diversify. When I have a ring on every finger, I'll go back to Paris to live a life of luxury."

He jiggled the rings like a puppeteer.

"Very clever . . ." Étienne said. "Tell me something, Gaston. I'm dealing with a claim for war reparations filed by a shipowner who says his warehouse was razed by a bomb."

"These things happen."

"He's provided witness statements, expert opinions . . . How do we go about verifying them?"

This was a question that Gaston had obviously never asked himself.

"Why would you need to verify them?"

"Because that's what the Exchange is supposed to do . . ."

"No, no! It's not our job to check, it's our job to ensure they're reimbursed. So that economics can continue its civilising influence!"

Jeantet confirmed as much to Étienne the following day.

"Look, there's a lot of war damage, and there's more and more every day, how do you expect us to verify these things?"

He huffed and puffed like a walrus, fanning himself with whatever was to hand – a sheet of paper, a hat, a cardboard file.

Étienne had anticipated the objection.

"We could go to the scene, interview witnesses . . ."

"I see. But we would be in an invidious situation. You have to understand: there are witness statements, reports . . . The insurance companies, the gendarmes . . . If we start questioning them, it would constitute a "second opinion", it would mean casting doubt on the probity of the experts, it would set the cat among the pigeons!"

Jeantet tilted his head.

"And besides, why would we do such a thing?"

Étienne took the plunge.

"It occurred to me that the Việt Minh might be tempted to use the traffic in piastres to acquire supplies. Equipment, weaponry . . ."

Jeantet suddenly reared up, his face beet-red.

"This is sheer speculation . . . I . . . I . . ."

He searched for a word that refused to come.

"I am not about to launch an investigation that would dispute the findings of insurance experts and the police."

"Why not?"

"Because I'm sick to the back teeth of you and your theories, that's why! We authorise transfers because the government tells us to authorise transfers. If and when they tell us to investigate war reparations, then we'll do so!"

His neck was bloated, like a turkey cock trying to intimidate a rival. He grabbed a small wooden frame and handed it to Étienne.

"My ex-wife, have I ever shown you? She's a—"

"Complete bitch."

"Do you know her?"

Suddenly Jeantet's anger had given way to infantile excitement. His eyes were wide as he anticipated some reassuring revelation.

"Not personally, no," said Étienne.

"Oh . . ."

Reluctantly, Jeantet set down the frame. He stared at Étienne as though struggling to remember what they had been talking about. But this was clearly a pretence, because as Étienne was about to leave, he said:

"This theory of yours . . . Keep it to yourself, all right? It's not good to meddle with these things . . . Life's complicated enough."

Then, cryptically, he jabbed his chest. "Take me, for example . . ."

*

It took Étienne several days to accept that Jeantet was right. His evidence was worthless, the clues he had found could be twisted to say anything. The passion he had felt was no more than another part of mourning, of the constant desire to avenge Raymond's death, a sign that he was still sick with grief, that he had not recovered.

He went back to Le Grand Monde, more elated than ever, squandering almost everything he had, then racking up debts in the smoke shops, which he paid off using his backhanders.

It had been about three in the morning, Vĩnh was helping Étienne into a cycle rickshaw when he was brutally shoved by a tall, obese man, who ran at him, his whole body tilted, as though on stilts. Vĩnh collapsed in the street and did not get up.

An exhausted, teetering Étienne watched as the man lurched towards him. He was a chubby Chinese man with no neck, his eyes sunken in massive cheeks that seemed to merge with his brow. Without a word, he slammed Étienne violently against the door, jammed a forearm under his throat and drew a sharp blade.

Étienne gasped for air, he struggled, tried to lash out, but the man was so massive, the sheer inertia was such there was nothing he could do. The man had ripped Étienne's shirt open and was running the blade across his chest. Before Étienne could see what he was doing, it was over, the man let him go and sheathed the knife. He smiled good-naturedly, then he turned and lumbered away, with an elephantine tread.

Étienne stared down at his chest. The man had carved a cross over his heart.

He did not sleep a wink. Neither did Vĩnh. They lay next to each other, neither saying a word, a threat had come between them. A dozen times, Étienne rehearsed the list of those who knew about his investigation: Loan, Jeantet, Gaston, Annie ... Any of them could have mentioned it to someone else, who, in turn ... The possibilities were endless.

It was at dawn, as rain lashed the windows, that Étienne finally broke the silence.

"I was right," he said.

Vĩnh nodded, but did not look at him.

It was a joyless victory, but now that his suspicions had been confirmed, Étienne felt better. He felt threatened, but the issue he had raised went far beyond Raymond's death. This murderous war that had mobilised the peoples of two countries, which had cost billions and caused countless deaths, had been based on a flaw in the system, an anomaly. Étienne was not a crusader, but he felt the need to tell what he knew. Vĩnh knew this without needing an explanation. Both feared the consequences.

"What will you do?" said Vĩnh.

Étienne squeezed his eyes shut but said nothing. The following day he slowly mounted the steps to the High Commission and demanded to speak to a senior officer. He was no longer the greenhorn who had come here a few short months earlier. This time he was the one bringing the news.

"I work for the Indochinese Currency Exchange. I have information of vital importance for the High Commissioner."

Étienne was received by a secretary, a young man in a double-breasted suit he had often seen at Le Métropole. He reeked of Foreign Office bureaucracy, polished to the tips of his fingers, were it not for the fact that he bit his nails to the quick. He affected an Olympian stillness that had been inculcated in him. He was an Important Person – this was palpable from his solemnity and his prudence.

He set in front of him the file Étienne had brought and read through it without a word; the process took some fifteen minutes.

"There are a number of imports listed here which, if not suspicious, are, I grant, a little odd . . ."

"A little, indeed . . ."

"But the balance are principally claims for war reparations. I fail to see how you could draw the conclusion that the Việt Minh are somehow masterminding what are, in effect, perfectly legal transactions."

"I have no proof, of course, that's why I've come to you."

"I don't understand . . ."

The young secretary placed the tip of his thumb on his lips; he was aching to bite his nail.

"None of these claims for war reparations have been properly vetted," said Étienne, "and we have no record of where the monies went. Launching an investigation would make it possible to . . ."

"I'm sorry, monsieur, but you are putting the cart before the horse. We do not launch investigations to look for evidence of wrongdoing; it is only when we have evidence that we launch an investigation. That is standard procedure."

"With no evidence, there's no investigation, but with no investigation, there's no evidence . . ."

The young man gave an unexpected chuckle.

"You might put it that way, yes."

Étienne stood up and began to unbutton his shirt. The secretary, thinking he was spoiling for a fight, got to his feet, but, rather than summoning security, he clenched his fists and took up a boxing pose.

Étienne showed him the knife wound on his chest.

"I've been threatened, as you can see."

"Oh, here in Saigon, such things are commonplace. Indeed, I myself . . ."

Étienne did not wait to hear the anecdote. He picked up the files and stalked out of the office.

Now there was one more person who knew about his investigation. It was a vicious circle.

It was as he was walking along the street that Étienne thought about Vĩnh.

The notion that he might have been responsible for the leak was all the more unsettling since Étienne had never considered him a suspect. But, truth be told, he knew nothing about the young man or his family who lived in the north. Vĩnh had been foisted on him by Monsieur Qiao, a Chinese comprador involved in countless shady deals . . .

Vĩnh was perceptive enough to realise that Étienne was uneasy on his return from the High Commission and that his misgivings had nothing to with his unsuccessful visit.

They ate in silence.

Étienne had already broached the matter of war reparations with

Gaston, then with Jeantet, and, having failed to get an answer, he had approached the High Commission, but to no avail. Now he decided to see whether the trail led back to Monsieur Qiao and the following day headed up to the archives, where he was greeted by a young Vietnamese man, smiling awkwardly beneath his blue visor.

"Is Annie not here?"

The young man held out his hand.

"My name is Thien."

Étienne did not shake the outstretched hand.

"Where's Annie?"

The boy didn't care in the least.

"She has gone home. She has retired. As of last week. I am her replacement. Annie is my father's cousin, she was the one who got me this job." (His eyes were shining at the thought of being the new archivist at the Exchange.)

Étienne took a step backwards.

"I find that a little strange ..."

The young man's smile faded, as though he had done something wrong.

"She just upped and left, with no warning?"

"Oh no, monsieur, her retirement was planned a long time ago."

Étienne remembered that Gaston had mentioned this, but the abruptness of Annie's departure together with the threats he had faced made him worry that Annie had been the source of the leak, and had disappeared as soon as her mission was accomplished.

Étienne instantly realised that this notion was preposterous. How could Annie be the source of the leak since it was she who had given him the compromising dossiers and steered him towards Heurtin Frères?

No. It was more likely that Annie had been collateral damage. Murder was as common in Saigon as on the mean streets of Chicago.

"She wanted to go back to Bac Kan," said the young archivist. "It's the village in the north where we're from. She wants to take care of her youngest daughter, she's had so much tragedy in her life ..."

So it was that Étienne discovered that, three years earlier, Annie's two sons had been killed by the Việt Minh for refusing to pay taxes.

"You are Monsieur Étienne, I think?"

Étienne did not have time to answer before the young man went over to the door and closed it, then took a cardboard file from under the counter.

"Annie says that this is her retirement present."

Attached was a brief note in an elegant cursive hand: "Do not worry about me. Annie."

The box contained a record of all the transfers Monsieur Qiao had made over the previous six years.

30

If it rains, we roll down the awning!

After the arrest of Germain Cageot, Jean's initial relief about the investigation turned to disquiet that an innocent man was being charged with the crime. It was unjust. He felt the case should have been closed. Not that he felt remotely guilty. The girl was dead, it was unfortunate, but if she'd fallen under the wheels of a métro train, the driver would not have been blamed. If she'd thrown herself out of a window, the architect would not have been blamed. The real reason that an innocent man was languishing in prison was because Justice was not only blind, but deaf and pig-headed.

Geneviève, for her part, was increasingly obsessed with the case. She eagerly read all of François's articles about it.

"He's a deeply strange man . . ."

"Who, François?"

"No," she said without looking up from *Le Journal*. "Germain Cageot, the murderer arrested by the police . . ."

"The murderer . . .?"

"Well, you know what I mean."

She set the newspaper down on the table.

"What an extraordinary man!"

"The murderer?"

"No, your brother. What a star!"

Jean was concerned by Geneviève's increasingly fervent admiration for François. He wondered whether it might not spread to include Hélène, and one day he alone would find himself excluded from the vast object of her admiration.

The day before, François had been unable to find an excuse to avoid the sempiternal "Sunday family lunch" that meant so much to Geneviève.

While their neighbour, Madame Faure, struggled to serve up the boeuf bourguignon, Geneviève, more regal than ever, had opened *Le Journal* and turned to François's interview with Mary Lampson's parents.

For some inexplicable reason, she had decided to read it aloud, as though she had penned it herself and wanted everyone to share in her pride. François did his best to dissuade her: "I know the piece by heart, Geneviève, and I'm sure Jean has already read it . . ." Glancing at his brother, François was not at all sure and, not for the first time, wondered what on earth was going on in their marriage, but that subject was a bottomless pit. And so Geneviève read: "A little detached house in Noisy-le-Sec . . . doilies on every piece of furniture . . ."

On the advice of their lawyer, Mary Lampson's parents had not until now granted any interviews, they had simply endured the tragic ordeal from which there was no escape. François had had a particular cachet since the early days of the case, because he had been in the cinema on the day the tragedy occurred, and because he had always been one step ahead of his fellow journalists. So as soon as he found out that Germain Cageot had been arrested, he telephoned them, arguing that an interview might bring them closure . . .

The Legrands's millstone cottage had an incongruous roughcast extension tacked on like an afterthought.

"It's a guest room with an en suite bathroom," Monsieur Legrand said. "We built it with money our daughter gave us . . ."

He was clearly unsettled by the presence of François's photographer.

"He's just going to take a few pictures, then he'll let us talk in peace . . ."

The Legrands had been wise to follow the advice of their lawyer, since they did not know how to say no. It had been easy to persuade them to pose in their living room, clutching a photograph of Mary, and in the spare room where no guests would ever sleep. François felt a pang of guilt.

"That's enough," he said to the photographer, who continued taking shots of the house until he was ushered outside.

Everywhere, there were doilies, knickknacks and photographs of their daughters. The interview was more excruciating than François had expected. He was dealing with a couple who had been devastated by tragedy. "The Legrands have lost both their daughters," he wrote in *Le Journal*. "Since Mary's murder, their younger daughter, Lola, furious that her parents suspected Marcel Servières, has refused to speak to them."

It was not difficult for François to gauge how much of this had been due to pressure from Juge Lenoir.

On Germain Cageot's arrest?

"Why would he do such a thing? He didn't even know her . . ." The feud with their daughter Lola?

"Now we know it wasn't Servières, she might come back to us . . ."

Everywhere François turned, there were photos of Mary that had been clipped from magazines and framed; these were surrounded by unexpected items of furniture, gifts from Mary.

"It was she who gave us the television set," said Adrienne Legrand. "We don't really know how to use it. My husband prefers to read the paper."

"IT WON'T BRING HER BACK"

say Mary Lampson's parents after Germain Cageot's arrest

François, who had been deeply moved by the Legrands's terrible grief, wanted only to forget this interview. So Geneviève reading it aloud was a long and painful ordeal.

Especially since no sooner had the investigation been opened than it had been closed again: no charges had been brought, and Germain Cageot was once again a free man.

*

Geneviève was also free. And she was overjoyed. The previous day, she had gone out and bought a typewriter. After dinner, she threaded a sheet of paper into the machine and began typing, very slowly, with one finger, looking up after each letter to assess the result. She seemed entirely satisfied.

She had good reason: three days later, Georges Guénot was summoned to the tax office where he was greeted by an inspector.

"Eugène Terret. Committee for the Confiscation of Illicit Profits."

Georges Guénot was devastated.

Since 1946, he had been exceedingly careful to sell off his black-market stock in dribs and drabs as products were gradually made exempt from rationing. He had managed to stay under the radar until 1948, so it was ironic that he should be caught now, when the textile industry was gradually being opened up, the "purge" on racketeers was flagging, and the committees set up in the wake of the Liberation were winding down. Within inches of the finish line. It was a poor return on his investment. The committee, set up in 1944, had swept up an impressive number of war profiteers who had "traded with the enemy powers" or benefited from "lucrative operations". Now it was his turn.

He was informed by the official that he would not be questioned until later, since, at that very moment, local officers were executing a search warrant on his premises, and his order books and accounts were being forensically examined.

Georges Guénot said nothing.

This was not a promising start.

At eight o'clock that evening, someone brought him a sandwich, he was allowed to go to the bathroom for a drink of water and, since there was nowhere else, he slept in the drunk tank with the winos and the tramps. The following day, at around 5 p.m., as he shambled into Eugène Terret's office, frantic and exhausted, he saw his ledgers, his order books and his archives spread across the desk. Together with the letter that prompted the investigation, crisply typed and sufficiently detailed to draw attention to someone as yet unknown to the Committee, which was rare.

Anonymous letters provided endless allegations – both real and fabricated. But a number of these letters had been of sufficient use that the Committee could not ignore them. This particular letter was both succinct and precise.

301

"You have two warehouses stocked with fabric."

Monsieur Guénot was about to say something, but Terret did not give him time.

"Yesterday, those warehouses were searched and they have now been sealed by the police."

He picked up an inventory.

"The stocks discovered are so extensive and so varied (there are even furs) that it would take months to check this inventory ... and more staff than we have at our disposal. We will therefore assume that this list is accurate."

This was the "official" inventory, in which Georges Guénot noted only a small part of the stock he purchased. He caught his breath.

"But given the discrepancy between what is listed here and what is in your warehouses, we will multiply it by ten."

"No!"

It was a heartfelt cry.

Eugène Terret had heard many such cries; this was the cry of a hard-bitten racketeer. His judgement, he decided, had been accurate.

"All of these fabrics were purchased legally," Guénot protested. "There's nothing illegal!"

Eugène Terret nodded in apparent agreement.

"As you say."

He picked up a file and spread it out before him.

"All your purchase invoices are here. Well, when I say all ... I can only assume, of course. But whether or not they reflect your actual stock is not particularly important. Those we have clearly show that the fabrics were purchased for considerably less than their actual price. Could you explain that to me, Monsieur Guénot?"

"Well ... these are products I bought from ... from traders who needed to get rid of them, that's all!"

"Once again, you are correct."

He leafed through the invoices.

"Dreyfus and Sons, Emmanuel Cohen and Company, Herschel

Ltd., Reichelberg Fabrics ... I notice that many of the sellers are located in the Sentier district of Paris. Or rather 'were', since most of them no longer exist."

"It's hardly unusual to buy in Sentier," snapped Guénot with a forced laugh. "That's where the rag trade is based!"

Terret set down the inventory, he waited for a long moment and then, speaking slowly and gravely, he said:

"Monsieur Guénot, you took advantage of the situation of Jewish merchants threatened by the occupying forces. When they were about to flee, they had no other choice but to sell off their stock, and everything I can see here proves that you profited from that situation to an extent that goes far beyond reasonable negotiation."

"It's not illegal to buy goods. Even at reduced prices."

"Once again, you are correct, Monsieur Guénot. It is not illegal. But making exorbitant profits reselling such goods to the occupying forces ..."

"Come on! Twenty metres of fabric here and there, what difference does that make?"

Three times! Three times in five years, he had sold fabric to the Germans! No one had been more careful.

"It's not fair to compare me to people who were trafficking during the war!"

"You are correct! Which is why we will do no more than confiscate your remaining stock."

"Wait a minute, that's a bit much!"

"I will tell you precisely what is going to happen, Monsieur Guénot. In a minute, I will open the door to my office and you will walk out delighted and relieved because the government, which I represent, has elected to simply confiscate the goods and allow you to go about your business. If I were you, I would consider myself very fortunate. If, however, you choose to challenge this decision, which I would argue is generous, I will have you arrested and brought before a magistrate and you will remain in prison while your case is thoroughly investigated, something that will take time, a lot of time. At the end of this investigation, you will be tried for illegal profiteering and fined fifty times the total of your profits, which sum will be tripled because you collaborated with the enemy. The magistrate may impose the forfeiture of your civic rights, resulting in a lengthy ban on any and all commercial activity, which is the only thing you know how to do. Furthermore—"

Georges Guénot held up his hands.

He looked at his ledgers and his records. The desk on which they lay looked like a bombed-out city.

He was about to leave without a word when Eugène Terret called him back.

"One last thing, Monsieur Guénot. You may be losing much of what you stole, but you have the chance to remain a free man. If, in future, we discover that you have been involved in a shady deal, a trivial infraction, a simple blunder, that miracle will not occur again. You will be brought before the magistrate and go straight to prison."

*

During this period, Jean watched as, every morning, Geneviève got up early, got dressed, put on her face and went out. She would go to the offices of the State Property Department. The female clerk she usually dealt with had taken a liking to this smiling, well turned-out young woman, who always addressed her as though fearful she was intruding. Geneviève had told the woman that she was hoping to go into the fabric trade. When might there be an auction? But there was nothing at the moment.

"It can happen overnight," she told Geneviève. "Sometimes there will be nothing for weeks, then suddenly goods come in from bankrupt businesses, from foreclosures . . ."

The clerk was right.

"I think I finally have something for you . . ." she whispered. "Two warehouses of fabric, but they won't go to auction for a little while yet, there has to be an inventory . . . But don't say I told you!"

In the end, there was no inventory.

Geneviève and Jean arranged to meet with the official responsible for the valuation and offered to buy all the stock.

"There must be at least four hundred thousand francs' worth."

Geneviève offered a third; Jean stared at his shoes.

"A hundred and thirty thousand francs?"

The official baulked, but only for form's sake, he was keen to make it clear that he was motivated by the common good, not merely selling the treasures of the Republic at cut price. In fact, he thought the deal a good one. There would be no inventory to arrange, no employees to mobilise, no checks to carry out, no transport to organise, no lengthy auction that would go on for months and risk the state being lumbered with the goods no one wanted . . . Of course, what was being offered was only a third of the value, but these clients were prepared to pay in cash.

First, he had to check the confiscated goods no longer legally belonged to the owner, but to the state.

"I need to ask Monsieur Terret . . ."

"Who is he?" asked Geneviève, with a broad smile.

"An inspector with the Committee for the Confiscation of Illicit Profits."

Eugène Terret quickly confirmed that Georges Guénot no longer had any rights to the goods he had stolen.

Geneviève and Jean paid for Georges Guénot's stock with the advance provided by Monsieur Pelletier. They were utterly elated. At least until the following day when they visited their shop. Geneviève did not say as much, since she had insisted on renting the place, but now that they had to think about furnishing the shop it was clear how cramped it was. It was much too small. But there was no going back, the lease had been signed, they had bought the fabric.

Jean had been well aware of the problem, but he never had the strength to contradict Geneviève, since he never managed to convince her.

When a carpenter measured the space for the sales counter, it was clear that there would barely be room to move between the displays. The shop could just about accommodate half a dozen customers.

"The best thing would be to see it on the pavement," said Jean.

"On the pavement?" Geneviève looked horrified.

"Yes, that's the only solution I can see ..."

"On the street, like some flea market? We're not running a stall in a souk!"

For once, Jean, unruffled by his wife's withering scorn, argued his point – and it was this that unsettled Geneviève.

"If it works in a market, why not here on the pavement?"

"But ... this is a boutique, Jean, a bou-ti-que!"

"The most important thing is to sell the stock, isn't it?"

The argument was unassailable. But Geneviève was not about to admit defeat.

"And if it rains, we simply shut up shop? Let's hope for fine weather, or maybe you think we should move to Africa!"

"We'll put up an awning," said Jean. "A large awning that covers the whole pavement. We'll put the displays outside. Except for the bedlinen, we keep that inside, but everything else can go on the pavement. And if it rains, we roll down the awning." Geneviève was forced to agree that it was the only practical solution, but it offended her aesthetic sense as the future owner of a boutique. As it was, she thought it a little undignified to have to sell household linens when she longed to sell fashionable dresses and blouses, but to have to sell things on the pavement ...

Inclined as she was to sneer, there was no time to make other arrangements.

The awning was the most expensive part of the renovation. There was some carpentry, some plastering, a lot of cleaning, but the bulk of their budget was spent on the oversized awning. It ran the full width of the shop and extended more than four metres across the pavement – a permit had been obtained from the town hall.

For once, Jean seemed to know exactly what he was about. He drew up a scale model of the perimeter of the shop, including the section of pavement allocated to them by the municipality – as far as he was concerned, it was all one. He set out small squares of paper to represent the stalls and the displays.

Geneviève watched his preparations disdainfully. Living with Jean meant always having to come down a peg or two, nothing was ever as good as one hoped. Her idea for a boutique had been turned into a flea market; she felt sullied.

It quickly became clear that Jean was tinkering with the renovation project as a way of deferring the moment when he would have to find linen manufacturers.

"I wouldn't mind," nagged Geneviève in the shrill voice that pierced Jean's eardrums, "but the sheets and tablecloths aren't going to make themselves!"

Reluctantly, Jean put down his pencil and set off for northern France.

*

Hélène and François had moved into the apartment on the rue des Arquebusiers.

It was a beautiful apartment with a long balcony with views over Père-Lachaise. They each had a spacious bedroom and shared an airy living room and a kitchen large enough to serve as a bathroom; the toilet was out on the landing, but was private.

It was the happiest period in their relationship.

Unfortunately, it lasted only a week.

Hélène had headed off to the École des Beaux-Arts on the rue Bonaparte with little hope, fearing that she would look a fool, but she had promised her father, so she went . . .

Instead of being turned away, she was greeted by the Head of Studies, Monsieur Ferdinand Graux, a podgy man in his fifties with blue eyes, a blond moustache and such a radiant air and beatific smile that it seemed as if, at any moment, a halo would encircle his head.

"I've never passed an art exam . . ." said Hélène, prepared to turn tail.

"Yes, that's a shame . . ."

He leafed through the portfolio she had brought: a half-page CV and four drawings she had dashed off the night before. They were absolutely terrible, but Monsieur Graux was nodding his big round head contentedly.

"The thing is, I've only been in Paris a few days ... I hadn't planned ... I mean, my portfolio ..."

"Yes, that's a shame ..." said Monsieur Graux again. "Did you have a particular subject in mind? Architecture? Sculpture?"

"Painting ..."

"I see."

He closed the portfolio, folded his arms and gazed at Hélène for a long moment.

"There can be no question of you entering the École without matriculating."

Relieved that the ordeal was over, Hélène made to get up.

"But if you're interested, the École allows students to join as 'observers'. It's something that fell out of favour before the war (the First War!). But I think ..."

Monsieur Graux explained to a dumbfounded Hélène that the status of "observer", previously reserved for foreign students wishing to observe the methods of the École so they could benefit their own country, had never officially been revoked.

"You would be allowed to attend lessons. Needless to say, you would not be allowed to sit the exams, but if you were to do so for a year, you would have the best possible chance of succeeding in the entrance exam next year ..."

Hélène squeezed her eyes shut; instantly she saw Monsieur Graux in a very different light.

Here, as elsewhere – as everywhere – women got what they wanted only if they were prepared to give in to a man's advances. It was something they learned from a tender age, a dictum that seemed part of their condition. She was about to put on her coat but stopped as she beheld the vision that was Ferdinand Graux. He was so flamboyantly homosexual that either Hélène's theory was wrong or he was acting on behalf of someone else, or from some ulterior motive. The shadow of the halo over his head was surely the mark of the hypocrite, the deviant, the pervert?

Graux sensed what she was thinking and was offended.

"Had you come here last week, mademoiselle, I would have sent you home."

He rummaged through his in tray and took out a memorandum.

"But as it so happens, at last night's board meeting" – he stressed the enormity of the coincidence – "it was realised that the status of 'observer' had become dormant, so we were requested to resuscitate it, so to speak. Apparently, we need to 'thrive'."

He scanned through the text, picking out various words and intoning them as though they were from a foreign language.

"Thrive."

"Shine."

"Excel."

He set down the memo.

"So, mademoiselle, if you wish to . . . 'thrive', then the doors to the École des Beaux-Arts are open to you."

At the time, her home life with François was still in its honeymoon period. They joyously cooked together, joked from room to room, and François grumbled as he carried up the numerous packages Hélène had delivered. When Hélène was accepted to the Beaux-Arts, they had a celebration dinner of sardines and black-market butter, during which their parents' ears must surely have been burning. After that, conversation moved on to Bouboule and Geneviève, an undemanding subject. A poignant quarter of an hour was spent talking about Étienne, and Hélène read out snippets from his letters. Everything between them was rosy. It was possible to imagine that things might go awry, but impossible to imagine quite how quickly and how seriously they would deteriorate.

Firstly, because a week at the École des Beaux-Arts was enough for Hélène to realise that, while painting might be (perhaps, nothing could be less certain) a possible career, she would never "thrive" in this viciously chauvinistic atmosphere, this dry pernicious studio. By way of welcome, René Chevalier, head of the atelier, had seen fit to remind her of the house rule: "no women, no dogs, no politics, no religion". In terms of dogs and women, this rule was generally observed. A handful of women were accepted to various ateliers, only to be quickly ejected. It was clear to everyone that Hélène, having been admitted without matriculating, on a status that had not existed a day earlier, had been accepted as the result of some questionable "favour". Having discovered she was not welcome, indeed barely tolerated, that the study of old masters was tedious, the serried ranks of easels promoted a competitive spirit she found uninspiring, and the few students who expressed an interest in her had less than artistic intentions, Hélène quickly found herself out of her depth. The ethos of the École, like an invisible shroud that floated over classes, acted like a corporatism. The fervent hope that they might be "chosen" led many students to cleave to the maxim that neophytes "speak only when spoken to, and they are never spoken to".

Scarcely had she joined the École than Hélène had only one thought: to leave.

The glares of the students, the crude jokes, the wandering hands of the "chauvinist-in-chief" responsible for tutoring those planning to take the entrance exam, all these things simply reinforced her decision.

Hélène realised that she had never really believed it would work.

Studying at the Beaux-Arts had never been a plan, merely a notion; she did not have enough passion for art and painting to take on the institution. She felt lost, adrift; the apartment she shared with François had begun to feel like a boarding school, and her bedroom like a prison cell. She longed to go out, but did not know where to go, she smoked too much, she seethed with the same anger she had felt in Beirut, but now she could not vent it on her parents. In coming to Paris, she had somehow lost her way, but now she could see no new horizon towards which she could run.

Although she had stopped attending classes, she continued to hang out at the Café des Artistes, the favoured haunt of Beaux-Arts students. They thought her an idler with the delusions of a courtesan, languid, sultry and scandalous, someone who smoked endless cigarettes and let others buy her coffee . . . By mid-morning, she would be ensconced in the café, and it was not unusual to find that she was still there at dinner time. The men began to wonder whether she was working as a prostitute. Wild rumours began to circulate about her, their lurid aspect fuelled by Hélène's devil-may-care beauty; it seemed as though one could simply reach out and fondle her breast or her arse, but no one dared do so. Her mere presence put to shame those who considered themselves free spirits. She would chat with the worst elements of the École, those who skipped classes and shunned the ateliers so they could drink aperitifs.

She made the acquaintance of a young man named Jonsac (Bernard de Jonsac, to be precise), a former Beaux-Arts student like herself who made his fortune by supplying current students with all manner of illicit substances. He was often accompanied by one of his acolytes, Max Bernat or Ferdinand Lagre, who served as henchmen. "Drugs are driven by fashion," he insisted. "Just now, everyone is taking amphetamines." The little pills gave Hélène a pleasant lift, and she did not find the eventual palpitations unpleasant. Since she had no money, she made a deal with Jonsac. What he asked in return was not particularly onerous and did not take much time, so as long as things did not go any further ...

She wrote letters to Étienne in which she told him (almost) everything: the truth about François ("He's constantly pestering me about going to the Beaux-Arts, when he's never even set foot in the École Normale Sup, and spends his time writing about stray dogs for *Le Journal*!"), the pusillanimity of Jean ("Bouboule is a spineless little man, you can't imagine, and Geneviève is a complete bitch!"). Then, because for all her anger, Hélène had a good heart, she would add in mitigation: "François is the one who has been covering the Mary Lampson case I mentioned, he writes these amazing articles. And they're always on the front page!" Or: "Jean and Geneviève are opening a shop selling linens, so at least he won't have to spend weeks trekking around the provinces."

Étienne wrote back: "I am planning to give His Holiness Pope Loan I some tiny bells to replace the tassels on his mitre so we can hear him coming, like cowbells on cattle." But Hélène knew her brother too well not to realise that humour was just a mask for his grief. She wanted to know his true feelings and the more light-hearted he seemed, the more she worried what he was hiding. "So, the hero of the Syria Campaign of 1941 has chosen *Le Journal du soir* over the École Normale?" Étienne wrote. "It'll be the death of Maman when she finds out!" But now and then Étienne talked about his fears, though they never seemed to involve him directly. "This is a savage country. There are assassins everywhere, you only have to go to Cholon to find someone who'll kill anyone you want for a few piastres." But he could never remain serious. "If Bouboule brings his beloved to visit, he'll easily find someone who can make him a widower ..."

Even Étienne's letters were the subject of arguments with François.

"At least Étienne sends you letters," he would say curtly when a letter arrived from Saigon. "I suppose that's good ..."

"He doesn't send me letters, he replies to my letters," said Hélène, pretending to be engrossed in reading.

François also resented his sister, who he accused of telling their father that he had lied about attending the École Normale Sup, something Hélène denied.

"How did he find out, if not from you?"

"I don't know! From Bouboule. Or that bitch Geneviève."

This put François in a difficult position, since his suspicions were equally divided between his brother, his sister and his sister-in-law. He would probably never know who had betrayed him, and living with this uncertainty was all the more painful since he knew he had no one to blame but himself.

His relationship with Hélène never slipped into something easy, relaxed, fraternal. Hardly had they agreed the house rules for the apartment than they were broken. Hélène's slovenly habits invaded the living room and the kitchen; she ignored the rota for cleaning and shopping.

They argued constantly.

In fact, they did little else on the rare occasions that they bumped into each other, because Hélène usually slept until mid-morning ("The atelier doesn't open until late," she would say lazily) and did not come home until two or three in the morning.

Ever since they had moved in together, François had been on the back foot. He never knew how to deal with Hélène and alternated between threats and pleas.

"Yes, it's tough being a father . . ." Mathilde would say with a laugh.

If François had worried that living with his sister would thwart his relationship with Mathilde, he was quickly reassured. His lover had long since left by the time Hélène came home.

Less than two weeks after they moved in, François came face to face with Vladimir Ulyov, a student from Hélène's atelier, who claimed to be an exiled Russian revolutionary. (In fact, he was born in Romorantin, and owed his name to a grandfather who had done nothing more revolutionary than marry a farmer's daughter and get run over by an oxcart.) François had peered like a zoologist at the young man before reluctantly shaking his hand. Vladimir was a skinny boy with yellow teeth and yellow skin who constantly scratched his head and flicked away the dandruff with his fingernail. Within seconds, Vladimir and Hélène were holed up in her bedroom. François heard the key turn in the lock.

He felt completely helpless.

François had carped about Hélène's timetable, grumbled that she did not go to class in the morning, complained about her refusal to clean and tidy the apartment, but so far his sister had spared him the question he most dreaded. Was she a virgin? Surely she had to be; she was only eighteen, well, almost nineteen, but even so, girls don't sleep with men at that age.

"Had you ever slept with a man when you were her age?" François asked Mathilde who was sprawled on the bed, one elbow propped on the pillow, languidly smoking a cigarette as she stroked the hair on his chest, his belly . . .

"Well, had you? Slept with men at her age?"

Mathilde folded her arms and carried on smoking.

A minute elapsed, then two.

Mathilde stubbed out her cigarette and lit another one.

Her silence made François uncomfortable. His tactless question had offended her.

"I mean," he ventured, "when you were nineteen . . ."

"Be quiet, will you? I'm trying to count!"

They both burst out laughing, François threw a pillow at her.

He never felt he really knew Hélène. He was angry with his father. You don't entrust your teenage daughter to someone without telling them everything you know.

He stared at the locked door, knowing Hélène and Vladimir were on the other side.

He should have done something straight away; it was too late to do anything now. Would he look like a fool if he knocked on the door? Was it his job to be a wet blanket? Hélène was a complete pain ...

He settled down to work.

As the reader knows, Germain Cageot, the man arrested after the identity parade, had quickly been released, because, aside from the lack of any evidence or any motive, the witness had recanted her statement, she now said she could not be sure, in fact she was convinced that she had made a mistake, and that she would be unable to recognise the man she had seen. Juge Lenoir had wanted to keep the suspect in custody, but the supervisory authority recommended that he be released, and Lenoir was not a man to flout authority.

It was at this point that François decided to interview Mary Lampson's husband.

He had found Marcel Servières to be edgy and tense, nothing like the image of the handsome, debonair Parisian actor who invariably played the ladies' man. Servières was unshaven, wearing a tattered dressing gown and a pair of house slippers. He chain-smoked throughout the interview.

François asked him how he had first met Mary Lampson, about their careers, and Servières answered mechanically as though he had learned the role and was rehearsing it. He insisted that he had been shocked to discover his wife had been pregnant, and dismissed rumours of a divorce with a wave.

François had learned nothing new. He had enough material for an article, but no answers to the countless unresolved questions.

Had Mary Lampson planned to sue for divorce? If so, why? Had it been Servières who wanted to divorce? Why? Did he have a mistress? Did Mary have a lover? Whose child was Mary Lampson carrying? Had Servières written the note found in the victim's handbag?

François was brooding over these points when he noticed a hissing sound.

No, it was not a hiss, it was . . . a moan. And it was coming from Hélène's bedroom. He could hear panting.

François blushed to the roots of his hair.

Was this the sound of Hélène . . . making love?

Hesitantly he got to his feet. Did he have the right to press his ear to the door? No, he couldn't do that . . . But . . .

The sound of ragged breaths and sighs.

And that steady, pounding rhythm . . .

François stood helplessly. He could not have felt more distressed if he were prevented from saving Hélène from being violated.

He laid a hand on the doorknob, but already he knew he would not do anything. The gasps were louder now . . . It was a man grunting . . . François strained to hear. It was Vladimir! It was not the sound of Hélène sighing, it was the Russian! Which made it all the more stomach-turning.

Images flashed through his mind, the Russian lying on top of Hélène, grunting like a wild beast, it was enough to drive him mad . . . François picked up his pad, his notebook and his typewriter and locked himself in his room, but still he could hear the muffled panting. He set about typing up the interview, humming angrily to drown out the moans. He was terrified that one of them would start screaming; this sometimes happened when he and Mathilde forgot themselves. He hummed louder and louder.

The situation was now impossible.

He could not reasonably be expected to share the apartment with Hélène.

31

It sounds pretty complicated

The list of transfers made by Monsieur Qiao over the previous six years ran to about forty pages; it took Étienne less than an hour to go through them.

With the help of Gaston's rubber stamp, and that of a number of other clerks at the Exchange, Monsieur Qiao had managed to transfer a large amount of capital to France. The supporting documentation made it possible to trace the transfers through banks in Hong Kong and Singapore, at which they vanished without trace.

If Étienne's theory was correct, the monies were then channelled to arms dealers on behalf of the Việt Minh.

But there was something else.

Two documents proved that the Exchange had authorised the transfer of vast sums to France (hence, at an exchange rate of seventeen francs rather than eight francs) which had ended up in personal accounts in a number of Paris banks.

The recipients were designated only by their initials: E. N., P. R., D. F., A. M., S. R.

Whoever these people were, they were war profiteers.

But.

But although Étienne's assumptions were probably true, there was no conclusive proof. All he had was a record of transactions made by the Exchange.

What Étienne was dealing with had the potential to trigger a political storm, but there was not a chance in a million of doing so with the physical evidence in his possession, since he could prove nothing.

Vĩnh, who was sitting at the table, turned his head. On top of the fridge, Joseph had just got to his feet, stretched, leaped down onto the floor and was now sitting, staring at Étienne. Sometimes the cat had a sixth sense worth listening to ... Étienne felt a wave of anxiety, as though an accident were about to happen, a cataclysm that he could do nothing to prevent.

He felt crushed, and the fact that he could do nothing made him utterly miserable.

Raymond was still dying a long slow death. He was a pawn to be manipulated by dark forces. His death and the agonies he had suffered counted for nothing.

Just as one more shower goes unnoticed in the rainy season, so Étienne did not notice the tears trickling down his cheeks. Vĩnh and Joseph gazed at him sadly.

At length, Vĩnh went and sat next to Étienne. He took the cardboard folder bearing the logo of the Indochinese Currency Exchange from his lap.

"You're in real danger," Vĩnh said gravely.

This was the irony of the situation.

These files which he could not use to prove anything were now a threat simply because he had them in his possession. Vĩnh was merely confirming something Étienne had heard a thousand times. The Việt Minh were everywhere, they saw everything, knew everything ...

This conspiracy theory, which had long circulated in Saigon, had always seemed to Étienne as fanciful as the Gunpowder Plot or the antics of Robin Hood. But while Vĩnh was naive enough to believe in the Pope of the Siêu Linh, Étienne could not help but admit that, in this case, it would be just as naive not to trust him. The power of the Việt Minh was amply demonstrated by the spate of street assassinations and their endless ambushes on the Expeditionary Force. But there was more to it than that. Philippe de Lacroix-Gibet had been right when he said that, in war, information was the ultimate weapon. Strictly speaking, the Việt Minh had no army, only armed factions, so its ability to terrorise French troops was based on a vast network of informants and spies unrivalled by anything in the Western world.

Étienne was afraid not for his life, he was afraid that he would

317

not be able to finish what he had started, that everything would founder in the turbid waters of this dirty war.

His infantile honesty had also put Vĩnh and Joseph in danger.

"We must leave," said Vĩnh.

"Absolutely not."

The answer came unbidden. Although Étienne could think of no way to carry out his plan to expose what was happening, to run away would be tantamount to desertion; he did not have the strength to give up.

"We must leave," Vĩnh said again.

Étienne got up and walked over to the window. Saigon had never looked so much like a murky swampland. He shook his head, surprised by his own resolve.

"I can't do that. I will not leave here, until . . . until . . ."

Étienne did not know what to call this thing.

". . . until I've told the truth."

He instantly regretted the phrase; it was pompous and completely out of character. Étienne did not care about the truth. What he wanted was justice.

But even that sounded like something from a novel. In real life, there is no way to say such words. He did not say them, but Vĩnh clearly understood, because he got to his feet and picked up Joseph.

"Can you find a way for us to get out?"

The young man was not looking at him, he had closed his eyes and was stroking Joseph's head, as though things were finally going as he had wished and hoped for.

"Monsieur Qiao is my uncle by marriage," said Vĩnh. "I can gain access to his house. I should be able to get the documents you need, but if I do, we'll have to be ready to leave, we won't be able to stay in Saigon a moment longer. I want you to give me your word."

In that moment, Étienne realised that the suspicions he had once harboured about Vĩnh still lingered in some corner of his brain, like a latent poison for which the young man had just calmly and decisively offered the only possible antidote: risk in exchange for trust.

"You have my word," said Étienne. "Loan is powerful enough

to discreetly get us out of Saigon. I helped him and I know that he will help us in return."

Vĩnh nodded. He was happy with this answer. Joseph jumped down from his arms and within a second he was curled up on top of the fridge. As far as he was concerned, the matter was settled.

But Vĩnh added:

"If you do not keep your word, we will be dead."

It was a simple statement, which made it all the worse.

In Étienne's eyes, Vĩnh had been a man of many faces. First, the frightened, docile and willing adolescent offered by Monsieur Qiao, whose sacrifice Étienne had refused. Then a different Vĩnh had come to him without compulsion. This was a placid and resolute young man whose face was that of the friend who supports and cares for you and does not judge you for putting yourself in danger. Then there was the Vĩnh of their shared life together, a face Étienne now regretted not looking at enough, the face of a graceful, slim, yet powerful man, who slipped between the sheets like a warm, reviving spring. And now, suddenly, Étienne saw a new face, one he had never imagined, the face of a man willing to risk his own life, who asked nothing in return but to leave with him . . .

It moved Étienne to tears.

*

Étienne immediately gave Captain Moinard an alarming letter to deliver to Pope Loan. "Come quickly. I desperately need your help. Tell no one that this concerns me, I will explain . . ."

Three days later, His Holiness arrived in Saigon to find Étienne in a terrible state.

"What has happened to you, my friend?"

Étienne was haggard, exhausted and clearly at the end of his tether. He found various excuses to be absent from the Exchange, and every night he smoked a terrifying number of opium pipes which he had to prepare himself since Vĩnh, in an attempt to gain access to his uncle's files, was spending more time with his family and made only brief visits to the apartment.

Étienne took Loan's hands in his.

"I can't tell you how, Loan, but in a few days, perhaps even a few hours, I will have concrete proof that the Việt Minh is exploiting the traffic in piastres to procure weapons."

Loan gave a sigh; he had never believed this rumour.

"My friend . . ."

Étienne cut him short.

"Incontrovertible evidence, take my word for it. But I need your help, we have to get out of the country."

"Who is 'we'? You and who else?"

"I'll tell you when the time comes. But, right now, you are the only one who can help me . . ."

He was haunted by the feeling that he was forever forgetting some crucial detail that might be catastrophic. Loan scratched his head, clearly moved by Étienne's sense of urgency.

"Very well . . ."

Étienne hung on his every word.

"We shall do something . . ."

"Tell me . . ."

"The papal plane is at Georges Guynemer airfield, about thirty kilometres from here near Biên Hòa. The place is heavily guarded, the Việt Minh never venture there. We'll find a car to drive you there discreetly. From there, our plane will fly you to a commercial airport."

In a flash, Étienne remembered his first flight, the flushed face of the alcoholic pilot, and banished the thought.

"As for payment . . ."

"Come, my friend! There will be no talk of money between us! I owe much to you . . . And everything that you did for Diêm, Loan is now able to repay."

On a sudden impulse, the two men hugged. Then Loan also found it necessary to regain his composure.

"By the way, where is it that you want to go?" he asked.

"Paris."

✻

In telling him that François worked at *Le Journal du soir*, Hélène had given Étienne one last hope. The hope that some journalist would pick up the story, launch a full investigation and reveal the truth. Étienne had no real idea what his brother's role was at the newspaper, since Hélène's comments had been self-contradictory. On the one hand she had written that François was covering an important murder case ("on the front page!"), only to later sneeringly comment: "He spends his time writing about stray dogs." But whatever his own role, François was bound to know someone who would be interested in the "Qiao dossier" – such a scoop could hardly fail to interest a major daily newspaper.

It took Étienne two days to contact his brother at *Le Journal*. He initially tried calling from a private office in the Exchange, then from the general post office, and later from a telephone booth – he mistrusted everything and everyone. Eventually, he managed to get through. Initially François seemed rather uninterested. The Indochinese traffic in piastres – an abstruse subject – was far removed from his usual news articles, and he could not see what he could be expected to do with a story that was out of his bailiwick. But he was moved and a little worried by Étienne's insistence, and the unfamiliar urgency of his tone. Holed up in a booth on the docks, endlessly feeding coins into the payphone, Étienne watched as his salary and his attempts at persuasion melted away.

"The illicit profit made by the traffickers comes directly from the French treasury!"

"OK, and . . .?"

"But this is much worse: the Việt Minh are exploiting the traffic in piastres! France is unwittingly funding weapons for the very enemy it is fighting. A Chinaman named Qiao submits falsified transfer documents to the Exchange, and the profits from these transfers are channelled directly to the Việt Minh."

Étienne was clearly nervous and speaking very quickly. François had heard "a Chinaman named Ciao", which sounded oddly Italian. The whole thing was clear as mud.

"This story of yours sounds very convoluted."

"Christ's sake, François, listen to me!"

"All right, all right, don't get worked up!"

François was finding it difficult to sound enthusiastic.

"This story you're talking about ... it's not really my area. I work on the general news desk. Anything about Indochina would be handled by the politics desk. And besides, the war is happening on the other side of the world, so most readers can't really relate to it ..."

Étienne did not want to bring up Raymond's death. He knew that his note of pathos would make his talk of exposure sound like a petty act of revenge, make the scandal seem infantile. He felt so crushed that he was tempted to give up. Then, in a last-ditch attempt he said:

"Vast sums of money are diverted to Paris, to the bank accounts of public figures ..."

"Who exactly are we talking about?"

Étienne relaxed; he had finally got François's attention.

"There are at least five public figures involved in the scam. I only have their initials – E. N., P. R., D. F., A. M., S. R. – but it shouldn't be too difficult to work out since they have to be people with connections to Indochina who have the means to exploit the system. The sums they've received run to millions of francs just this year!"

A financial scandal involving the Indochinese war would not add a dozen copies to the circulation of *Le Journal*, but French public figures raking in the illicit profits was a very different matter. This could be an opportunity for François to move from general news to tackle more serious, more exciting topics.

"What exactly do you have on them in this dossier of yours?"

Étienne's mind was racing. He realised that, at this juncture, his self-confidence was as important as the nature of the evidence.

"It's hard to explain over the phone ... I have the payments, the dates, the initials. I just need to link those to the names."

"You don't understand, Étienne: what documentary evidence have you got?"

Étienne lied.

"Notes made by those making the payments ... That's why I only have the initials of the payees."

He sensed that this would not be enough.

"Their accounts are with Banque Godard and with Hopkins Brothers."

François jotted this down.

"Can you send me a copy?"

"No, no copies! I'm not prepared to part with anything, François. I'll bring the dossier to you and you publish it, agreed?"

"Hang on, hang on, I need to see whether the dossier can be published . . ."

"But . . ."

François could tell from Étienne's tone and these shrill outbursts that he was in a panicked state and needed to be calmed down.

"If you have conclusive evidence, there won't be a problem, Étienne. Do you trust your sources?"

"A hundred per cent. My source is Monsieur Qiao's nephew."

The Chinaman again, thought François, who still did not understand his role in this affair.

"So, who is he, this nephew?"

"He's . . . he's my manservant."

François closed his eyes. Stories involving maids and manservants were two a penny, and they always reeked of revenge.

"I'll need hard evidence, you do understand that?"

François said this in a tone that expressed grave doubt, but Étienne did not seem to hear.

"I understand. So, if I bring you the evidence, you'll publish? Promise?"

If the evidence held up, how it would be dealt with would be decided not by François, but by Arthur Baron, or Denissov, the story would be taken out of his hands – but how could he explain this to his brother? He decided not to try, since it was the most expedient solution.

"I promise."

There was a long silence.

"Thanks, François, this is really important . . ."

"I understand."

"I'll work out a way of getting to Paris and I'll bring you the dossier."

"All right."

∗

"Étienne's coming to Paris?"

"That's what he said . . ."

"When?"

"He's not sure, it sounds pretty complicated."

At his sister's insistence, François was forced to relate everything that had been said, and, as he did so, he began to worry. Had he stuck his neck out too far? If the dossier did provide conclusive proof, would Denissov give the story to someone else?

Hélène could not work out how Étienne could have got involved in this affair. He had never had the slightest interest in current affairs, so the idea that he had been caught up in a political and financial scandal seemed utterly far-fetched. As François explained what he had been told, he found it difficult to hide the fact that Étienne was in a tricky situation.

"Is he in danger?"

The only honest answer was "yes".

"Of course not, don't be so melodramatic."

The rebuke sounded forced.

"What are you going to do?"

"I'll wait for him to get here, study the dossier and if the evidence is compelling . . ."

"Let me rephrase: what the hell are you going to do?! Étienne's in Saigon, he's in danger, but you're not planning to alert anyone, you're not going to ask someone for help, oh no, you're just going to wait for him to show up in Paris to see if his dossier is worthy of two column inches on page eight?"

They argued.

No matter the trigger, no matter the subject, it always came to this; they could no longer abide each other.

＊

One of Loan's disciples came to Étienne's door with a copy of the Gospel of the Siêu Linh. It was a beautiful glossy book. In it was an account of how Loan had had his Revelation (there was a handsome portrait of the Pope gazing at the horizon; it was clear the man was imbued with something spiritual), together with potted hagiographies of various saints recognised by the Siêu Linh and the tenets of the sect (peace, progress and fraternity in various guises). This was followed by an impressive list of prohibitions for men – killing, coveting one's neighbour's wife (to say nothing of screwing her), stealing, abusing alcohol, gambling, eating meat, blasphemy, making threats, speaking ill of others, etc. – and for women: lying, flirting, seducing one's neighbour (to say nothing of getting screwed by him), spicing octopus, showing one's ankles, etc.

The idea that any sane person would adhere to a creed that deprived them of almost all of life's pleasures was a mystery to Étienne, although thinking about it, Western religions offered little more in the way of joy or pleasure than the Siêu Linh.

The disciple bowed before the Papal Nuncio and withdrew.

On the last page of the booklet was a small handwritten note: "Destination Phnom Penh, then by commercial airline to Paris. Our plane will be waiting for you at the Guynemer airfield anytime in the next ten days. If that is too soon, we will rearrange. If you need a car to get you to Biên Hòa, let me know. Look after yourself."

It was signed "Your friend, Loan".

32

Murderer!

The interview with Mary Lampson's parents had had a huge impact on the readers of *Le Journal*; Denissov was over the moon. The story, it seemed, would run and run. Barely two weeks later, there was another scoop. Having carefully reviewed a number of photographs, in particular those of Mary Lampson and Marcel Servières's wedding, Madame Soubirot, always referred to as "the surprise witness", who had mistakenly identified Germain Cageot, was now categorical. It had not previously occurred to her, but the man who had pushed past her as she emerged from the toilets at Le Régent only minutes before Mary Lampson was murdered could well have been Marcel Servières.

"Are you certain?" insisted Juge Lenoir, glimpsing light at the end of the tunnel.

"Well, what I mean is . . ."

It was a curious thing. Madame Soubirot always began by being absolutely certain, but quickly started to doubt herself.

"What Monsieur le Juge wants to know," said Commissaire Templier in his fluting voice, "is whether you are absolutely certain."

"Well, I mean . . . certain . . ."

The commissaire took the magistrate aside.

"The witness doesn't seem very sure of herself."

"She's simply nervous."

"The handwriting analysis did not—"

"I've been thinking about that. We'll have it redone; I'll appoint a new expert."

Commissaire Templier had the fatalistic look of a man on a railway line who has just seen a train hurtling towards him.

"What I suggest . . ." he said patiently.

But the magistrate had already seized the case file to check the statement given by Marcel Servières.

While he did so, the commissaire was listening sympathetically to Madame Soubirot, who was saying: "Yes, I think so, I can't be certain, but I think so . . ."

In his article, François pointed out: "The difference in opinion between Commissaire Templier and Juge Lenoir is clear from their use of language: what the police officer soberly refers to as Marcel Servières's 'schedule', the magistrate calls 'his alibi'."

"I was playing billiards that Sunday," Servières had said in his statement.

This had been confirmed by friends from the club where he usually played. He had left the club at about 3.30 p.m. but had not arrived at his home in Neuilly until 4.45 p.m. On a Sunday, this journey would take no more than half an hour. This forty-five-minute discrepancy posed a problem.

"I visited a number of tobacconists trying to find Silver Star cigarettes, an American brand. There aren't many tobacconists open on Sundays. In fact, I didn't manage to find any before I came home."

The investigating magistrate, who had previously been satisfied with this answer, suddenly saw things differently.

"It's hard to imagine he used the time to go to Le Régent to murder his wife," said Commissaire Templier.

But Juge Lenoir had found a bone, and was determined to gnaw on it.

"The witness has made a categorical identification . . ."

"I'm not sure I'd say it was categorical . . ."

"And then there's the gap in his alibi. Forty-five minutes. More than enough time."

The magistrate issued an arrest warrant for Marcel Servières.

Commissaire Templier executed the warrant, braved the flashbulbs of the photographer hiding outside Servières's home, responded evasively to François Pelletier's questions, and drove Marcel Servières back to the Palais de Justice. Only at this point did the magistrate begin to consider the delicacy of the situation.

While it was true none of the tobacconists open that particular Sunday remembered a visit from the celebrated actor ("And it's not as though people wouldn't recognise him," growled the magistrate, "his face is plastered all over the newspapers!"), this was merely negative evidence. To make matters worse, Commissaire Templier pointed out that Marcel Servières had not had forty-five minutes to kill his wife, only ten.

"What do you mean, ten minutes?"

Juge Lenoir had a habit of standing on tiptoe when he wanted to express his outrage. The commissaire was not impressed.

"It would take Servières thirty minutes to get from the billiard club to Le Régent. If we assume it would take another thirty minutes to get from the cinema to Neuilly, we're left with ten minutes."

"It's still possible," said the magistrate.

"Perhaps, but barely. He would have to park his car, slip into the cinema without being noticed, find his wife, kill her, leave the cinema, get back in his car . . . All that in the space of ten minutes, it would be tough, very tough."

"But he's a tough customer!" said the magistrate, oblivious as always to the commissaire's sarcasm.

A visit to the crime scene confirmed that the lock on the emergency exit was broken, so it would be easy to get in and out of the cinema. Servières was well aware that his wife always hid until the film had started, and it was possible to walk from the emergency exit to the toilets without being seen by anyone in the audience. He would have been able to leave as discreetly as he had arrived.

As far as Juge Lenoir was concerned, the case was all but closed. He had Servières arrested and was convinced of his guilt. Who but Servières had known that Mary Lampson would be at that particular cinema? Who else could have known which screening she had decided to attend? These were questions that the magistrate could temporarily ignore. Right now, the only important thing as far as he was concerned, was how to shoehorn his theory into the Pandora's box he had just opened.

Le Journal ran with the headline:

SERVIÈRES ARRESTED IN MARY LAMPSON MURDER CASE
HUSBAND IS NOW CHIEF SUSPECT

There remained, of course, the matter of a motive.

"Mary Lampson wanted a divorce, Servières was furious," the magistrate said.

"That's just a rumour, Lampson hadn't filed for divorce ..."

"He was jealous. The brutal way she was killed makes it clear this was a crime of passion!"

At the doubtful look on the face of Commissaire Templier, the magistrate added:

"She wanted a divorce, she had a lover, Servières had admitted as much. He was jealous, that much is certain."

At this point he crowed triumphantly:

"And another thing: if Mary Lampson didn't have a lover, why didn't she tell her husband that she was pregnant?"

"Maybe she wanted to be sure. She was only two months pregnant, so maybe she didn't want to give him false hope."

Every man in the starlet's entourage had been investigated in an attempt to identify Mary Lampson's "lover". Her relationships had been scrutinised. Every man whose first name began with "M" had been questioned. But to no avail. The fact that the magistrate believed in the existence of this lover made Commissaire Templier deeply uncomfortable.

François had been right when he suspected that the two men's theories did not agree: after making his reservations clear, the commissaire, aware that he was an officer of the law and not a friend of Juge Lenoir, threw up his hands as if to say: "You go ahead, do what you like."

"The only way to know for sure is to try for ourselves!" said Juge Lenoir.

"Murder a woman?"

"No, no," said the magistrate, who took every statement literally. "See whether the journey can be made in that time."

François chose the headline:

COULD MARCEL SERVIÈRES HAVE MURDERED MARY LAMPSON?

Reconstruction to prove whether he had time . . . or not

*

Hélène, who had been sitting at the back of the Café des Arts for more than an hour, was beginning to fret. Ever since François had told her that Étienne was coming to Paris, she had been frantic. It was clear that her brother was in danger, but Hélène could not begin to imagine what kind of danger. What kind of enemies might he have made? She was convinced that François had not told her everything. She couldn't see through the whole thing. If anything happened to Étienne, she would never forgive herself. What she needed right now was a shot of amphetamine.

This thought simply exacerbated her panic. Nervously, she drummed her fingers on the table and glared at the door. Jonsac had promised to be there by noon, but Hélène had never known him to be on time.

A customer had left a copy of *Le Journal* on the banquette. The Mary Lampson case, which should have been solved in a matter of days, had now been dragging on for months. Everyone was completely obsessed with the case, especially François. Meanwhile, Étienne was risking . . . "Risking his life" was what she had thought; why did she always assume the worst?

She read François's article and then found herself studying the front-page picture of Marcel Servières. He was typical of the kind of men she did not like but slept with; he looked a little like Lhomond, a future ageing Lothario. She had barely slept with anyone since Lhomond, she had been pure and chaste. Give or take the occasional lapse. The first had very nearly been Vladimir Ulyov, who had since disappeared without trace. When she brought him back to her bedroom, she had made up her mind. She didn't particularly like him, but, on the plus side, he didn't look like her former maths teacher. He would not hit or humiliate her. That evening, Vladimir had launched into an interminable disquisition on the comparative merits of Lautréamont and Baudelaire and fallen asleep fully clothed. Then, it turned out that he suffered from a form of sleep apnoea; he grunted and moaned in his sleep, in the throes of some erotic dream. Hélène had not got a wink of sleep all night.

The second exception had been Jonsac. While at first he had been happy with very little, in recent days there had been doubts hanging over their relationship . . . Just then he strode into the café, alone for once, smiling, relaxed, wearing a flower-print waistcoat that shrieked bad taste and a lurid cravat that made him look like a clown masquerading as an artist, which is what he was. He walked through the café, shaking hands with everyone he passed, kissing a number of the girls; Hélène could have sworn that he was deliberately dragging his feet, trying to make himself seem desirable. As if she could desire such a man.

"You're not reading this, are you?"

As he sat down, he grabbed *Le Journal* and tossed it across the table, as though it stank. Hélène was offended, but made no protest.

"Just give me a pill," she said.

"Thing is . . ."

Jonsac did not look at her, he was staring at the other side of the café. Then, abruptly, he turned to her.

"It's a bit of a rare commodity at the moment . . ."

Relieved to have delivered the bad news, he carried on in the tone of a trader:

"Maxiton, Corydrane, Préludine . . . they're all in short supply. But, while we're on this subject . . ."

Hélène pricked up her ears. Jonsac dropped his voice to a whisper; he still could not bring himself to look at her.

"We're off to get fresh supplies."

"Who is 'we'?"

"Bernat, Lagre, me. Maybe you. What I mean is . . ."

Hélène had no idea what he meant, but knowing that it would be some hare-brained idea, she sat, mute, making no attempt to help him. It was she who was silent now, who stared towards the front door.

"It's a pharmacy, right? A dead cert. We've got a deal with the lab assistant who only takes a fifteen per cent cut. They've got everything you could possibly want."

"And how are you supposed to get in?"

"I can't tell you that. Security reasons . . ."

He shot her a conspiratorial look.

"Thing is, we need someone to keep a lookout."

He rummaged in his pocket and fished out a little pink pill that he offered to Hélène, who simply shook her head.

A little flustered, Jonsac reached for the bottle of water on the next table, poured a thimbleful into Hélène's empty coffee cup. The result was an unappetising brownish liquid, but Jonsac did not look. He popped the pill and washed it down with the contents of the cup.

"You don't have to actually do anything. We'll put you in a strategic place so you can stand lookout. If anyone approaches, you blow your whistle and get out, that's it."

"I don't have a whistle."

"We'll give you a whistle."

"Like a police whistle?"

"Exactly like that."

Hélène was about to tell him to get lost. It was the coffee cup that changed her mind. Suddenly she didn't feel she needed a pill any more. Maybe she would never take one again. Once she knew that, there was no reason to refuse.

"Five thousand francs."

"Ha! Who the hell do you think you are?"

"Someone who's about to act as lookout for three guys breaking into a pharmacy, who'll be able to line their pockets if they don't end up in prison."

"Yeah, but, five thousand francs . . ." Jonsac shook his head.

From his tone, she knew that she could have asked for more. But it didn't matter; Hélène wanted to do it for the thrill. For the fun of it, she told herself. Robbing a pharmacy was more exciting than a handful of methedrine pills.

*

"I'm convinced he had time to murder her!"

Geneviève had always loathed Marcel Servières for reasons Jean could never quite understand. Could she reasonably question his guilt?

"I don't like the look of him," she said. "He plays the juvenile lead, but I can tell he's a pervert ..."

Jean was at the local post office in Lamberghem, a village of a few hundred souls north of Béthune where he hoped to sign a contract with a small family business to make household linens.

It had been raining since he got here. Through the windows of his booth, he could see, beneath a leaden sky, the torrent lashing at the post office windows.

"They're going to do a simulation ..."

Jean did not understand, so Geneviève had to explain.

"In order to find out whether he had enough time to kill his wife. They'll take a car and drive the route he would have driven, so they'll find out ..."

"It's useless," Jean interrupted.

"We don't know that – they're not doing it until this afternoon."

"No, not that, the negotiations with the linen factory in Lamberghem, they didn't work out."

There was a long silence while Geneviève absorbed the blow.

"What in God's earth did you say ...? Or have these people got so much work they can afford to turn down orders?"

Jean had prepared a plea of mitigation, but was prevented from giving it by a passing column of army trucks that made the ground tremble and the walls of the post office shake. Instinctively, like a man watching a passing train, Jean mentally counted the trucks: ten, twelve, fifteen – the convoy seemed endless. Northern France was in turmoil, the miners' strike had become aggressive, the government had cranked up its rhetoric, the confrontation had begun to look like a civil war, the police had been sent in, and after them, the army, now both camps were brutally vying with each other,

333

blaming each other for events far beyond their control, the strikers had turned "scabs" out of their offices, had baited them in their own homes, women had had their heads shaved. The socialist government sent in armoured cars to subdue the demonstrators, whom they considered communists intent on overthrowing the Republic. Striking miners had set up barricades around the pit heads and shut down power stations. There was a rash of power outages, no one knew what would happen next, tens of thousands of people had taken to the streets of Verquin and Béthune. The riot police were launching "tear gas grenades", a weapon first used a year earlier against other striking workers. No one had ever seen so many gendarmes, police officers, riot troops and soldiers launching a concerted attack on demonstrators, everyone was on edge. This was the area that Jean had to drive through.

"Well, you'll be pleased to know that everything here is going fine," Geneviève said curtly. "The renovations to the shop are going full steam!"

In other words: Geneviève was up to the task; Jean was not.

"They've had to lay people off in the past few months," said Jean. "And now they don't have enough staff to take on an order like ours . . ."

He saw the postmistress, a rather young woman, plain-featured with a muddy complexion. The accordion door to the phone booth was so thin that she could hear every word. A substitute postmistress, she had explained after it took her three attempts to connect the call. She did not even pretend she was working, she rested her chin on her hands and listened to the conversation, as though it were a radio show. Jean turned his back and lowered his voice.

"Speak up, Bouboule," snapped Geneviève, "I can't hear a thing!"

"They don't have enough staff . . ."

"Did you suggest that they subcontract the work?"

"Um . . . no, I thought that . . ."

"What did you say? Articulate, for God's sake! Ar-ti-cu-late!"

Jean sighed then whispered: "I thought . . ."

"So, you've started to think, have you? Well, then we're doomed!"

"I'm heading to Berquieux this evening . . ."

"To where? I can't hear you!"

"BER-QUI-EUX ..."

It was articulated in a breath.

"And if it doesn't work out, where are you planning to go? Belgium? Holland? The North Pole?"

"They have more staff in Berquieux ..."

"Are you going to sort this out?"

Jean longed to hang up. He could feel the postmistress's eyes boring into his back. She had little else to do, the post office was completely empty. He wondered whether she could hear Geneviève's side of the conversation.

"Everything will be fine," he stammered, "I promise ..."

"Useless idiot!"

Geneviève slammed down the receiver.

Startled by the unexpected disconnection, Jean pretended to carry on the conversation.

"Yes, yes ... all right ... I'll do that then ..."

He deliberately left long silences during which he nodded at what his imaginary interlocutor was saying. And to give further weight to his fiction ("All right, I'll tell him that, all right ... Sorry"), he turned to the postwoman, who was beaming broadly as she brandished the blue telephone cable from which dangled the plug she had removed as soon as Geneviève hung up.

Jean blushed furiously. Then, unsure what to do, he pretended to finish his conversation:

"All right, I have to go, all right, bye ..."

He was still holding the receiver and staring at the walls of the booth, which were scrawled with phone numbers and various phrases, innocent and lewd. There was a length of string from which hung the Pas-de-Calais telephone directory, soiled by various hands, the dog-eared pages half-torn out.

He had no strength left.

"We're closing up now!" said the postmistress.

Jean dropped the handset and let it dangle, pushed open the creaky accordion door. He was pouring with sweat.

"How much do I owe you?"

He could not bring himself to meet her eye; he pretended to look for change in his wallet. He could tell that she was grinning, could feel her mocking expression. The postmistress and Geneviève were both right, he was a useless idiot. He paid. He wished he could die. He headed for the door.

"Goodbye . . ." called the postmistress, in a clear, sing-song voice. The lights went out behind him.

It was still raining. Jean stood in the doorway, watching as sheets of rain swept along the street and storm drains overflowed onto the pavement.

As he pulled up the collar of his gabardine, he turned and saw the postmistress, who had just opened the door and was searching for the right key on her keyring, trying one and then another. She assumed that Jean was trying to help when she saw him grip his walking stick, but already he had thrown the door open and brutally pushed her back into the post office where she stumbled, her arms flailing as she attempted to steady herself on the counter, then slipped, twisted her ankle, lost her balance and crumpled. Jean slammed the door behind him and lunged at her. By chance, the young woman had fallen next to the phone booth. Jean grabbed the dangling black receiver and beat with all his strength again and again. Blood spurted everywhere. Still Jean carried on. The woman's head had caved in and she had slumped onto her side. The telephone cord was too short. Jean tugged at the handset, but he could no longer reach her. He stopped. The broken nose, the shattered brow ridges and the mouth full of broken teeth made her unrecognisable. The dark pool of blood began to spread. Jean dropped the receiver and stood up straight. The post office was plunged into darkness. Jean lurched towards the door and opened it. He stood on the threshold for a moment; it was still raining heavily. As he pulled up the collar of his gabardine, he noticed a smudge of blood on the edge of his palm. He looked around for somewhere to wipe his hands, but could see nothing, so he knelt down and rinsed them in the gutter. Then he set off along the deserted street, crossed over and walked back to his car. He climbed behind the steering wheel, started the engine.

The wipers flicked ineffectually and Jean had to wipe the misted windscreen.

On the passenger seat lay a road map, which Jean spent some time consulting.

Berquieux was no more than ten kilometres away, and he would easily find a hotel there.

*

It was not difficult for François to work out the route for the re-enactment of Servières's drive from République to Le Régent and on to Neuilly. It would inevitably be the quickest route.

He traced a map of the main thoroughfares the car would take. Malevitz picked it up and eyed it sceptically.

"It's not exactly ... attractive, your little drawing. Not very graphically interesting. There's no way it's going on the front page!"

Denissov also studied the map, but reacted very differently. Grabbing one of the thick blue pencils he used to slash articles he considered too long, or to scrawl angry notes over sentences he thought garbled, he traced large incriminating arrows along the streets and circled the main crossroads. From a distance, the map had the dramatic, ominous look of a poison-pen letter. Once neatly redrawn, the map appeared on the front page, where it had a singular dramatic power: you could sense that something terrible was about to happen on those streets.

This was also what Geneviève thought as she flicked through her *A–Z* of Paris and inspected the route. Having completed her study, she jabbed at one of the pages and said: "There!"

She glanced at her watch and decided she had time to make a brief detour to a fishing tackle shop before setting off for the place de la République.

Meanwhile François and many of his colleagues joined the group that was about to set off from the rue des Filles-du-Calvaire. Cameras clicked incessantly and photographers vied for shots of Marcel Servières, looking pale and tense, surrounded by his three lawyers, Juge Lenoir, who did not know which way to turn, and

Commissaire Templier, who calmly continued issuing instructions to the motorcycle escort and ensured that the route was correctly marked out.

The plan was that Servières would drive his own car, with the magistrate, the commissaire and one of his own lawyers. The car would be led by two outriders, whose job was not to clear the streets (it was crucial that the journey be made in actual traffic conditions), but to ensure that no unexpected complications interrupted the rigorous reconstruction.

Commissaire Templier turned around and gazed at the swarms of cars (lawyers, reporters, onlookers) intent on following the cortège. They were lapping it up.

Juge Lenoir could not resist the urge to saunter over to the reporters and explain his stratagem. From the smug smile that lit up his face, it was clear this was one of the greatest days of his life. He talked about "the rumblings of justice", about his "fair and scrupulous investigation", about the "march of truth"; then, bloated with pride, he climbed into Servières's car and gave the starting signal. It looked like a rally.

Lenoir had brought a huge stopwatch, which he had probably bought specially for the occasion. The trip would be made twice to ensure an accurate journey time.

Servières disengaged the clutch, shifted into first gear and drove off without a word.

The caravanserai set off, only to encounter some teething problems as they approached the first red light.

Realising that there was a risk they would be separated from the convoy, a number of reporters overtook Servières and waited on the far side of the junction, causing a traffic jam that the outriders had difficulty in dispersing. The lawyer who was sitting in the back, feverishly taking notes, announced: "These hold-ups will be of crucial importance if this should come to trial." Juge Lenoir paled as he saw several more vehicles pass as photographers tried to get shots of Servières at the wheel. A reporter on the back of a motorbike shouted:

"Marcel, how are you feeling?"

The lawyer lost his temper, the magistrate screamed: "For God's sake, get out of the way," then turned to the commissaire, prepared to blame him for the chaos.

"There are insufficient officers patrolling the route, Commissaire!"

"There are officers in front, officers behind, and officers stationed along the route. If you required a security detail on the scale of a state visit by the King of Saudi Arabia, you had only to ask, I would have requested further reinforcements."

And, seeing the magistrate open his mouth to say something, the commissaire added:

"This is what happens when you notify the press rather than conducting the re-enactment discreetly. To say nothing of doing it on a weekday when the crime was committed on a Sunday, when traffic would move more freely."

The comment left the magistrate stunned. He had made two grievous errors. He had yielded to temptation by inviting the press so they could see his work and commend his judicial prowess, and he had forgotten that this was a Saturday, not a Sunday. He turned to the lawyer in the back seat, who had put away his notebook and was now languidly gazing at the streets of Paris. The re-enactment, he had decided, was an abject failure, it would be given short shrift by a magistrate when the case came to trial . . . if that day ever came.

Juge Lenoir watched helplessly as photographers on motorcycles weaved around the car, as Servières clenched his jaw and turned his face away every time one of them approached, at the cacophony of car horns. The re-enactment had quickly become a Calvary, and the junction at La République would prove to be his Golgotha.

As Servières pulled up at the traffic lights, he drew alongside a woman who was sitting on an angler's folding chair.

"Murderer!" she shrieked.

Everyone turned to look, Servières first.

"Bastard! Murderer!"

This particular junction had been carefully chosen. It was the longest red light on the route.

"Oh, my God . . ." babbled Servières.

"The guillotine, that's where you belong! The guillotine!"

The lawyer made to get out of the car, as did Servières.

"Stay where you are!" stammered Juge Lenoir, then turned to the commissaire. "Aren't you going to do anything?"

"If I take the time to get out and have this woman moved along, it will interfere with the timing of the re-enactment. But it's your decision."

Perched serenely on her folding chair, Geneviève continued to scream:

"Murderer! The guillotine! Murderer!"

The magistrate peered through the window.

"Oh, good God!"

It was that woman who had insisted that her husband take part in the identity parade. The torrent of abuse came so thick and fast that he could not think of her name ... Pelletier, that was it, Pelletier! She was dogging his every step.

"Murderer! Bastard! The people will get you!"

The magistrate racked his brain trying to work out which articles of the penal code this woman was violating, but could think of none. If he had this madwoman forcibly removed, she would pester him for weeks, for months, she would become his nemesis.

"Shut up!" he said in a pathetic, almost inaudible voice that testified to the extent of his failure.

Servières had rolled up his window and was glowering resentfully at the red light. But it was not enough; through the closed window they could still hear her.

"Bastard! They'll lop your head off!"

The reporters in the cars behind could hear the screams, but it was difficult to tell where they were coming from. None were prepared to get out of their car to look for fear of being left behind.

At last, the light turned green.

The caravanserai set off again.

By the time François's car drove past the junction, Geneviève had quietly folded her angler's chair and self-righteously scurried away.

33

Unless he can find someone to help him, it will all be over

Étienne was sleeping little, smoking too much opium, and gradually sinking into a paranoid delirium that made him skittish and nervous. He jumped at every noise and shadow, spent hours standing by the window scanning the area, restricted his outings to the strict minimum. Joseph had come to terms with this and spent his time perched on top of the fridge, curled around the Buddha, watching as Étienne paced and sighed.

Étienne kept changing his mind about the details of their departure.

On the second day, he began to worry about how to get from Saigon to the airfield at Biên Hòa. He had considered asking Loan to send a car, but if news of his departure were to leak, someone would try to intercept him on the ride there. Whatever the nature of the attack, there would be no way to escape it in an ordinary car. This thirty-kilometre stretch of road seemed to him the weakest link in their plan.

He brooded for two days, then took all the money he had, said goodbye to Joseph (every time he left the apartment, he cradled the cat and said goodbye; Joseph was growing a little tired of the routine) and headed for the Café Camerone where his appearance caused a stir.

The two soldiers who had beaten him up in Hiến Giang a few days earlier instantly recognised him and burst out laughing. Étienne thought he heard them say: "He's come back for more," but this did not stop him. He walked over to the square-jawed, blue-eyed veteran, who had not joined in their laughter. He could tell that some higher logic, some grave reason, had brought Étienne here. He got to his feet and stepped out onto the terrace. The legionnaire said nothing, but simply waited, as was his style.

Étienne summed up the situation in a few short words, and was surprised that it did not provoke the reaction he expected.

"Gooks trafficking in piastres ...? Yeah, there's been rumours circulating for the past few months. If it's true, it's depressing, because it means my men are dying for nothing, for nobody. I just hoped it was a lie."

It was a simple statement, but as the legionnaire stood, staring into the distance, it was clear his mind was teeming with conflicting images.

"I'll have proof within a couple of days," said Étienne, "maybe a couple of hours. Concrete proof. I'm planning to take it to Paris so a major newspaper can publish it."

The soldier gave a fatalistic shrug; he had little faith in such a plan.

"Many of your comrades—"

"Stop!" The legionnaire interrupted Étienne and stared him in the eye. "Don't try that emotional blackmail, I'm a soldier, you don't stand a chance."

"This isn't about emotional blackmail, it's about justice. The soldiers" – he no longer used the word "comrades" – "of the 2nd Regiment were slaughtered with weapons funded by the French government. I'm going to expose these people ..."

He paused.

"I need an armed escort to Guynemer airfield near Biên Hòa. Thirty kilometres, a thirty-minute trip. If anyone's going to try and stop me, it will be then. If I can make it to the airfield, there's a plane waiting."

"Bon voyage."

That was it; the soldier gave a curt nod, turned and disappeared into the bar. Étienne listened as lively conversations started up again, heard a burst of laughter. He had failed.

He reverted to his original plan.

For their escape, Vĩnh would leave first, taking Joseph in his basket. Étienne would follow with the dossier. They would take nothing else, no suitcases, no bags, nothing conspicuous. The three would meet on rue Catinat where they would take a taxi, and a second, and a third if necessary, only giving the last driver their final destination in Biên Hòa.

As he headed home, Étienne, who had no illusions about the prospect of his plan succeeding, deliberated. Was it really wise to go and buy a gun? Not because the transaction was inherently dangerous, but given that in Saigon everyone knew everything, to buy a pistol (or a revolver? Étienne did not know the difference) would draw attention to him. But by now Étienne was impervious to reason, to logic. So, he wandered into the alleys lined with the smoke shops he used to frequent. He spoke to someone who referred him to someone else who referred him to a third man, leaving traces everywhere.

Eventually, he emerged with a Nagant 1895. He had handed over two-thirds of everything he possessed, and had come away disappointed: because the gun was a revolver (he'd hoped for a flat sleek pistol of the kind he'd seen in spy movies; this looked more like something out of a western), because it was Russian (instinctively, he mistrusted communist weapons), and because he had only been given six bullets (he wasn't planning to mount a siege, but even so, six bullets, when you thought about all the shots that went wide . . .).

It is difficult to recount what happened next, because everything happened so fast.

Shortly before eight o'clock, Joseph suddenly jumped down from the fridge and leaped up onto the windowsill. Then came the muffled sound of footsteps on the stairs.

Joseph crept down from the windowsill and climbed into his basket.

Étienne's first thought was that they had come to get him, perhaps to kill him. He raced over and lifted the two floorboards to reveal the place where he had hidden the revolver, and frantically felt for the six bullets, which he was sure he had left right next to it . . . Hardly had he found them when Vĩnh raced in, terrified and panting. He was carrying a large grey box file, and had the haggard look of a child who is wondering: "What have I done?"

He did not say a word; he could barely catch his breath.

Étienne stared at the box file, thinking: "I hope it's all there." Though he did not say as much, Vĩnh could sense it.

Étienne set down the revolver, took the box file over to the table, and untied the strings.

Inside were invoices bearing the letterheads not just of Indochinese companies but of French ones, bank transfer receipts, account statements, letters, names, addresses, signatures, this file was dynamite ... Leafing nervously through the contents, he discovered orders from armaments companies in Bangkok and Manila. A lot of the documents would need to be translated from Chinese or Vietnamese, but it was all here. Monsieur Qiao, being a canny comprador, kept a record of the proceeds from the illicit transfers, since he received commissions at each stage. His total profits must have been colossal.

Étienne closed the file and tied it up.

"We need to leave."

But, turning, he saw Vĩnh was curled up on the floor, his back against the partition wall, his fists clenched, sweat streaming down his face. What had he had to do to get the dossier? From his panic, it seemed clear that someone was already after him ...

Étienne grabbed him under the arms, but could not lift him to his feet.

"Everything will be all right," he crooned.

But everything was not all right. Vĩnh was limp, lifeless.

"I'll go get a taxi," said Étienne. "You wait here. Don't try to move."

Vĩnh did not seem to understand.

"You wait here," Étienne said again. He took the file and hid it in the recess under the floorboards. He placed the revolver in Vĩnh's hands, but the boy could barely grip it.

"If anyone comes, shoot ..."

It was a foolish thing to say. To shoot, he would have had to be able to cock the hammer, raise the gun and aim. Right now, he could not even hold it.

Étienne raced across the landing and down the stairs.

He was panting for breath by the time he reached the street, but he forced himself to walk casually – quickly but casually. The hustle and bustle of the rue Catinat fuelled his anxiety; there were too many people, too many risks. He wanted nothing more than to give up, but it was too late for that.

He hugged the shop windows, stayed as far as possible from the edge of the pavement. The taxi rank was up ahead, next to the line of parked cars. It took almost ten minutes for him to reach it.

There were no taxis waiting. Étienne was bewildered, he had never seen the rank empty. Usually there was a huddle of drivers standing around smoking, and as each taxi left, the remaining drivers would push their cars forward to save on petrol.

Could this be a sign? But a sign of what? Not wanting to loiter on the corner, Étienne slowly wandered across the road and stood there, trying to look unruffled as he kept one eye on the rank. A moment later, a taxi pulled up. But Étienne did not like the look of the first driver, or the second – it was completely irrational. Within minutes, there were half a dozen cars. Still Étienne did not move. Something inside him balked, told him to turn back. He had to stop; this whole plan was madness.

The thought of Vĩnh finally forced him to decide: Vĩnh, lying on the floor of the apartment, clutching the useless revolver, and Joseph curled up in the basket. They were depending on him.

He crossed the road, spoke to a driver, climbed into the cab and they set off.

The elderly Vietnamese cabbie floored the accelerator. In the back seat, Étienne was tossed about.

"Just here," he said, and the driver slammed on the brakes.

Étienne ran inside and raced up the stairs.

Then, suddenly, he stopped dead.

The door to the apartment was ajar.

He pushed it open.

Vĩnh was lying in a pool of blood, his throat slit from ear to ear. Black blood gushed from the still-pulsing jugular vein.

Étienne collapsed in the doorway and burst into tears.

The apartment had been hastily ransacked. Joseph's cat basket was empty. The revolver, which Vĩnh had not been able to use, had been kicked across the room.

Étienne crawled over to where Vĩnh lay, and reached out a hand. The body was still warm, the young man's eyes were wide, staring, vacant.

Étienne rolled on the floor, but in a reflex that surprised even him, managed to clap a hand over his mouth to stifle a scream. Sick with grief and fear, he wished that he, too, could die. When he tried to get up, his found his hands were slick with blood. Moving on all fours, lest there was a gunman aiming through the window, he crawled over and lifted the floorboards.

The box file was still there.

Seeing it, his decision was made. He took out the dossier and hugged it close, then moved around Vĩnh's body looking for Joseph. Where could he be? Suddenly, nothing in the world mattered more to Étienne than finding his cat. Joseph! Joseph! Picture the scene, Étienne in tears, his hands smeared with blood, stumbling around the apartment looking for his cat.

The sight of the revolver jolted him back to reality. How long did it take him to get to the taxi rank? Twenty minutes? Whoever had done this had showed up just as he left; he had only just missed them. The apartment was big, but there was not much furniture, it wouldn't take long to search. *Joseph!* How many men had Vĩnh seen burst through the door? They didn't spend long questioning Vĩnh, they knew that Étienne had what they were looking for, what they had to find at all costs. *Joseph!* The bed had been upended, the mattress slashed with a machete – where would Joseph hide?

He hears a noise in the stairwell!

Étienne turns and stares at the doorway, so terrified that he instantly empties his bladder, a hot, wet feeling as though he were bleeding heavily.

A woman. She stands on the threshold and pops her head around the door. Étienne has seen her once or twice, but does not know her name. She stares at Vĩnh's body lying in the black pool that has spread almost to the doorway. She glances at Étienne and then, without a word, she vanishes.

She does not want to get involved.

Or she has gone to alert someone.

Étienne staggers out onto the landing, stumbles down the stairs, his feet missing the treads, clinging to the banister and clutching the dossier to his chest.

They will be back. They are searching for him now. Combing the streets. Questioning their informants. Sharpening their machetes. Turning the city upside down.

Étienne reaches the foot of the stairs, turns into the hallway, then flattens himself against the wall.

He had forgotten that the taxi is parked just outside.

Could they be waiting for him in the shadows? There is nothing he can do, so he sets off at a run, all but rips the front door off its hinges, throws himself onto the back seat of the cab.

"Le Camerone."

The elderly driver takes off at top speed.

The box file falls, spilling its contents on the floor.

Étienne clumsily gathers up the papers. The taxi driver has had his fair share of dodgy customers, but this man with the piss-soaked trousers and blood-stained hands seems particularly suspicious.

The moment he discovered Vĩnh's body, the moment he lost Joseph and found himself alone in the world, Étienne stopped thinking, stopped relying on reason, he is driven now by sheer instinct, and it was instinct that provided the address. Le Camerone. In theory, it is a clever move. Before long, the taxi driver will be telling everyone about this escapade, Vĩnh's killers are looking for him all over Saigon. Without an escort, Étienne is a dead man. Unless he can find someone to help him, he might as well throw himself in the river, it will all be over.

The streets flash past as they hurtle towards the legionnaires' bar. Étienne feels a wave of nausea and quickly rolls down the window. As he spews up his guts, the taxi driver does not even slow, he is eager to be rid of his troublesome client.

They have arrived.

The driver does not move a muscle. Étienne fumbles in his pocket, finds a wad of crumpled notes, tosses them onto the front seat, grabs the box file and gets out of the car. Before he can close the door, the driver has already roared away.

There are soldiers on the café terrace.

Seeing the taxi pull up and Étienne get out, one of them races inside and almost immediately the square-jawed legionnaire appears, calm and unruffled as always. He takes Étienne by the shoulder and steers him into the bar and shoves him onto a chair. The dossier flies open, documents flutter everywhere. Étienne kneels down to pick them up and stuff them back into the box. He is on all fours, freezing in his sodden trousers.

Around him, there is a deathly hush.

The soldiers are all holding drinks and cigarettes. None of them says a word, they simply watch as he gathers up his papers, his body racked by dry sobs, he looks as though he is having a nervous breakdown.

A strong hand catches him just as he loses consciousness.

*

A glass of water in his face.

Étienne thinks he is drowning, he gasps for breath, then sits up.

"We need to go now."

The veteran legionnaire is standing in front of him.

Étienne frantically struggles to remember. Le Camerone. He hears voices, but these are not bar-room conversations. They are muffled, whispering.

"Get up," says the legionnaire.

Gripping him under the armpits, he drags Étienne to his feet and steers him back into what he now realises is the bar.

The atmosphere is very different from when he arrived. He can see a dozen soldiers armed with machine guns and, as he is pushed towards the door, he hears the hum of the engines, three armoured cars, two equipped with machine guns. Étienne is hoisted into the back seat, someone forces him to lie down, covers him with a blanket.

"Guynemer, Biên Hòa, right?"

The convoy sets off.

Étienne cannot tell how fast they are driving, but the truck judders violently. Though he is struggling to breathe, he forces himself to lie still. He remembers Vĩnh's slumped body, the gaping throat, the lifeless eyes. He feels his heart hammer in his chest. What about Joseph? Did the cat manage to slink away, or was he thrown out the window?

Suddenly, the trucks brake hard.

The blanket is jerked away. Étienne is lifted down.

They are on a tiny airfield with only one runway. There are lights on in the low building; they approach on foot. It looks like the officers' mess of a makeshift airfield built twenty years earlier.

Étienne is surrounded by eight heavily armed legionnaires whose machine guns sweep the area in a full circle. Those at the rear are walking backwards. The veteran officer knocks on the door and, without waiting, opens it.

"Ah, so you finally got here!"

Étienne recognises the sepulchral voice of the German pilot. The man gets up from the table in the middle of the room, which is strewn with empty beer bottles. There is someone else, a Vietnamese man with a weathered face and grey hair who is wearing a strange green cap. His lower lip droops, it is hard to tell whether he is stupid or drunk.

The German pilot comes and stands in front of the soldiers. He seems unsurprised.

"Right, then, let's do this . . ." His words are slurred.

He stumbles outside, and they walk away from the building towards the ancient plane that Étienne has only just noticed.

Two rows of lights set into the ground create a path across the tarmac. The pilot's sidekick must be operating runway lights from the mess hall, since there is no control tower.

When they get to the plane, Étienne turns to the soldiers. He wants to say something. The old legionnaire gives him a faint smile and winks, nodding at the pilot who is clambering into the cockpit.

"Don't worry. He's flown drunk more times than he's flown sober. He's used to it by now."

Étienne extends a grubby hand. It is a mute question to which the legionnaire gives no answer.

"Right, we're done here," he mutters, beckoning the others.

Seconds later, they are in their trucks and heading back to Saigon.

The engine splutters into life, the whole cabin is shaking. Étienne manages to climb in. He is exhausted.

The pilot nods to one of the four empty seats, then takes the controls. If his eyes seem unfocused, his gestures are surprisingly precise. He turns and says something Étienne cannot hear, but seeing him gesture, Étienne looks around for the seatbelt. When he does not find it, he gives up.

Quivering like a leaf, the plane slowly begins to taxi. It pauses for a second as it reaches the middle of the runway, the engine revs, then gradually slows, the plane moves off, slowly at first, then quickly gains speed.

Despite his exhaustion, Étienne feels an almost physical sense of relief, as though a vice around his chest has been loosened. He is frozen from head to toe. He is still hugging the box file to his chest.

The plane takes off.

Looking through the window, Étienne sees the runway and the airfield grow smaller, and, further off, the line of armoured cars from which, he assumes, the legionnaires are watching.

The plane banks sharply to the west, passes over the tiny aero-drome. Through a gap in the treetops, he sees a parked car with its headlights on.

It looks like a limousine.

Idling.

The plane is flying at several hundred metres. Étienne peers out the window at the parked car.

A state-of-the-art limousine.

Although they are much too high for him to make out who is inside, Étienne instinctively knows.

It is Monsieur Qiao.

Instantly realising what is about to happen, he turns back to the pilot.

It is then that he hears the explosion.

The cabin jackknifes, and Étienne just has time to see the shattered windscreen of the cockpit as it plunges into the darkness. The door next to Étienne has been ripped away, the wind rushing in is like a hurricane. The pilot is slumped back in his seat, the plane is plummeting, its trajectory almost vertical.

Étienne slides across the steel floor and slams against the tattered partition. He is dazed by the blow and deafened by the ear-splitting roar of wind and engine and propellers.

In a brief flash, he sees his mother cupping his face in her hands and saying, "When will you be content with what life has to offer you, Étienne?"

He does not have time to answer.

He is still clutching the box file when what is left of the plane crashes into the ground and explodes.

III
October 1948

34

He doesn't take planes often enough

Louis trudged along, surprised to find himself opening his mouth slightly every time he inhaled, as though short of breath. Like an old man, he thought. No one reaches the age of sixty without suffering great hardships, and Louis had had his share, he would admit, without ever specifying what they were. But to lose a child . . . There was nothing worse. Only now, after he and Angèle had struggled to take in the news, after he had been to the post office to put calls in to Saigon and then to François, only now as he walked home along the avenue des Français did he finally start to weep, right there on the street. Caught off guard by the violence and abundance of his tears, Louis looked around for somewhere he could stop. Seeing a small space between two shops windows, he squeezed inside and there, with his forearm over his eyes like a child playing hide-and-seek, abandoned himself to his tears, his grief, whispering: "Étienne, Étienne," over and over, there was nothing he could say but the name of his son he had just lost.

The postmaster, Monsieur Cholet, had delivered the telegram in person. Geneviève's father usually revelled in the calamities that befell the Pelletier family, but on this occasion he could find nothing to say, he felt a lump in his throat, and, when the door opened, he simply handed Louis the telegram from the High Commission in Saigon. From Monsieur Cholet's expression as his trembling hand delivered the telegram, Louis knew that something tragic had occurred and that it had something to do with the children – what else was there to fear?

Instantly, he knew it was about Étienne. As though he had always feared this moment, sensed some vulnerability in his son that destined him to tragedy.

Louis accepted the telegram and silently closed the door on Monsieur Cholet, who was relieved that he had not had to say a word.

Angèle appeared from the kitchen, wiped her hands on her checked apron and brushed a lock of hair from her face. Seeing her husband, she opened her mouth to say something, then let her hands fall to her sides when she saw the telegram, the time bomb that seconds from now would reduce her life to dust. Neither of them moved. Eventually, Louis looked down, opened the telegram and read it. Angèle stood, motionless, waiting for the verdict. Which of my children is dead, she wondered, it could only be that.

Although they never talked about it, Angèle also knew instinctively that it was Étienne.

Louis did not need his glasses.

"It's Étienne," he said without looking up. "He's dead."

He laid the slip of paper on the table, walked over to his wife and took her in his arms and she wept, saying over and over: "How, how did he die?"

"A plane. A plane crash."

He had held her for a long time, and then Angèle had turned away, not wanting her husband to see her like this. She had gone to her room and gently closed the door; he had not dared follow. That soft click of the lock broke his heart.

Louis felt a hand on his shoulder.

He came to, he was on the avenue des Français, a hundred metres from the post office. He turned round, but his eyes were so blinded with tears he could not see.

"Are you all right?" a bell-like voice asked.

Louis rummaged for a handkerchief and dabbed at his eyes. She was a rather short woman of about thirty, a woman who looked much like any other, she was leaning close to him.

"It's Étienne," he said, "he's dead."

She nodded as if he were talking about a vague acquaintance, someone she did not know well enough to weep for, yet close enough for her to feel sad. She slowly shook her head, then walked away, her curiosity satisfied. Now that she knew why this old man was sobbing in the middle of the street, she could go on her way.

*

"ÉTIENNE PELLETIER DECEASED – STOP – PLANE CRASH – STOP – SINCERE CONDOLENCES – STOP."

Louis had sat down at the dining room table, dazed, unsure what to do. Much later, Angèle came to find him. She had taken off her apron, changed her clothes and brushed her hair. She picked up the piece of paper and unfolded it, as though she needed to check: plane crash.

"We need to tell the children . . ."

She had almost said "the other children". She sat down and stared blankly out the window. Louis knew that they would not talk about it now, so he got up, put on his jacket and slipped the telegram into his pocket.

At the post office, he requested the phone number for François's newspaper in Paris. News did not travel fast, but surely they would have heard about a plane crash in Indochina. Then he changed his mind.

"Could you put me through to Saigon?"

It was an uncommon request, and the operator did not quite know what to do. "Yes, of course," she said, turning to an older colleague who got up and walked over to the switchboard.

Louis made a quick calculation. It would be 3 p.m. there.

"The High Commission, Saigon, please, I'm afraid I don't know the number."

What Louis most feared was being passed from one office to another, having to repeat himself, to ask over and over whether anyone knew anything about the death of Étienne Pelletier. In the end, it did not happen.

"I am so sorry for your loss, Monsieur Pelletier . . ."

It was the calm voice of authority. Measured. Youthful. There was a brief silence. The man spoke slowly, as though talking to a foreigner who has not mastered the language.

"Your son was on a flight from Biên Hòa, a few kilometres from Saigon, heading for Phnom Penh. It was a private plane, it came down shortly after take-off."

Came down. Whoever was speaking did not say it had crashed.

"Were there many fatalities?"

"Not many, as far as we know."

"What does that mean?"

"We believe that the only people aboard the plane were the pilot and your son, Monsieur Pelletier. No one else."

How could Étienne be the only passenger? Could he afford to rent a plane? The man had said it was a private plane, perhaps Étienne had been going on a tour? When his son had first heard about the job at the Exchange, Louis had pored over a map. Phnom Penh was to the west of Saigon, in Cambodia.

Was that where Angkor Wat was?

"Of course, Papa." Étienne had laughed. "It is the eighth wonder of the world!"

"I thought there were only seven wonders of the world?"

"Yes, Papa, but since only one of the original seven is still standing, and tourism constantly needs new wonders, the old list has been replaced and expanded. Maybe next time your soap factory stands a good chance."

Étienne has an answer for everything, his father often said.

"Hello? Are you still there, Monsieur Pelletier?"

"Yes, yes . . . How did it happen? The accident, I mean . . ."

"It was an old plane, a Lockheed Vega decommissioned eleven years ago . . ."

"The plane was decommissioned?"

"Yes, but that's not uncommon. Just because a plane has been decommissioned doesn't mean it can't fly, but . . . well, let's just say that it requires more regular checks."

"Why did it come down, then?"

"I'm afraid we don't know yet, sir, we'll have to wait for the results of the investigation, but I have to tell you, it won't be easy."

Louis was trying to piece the thing together. A decommissioned plane, regular checks, an investigation that would not be easy . . .

"The area where the plane came down is difficult to access. In fact, from a military point of view, the whole region is unstable."

"What about the body . . . What about my son . . .?"

This was the difference between him and Angèle: had she been here, this was the first question she would have asked.

"Well . . . a unit has been dispatched to . . . recover the fuselage . . ."

The official was clearly weighing every syllable.

"And repatriate the remains."

"We'll come as soon as we can."

"That will not be necessary, Monsieur Pelletier. As soon as the unit returns, we will have your son's remains sent to Beirut – that is where you are currently?"

"Yes, but I wondered whether . . ."

"There is nothing you can do here, Monsieur Pelletier. Obviously, if you wish to bury your son in Saigon, then you are welcome to come. If, however, you prefer to have him laid to rest in your family vault, then it would be best to leave everything to the authorities."

Louis could not think straight. Angèle would never agree to burying Étienne in Saigon.

"Perhaps you're right . . ."

"This is what I suggest, Monsieur Pelletier. As soon as your son's remains are brought back to Saigon, we will have them repatriated to Beirut. I will confirm the details by telegram, if that suits."

Louis replaced the receiver, left the booth, paid at the counter and left the post office.

Images flickered through his mind. A smiling Étienne was boarding a tourist plane, the pilot was a friend, the plane was due to land a few hours later in Cambodia. The temples of Angkor Wat.

The last real image Louis had of his son had been at that long-ago meal. Louis had spent much time considering the toast he would give, and thought himself clever when he raised his glass and said: "To Saigon." It was there that Étienne had learned of the death of his friend Raymond, and there that he had lost his life. Louis could have kicked himself.

He was halfway home when he remembered that he had to let his other children know.

He was utterly shattered. He prayed that François would be out of the office working on a story, he could leave a message, he simply did not have the strength for anything else.

*

"Here, drink this," said Denissov, handing him a glass of whisky.

François waved it away, he loathed whisky. He was in his boss's office. Don't cry, he thought, don't cry. But it was such a brutal blow.

He had been in Denissov's office discussing the Mary Lampson case when the call was put through.

"It's François's father," said Monique, popping her head around the door. "Apparently it's urgent . . ."

Denissov had handed him the phone.

"Étienne is dead," his father said, tonelessly.

The whole room seemed to founder.

Behind his desk, Denissov seemed to be floating, pitching from left to right, sinking into air. François knew this feeling of looming panic; he had felt it once before during the war.

"How did he die?" he faltered. "How is this even possible?"

His voice was choked.

Denissov got up on the pretence of looking for something and left the office. François broke down; he collapsed onto a chair. The cord was short and the phone fell onto the floor. François rushed to pick it up.

"Papa, are you still there?"

"Yes," said Monsieur Pelletier. "A plane crash. On the way to Angkor Wat . . ."

There was a long silence.

"When did he die?"

Louis had not thought to ask.

"We got the news earlier today."

It was all he could say.

"The authorities will send his body back to Beirut."

So, it was true, thought François, Étienne really was dead.

360

"I'll send a telegram as soon as they tell me when Étienne's coming home."

The wording was ambiguous, but François could well understand that his father was finding it difficult to express himself.

"Can you please let Hélène and Bouboule know?"

François was about to say: "Hang on a minute!", but his father was already finishing.

"I have to go now, I need to take care of Maman. I love you, son."

He hung up.

François was dumbfounded.

Denissov came back in and walked around his desk.

"My brother," François felt he needed to explain.

He felt embarrassed to be crying in front of Denissov, but did not have the strength to get up and leave. It was at this point that his boss had offered him the glass of whisky – the American equivalent of a handkerchief – which François had waved away, afraid that it might make him throw up, as if things were not bad enough already.

"How?"

"A plane crash. In Cambodia."

Then the penny dropped.

Had he been at home, it would not have occurred to him, but here, in Denissov's office, the news took on a very different meaning. In any other situation, "a plane crash" would simply mean "a plane crash", but not here, not at *Le Journal*, not under the circumstances. He almost found himself telling Denissov the whole story, how his brother had promised to bring a dossier, a scoop, a political scandal in which high-ranking public figures were illicitly profiting from the traffic in piastres ... But he knew that he had no evidence. Especially since the dossier had doubtless disappeared along with Étienne. "No, no copies! I'm not prepared to part with anything, François."

"Was he a soldier?"

"No, he was working for the Indochinese Currency Exchange in Saigon."

"If you need a leave of absence to go there ..."

"No, thanks but no, they'll send his body home to Beirut, I mean, to my parents' home ..."

He too was finding it difficult to express himself; he simply could not find the right words.

"I need to break the news to Hélène, my sister. And to my older brother."

François had managed to get to his feet.

"Of course, of course," said Denissov. "Let Malevitz know, and go ... Take all the time you need."

Étienne's death felt just a little less cruel now that François saw it differently, as a tragic event that might not have been an accident ...

*

He never knew what time Hélène would come home. Or with whom. Or what state she would be in.

François sat chain-smoking, without even thinking to open a window. The thick haze in the room mirrored the confusion in his mind. He already felt that he was somehow to blame for Hélène's messy life, and with Étienne dead, he was afraid that she would sink even further into whatever debauched life she had been leading. Her breath often smelled of alcohol and tobacco smoke, but it was her glittering eyes with their pinpoint pupils and her violent mood swings that made him fear that Hélène was already in the grip of some deadly habit that would only be exacerbated by her taste for provocation.

He had decided to wait for Hélène to come home, to tell her first, because right now it required the least effort, and he felt exhausted, drained. That done, he would go to the Porte de la Villette and break the news to Bouboule.

He had not bothered to turn on the lights. He sat, stolid and unmoving, as if he had melted into the armchair, consumed by an emptiness that had sapped him of strength. Images of Étienne surfaced. Although there was only a year between them, they had

had nothing in common, and everything had pushed Étienne closer to his sister, though she was five years younger.

He pictured his brother at school, where he had been so lonely. He and François had not had the same gang of friends, in fact Étienne had had no friends. It pained him now to remember Étienne's solitude, and the permanent smile that, in death, took on an aching poignancy. They had rarely played together. François was ashamed to remember how he had distanced himself from his brother, because Étienne's "delicate side", as their mother put it, offended his burgeoning manhood. He was keenly aware of the playground jokes that quickly turned to insults that François pretended not to hear. "I defended him!" he would say in his defence, and it was true that he had never left Étienne to face the ordeal alone. But he always intervened at the last moment, and then almost reluctantly, and when he punched some boy who had insulted Étienne, it was actually his brother he was punching, hence his strength . . . It was past mending now, Étienne was dead, François would never be able to tell him how sorry he was, how wretched he felt. Death had planted a splinter of remorse in his life.

François looked up. The room was bathed in a pale glow.

The doorbell was ringing.

Hélène. He struggled to his feet. The bell continued to ring, angrily, impatiently. François trudged towards it, already crushed by the weight of the task he had to perform. It was as he reached for the handle that he remembered Hélène had her key, and that she never rang the bell.

He opened the door; it was not Hélène.

Geneviève, her face a mask of fury, stormed into the apartment then wheeled around to face him.

"So, I see family doesn't matter to you!"

François was bemused.

She was waving a slip of paper he could not read.

"I am sick and tired of this disrespect, do you understand? I know that I've never been more than an afterthought to all of you, I'm belittled, I'm barely tolerated, I don't matter."

She rushed at François as if about to push him out the window, stopping only when she was inches from his face. He could feel the rage radiating from her whole body.

"But because monsieur here writes for a newspaper, he thinks he can look down his nose at people, even his elder brother. Well, I won't stand for it!"

"I've no idea what you're talking about ... What the ...?"

"Really? You've no idea?"

She continued to wave the scrap of paper as she stalked about, as though intent on breaking everything in the room.

"So, Jean's got no right to be told, is that it? Everyone else gets to know, but Jean and his wife are treated with contempt, hmm?"

"What the bloody hell are you talking about?" François roared.

Geneviève was not remotely chastened.

"Jean had no right to be told about his brother's death. I suppose you think that's normal? Well, bravo! He's the eldest son, I'll have you know! Telling Jean should have been your number one priority! Instead, you sit here in an armchair, drooling and chainsmoking and waiting for what ...? A blue moon?"

François could now see that the piece of paper she was holding as she strutted around the room like an angry turkey cock was a telegram.

"But Jean's a weakling, he's always let this family walk all over him. A coward, that's what he is! Oh, if only I'd known! Not that anyone told me that when it came to the wedding. They were only too happy to get the idiot off their hands!"

François had regained something of his composure. So Geneviève's first thought, when she heard that Étienne was dead, was to make a scene.

"Thankfully, I have my own father!" she went on. "I have my own family, because otherwise ..."

"Shut up!" François shouted angrily.

I'm going to kick her out, he thought, and marched over to Geneviève, but she was looking straight past him, and, when he turned, he saw Hélène, her eyes glistening.

"You can be heard down in the street," she said.

The scene seemed strange, she had never seen François and Geneviève argue. What could have happened for them to end up fighting?

"Oh really?" said Geneviève in a shrill voice. "Well, I'm glad we can be heard down in the street! I want the whole world to know that your brother … that your brother …"

She gaped like a fish, searched for words that would not come. There was a silence. She tossed the telegram on the floor.

"I think your brother Bouboule doesn't take planes often enough!"

She made a gesture that was intended to be stately, as though draping herself in an invisible cloak, and with a spirited pirouette and a step as determined as when she entered, she left, slamming the door behind her.

Hélène looked from François to the telegram on the ground. They both stepped forward, but it was Hélène who grabbed it first.

She read it, blanched, and burst into tears.

She rushed at François, pounding his chest with her fists. "Étienne, I can't bear it, Étienne …" François made no attempt to stop her, he simply wrapped his arms around her and raised his chin to avoid the blows. After a moment, Hélène relaxed, she pressed her face into her brother's chest and sobbed for a long time. Then, suddenly, she pulled away, rushed to her room and slammed the door.

The telegram lay on the floor.

François could not help but pick it up.

"ÉTIENNE PELLETIER DEAD IN PLANE CRASH SAIGON – STOP – REMAINS REPATRIATED TO BEIRUT SOON – STOP – MONSIEUR PELLETIER PHONED FRANÇOIS WHO WILL TELL HÉLÈNE AND JEAN – STOP – PAPA"

Being the postmaster at the Beirut office, Monsieur Cholet did not pay to send telegrams.

35

Étienne wasn't that kind of person

Even the weather seemed to conspire against him. A day earlier, an icy, unpredictable wind had begun sweeping through the city, whipping the faces of anyone who stepped outside. For Louis Pelletier, this turbulent, unsettled weather was at odds with his need for order and structure. It had all begun when Étienne's remains arrived home.

Angèle had broken down, in her furious grief she could have killed the whole world. Louis had to hold her back, since Étienne's body had been shipped home in a coffin cobbled from scrapwood fit only to be thrown away. The undertakers hurriedly removed the makeshift casket. Angèle sobbed inconsolably all day.

Louis was haunted by another thought. What was in the box? What remained of his son? A jumble of pieces stuffed into lead-lined bags? His heart ached to think that Étienne was here in this crude coffin, and not even Étienne, but only what they had been able to find.

This was merely the first act of a long and complex episode that unfolded without order or method, a series of improvised decisions made by no one that seemed to emerge from the ambient chaos. Louis sensed that no one could help them.

The first decision was that the funeral procession should leave from the house. It was Angèle who had insisted, her tone so determined, so brittle, that it seemed this mattered to her more than anything; Louis acquiesced. As a result, between the undertakers and the family, the apartment was crowded, while friends and neighbours gathered on the stairs until one of the funeral directors gently suggested that they wait outside in the freezing cold. Furthermore, though the apartment was spacious, many of the rooms were difficult to access. The coffin had had to be tilted slightly to fit through the door and down the narrow hallway. Louis was dreading the removal because, with Étienne's remains inside, there was no room for trial and error. He fretted and paced. There was no one he could talk to.

Then came the funeral mass.

Étienne had not set foot inside a church after his first communion. The new parish priest, who had arrived three years earlier, was unknown to the Pelletier family – which spoke volumes about their religious zeal. But despite her secular leanings, Angèle insisted that there be a funeral mass, and so there was.

Louis agreed to everything, grumbling only to himself. His heart was heavy, but he did not let it show. It was up to him to buy the place in the cemetery and the grave which, in his mind, had quickly become the family vault. It was to bury Étienne, the youngest son, that a monument was to be inaugurated, which Louis, the oldest of them all, had never even thought of for himself. It was the one subject on which he and Angèle disagreed.

"It's pretentious," Angèle said when Louis showed her the photograph he had seen in the monumental mason's catalogue.

"It's dignified," he said.

It was obvious what he meant.

Angèle realised it was simply the memorial version of his need for respectability, the same need that had prompted him to have "Maison Pelletier et Fils" painted in large letters above the gateway to the soap factory. But this inscription embraced the whole family, and that thought chilled her. Not because she saw herself, or even Louis, in this vault, but because she imagined all of her children lying there, as though they were all fated to die prematurely. She felt as though the family might be obliterated overnight, as though they were all in the anteroom of death. But despite her misgivings, she agreed.

It was a roughcast mausoleum in the form of a Greek temple with a triangular pediment, two steps leading up to a stylobate on which stood three fluted columns (carved volutes and acanthus leaves, cyma recta cornices, dentils on the pediment), a pronaos set behind a wrought-iron gate and, inscribed on the tympanum, in high relief, "Famille Pelletier". It was vain, but the children said nothing because, in their grief, each was getting by as best they could.

Thereafter, things were a little more prosaic. At the cemetery, the coffin was lowered into the vault. The priest who had accompanied the cortège was a disillusioned man. During the obsequies, the family had had no idea when to sit and stand, to sing, respond, or make the sign of the cross: it was obvious that they had no religion. Louis surreptitiously observed the Cholets and did as they did. The priest had found it painful to watch such an ungodly spectacle. So, when they reached the cemetery, he simply said a few words; he considered that his presence was an indulgence.

Then came the litany of condolences.

The funeral directors had not mentioned this, they assumed it was taken for granted, but the Pelletier family felt dazed as they saw the mourners form a line – my God, how many were there, dozens, hundreds? – each stepping forward to throw a flower onto the coffin, shake the hands of the bereaved, and mumble the awkward, self-conscious words that go unheard. This proved too much for Angèle, who gripped Louis's arm and said: "Take me home." Hélène, exhausted with weeping, took her mother's other arm and, with faltering, hesitant steps, the three of them left the cemetery.

The two brothers stood by the graveside, forlorn, bewildered, utterly at sea. Then Geneviève, in her brand-new mourning dress, reached out and took the hand of the first mourner, she bowed her head sadly, and accepted their condolences with an anguished, whispered: "Thank you." Jean turned to suggest that perhaps it was not her place to . . .

"Please, Jean," she cut him short, "it's my duty."

One by one, the crowd filed past, shaking her hand, giving a brief embrace, and offering words of comfort which Geneviève accepted with the inexpressible mask of a *mater dolorosa*.

*

This time, given the urgency of the situation, the children travelled from Paris by plane. They were to fly back the following day. Monsieur Pelletier had paid for the tickets and, for the first time, he could not help but wonder when his children would be "on their own two feet". He was more than happy to pay, but would have been reassured to know they were financially secure.

The fact that Angèle allowed Louis to have a restaurant cater the funeral dinner was a sign of just how badly she was coping. In fact, she went to bed without eating. Hélène went with her.

The three men gathered in the living room. (Geneviève was spending the evening at her parents', where she was lavished with sympathy, both for her marriage to Jean and the sudden painful loss of her brother-in-law.) After asking François about his work and how he was finding living with his sister – "Everything's fine," said François, keen to get off the subject: there was too much for him to explain – Monsieur Pelletier turned to Jean to ask about his plan to open a linen shop. A plan in which Louis Pelletier had little faith, not because of the business model, but because he believed that a man who could not run a soap factory could never succeed at anything. "Everything's fine," said Jean. No two words filled Louis Pelletier with greater dread.

There was a lull in the conversation, the men smoked cigarettes, and each of them stared at his glass of fine wine, engrossed in his thoughts.

In the bedroom, Angèle and Hélène were sitting side by side on the counterpane.

"I didn't even think to ask, darling, how are things at the Beaux-Arts?"

"Wonderful."

The word came without a flicker of hesitation; she put all the energy she could still muster into the lie.

"But I don't really want to talk about it . . ."

"Of course," said Angèle, sympathetically.

This answer was enough to satisfy her, her mind was on other things.

It was Hélène, who had only gone along to keep her mother

company, who dozed off while Angèle sat next to the bed, holding her daughter's hand and brooding about her dead son.

Where were his belongings, she wondered. They had telephoned the High Commission again, someone had promised to make inquiries, but they had heard nothing since. Where were Étienne's clothes, his trunk, his possessions? Louis had promised to call Saigon again, but he had had so much to do. It was gruelling ... Angèle suddenly remembered the last time they had celebrated the factory's anniversary, when she and Étienne had walked home together and he had laid his head in her lap while Joseph ... No one had given a thought to Joseph. What had become of the poor cat?

Hélène woke with a start. "I'm sorry, Maman, I fell asleep ..."

Given that all the family were haunted by the same question, it was unsurprising that, in this moment of calm, the men in the living room and the two women in the bedroom were engaged in the same conversation.

Talking about what had caused Étienne's death.

François told his father about Étienne's telephone call, his plea that François write an exposé, the dossier he was planning to bring to Paris with concrete evidence of a financial scandal ...

"What scandal?" said Monsieur Pelletier.

"Something to do with the exchange rate between the piastre and the French franc."

Louis's eyes widened.

"What possible scandal could there be about exchange rates?" he said, then announced: "Besides, Étienne wasn't that kind of person."

"What kind?"

"The kind who goes around unearthing scandals. Étienne was a poet, not some knight in shining armour."

"Then why did he call me?"

"Oh, he may have heard some gossip, but can you seriously imagine Étienne as a detective?"

François had had precisely the same doubts from the outset. He was perplexed by the nature of this scandal and questioned his brother's ability to find hard evidence.

"You're saying he was planning to come to Paris? Then why was he on a private plane heading for Angkor Wat?"

In the next room, Angèle reacted just as sceptically to Hélène's professed conviction that Étienne was the victim of some sinister plot. When Hélène said that he had been on a private plane with only the pilot, Angèle assumed it had been just another love affair ...

"You should try to sleep, darling."

36

Another dead end

The children returned to France bitterly divided about the truth of the story.

The least persuaded was Jean, who had not even known the piastre was the currency of Indochina and could not understand how it amounted to a scandal. Hélène, on the other hand, was an avenging fury. She demanded that François investigate, that he rally the entire editorial staff of *Le Journal*, but nothing seemed to happen and she thought her brother a coward.

François, for his part, read up about the piastre and quickly found that what Étienne had said about the exchange rate was true. It was not difficult to imagine how people might be tempted to transfer piastres to France, where their value doubled, as if by magic.

He found himself in a predicament, one aggravated by his guilty conscience. On the one hand, he hoped he had just stumbled on the stuff of every journalist's dreams; on the other, he felt that he was using his brother's death as an excuse. He had no idea where to start. He could talk to his colleagues at *Le Journal*, but he knew they would not give him the resources to launch an investigation unless he could provide concrete evidence, and he could not get concrete evidence without the paper's editorial resources. It was a vicious circle.

He had spent his time in Beirut and his journey home brooding on the subject, reading and rereading the list of initials provided by Étienne (E. N.; P. R.; D. F.; A. M.; S. R.), five public figures who – supposedly – were illicitly profiting from the traffic in piastres. It all seemed very flimsy.

He sought out a colleague, André Lucas, a seasoned newshound who'd seen it all and had been navigating the cesspit of politics since the 1920s. Lucas was a decent guy who would be happy to answer his questions. When François did not find him in the editorial office, he made to leave.

"Why are you looking for him?" said Baron, clearly annoyed by François's intrusion.

"Nothing, just some information."

"Information is not nothing."

"No, what I mean is . . ."

"About?"

"Banque Godard. And Hopkins Brothers."

Baron raised an eyebrow.

"In what respect?"

By way of answer, François simply smiled, and Baron accepted this, though he did not smile.

"They are private banks," he said, "inaccessible to the *vulgum pecus*. Banque Godard requires that one deposit an exorbitant sum before it will open its doors. In exchange, it guarantees absolute opacity about all your transactions. Hopkins Brothers works hand in glove with the miscreants who dabble on the Stock Exchange and in illicit profits. Taken together they are two of the most vicious sharks to infest the morally turbid waters of international finance."

The low-key alarm ringing in François's head was suddenly a wailing siren.

"Are you considering opening an account with them?"

"That's right," said François with a forced laugh, which allowed him to leave without offering any further explanation.

Since he had no chance of persuading these banks to part with a list of their clients – even the tax authorities themselves had failed to do so – he found himself at another dead end.

He had the list of initials pinned over his desk, though he hardly glanced at it since he now knew it by heart. He found himself reciting it over and over, like a nursery rhyme. Whenever he tried to put it out of his mind, it came back, obscure and fascinating.

He was shaken from this fixation by a young woman of about thirty.

She had been waiting on the pavement outside the office. "There he is, that's him," said a colleague she had just asked. She approached him with a reticence he initially attributed to shyness, and stood, gripping the straps of her handbag. She exuded anxiety.

"Monsieur Pelletier ..."

She spoke in a whisper, glancing around as if for help. She was younger than François had first thought – twenty-five, perhaps not even that – and very pretty. She was dressed with a simple elegance intended to go unnoticed. She looked as though she were playing a role, a young woman dressed up as a wife.

François was immediately struck by this thought.

He took her by the arm, "Come with me," he did not want anyone else to see her, "There's a café nearby," and she meekly allowed herself to be led. When he turned to look at her, she looked as though she might burst into tears. He quickened his pace, and as he reassured her – "We're almost there, it's just up here" – his mind was racing, strategies already forming in his mind.

He chose a table at the back of the café.

"Please," he said, gesturing for her to take a seat.

He took her coat and laid it on the chair next to him. She was wearing a subtle perfume. As he sat opposite her, it was clear that she was extremely pretty. Her eyebrows were like slender wings above smouldering eyes and small, perfectly shaped lips.

"So, you were in Le Régent on the day Mary Lampson died, am I right?"

Her mouth fell open in a perfect "O". Why else would she have sought him out?

"How can I help you? By the way, what's your name?"

The young woman swallowed hard.

"In a way, that's why I'm here ..."

It was puzzling, she spoke in a whisper and seemed determined to be discreet, yet she was staring at him with a singular intensity.

"Ah," said François. "You would prefer not to give your name? Is that why you didn't respond to the police appeal?"

Immediately, she looked relieved. She smiled. My God, her smile ...

374

"My name is Nine. Well, actually, it's ... Everyone knows me as Nine ..."

She was speaking so softly that François had to strain to hear. Her hands were folded on the table; she was not wearing a wedding ring. When the waiter appeared, she looked up and François took the opportunity to glance at her bosom. From the graceful curve ...

"I wanted to ask your advice ..."

Did he detect the trace of an accent?

"Why me?"

"Because you are covering the case for *Le Journal*, and because you know the magistrate ..."

Was the accent Dutch? Scandinavian? She spoke in short bursts. If François did not help her out, they would be there all day.

"You want to know whether the magistrate would be prepared to take your testimony anonymously, is that it? For your name to be covered by the secrecy of the judicial investigation ..."

The young woman nodded.

"Who was with you at Le Régent, Nine?"

It was cruel, and it was intended to be, he wanted to discomfit her a little. But when she did not answer, it was François who felt embarrassed, so, to save face, he took out a notebook and a pen and laid them on the table. She did not watch what he was doing, she was staring at his face, she could not take her eyes off him. François was beginning to feel uncomfortable.

"Did you see something that might relate to the murder?"

"No, nothing! That's why I didn't go to the ... You see ..."

When she spoke like this, spontaneously, the accent was more noticeable, though still hard to pinpoint.

"And your ... And the person who was with you?"

"Nothing ... we heard a woman scream and we left the cinema as fast as we could, like everyone else."

If François understood why Nine had not initially gone to the police, he had no idea why she had come to see him today. Nine blushed, and the fingers holding her cup trembled.

"Because of your friend?"

François could not resist coming to her aid once more. She

nodded. The rest did not matter to him. Things had gone sour between Nine and her lover, the guilt of not going to the police had come between them, she wanted to rid herself of the burden.

Behind the counter, a waiter dropped a glass which shattered on the floor. "Fuck!" Like the other customers, François instinctively turned to look. The young woman also turned, but with a quick, wary movement, as if she feared being recognised.

"All right," said François as she turned back to him. "I'll go and talk to the magistrate and try to persuade him to keep your identities secret. But you do understand that your friend ... that he will also have to appear before the magistrate?"

She understood.

My God, her eyes ...

"If I can get him to agree ..." François said.

"What if you can't?"

"Then you stay in the background. Besides, if you have no new information about the crime, it won't make any difference."

"And if you can persuade him ...?"

He wished he could say: "If I persuade him, you sleep with me, you spend the night with me." The very thought of it brought a lump to his throat.

"What will I owe you?" said Nine.

A quid pro quo. François gave a half-smile.

"You can pay for the coffees."

She seemed flustered. Every favour implies some form of recompense, but François was making it impossible for the young woman to pay her debt. They were both embarrassed. François got to his feet.

"Do you have a number where I can leave a message?" he said, dropping some small change onto the saucer. The situation was so awkward that she did not even offer to pay.

She hesitated, glancing towards the terrace then back at him, like someone who has considered a response but is still hesitant.

"If you don't have a number or an address," François said irritably, "you can call me tomorrow at the newspaper."

He was furious that she had asked him for a favour and given nothing in return.

"You won't have to compromise yourself." He could not resist the barb.

She held out her hand. François took it reluctantly. If only to feel the touch of her hand, to take something from her.

37

The urge to hurt her

"Out of the question!" snapped the magistrate.

But he was disconcerted to see François calmly accept his verdict and head for the door.

"Wait," the commissaire murmured in his girlish voice.

François paid him no heed and walked out.

"Stay where you are!"

The magistrate scuttled after him and caught up with him in the hallway, followed by the commissaire with his purposeful stride.

"This woman is obliged to give a statement! It's ... it's ..."

He searched for the word, turned to the commissaire who was unwilling to help him.

"It's mandatory!"

"Very well," said François, "go tell that to the witness."

"But I don't know who this person is! I've never met her!"

Again, he turned to Commissaire Templier for support but the officer simply stared at him, which made the magistrate all the more uneasy. François headed for the stairs.

"You can read her testimony in *Le Journal* ..."

"Wait!"

Again, the magistrate hurried after him, this time overtaking François so he could block his path.

"You have no right!"

François glanced briefly at the commissaire, who was clearly amused by the whole episode.

"What exactly do you expect from their testimony, Monsieur le Juge? Here I am offering you the two missing witnesses on a plate. But these two witnesses were seated in the middle of a row."

The magistrate screwed up his eyes. He pictured the cinema on the day of the reconstruction, the two empty seats in the middle.

"Do you really think they would force the whole row to get up so they could go and murder Mary Lampson?" François said. "Do you really think they might have seen what people sitting closer to the toilets missed?"

Juge Lenoir was at his most touching when utterly out of his depth. At such moments, his features took on the bovine bewilderment one might expect to see on the face of the archetypal village idiot.

"Let me tell you what's going to happen," François said. "*Le Journal* will publish these witnesses' story, making it clear to our readers that their names have been changed to protect their privacy. And you can read their witness statements at the same time as our readers."

Once again, the magistrate realised that he was beaten.

The re-enactment at Le Régent had not been a success; the one with Servières had been a fiasco. The fates were against him.

He simply nodded. He could not even summon the strength to say the word "yes".

*

She did not call *Le Journal*, instead she came to the office. François spotted her standing on the opposite pavement, nervously twisting the handles of her handbag. But this time she did not approach him, but waited for him to cross the street. She stared at him with that singular intensity.

"Excuse me . . ."

At the sound of her voice, François felt his stomach lurch.

"The magistrate has agreed to hear your testimony *in camera*," he said, "and he has guaranteed you can remain completely anonymous."

He could not help but add:

"Assuming that no charges are brought against you."

"What do you mean 'no charges'?"

"I know what you said to me. I don't know what you plan to say to the magistrate."

It was cruel, but he could not suppress the urge to hurt her.

"I'll tell him exactly what I told you."

"In that case, you're fine."

He waited but nothing came. Then, after a long silence:

"Thank you so much."

About time too!

"You're more than welcome. Goodbye."

∗

Mathilde had an authoritarian streak that François found infuriating. Beneath her apparent indifference, he thought, was an overbearing woman. It was sheer bad faith on his part. Mathilde simply wanted to have sex, and, as always at such times, she was very persuasive, as François knew from experience.

"I prefer your body to your mind," she said. "It's your body I'm talking to now."

As she said this, she leaned over and François felt a rush of desire. He tried to pull away, but Mathilde interpreted this as flirtation. And she was not entirely wrong: François did give in, but that simply made matters worse, since Nine's face floated between them, making any attempt to give up futile.

"Right," said Mathilde, getting up from the bed.

She slipped on her skirt and her blouse, she smiled at him. None of this was of any great importance.

"I'd better be going."

"Wait a minute!"

François pulled her close and she yielded to his embrace, squirming a little as she pulled on her coat and planted a kiss on his lips. As he watched her leave, he was not sure whether he was relieved, frustrated or sad; it was all very confusing.

In his mind was the last image of Nine, a woman who had given him only a nickname, he did not know her real name, nor where she lived. He knew absolutely nothing about her, and this fact served only to fuel his fascination. François was deeply frustrated. He felt caught between two mysteries: an enigmatic young woman and a set of indecipherable initials.

Things were spiralling out of control. He was still reeling from his brother's brutal, disquieting death; Hélène had returned to her saturnine ways and was more irritable and more volatile than ever; his investigation into the piastre scandal had gone nowhere; and now Mathilde was clearing out.

She had brought along a bottle of Muscadet – "For afterwards!" she said – but it had not been opened. It would be lukewarm now, but François didn't care. Not being much of a drinker, by the third glass his head was spinning.

He turned off the lights and lay down, the dark room pitched and rolled, several times he had to sit up to stop the room from spinning – was he going to throw up?

The image of Nine danced before his eyes. He wanted this woman so much it was ruining his life. He got up and walked around for a little, struggling to keep his balance. He was not drunk so much as lost. The image of Nine's face gave way to the set of initials Étienne had given him, which he had desperately tried to decipher.

As often with men who think more clearly when they write, François had scribbled down the sequence of letters over and over, so often it had become an almost unconscious act. He pulled his notepad towards him and, having pouring himself a cup of coffee, set about writing them again: E, N, P, R, D . . .

"Shit!"

An inattentive gesture sent his cup crashing to the floor. He got up, fetched a sponge, wiped the floor and picked up the shards. By now, he was in a foul mood.

He sat down again and stared at the pad.

E, N, P, R, D . . .

The sudden revelation was like a slap in the face. His clumsiness over the cup had interrupted his flow, but now forced him to see the letters as a different sequence.

E, N, P, R, D.

He tried to remember what Étienne had said. "At least five public figures involved in the scam . . ." François struggled to marshal his thoughts. Who had told Étienne that these initials represented five people? Why had he jotted down the initials in groups of two – was it something that Étienne had said? Because if not, there was a different possible sequence: "E. N. – PRD." and "F. A. – MSR", and that was a very different kettle of fish.

Now that this doubt had occurred to him, and given that he could not precisely recall the brief, panicked phone call with Étienne, this new sequence suddenly seemed self-evident.

PRD: Parti Radical Démocratique.

MSR: Mouvement Social et Républicain.

Two political parties in government.

In an instant, François was rifling through the old chest of drawers where he kept various bits and pieces in a disorganised jumble. Somewhere in here was a Civil Service Directory. It was probably not up to date. Governments rose and fell – France was on its fourth government of the year – while ministers came and went in the blink of an eye. Even so, it might prove useful . . . François rooted through the drawers, taking out handfuls of documents he might just as well have thrown in the bin. He knew it was a long shot, but he wanted to be sure. He tipped everything out onto the floor. Searching sobered him up a little. Then, finally, he found it.

The 1946 Almanac. Not so old.

He wasted no time going back to his desk but sat cross-legged on the floor, feverishly reading through the list of members of successive government. It was a task that required a meticulous eye, something he felt ill equipped to deal with after a failed attempt at sex and three glasses of lukewarm white wine.

He was still thumbing through the pages when Hélène came home.

"Are you all right?" he said.

She looked deathly pale.

"It's nothing, I'm just tired."

A facile excuse. François went back to his almanac.

Hélène reeked of booze.

Everything was falling apart.

"What are you doing?" she asked, but seemed uninterested in his answer. She went to her room, threw her coat on her bed, then went out to the toilet where she threw up.

In the métro, there had been a man reading *Le Journal*. On the visible part of the page, Hélène had read:

NEW SMASH-AND-GRAB BY "PHARMACY GANG"
One dead in place des Ternes robbery

When Hélène did not come back from the toilet, François began to worry. He needed to do something. What the hell was going on?

Just as he was about to get up, he was stopped short by the line immediately above his finger.

Edgar de Neuville – Parti Radical Démocratique.

"E. N. – PRD."

Edgar de Neuville, sixty-four, brief stint as Under Secretary for Foreign Affairs two years earlier, but as François read on he discovered that Neuville had spent a decade with the Department for Colonial Affairs in Saigon.

"What are you doing?"

Hélène reappeared, having rinsed out her mouth. There was a knot of fear in her stomach, but she tried to put on a brave face. What time was it? She glanced at the clock. Four o'clock. She had had no lunch, her stomach was empty and aching.

François read aloud:

"Félix Allard – Mouvement Social et Républicain. F. A. – MSR."

Allard had spent five years as Secretary General of the French High Commission in Indochina.

Hélène peered over his shoulder.

"Is it to do with Étienne?"

François explained what he thought he had worked out. It was a curious tableau: brother and sister, both a little drunk, staring at a series of initials like some code they hoped to crack, a code that might have led to their brother's death.

"I need to think," said François.

He still felt unsure. Hélène's face was pale and haggard.

"You're not feeling too good, are you?" he said gently.

Hélène huddled close to him; she was shivering.

She fretted about the dead man in the place des Ternes pharmacy.

About Bernard de Jonsac.

Had she been involved? Everything was a blur.

"I miss Étienne so much," she said softly.

François hugged her tighter.

38

Oh, what a shame!

François did not expect André Baron to sit on his hands after their brief conversation about private banks – he knew how jealously the man guarded his territory. What he did not know was where the counterattack would come from. Baron himself? Denissov? In the end, it came from Malevitz.

"Did you go to see Baron?" snapped the head of department. "What kind of bullshit are you playing at?"

His furrowed black brows gave him a satanic air that could be terrifying to those who did not know him. François had decided to say as little as possible. If this was a scoop, he was not about to let anyone take it from him; if it was nothing, he wouldn't look like a fool.

"I'm working on something, but it's early days."

"Is it one for us?"

Although "us" referred to the general news desk, it could be heard as an extension of the "royal we". Malevitz firmly believed that the news desk was the heart and soul of Le Journal, and in this he was not entirely wrong. The concept of "human interest stories" was one of the innovations Denissov had brought back from the USA. "Readers want stories they can identify with, stories about their lives – only worse," was how he had put it. It was Malevitz's job to unearth and write up the stories that regularly made the splash headline, the stories that captured the public imagination. As a result, Malevitz considered himself to be the heart and soul of Le Journal.

"Possibly," replied François. "I'm not sure yet."

This was the sort of answer every news editor despised.

"That's tough, because it's your job to be sure. So, if you're not sure, you move on, got it?"

François shrugged defeatedly.

All right.

"Where are we on the Lampson story?"

This was the one story where Malevitz acknowledged that his junior was doing a "good job". François had regularly managed to get stories that ran over several editions, and the other major papers had never managed to catch up. François explained to Malevitz that two of the missing witnesses had come forward, but he quickly added that it was a boring story of adultery between boring people and was probably not worth the column inches.

"On the other hand, Juge Lenoir did say something stupid," said François. "But I don't know if we can print it . . ."

"If we printed all the dumb shit that man said, we'd have him on the front page every day. What was it this time?"

It was a deeply unprofessional move from François; in an attempt to downplay the magistrate's interview with Nine lest Malevitz decide to run with it, he was deliberately trying to amplify a minor detail.

"The last witness. The magistrate is convinced that 'he's our man'."

François was truly gifted. This phrase "the last witness" reeked of printing ink. Malevitz's eyes lit up.

The comment had been made in the judge's chambers. Nine and her lover had already given their statements, and François had come to check that there was no new information. Secretly, he hoped he might get to see Nine, and especially her lover – he wanted to see the look on the man's face.

"How do you explain that?" Juge Lenoir had asked. "Only one witness has not come forward."

The magistrate was disarmingly forthright. It was easy to get information from him; he simply couldn't keep his mouth shut.

"I can't explain it," replied François. "What do you think?"

"I think that he's our man."

"Do you mind?" said François, taking his notepad from his pocket.

The message was clear. You are speaking to a journalist who is writing an article. Far from being surprised, or even alarmed, the magistrate was thrilled.

"What reason could he have for staying in hiding? He is the only one of the 229 members of the audience who has refused to cooperate with this investigation. Why would that be – if he's got nothing to hide?"

There were as many reasons as there had been witnesses who came forward late, but it was not in François's interest to point this out. Though Commissaire Templier would have done so had he been present. But here, face to face, Juge Lenoir belonged to François.

"I hadn't considered it from that angle . . ." said François, taking notes.

Juge Lenoir's problem (or, rather, one of his problems, because he had many) was that he was too inclined to say what he thought, and, to make matters worse, once he said something, he invariably ended up believing it.

François's prompt was all that was needed. Already Juge Lenoir was pacing his chambers, expounding on what he had just said, which he mistook for a theory.

"After the appeal for witnesses, the re-enactments, the identity parades, there surely can't be anyone who hasn't heard about the case."

He rushed back to his desk and dug out a couple of newspaper clippings. A German magazine had written a short article about the case, but the magistrate was jabbing his finger at one from an Italian newspaper, because it had his photo.

"Everyone in Europe has heard about the case. Do we really believe that this witness, the last witness, is the only person who doesn't know? Come off it!"

"Indeed, I wonder what reasons he might have?" François prompted.

"There's only one possible reason, dear boy, if you know what I mean . . ."

The next day, François wrote the headline:

JUGE LENOIR WONDERS:

Why would the last witness insist on staying in hiding?

François had decided – as Malevitz rubbed his hands in glee – to run the story over several editions.

He would fire the second salvo the following day, revealing that the investigating magistrate was in no doubt that the last witness was the murderer.

This delay allowed François to focus on a more pressing concern.

"Stan," he said, "I could do with a couple of days off. Would that be all right?"

Malevitz, out of tact, had not asked François about his tragedy.

"I need to take care of my little sister, this hasn't been easy for her, so I'd like . . . Well, I'm sure you understand . . ."

"Of course, of course. Just make sure we can get in touch if we need to."

Heading home on the métro, François took out his notepad and assessed the work ahead.

First he had to sketch the broad outlines of the careers of Edgar de Neuville and Félix Allard; try to get a sense of them.

Then investigate their lifestyle. If they were receiving large sums of money, it was possible that they were stashing it abroad, but equally possible that they were spending it. Had they recently married off a daughter in lavish style? It was also important to trawl the banks. Could he find someone on the inside prepared to provide information? If the story seemed promising, Denissov would give him the money to salve a conscience or two . . . François's goal was to research the story, make sure it was rock solid, then sell it to Denissov.

Because once that was done, there was only one way to conduct an investigation.

Finding out how and why Étienne died would mean starting with the Indochinese Currency Exchange.

Find a loose thread and pull.

And there was only one way to do that.

Go to Saigon.

It was at about this time that the first delivery of linens arrived at the Dixie Boutique.

A van filled with boxes and crates.

Standing on the pavement, as stern and upright as the Lady of Justice, Geneviève looked as though she were trying to block the delivery man. She demanded to see a number of samples before accepting delivery.

"Really?"

The driver was Monsieur Steuvels, who ran a small delivery company in Berquieux with his son.

"But, of course, monsieur!" Geneviève pursed her lips, articulating each syllable, as though he had just insulted her. "Because if the work does not meet our impeccable standards, you will unload nothing and I will pay for nothing!"

The driver pushed back his cap, scratched his forehead and glanced at Jean, who looked mortified.

"Well, I suppose it's your call . . ."

It proved an acrobatic feat to find a sample sheet, a sample towel.

"What about the pillowcases and the tablecloths?" said Geneviève. "And where are the napkins?"

The samples were all laid out on the shop counter. It was clear that Monsieur Steuvels considered Geneviève's demand a little excessive. The workmanship was immaculate.

Having spent an hour lugging boxes to find a set of bedsheets and a checked handkerchief, Monsieur Steuvels seemed about to lose his temper.

"Very well," said Geneviève in her most ladylike tone, "you may unload the goods."

"Might I suggest we settle the account first?"

Monsieur Steuvels was a cautious man.

He and Geneviève pored over the order, the waybill, the invoice, examining every line – it was interminable. In the end, Geneviève wrote a cheque which Monsieur Steuvels slipped into his wallet.

Jean had to lend a hand; he was sweating profusely.

The rather tense atmosphere became a little more relaxed. By the time the goods had been unloaded, client and supplier were almost friends. So much so that Geneviève, who was even more miserly now that she was a shopkeeper, suggested that they all go and have a drink at the nearby Café Balto.

Monsieur Steuvels's son ordered a grenadine. When it was Jean's turn to order, Geneviève glared at him, and he humbly asked for a glass of mineral water and watched as Monsieur Steuvels and Geneviève sipped glasses of Byrrh. After they had run out of things to say about the business and household linens, Monsieur Steuvels turned to Jean.

"When was it you came and placed the order?"

Jean gripped his glass. Instinctively, he felt the wind shifting.

"It would have been around 20 October, wouldn't it?" said Geneviève. "Jean, the man is asking you a question."

"Yes, that's right, sometime around 20 October."

Despite the glass of Vittel, his throat felt dry.

Monsieur Steuvels nodded gravely.

"Around the time you were there, the family suffered a terrible tragedy ..."

"Really? Do tell ..." said Geneviève, who was always thrilled when tragedy struck others.

"My little niece ... Well, I say 'little', but she'd have been twenty-two. My sister's lass."

Geneviève saw Jean's face flush and he looked towards the billiard room as though someone had asked him to play and he was reluctant to get up.

"So, what happened to the girl?" Geneviève said.

"Murdered, madame, you'd scarcely believe it. She was working, temporary like, at Lemberger post office. An hour after closing, we got worried cos we hadn't heard from her, and she was found dead right there in the post office. My sister's eldest, she was, and about to get engaged. A terrible thing, it was."

"And ..." ventured Geneviève, "what exactly happened ...?"

"In a brutal, very brutal ..."

Jean got to his feet, signalled that he was going to the toilet, and walked off.

"In what way brutal?"

Geneviève had dropped her voice to a whisper.

"Bashed her head in, madame, there's no other way to say it."

"Oh my God! With ... with what?"

"With the telephone receiver. The one in the public callbox. Police, they say she was hit ten times or more, died almost instantly she did, from what they told me."

"Well, I suppose that's a blessing – in a way ... But who could have committed such a heinous crime?"

"We still have no idea. The gendarmes round our way are lazy so-and-sos. One day they'll say one thing, and the next ... They even came round looking for lice from the girl's fiancé and from my sister!"

"That's disgraceful!"

Jean had returned from the toilets.

"Did you hear that, Jean, it's terrible!"

Jean did not sit down, he simply stood, waiting for the party to break up.

"Monsieur Steuvels's niece was murdered ... How old did you say she was?"

"Twenty-two."

"Beaten to death in a post office. With a telephone receiver. Several times, obviously ..."

There was a long silence as everyone considered the dreadful circumstances.

"Tell me something, Monsieur Steuvels ..."

Geneviève was gripped by a sudden doubt; you could see it on her face.

"These young girls ... I'm sorry, I meant this young girl ... Was she raped?"

Jean opened his mouth, but Monsieur Steuvels cut him off.

"No, no, thank God, small mercies, Madame Pelletier ... Bad enough that she was murdered."

"Of course, of course," said Geneviève. Her cheeks once more had the pink glow of a Norman farmwoman.

"They got some fingerprints," said Monsieur Steuvels, draining his glass.

"Fingerprints, what fingerprints?" exclaimed Jean.

Monsieur Steuvels attributed his nervousness to the magnitude of his revelation, which was not entirely untrue.

"On the telephone receiver, they found the murderer's fingerprints, that's how they excul ... how they exculp— how they proved her fiancé wasn't involved, see?"

Jean looked at Geneviève, whose eyes were half-closed, as though she were adjusting to this new perspective.

"There would be dozens of fingerprints in a post office," she said. "Hundreds."

"That's true," said Jean.

"There could be thousands ... I know what I'm talking about – my father is a postmaster."

"Aha!" said Jean triumphantly.

"Maybe," said Monsieur Steuvels, "but in this case ..."

He was building up suspense.

Jean's mouth was half-open, Geneviève's eyes half-closed.

"But in this case, they found fingerprints in the girl's blood, you see? So they've got to be his."

Geneviève's eyes flickered wide.

"Well, then, why haven't they arrested the murderer?"

"Thing is, they've got the prints, but they don't got the man whose prints they are."

"Oh," said Geneviève, "what a pity ..."

She seemed almost as disappointed as Monsieur Steuvels.

Jean's throat was still dry, his hands were clammy.

He would have given ten years of his life for a glass of water, but was unable to move.

"That's not the whole story," Monsieur Steuvels said at length, clapping his hands on his knees, "but we need to get back on the road, don't we, lad?"

*

However much Geneviève stacked sheets and tablecloths in the wall racks, she loathed the shop. It was nothing like what she had dreamed. The confined space and the fact that they had to have stalls out on the pavement meant that, rather than welcoming an elegant clientele and discreetly unfolding tablecloths and linens, they had to pile up linens on market stalls. It was humiliating. Geneviève blamed Jean, because she had long since learned to blame him for everything, but today she understood his pain and did her best not to burden him unduly.

"What on earth are you doing?" she would say if he dropped something or bumped into a piece of furniture.

She did not shriek, but said it in a patient, motherly, almost amused tone.

"Go on, give it to me, I'll take care of it . . ."

Jean slumped into a chair, overcome by dread.

Knowing that his bloody fingerprints had been found in the post office at Lamberghem was petrifying. The rest of the day was a nightmare. He was plagued by cold sweats and blurred vision, he had to grip the furniture to steady himself. Worst of all was the torrent of images. He saw himself being arrested, being dragged before a magistrate. It was a version of Juge Lenoir ten times more frightening than he was in reality who loomed over him growling: "Show me your hands . . ." And as Jean held out his sweaty hands, the magistrate, like a palm reader said: "I can see that these hands have held a telephone receiver . . . Am I wrong?" The magistrate was flanked by two hulking gendarmes with black moustaches.

Once she had finished tidying up, Geneviève sat down, her knees splayed, like a farmer's wife on a milking stool.

Jean was standing at the door, peering into the street, as though expecting someone to appear.

"I've been thinking about Monsieur Steuvels's niece . . ."

Jean wheeled around. His wife was shaking her head, her mouth set in a cynical rictus.

"They're not going to find the killer anytime soon . . ."

"They have his fingerprints," Jean managed to say, despite the lump in his throat.

"But if his fingerprints were on file, the police would have him banged up already. The way I see it, he'll be much more careful now. The police won't find any more fingerprints, you take my word for it."

That evening, as Geneviève lay stiffly on top of the bedsheet, her arms by her sides, Jean, who was lying on his back next to her, heard her say:

"At least you're lucky enough to get to travel, Jean . . . And then, when something curious happens down there in the provinces, you don't even think to tell me . . ."

This was not the dry, metallic tone she used when upbraiding him, but an amused, affectionate, almost childlike voice.

Slowly, she slipped her hand beneath the sheet.

"But there's a lot going on down there, isn't there, Bouboule?"

39

Not now, not ever

He lacked the skill. When it came to human interest stories, François was an expert, but this story was not about interviewing witnesses, worming out some lurid detail that would fascinate the public. He needed to probe elite groups who fought shy of speaking to the press. It was an investigation that required an address book, contacts, a network – and François had none of those things.

From the National Assembly archives, Senate directories, party political pamphlets and documents at the National Library, he had managed to build a picture of the lives of Félix Allard and Edgar de Neuville: he knew their wives' maiden names, their children's names and ages, and every post they had ever held – which information was available to anyone and led precisely nowhere. He could just about write a pen portrait of them, using only his imagination.

As François saw it, Edgar de Neuville had all the makings of a local country squire. His marriage to a certain Mademoiselle Gendreau-Balthazar and the strings pulled by his father-in-law had opened the doors to the colonial administration. What was most interesting about Neuville was his extended posting to Saigon, which, in addition to a good working knowledge of French–Indochinese relations, would have garnered him a long list of friends in high places. He had joined the Parti Radical Démocratique – a ragbag political party – and been elected senator.

According to François's timeline, he was unlikely to have met Félix Allard in Saigon, since he had been posted there two years after Neuville's departure. Allard had also worked at the French High Commission, so would be well versed in Indochinese relations. After various roles, he had finally climbed the greasy pole to become a member of parliament.

By the end of the first day of his investigation, François knew only two things for certain. First, that he did not have a shred of evidence and second, that, without help, he had no chance of getting any further.

He had spent the whole night brooding over this conundrum and had decided that there was only one solution.

Mount an assault on the front lines.

The following morning he called the parliamentary office of Félix Allard. The député was in his provincial constituency and would not be back until the following day. By some miracle that François was too inexperienced to appreciate, Edgar de Neuville happened to be in Paris. Having managed to get him on the phone, François launched into a panegyric about Neuville's knowledge of Indochina.

"I'm working on a major article about the situation in Indochina, Senator. I've been talking to people who truly understand the issues, which is why I've taken the liberty of calling to ask whether you might help. You know the region intimately . . ."

The senator cleared his throat, he was deeply flattered. It was clear that he was rarely asked his opinion on anything.

"When am I free . . .? Let me see, let me see . . ."

"I'm terribly sorry, Senator, but we go to press tomorrow morning. And I'd be bitterly disappointed not to have your insights on the issues. I think half an hour of your time would be enough to . . ."

"Very well, let's do it! Give me a time."

So it was that, late afternoon the same day, François was ushered into the senator's private residence and was surprised by the simplicity of the accommodation. The apartment was barely three times the size of the one he shared with Hélène. The modest office, at the far end of the hallway, was dominated by a mahogany bookcase and an old-fashioned desk strewn with papers and cigarette ash. There was a pipe rack containing at least a dozen pipes and the pall of smoke cleared only slightly when the senator, solicitous of his guest, opened the window.

Neuville seemed all the more imposing because the office was so small. He was broad-shouldered, with a farmer's build and strong features, a thick nose, bushy eyebrows, a lush moustache. He seemed a remarkably composed figure. François immediately suspected that he was on the wrong track. Why would Neuville be involved in the sordid traffic in piastres? He was clearly a man of simple tastes, which would be amply covered by his parliamentary salary.

He was a vain man who liked the sound of his own voice, and being cast in the role of an expert boosted his ego such that he greeted the young journalist with a smug, self-satisfied smile.

Before the conversation could begin, Neuville held up a copy of *Le Journal* bearing the headline:

"MISSING LAST WITNESS IS LAMPSON KILLER," SAYS JUGE LENOIR

Exclusive interview with François Pelletier

"That's you, isn't it? François Pelletier . . ."

The tone was accusatory, which caught François off guard.

"I wear two different hats at *Le Journal*. Human interest stories and extraordinary investigations."

The word "extraordinary" appealed to the senator. It confirmed and indeed bolstered his sense of importance. As he put away the paper, he said conspiratorially:

"The manhunt season is well and truly open, isn't it? All the other newspapers will be hot on your tail . . ."

François modestly accepted this tribute.

He had prepared a handful of questions that he had filched from the archives of *Le Journal*. At no point did Senator de Neuville express surprise at the clichés, or at the fact that the newspaper was treating him as an expert on a subject about which no one had spoken to him for more than a decade. François set his notepad in his lap, but although he scribbled a lot, he wrote nothing. Nothing except the single sentence he had come here to say, which here, in the senator's office, seemed preposterous.

Neuville held forth at great length about France's military

strategies, its beneficial influence on Indochina and the threat posed by Chinese communism to Asia.

François closed his notebook.

"My sincere thanks for this extremely enlightening contribution, Monsieur le Sénateur. It will be invaluable in writing the article. And to our readers, of course."

"You say it's going to press tomorrow?"

"Well, that's what my editor told me!"

François stood up and the senator came out from behind his desk to accompany his visitor to the door.

François studied the corridor and decided that he would stop and turn about two metres from the door – not too far, not too close.

He wheeled around with a worried look, as though he had suddenly remembered something.

"Just one more question, Monsieur le Sénateur: do you happen to have a private account with Banque Godard or with Hopkins Brothers?"

The reaction was instantaneous.

The unexpected question hit the senator like a thunderbolt. His face flushed purple, his expression hardened, his mouth fell open.

"What did you say?"

The senator's cogwheels whirred as his mind frantically processed the situation, his answer, and the untold consequences implied by the question itself.

François repeated himself word for word.

"Absolutely not!" bellowed the senator.

"And you have never held any such account?"

"But, but . . . why would you . . .?"

"There are allegations that these private banks have allowed certain people to make substantial, not to say illicit, profits from the highly favourable exchange rate between the piastre and the franc. Or, to put it bluntly, to engage in currency trafficking at the expense of the French taxpayer."

Patrician arrogance is a common tactic used by those in power, the conversational equivalent of the *argument from authority*.

398

"I have no dealings and have never had dealings with either of those establishments, monsieur, not now, not ever."

This told François that he was right.

As he went back downstairs (the senator slammed the door without shaking his hand), François wondered where Neuville spent his money. Did he have a string of mistresses? Secret vices? Was he a gambler? Perhaps he used it to fill the coffers of his political party.

François felt electrified, and had to take deep breaths to slow his pounding heart.

He put in another call to the parliamentary office of Félix Allard, explaining the nature of the article he was writing, his need for an expert on Indochinese matters and requesting an interview for the following day, as soon as the député returned.

If Neuville knew Allard, would he warn him in advance? It hardly mattered. If he did, Allard would have to devise some convoluted excuse not to meet with François, and that would be as damning as a bare-faced lie.

Finally, the ball was rolling.

François thought about Étienne, as though suddenly he felt he might be able to repay a debt for never having understood his brother.

*

François had fervently hoped that Étienne's death, the heart-wrenching funeral service and their return to Paris might heal his fragile relationship with Hélène. When their father had asked how things were going at the École des Beaux-Arts, and François had lied for her, *Oh, everything's fine, as far as I know*, she had shot him a grateful look. François did not know whether she was still attending classes. She never talked about school, she never talked about anything, he knew nothing whatever about her life.

He hoped that, by lying for her to their parents, he might earn himself a little gratitude. Or at least some peace of mind.

In this, he was quickly disillusioned.

If at first Hélène proved more tractable, consumed as she was by tears and grief, within two days of their return to Paris she had reverted to the furious tormented soul he found impossible to live with. François did not know what triggered this sudden change.

After the break-in at the place des Ternes pharmacy, Hélène was terrified. She spent a sleepless night tossing and turning, but by morning she felt much calmer. After all, she had nothing to do with the break-in. She knew it was the work of Bernard de Jonsac and his gang, and knew she should probably go to the police. If they came to interrogate her, she would say that it hadn't occurred to her, that Jonsac said so many things ...

Her fears faded a little when François told her his news. He was convinced that Edgar de Neuville was one of the men on Étienne's list, and that he was mixed up in the currency-trafficking scandal. The thought that Étienne's death was related to this scandal preyed on Hélène's mind, but she was quickly brought down to earth when she saw the front page of *Le Journal*. All the colour drained from her face.

GANG LEADER BERNARD DE JONSAC TURNS STATE'S EVIDENCE!

Hélène thought she would pass out.

Following a six-month undercover investigation, the so-called "pharmacy gang" has been smashed. The news comes two days after the death of Monsieur Bouvet during a break-in at his pharmacy on the place des Ternes. The gang, led by Bernard de Jonsac, a former student at the École des Beaux-Arts and known cocaine addict, has been responsible for more than twenty-five violent break-ins at pharmacies throughout Paris and the suburbs over the past two years. The highly organised criminal network of thugs, scouts, lookouts, drivers, dealers, etc. is alleged to have stolen several million francs' worth of drugs that were sold on to junkies,

particularly in the area of Saint-Germain. A large quantity
of amphetamines was seized during the raid.

The leader, Bernard de Jonsac, who proved less reckless
in front of the police than in front of the shop windows, is
said to have "grassed up" his accomplices, who, like him,
are facing long prison sentences for drug trafficking, criminal
conspiracy, robbery and other crimes. A dozen members of
the gang were arrested in dawn raids this morning. Further
arrests are expected over the coming days.

From that moment, Hélène's life was reduced to fear and
loathing. Her first reaction was to run away, but where could she
run, and how would she find the money? She could ask François,
but he had no more money than she did. The police would come
knocking. Then again, why hadn't they come for her already? And,
in the end, what had she done? Nothing! She had agreed to act as
a lookout, but after Étienne's death, she had left Paris. She had not
been involved in any of this. She had nothing to be ashamed of.
Even so, the police would want to question her . . . Had she ever
taken psychotropic drugs? Had she bought them? From whom?
They would discover the nefarious reputation she had cultivated
at the Café des Arts. There would be witness statements. Bernard
Jonsac would grass up anyone and everyone if it meant a lighter
sentence. How do you prove that you haven't done something?
Would Jonsac tell the police what it was she did in exchange for
the pills? That in itself would be a crime.

Hélène lived in constant dread. She no longer left the apartment,
but was constantly at the window, peering out.

François asked what was wrong, but Hélène just waved his
questions away.

40

A rather awkward case

Jean watched Geneviève as she slept. This deathlike stillness seemed to him to be a foreshadowing of what was to come. It was dead of night, and in the deep darkness, the discovery of his bloody fingerprints at Lamberghem post office was an intolerable weight on his chest. He tossed and turned a thousand times in search of some position that might lessen his asphyxiating dread. He sat up, lay down again. Meanwhile Geneviève slept on. Nothing could disturb her. She awakened just as she fell asleep, in an instant. In the morning, she would sit up, throw back the sheets, get up and immediately begin her day.

By dawn, Jean was out of bed.

Still in pyjamas, he gazed through the kitchen window at the breaking day, a rose-pink sky streaked with white. Already, the city was beginning to hum, the clatter of dustbins, the purr of buses along the avenue, the first car horns. Every sound sent shockwaves through Jean, creating a tracery of cracks in the fragile shell protecting him. The police already had his finger-prints. "But if his fingerprints were on file, the police would have him banged up already," Geneviève had reassured him, and she had a point. It had been three weeks – why had they not come to arrest him?

If, by some quirk of fate, another incident like the one at the post office should occur (and every time, Jean sincerely believed that it would never happen again), he would be careful not to leave any evidence.

But that was not how it worked ... Such precautions were taken by people who acted with premeditation. For Jean, it was not like that. His actions were sudden, brutal, reckless, there was no forethought, just a vast outpouring of rage. There was no time to check for fingerprints.

Thinking about it, it was surprising that the police had not found fingerprints or other clues before. Jean could not really remember the previous incidents without great effort, since his mind quickly blotted out all memories – all except for Mary Lampson, obviously, what with everyone talking about the case, François writing his scoops and Geneviève lapping up every new detail.

"Haven't you made the coffee yet?"

Geneviève was up and already making the bed.

Being a devoted fan of Radio Luxembourg (she never missed an episode of *La Famille Duraton*), she always turned the radio on as soon as she woke. Jean absent-mindedly listened to the news. Coffee was made, Geneviève finished dressing, and Jean resumed his post next to the window.

It was then that he saw it.

Down below, a police car had appeared; it pulled up in front of the entrance, thwarting any possible escape.

Three uniformed officers climbed out, white truncheons hanging from their belts. Jean was in shock.

"Do you hear that, Jean?" he heard Geneviève's voice behind him. "What a curious world we live in!"

The officers were nowhere to be seen, they had just entered the building, they were coming upstairs.

Jean gripped the window to steady himself, his vision was blurred, his heart was racing. Slowly, he turned, he thought he could hear pounding footsteps on the stairs. Geneviève, who heard nothing but the radio, poured herself a cup of coffee and said again: "What a curious world we live in!"

"Genev—"

The name would not come. He took a faltering step and collapsed on the chair.

Somewhere in his mind, he heard a whispering voice: "Maybe they haven't come for you . . ."

But just then, there came a loud peremptory knock on the door.

"Well, I wonder who that could be?" said Geneviève, who never answered the door. That was Jean's job.

He simply could not do it.

Geneviève glanced at her husband, his face was contorted with dread. A gruff voice barked:

"Police! Open up!"

"What on earth do they want now?" said Geneviève, getting up from her chair. "Just a minute!" she shrieked as she opened the door. "We're not savages!"

This was not the reaction the police were expecting.

"Are you trying to break the door down? The polite thing to do is knock and wait!"

The two officers exchanged a bewildered look.

"Is Monsieur Jean Pelletier here?"

"What do you want him for?"

Geneviève folded her arms, making it clear that if they wanted to come in, they would have to get past her first. Over her shoulder, the officers glared at Jean, who sat in the chair staring back at them with a look of abject terror.

"Are you Monsieur Jean Pelletier?" said an officer, waving a piece of paper. "This is a bench warrant. I am going to have to ask you to come with us."

"What's all this about?" said Geneviève, still blocking their path, one hand on the door, ready to slam it in their faces.

"I'm afraid we don't know, madame. Our orders are simply to take this gentleman to the station."

"This is preposterous! You can't simply haul people away without giving a reason. What sort of country are we living in?"

"Madame, I think it might be best if you did not make a fuss . . ."

"Oh, really?"

The situation was rapidly becoming acrimonious when Jean said in a faint whisper: "I'll be right with you."

He stood up and tremulously set his empty coffee bowl on the table. The tension eased a little and the officers looked at each other, pleased with this new turn of events.

"Very well," Geneviève said. "If that's how it is, we'll go with you!"

Jean had pulled on his jacket and was walking towards them.

"I'm afraid not, madame," said the officer. "Our orders are to take the gentleman to the police station. You're not . . ."

"I'm not *what*?"

It was clear the officer had inadvertently put another coin in the jukebox. Geneviève had folded her arms again and taken a step forward. The words "police station" set Jean's nerves jangling, blood coursed through his veins, he reached out to grab the chair and collapsed again.

"Let us help you, sir," said the senior officer.

They side-stepped Geneviève, strode into the room, grabbed Jean under the arms and waved the warrant under his nose.

"Which police station?" Geneviève said in a shrill falsetto.

"The commissariat in the 19th arrondissement, it's on the rue Augustin-Thierry . . ."

"I demand to be allowed to go with my husband."

Once again, Geneviève blocked their path.

"I am his wife before God!" she declared, imperiously.

This was an unexpected line of argument.

The officers exchanged a look. But when they moved towards the door, Geneviève stepped aside.

"I shall file an official complaint!"

His shoulders drooping, his tread heavy, his heart in his mouth, Jean began the slow descent to the yard. As he passed, apartment doors opened to reveal faces and fleeting glances, then silently closed.

From upstairs, Geneviève railed: "I shall file a complaint! I'll have your badges!"

Once outside, Jean had to be helped into the car.

The courtyard was clear, the avenue was all but deserted, but for some unknown reason, as the driver pulled out, he felt it necessary to turn on the siren.

To Jean, the siren's wail was like a nail in his heart.

*

There was no coffee or bread in the pantry. No one had thought to do any shopping: François was caught up in his investigation, and Hélène was close to hysterical about the threat hanging over her in the Jonsac case ... She did her best not to think about it.

François knocked gently on Hélène's door and heard a muffled "yes" from under the bedclothes. He pushed the door. Hélène sat up. "What is it, what time is it?"

"I'm going downstairs to get some breakfast, there's nothing in the kitchen. I thought you might like to come with me ..."

In the month and a half that they had been living together, François had made the invitation a dozen times and always been rebuffed. Strangely, this time Hélène accepted. She was weak and at her wits' end; she needed someone to be present.

"Just give me two minutes."

She took ten. François was silently seething. Not because he was annoyed at having to wait, but because he had a long day ahead of him. As always when a promising story came up, his mind was teeming with ideas. Hélène emerged from her room; she was at her most beautiful when she did not wear makeup. For François, it was painful, she looked so terribly young and fragile.

"Let's go," he said.

They found a table at Le Petit Albert. They had been to this café on her first day in Paris; it was not a happy memory. Hélène thought about the path she had taken since then. She had tumbled down a steep slope and now could see no way back up.

As for François, he was reluctant to talk about his investigation. Partly, it was superstition, the fear it might bring bad luck, but mostly it was because Hélène was so volatile, so quick to get carried away ... Given that the story concerned Étienne, she would bombard him with questions, with demands. No, he decided, he would tell her about the story once he had talked to Denissov, when he had been given the green light.

He was convinced that, after his meeting with Félix Allard, the investigation would finally get underway. Because, after all ...

"Mademoiselle Hélène Pelletier?"

François had not seen the men arrive.

Two men in mackintoshes who looked almost identical. Plainclothes police officers.

He was about to get up when he saw Hélène's face.

Instantly, he knew that she had got herself into trouble.

"Yes," she said, staring at the floor.

"I must ask you to come with us."

"What on earth is this . . .?"

François had not finished his sentence when Hélène turned to him, her face streaked with tears. She got to her feet. She would never know where she found the strength.

"Now wait a minute!" François shouted as he saw his sister being handcuffed.

Hélène had not protested. It was a clear sign that she was guilty – but of what?

"Hélène, what on earth is going on?"

As she was led to the door, she glanced back at him, utterly distraught. Within seconds, she had been bundled into the unmarked car parked outside the café and driven off. François was dazed.

Was it serious? What would he tell their parents?

"What the hell has she got herself into this time?"

It was the voice of Jean-Claude, the waiter. He was not speaking to François, he was simply thinking aloud as he stared at the glass café doors.

Where had they taken her? François had not thought to ask.

He had to get to *Le Journal*. Some informant would quickly report that a young girl had been arrested, and he would know to which commissariat she had been taken.

He could ask Denissov for the name of a good lawyer. His heart was in his throat. What the hell had she got herself into this time?

*

It was not the local police station, it was probably the headquarters of the Police Judiciaire, Jean had not bothered to look. He was rushed into a building, up two flights of stairs and into a hallway with doors on either side. It was almost empty, with benches lining the walls.

"Sit there," was all he heard.

Since then, there had been nothing. He had seen almost no one – a woman with a box file tucked under one arm, two men having a whispered conversation who did not even look his way. Jean wondered whether he could abscond. He could simply get up, walk slowly to the end of the corridor and down the stairs. If anyone stopped him, he could say that he was looking for the toilets. And if he managed to make it outside, then ... Then ... nothing. Where could he run, and how would he find the money?

He had no wristwatch, no way of telling the time. He felt as though he had been here for hours.

How they had found his fingerprints, this was what he did not understand. There had to be some explanation. No one issues a bench warrant with knowing what you've done. Then, suddenly, a thought occurred to him.

What if this was about the other girl?

He racked his brain. No, not the actress, the other girl ... The one before that ... The girl in the restaurant out in the provinces. But that was so long ago. No, it could not be that.

So, it had to be the actress.

That was the only way it could be.

He had twice been subpoenaed to appear, for the re-enactment at Le Régent and for the identity parade with the witness who thought she would recognise the man she had seen coming out of the toilets.

What could the police have since discovered that they had not known then?

*

François did not even get the chance to go upstairs to the news desk; he was nabbed as he came through the front door.

An arrest so sudden it looked like a kidnapping.

No one had asked his name. He had simply felt hands grip him under the arms, and by the time he knew what was happening, they were shoving him into a car, banging his head against the bodywork, not that it mattered. Before he could marshal his thoughts, his wrists had been handcuffed and he was sitting in the back seat between two broad-shouldered men who stared straight ahead. Those in the front seats looked like twins.

It was futile to ask any questions. This was not a kidnapping; it was an arrest. It had something to do with Hélène's arrest an hour earlier. Whatever it was, it had to be serious for them to come and drag him away as though he were guilty. I'm a journalist, thought François, but he was too inexperienced to know how to profit from this status, or indeed what it might protect him from.

He had only one thought: to assert his legal right to a phone call, and to contact Denissov.

Denissov would know what to do.

The car hurtled along the ring road. No one had said a word. As they approached the boulevard Mortier, the car turned sharply, drove through a gateway into a huge courtyard and pulled up in front of a double door. François stumbled out, almost losing his balance because of the handcuffs. He was ushered into a hallway and the handcuffs were removed. Even more strangely, as soon as he was freed, the four men disappeared.

He found himself alone in the cramped lobby, feeling completely disoriented.

Was he a free man?

There was no one there. Looking round, he saw the car he had been brought in start up and drive away.

He turned this way and that, rubbing his aching wrists.

The whole situation seemed preposterous.

"Hurts, doesn't it? The handcuffs . . . They can be very painful."

The concern came from a rather elegant man in his forties in an elegant charcoal suit who stood smiling at him. He spoke as though François were a friend. Laid a hand on his shoulder inviting him to follow, and spoke in a simple clear voice.

"We'll have to take the stairs; we've never had the money to install a lift . . ."

They ascended a stone staircase, emerged into a corridor and followed it.

"My name is Lagrange," said the man, not by way of introduction, but as though it were a colourful detail. He was charm itself.

He opened a door to a tiny office lined with shelves groaning under the weight of endless files. In the room was another besuited man. He was heavyset, with an unremarkable face and bulging eyes that did not move. Had he not blinked, he could have been mistaken for a wax figure from the Musée Grévin.

"This is my colleague, Arnould."

Clearly, this was no place for pleasantries and handshakes.

"Could one of you kindly tell me . . .?" François began in a voice he hoped was emphatic.

He did not have time to continue before Lagrange opened another door that led into a large office with two desks. There, sitting side by side, were Jean and Hélène, both of them ashen. Lagrange waved at a man standing behind them and he immediately disappeared. The man named Arnould took his place, hands clasped in front of him.

"I won't trouble to introduce you," said Lagrange with a broad smile. "Right, I think we should begin, what do you say?"

Lagrange gestured to the chair next to Hélène, though he himself remained standing.

François sat down.

"Monsieur Pelletier, you have caused us something of a problem . . ."

"And who, exactly, is 'us'?"

Lagrange glanced at his colleague as though he had anticipated this question, and had won his bet. He did not answer, but carried on.

"You have been poking your nose into a rather delicate matter and we are here to persuade you to go no further with your story."

Hélène and Jean both turned to look at François. So that was it . . .

"Étienne?" Hélène said.

"What story?" said Jean.

These were genuine questions, of course, though they all had reasons to feel profoundly relieved.

Jean because the fear that he had been found out was now

fading; Hélène because her arrest had nothing to do with the pharmacy break-ins; François because now he knew that he was on the right track.

Lagrange was still smiling.

"Monsieur Pelletier here knows exactly what I mean, don't you?"

It was François's turn to smile.

"As a journalist, I have every right to investigate whatever I choose, and there is nothing you can do to stop me."

Lagrange gave a little pout intended to convey his disappointment.

"In principle, of course, you are quite correct . . ."

"What are you talking about?" said Jean.

". . . but I think you will decide not to pursue the matter."

"I don't see what could compel me to do so . . ."

Lagrange looked at the three of them in turn. He nodded to Arnould, who silently left the room. There were no smiles now.

Lagrange came and faced them. He was deadly serious.

"Because" – he quickly consulted his watch – "precisely three hours ago we issued an arrest warrant for your mother and father. Pursuant to extradition agreements between France and Lebanon, they are currently on a flight to France. And if you insist on pursuing this matter, Monsieur Pelletier, and given their criminal past, we will have your parents sent to the guillotine."

François laughed.

"What exactly are you talking about?"

The three siblings shot each other worried looks. Had their parents been arrested? Were they really on a plane to France?

"Who are you talking about?"

It was Jean who managed to ask the right question. All of them knew that this had to be a case of mistaken identity, but they could not see how to turn things around.

Just then, Arnould came back into the room and whispered a few words to his colleague.

"I have just been informed," said Lagrange, "that Monsieur Maillard and his wife are on the plane to Paris."

"Oh, Maillard!" François gave a sigh of relief. "You've made a mistake. Our name is Pelletier."

Hélène and Jean were equally relieved, they could finally breathe, soon all this would be over.

As he said the words, François realised that these men had to know the names of the three people they had brought here. A mistake was highly unlikely. The whole story was insane.

"Did you hear that, Arnould? Apparently, we've made a mistake."

The heavyset man once again took up his position behind them. François turned to look. He had his hands clasped in front of him. With his thick features and his blank stare, he looked like a bouncer at the Bullier.

"It's possible," said Arnould gravely.

Suddenly worried, Lagrange reached across the table for a cardboard file that no one had previously noticed.

"Well, that would put the tin hat on it . . ."

He reached for the breast pocket of his jacket.

"Old age," he said apologetically as he put on a pair of tortoiseshell glasses. "Let's have a look, shall we, and if we have made a mistake, then we will rectify it, won't we Arnould?"

"Absolutely."

Lagrange was beaming at them again.

"Now, let's see. We'll start with you."

He looked up at Jean, who felt a chill run down his spine.

"You are Jean Albert Gustave Pelletier, born Beirut, 11 February 1921. You have a degree in chemistry. On 26 April 1943, you married one Geneviève Cécile Henriette Cholet. You were previously general manager of Maison Pelletier . . ."

Whenever he paused, he removed his glasses and laid his forearms on the table, as though waiting for dessert.

"You weren't exactly a success as general manager, were you?"

He pulled a face, as though this observation pained him.

"Where was I . . .?" He put his glasses on again. "Until recently you were a sales representative for Établissements Guénot, but left your post to open a shop with your wife, a shop called the Dixie Boutique."

He took his glasses off again.

"While we're on the subject, do you spell Dixie with a 'y' or 'ie'?"

"Er . . . 'ie'."

"What did I tell you, Arnould? It's Dixie, spelled 'ie', like Dixieland jazz!"

"I shall make the necessary correction."

"I should hope so. So, aside from that little detail, it's all correct?"

Jean nodded.

"Good . . ."

Still smiling, Lagrange turned to François.

"According to our information – and I say 'according to our information' because perhaps we're completely wrong. What do you think, Arnould?"

"It's possible."

"You are François, René – oh, just like Chateaubriand! Maybe that explains the writing and *le journalisme* and all that. So, as I was saying, François René Auguste Pelletier, born 14 June 1923. High school diploma. On 13 May 1941, you joined the 1st Light Division of the Free French Army commanded by Général Legentilhomme. You took part in the Syria–Lebanon campaign . . ."

He set down his glasses.

"What a story, eh! The French fighting the French, such a tragedy . . . Now, where was I?"

"Legentilhomme," said a voice.

"That's right, thank you, Arnould. You are currently employed as a reporter at *Le Journal du soir*—"

"As a journalist," François interrupted.

"Is that so? Hear that, Arnould? He says he's not a reporter, he's a journalist."

"I shall make the necessary correction."

"I should hope so, because a reporter and a journalist are very different things. I'm relying on you, Arnould. You work in the general news department under Stanislas Malevitz. By the way, is old Stan still at daggers drawn with Arthur Baron? I suppose that Denissov always blowing hot and cold doesn't help matters . . ."

"How do you know all this?"

"You work in information, we work in intelligence, our jobs are very similar, and for that reason we have the same rule: our sources are confidential."

He looked down at his file.

"Now, we come to you, mademoiselle. You are Hélène Pauline Gertrude Pelletier, born 23 April 1930 in Beirut. You have a high school diploma and are a student at the École des Beaux-Arts in Paris. By the way, they don't see much of you at the Beaux-Arts, do they? I get the impression you don't like it much. Which leads us to . . . Well, let's not dwell on the kind of people you hang around with, but if you want a word of advice, you should choose your friends more carefully. I'm sure you know what I mean . . ."

He was about to close the file, but paused.

"Then of course there is our absent friend, Étienne Pelletier, poor bastard, who died in Indochina on 25 October. God rest his soul."

They all sat in stunned silence. François was the first to come to his senses.

"So what was all that rubbish about Magnard?"

"Not Magnard, Maillard. Didn't your father tell you?"

The three siblings looked at each other.

"Did you hear that, Arnould? He never told them."

"What a shame."

"We'll have to rectify that. I'm going to tell you a little story. Your father's real name is Albert Maillard. He fought in the Great War, and distinguished himself. But when he was demobilised, he had some minor problems . . . readjusting. So, he came up with a very clever scam. He began selling war memorials from a catalogue. In exchange for a large deposit, he would offer a generous discount on the price. He sold hundreds of memorials to local councils, veterans' associations, schools. And then, on 14 July 1920 . . . he disappeared, taking with him the money and his then fiancée, Mademoiselle Pauline Maudet. They left for Lebanon under the name of Évrard. There, they gave themselves a new identity: Pelletier. And using the money he made from the great swindle, they bought a soap factory. You know the rest."

Jean, François and Hélène were so stunned by these revelations that they could scarcely think straight. What they had just been told bore no relationship to the story they knew, or the parents they knew.

"If all this is true," asked François, "then why did you never arrest them?"

Lagrange dropped his voice to a whisper and leaned forward conspiratorially.

"It's a rather awkward case, as I'm sure you understand. Many people were duped by the swindle, tempers were running high. If we had extradited the culprits, it would have reopened old wounds, and the government had more pressing worries ... And, to be honest, the government at the time was ill inclined to pursue the matter since it would have raised the thorny question: how was it that no one had seen this coming, that no one had done anything to prevent this ... monumental scam, if you'll pardon the pun."

This story, which a few minutes earlier had seemed utterly implausible, was gradually becoming credible ...

"But you knew they were living in Lebanon ..."

François found it very difficult to imagine his parents as swindlers.

"Oh yes, we never lost track of them. And I have to say we are very pleased that we took this little precaution, since the information is of considerable use to us now."

"How so ...?"

"Because it might bring you to your senses, Monsieur Pelletier. I am sorry, but you are faced with the choice of continuing your investigation into the traffic in piastres – which, I have to say, is of no interest to anyone – and the fate of your dear parents."

"You say this took place back in 1920?"

The question came from Jean, whom everyone had forgotten, as usual.

"Yes, they ran away on Bastille Day. They had a dramatic sense of timing."

"In that case, it's covered by the statute of limitations."

Lagrange opened his mouth on a silent syllable. His looked up at Arnould.

"Did you hear that, Arnould?"

"I did."

"Bravo, Monsieur Pelletier, bravo! You raise a very good point, there is a statute of limitations."

"Well then," said Jean, "I don't see what we're doing here . . ."

"I'll be frank, Monsieur Pelletier, that little fact did not escape us, which is why we were forced to change our strategy. And, as it turns out, I think that the statute of limitations works in our favour, because we have come up with a better solution, have we not, Arnould?"

"Much better."

"We have decided to take the matter and the whole Pelletier family . . . to the court of public opinion! A magnificent press campaign, François, you would be proud. We will begin by telling your father's story, and explain that, given the statute of limitations, he is safe from any legal action. The general public will hate this. At trial, it's always possible to side with the defendant, but people really hate impunity. We plan to publicly expose the entire Pelletier family. Your father's soap factory will be branded "built by a war profiteer", he will never get another order, never be able to sell his business, the company will reek of treason – it will be like a hanged man's house, nobody will want it. Political pressure will ensure that you, François, are fired from *Le Journal*; you will be branded for life and should you manage to find a job, it will be for some minor provincial rag where you'll still be writing stray dog stories at the age of fifty. As for you, Hélène, you'll have to carry on sucking off every Bernard de Jonsac who comes along. And you, Jean, will never sell so much as a pair of boxer shorts from your boutique. The whole Pelletier family, parents and children, will sink without trace."

The words echoed in everyone's mind.

Sucking off who? François wondered whether he had heard correctly.

Jean, who was initially relieved that there had been no mention of his fingerprints, now saw his linen shop, the only business where he had hoped to succeed, going bankrupt. How would Geneviève react?

"You murdered Étienne," Hélène suddenly screamed.

"No, no, mademoiselle, that's really not our style. Is it, Arnould?"

416

"Not our style at all."

"To be candid, mademoiselle, we have had no information about your brother from our colleagues in Indochina. We were entirely unaware of his actions."

"What is it that you want?" said François.

"Silence, Monsieur Pelletier, your silence. You toss your notes into the bin and go back to reporting on stolen bicycles. If you do not, if you try to be clever and pass the story on to one of your colleagues, if you make the slightest fuss, and I mean the slightest, we'll wheel out Big Bertha and blow the Pelletiers to kingdom come. Parents and children alike."

Hélène and Jean turned to their brother.

"Don't look at me like that!"

Lagrange closed his dossier and sat back in his chair as he quietly awaited the verdict, about which he was in no doubt.

"You said our parents were arrested?"

"A slight slip of the tongue, mademoiselle. Thank you for giving me the opportunity to correct it. They are not, strictly speaking, under arrest. We have simply urged them to come to Paris."

"For . . .?"

"Parents – even if they are thieves – can often be a fount of good advice. We thought your father would be able to help your elder brother make the right decision."

"And until they arrive we're prisoners?"

This came from Jean, who was already worrying about what he would say to Geneviève.

"Prisoners! Did you hear that, Arnould?"

"I heard."

"No, no, not at all, what on earth put that idea into your head? Your parents will be here by the end of the day, you will take a little time to talk to them and together you'll make a grown-up decision. In the meantime, you, Monsieur Pelletier, will not move a muscle. Let us call it a moratorium of sorts. You will suppress the urge to do something you might regret and we, for our part, will load Big Bertha, but we will not light the fuse. Are we agreed?"

François nodded. He agreed.

417

41

Absolutely

They had gathered at Luigi's, an Italian restaurant on the rue Lamarck where the pasta was divine, and, more importantly, for those in the rear dining room it was possible to talk without fear of being overheard by other customers, since the tables were spaced well apart. "Well, well, Monsieur Pelletier, we haven't seen you for a long time," Luigi greeted them, though it was something he said to every customer who had not been there for a week.

Everyone had gravely studied the menu. Everyone knew that the main course would be humble pie.

Angèle looked gaunt, no one was in the mood for jokes. It had been less than a fortnight since Étienne's death, and it was obvious that she was still constantly weeping. Now she had been forced to make this trip to Paris, a city that stirred up old memories ... She sat silent and preoccupied. In the thirty years they had been living in Beirut, she had grown used to the idea that she would never have to explain herself; these days, it was something she scarcely thought about, but now the past had resurfaced and with it the foul stench ... If truth were told, she felt ashamed. She was not sitting at a restaurant table; she was sitting in the dock. The thought of having to explain herself to her children was devastating. Meanwhile, Monsieur Pelletier commented on the menu, made suggestions that no one listened to. François was angry, Hélène was furious, Jean was out of his depth. As for Geneviève, her husband had told her nothing. You'll find out tonight, he had said. Geneviève felt insulted; it was obvious from her starchy manner. She was as imperious as ever, but sat tight-lipped, with an air of injured majesty.

Somewhat unnerved by the stony silence and the grim faces of the diners, the waitress took the order as she might for any group who had been arguing before they arrived. Nobody knew what would be said this evening, nor who would start the conversation. In the end, it was Louis. When the wine had been served, and although they were still waiting for their starters, François opened his mouth to speak, but already his father had set down his glass.

"My real name is Albert Maillard, your mother's is Pauline Maudet. We arrived in Beirut in 1920, under the name of Évrard. There we bought false papers in the name of Pelletier, for which we paid twenty-four thousand francs."

"Please!" said Angèle who found such details squalid.

There was a curious silence. They were no longer listening to an intelligence officer telling them an unlikely tale and threatening them with the full force of the law, they were listening to their father relate *their* story, *their* origin. As they listened, Louis recounted a story that they would have found hard to credit in a novel, though the story was filled with characters who seemed familiar, only their roles were very different.

Jean was secretly satisfied. His father had been forced to confess a shameful secret for all of them to hear. It was good to see the tables turned.

"When I came back from the Great War (thank you, mademoiselle)" – seeing the waitress refill his glass, Angèle laid a hand on his arm, he was drinking at an alarming rate – "things were very difficult. There was no place for the likes of us. We had fought a war and won, we had sacrificed health, our friends, our youth, and then when we came home, we discovered it was impossible to find a job – there were no jobs. Even our military pensions weren't being paid. At the time, I had a comrade to support (he's dead now), which meant there were two mouths to feed, and we were living in a tiny little garret ..."

"Get a move on, Louis!" said Angèle. "At this rate, we'll be here tomorrow."

"Yes, yes, you're right."

"So, anyway, this friend and I talked about starting a business ... At that time, there was more money being spent on memorials to those who had died in the war than on veterans who had survived it . . . Well, cities and towns were buying factory-made war memorials. So, we printed up a catalogue with drawings of various kinds of monument – there was something for everyone – and we sold an awful lot. But instead of having the monuments cast and delivered . . . we took the money and ran."

Louis drained his glass.

"How much?" said Geneviève, her eyes shining. "How much money?"

Louis turned to his wife, who gave him a look that said: "Go on, tell them, we've come this far . . ."

"In today's money, I'd say . . . thirty million francs."

There was a stunned silence.

None of the children sitting around the table felt they had grown up in a wealthy family. The Pelletiers were staunchly upper middle class, nothing more.

Eschewing her imperious bearing, Geneviève rested her chin in her hands and gazed at her father-in-law as Josephine once gazed at Napoleon: "What a man, dear Lord, what a man!"

"With that money, we bought the soap factory . . . You know the rest."

What Louis was talking about was now a thriving business, with outlets in Tripoli, Aleppo and Damascus. The money initially invested had obviously increased exponentially. Everyone around the table was trying to figure out where it had gone . . . Was there a secret fortune stashed somewhere?

Angèle leaned over and whispered in her husband's ear.

"Ah, yes, of course . . . The soap factory was so successful from the outset that in 1922, I founded the Federation of Overseas War Veterans. To bring together all the ex-servicemen no longer living in France – and let me tell you, that's a lot of people. Veterans who were as much in the shit—"

"Louis, please!" said Angèle.

"As much in need as those in France. The Federation paid for operations, it helped to pay the rent of those most in need, we set up a pension fund that continues to pay pensions to this day.

Funds came from everywhere, but since the soap factory was doing very well, for many years we were the principal donors, weren't we, Angèle? Over twenty years, we paid out about three times the amount that we made ..."

"The money you stole!" muttered Jean, bent over his plate.

"Oh, come on, Jean!" said Geneviève. "They've just told you they paid it all back!"

"Bouboule is right," said Angèle, "paying the money back does not change the fact that we stole it. That would be too easy."

"Maybe," said Geneviève, "but if you give it back, it's not the same."

No one now knew what to say. All that remained of the original fortune was all that they had ever known. The wheel had turned full circle.

Jean felt disappointed now. His father was once again a great man and he was a spare part. He briefly wondered whether the curse that hung over his life was not punishment for the sins of his father.

"In my experience, the veterans appreciate subsidies more than they do war memorials," Louis ventured, "but that's just my opinion."

He drained his glass again.

"That's the story," he said, setting the glass down.

There was a lengthy silence.

"But, in that case ..."

It was Jean who again spoke up. He was staring at the tablecloth, following a complex train of thought that required concentration. He looked at his father.

"But in that case, the whole history of the Pelletier family, Maréchal Ney, all that ..."

Louis turned to his wife who shrugged as if to say: "You're on your own, you can't say I didn't warn you."

"Well, in a way it's true ... but it's not true. We are a very recent branch of the Pelletier family, if I can put it that way. But Pelletier is a common name. Very common. I'm willing to bet there was someone named Pelletier in Napoleon's entourage. So, what you were told ..."

"What *you* told them!" Angèle said pointedly.

"Yes, all right, what I told them ... well, anyway, it's mostly true! That's it."

He drained another glass. From his expression, it was clear that the matter was closed, and yet ...

"Legally, the statute of limitations means that you can't be prosecuted," said François, "but the intelligence services are threatening to drag the whole family through the mud."

"Oh no." Louis shook his head. "I'm going to see Andrieu tomorrow, we'll sort this whole thing out."

"Andrieu? Robert Andrieu?"

"Yes, I've got an appointment with him, we'll sort things out."

Once again, everyone was dumbfounded. Robert Andrieu, a senior civil servant, had headed up several government departments and was currently the préfet de police in Paris.

"Do you know him?"

"Robert? Pretty well, yes. When I set up the Federation, he was one of the founding members. He was posted to Jeddah at the time."

"To Cairo," said Angèle.

"You're right, my dear, to Cairo."

"Do you know any other people?" Hélène said.

This was the first time she had spoken. Her tone was suspicious.

"How do you mean?"

"Do you know other important people?"

"The thing is, when you've fought shoulder to shoulder with men, you always have a kind of bond ... Most war veterans who took up government posts, and those who now live abroad, are members of the Federation – that's quite a lot of people, as you can imagine."

"No, I can't imagine."

"What I mean is, I know lots of people ..."

No one understood this sudden internecine clash between father and daughter. Hélène was staring at her father with a venom that was much more intense than when he had recounted his post-war exploits.

"Do you know anyone at the École des Beaux-Arts?"

422

It was not voiced as a question. Louis turned to his wife for support, but she was thinking of something else.

"Well, now you come to mention it . . ."

"Who do you know?" said Hélène curtly.

"You'll laugh at this . . ."

"I don't think so."

"I know the director, Alain de Breuille. He's an old friend, we fought together at the Somme. We lost touch, but we met up again through the Federation, when he was appointed to . . ."

"Warsaw," said Angèle.

"Yes, that's right. So when you said you wanted to apply to the Beaux-Arts, I gave him a ring. Since applications for that year had already closed, he came up with the idea of bringing back some archaic rule . . ."

Hélène nodded. So, it was to her father that she owed her admission to Beaux-Arts under the derided status of "observer". Not that it mattered now, since she had hated the school and left. But she was still angry at him for meddling in her life. Why did he always have to meddle . . .?

Resentfully, she pushed her plate away.

"And Étienne? Was that you too?" she said bitterly.

Seeing Angèle silently weeping, Hélène worried that she had gone too far. Especially since it was not her father but her mother who replied.

"It was me," said Angèle between sobs. "I asked your father to pull strings to get him a job in Saigon. Étienne so desperately wanted to be with Raymond, you know?"

Hélène got up and put her arms around her mother.

François thought about how much he was losing in this whole affair. Jean was thinking back to his arrival in Paris a year earlier and the job with Monsieur Couderc that he owed to his father's connections.

"So, what do we do now?" said François.

Louis picked up the dessert menu.

"I'll have a talk with Andrieu. Then we'll talk again, if that's all right?"

✳

Andrieu opened his arms wide and hugged Louis, then, very softly, said:

"I was so sorry to hear about your son, Louis."

Louis simply nodded.

It was a vast office whose windows overlooked soaring plane trees, stripped bare by winter.

The préfet de police gestured to the chair reserved for guests, then sat down next to Louis.

"How have things been otherwise?"

They had first met in 1923. The memory of the Great War had still been very raw. What cemented their friendship was a curious coincidence. Although they had fought in the same battles on three separate occasions (the Somme, the Second Battle of Flanders and the Battle of the Aisne), they had never met. Unbeknownst to each other, they had fought side by side, and each believed he owed his life to the other being there, present yet invisible, like a shadow protector, a guardian angel.

They had met several times, mostly in Paris where Andrieu had worked in various ministries, and each time it felt as though they were simply picking up the conversation where they had left off.

Today their meeting sounded a little different. Neither felt inclined to broach the subject, and both were keen to avoid platitudes. But the schedule of a préfet de police is a busy one and Louis quickly sensed in his friend a hint of impatience.

"So, Robert, tell me, where do we stand?"

"Nowhere, I hope!" said the préfet with forced laughter. "The case is closed! It *is* closed, isn't it, Louis?"

"That depends on what you want of me."

At sixty, Andrieu had a deceptively kindly face and a deceptively benevolent smile. The man was a political beast, and Louis instantly realised that he was in deadly earnest.

"I had to fire a shot across your son's bows to convince him to drop the story. Now we can discuss the matter. François was about to dig up a story about currency trafficking that . . ."

"A true story?" Louis interrupted.

"True, false, who cares? It's a scandal that we don't need right now!"

The bronze mantel clock depicting a soldier with a rifle ticked loudly.

"You're suggesting we swap scandals, aren't you? Yours for mine?"

"More or less. Your son drops his investigation, and we muzzle the bloodhounds investigating your war memorial swindle. What's the alternative, Louis? We dig up your past and you get crucified?"

"After thirty years and another world war, I don't think anyone will care much. In fact, with everything I've given the War Veterans' Federation, I could come out of this looking like Robin Hood."

"You're right, Louis, but your family name would be dragged through the mud. And mud sticks. It's your children who would suffer. Of course, we would have a scandal of our own to deal with – it won't be the first and it won't be the last. We'll simply set up a commission and bury the thing, then, in a couple of months, we'll find some other scandal to distract people's attention and they'll forget all about it. But by that time, you will have lost everything."

The clock chimed nine.

Louis had done his best to fight François's corner. He had failed. He looked up at Andrieu.

"How long have you known about . . .?"

"The war memorials? Actually, I only found out when I became préfet de police. It's one of the secrets of the Republic that are passed down from one chief of police to the next."

Louis said nothing, but looked Andrieu straight in the eye.

"What?"

"Did the government have something to do with my son's death?"

"Nothing whatever, Louis. I spoke to the Minister of the Interior personally, so I can give you my word."

"And how much is your word worth?"

"As much as yours."

"To the nearest piastre?"

The préfet smiled.

"If you like, yes, to the nearest piastre."

*

Monsieur and Madame Pelletier had taken a room at the Hôtel de l'Europe, which Angèle had always joked was run by "your father's mistress". Angèle was so drained by the events of the past days that when they checked in she did not even notice Madame Ducrau. It was when she came back from lunch that she finally noticed the woman and smiled to herself. Louis was not far off the mark: she had to be at least two hundred years old.

While Louis went to see the préfet, Angèle decided to take a nap. It was always the same, she looked forward to the moment when she could get a little rest, but when it came, she could not sleep.

She felt strangely relieved that they had finally told their children everything. If her hand had not been forced, would they ever have explained? She was sorry that Étienne had not been there. She could hear his booming laugh ...

Even in the grimmest situations, it is not unusual to become preoccupied with some insignificant detail. Since Étienne's funeral, Angèle had been brooding about Joseph's disappearance and what had become of the trunk containing Étienne's belongings that had not been shipped back.

She absolutely had to talk to Louis about the trunk again. Absolutely. It was on this word that she dozed off, fully clothed. Her mind seemed fixated on the word because, when she woke, it was still there. *Absolutely.* It referred to her son's possessions. Until she got them back, there would always be something unfinished.

It was early November, the nights drew in early. The hotel room was bathed in a bluish twilight. She finally understood why Louis always stayed here on his visits to Paris. Although the room was not big, it was cosy, comforting. Angèle could have lived out her days here; she felt a little like dying.

Louis had arranged that they would meet the children in the small lounge on the ground floor so he could tell them about his meeting with the préfet de police.

What time was it? My goodness, six o'clock. Barely time to wash her face and put on a little makeup – oh dear, oh dear, I look a fright, and they're probably all waiting for me downstairs ...

Geneviève always contrived to arrive a little late; she liked the idea of people waiting on her arrival. So she was a little disappointed when her mother-in-law appeared a few minutes after she did. She felt sure that Angèle had done it deliberately to spite her.

Louis gave an account of his meeting with Andrieu.

The case was closed.

François said nothing, he simply stared at his feet.

"Robert Andrieu assures me that the government had no hand in Étienne's death."

"And you believe him?" Hélène said tersely.

Her father looked her in the eye for a long moment.

"Yes, Hélène, I believe him."

It was over.

They ordered aperitifs. Madame Ducrau did not have much to offer, but they made do with what there was. At about nine o'clock, Angèle began to yawn.

"We're going to head off," said Jean, getting to his feet.

"So early?" Angèle said.

Not wanting to draw attention to his mother's tiredness, Jean blamed himself.

"Yes, I think we should head home ... It's been a long day, hasn't it, Geneviève?"

His wife stood up, po-faced and prissy, as though she had just been informed that her presence was no longer required. She kissed everyone perfunctorily – "Come on, Jean, since you're so desperate to get home, let's go!" It was excruciating.

"That woman's such a bitch," Hélène said.

"Hélène!" her mother said reproachfully, though she had been thinking the same thing.

"François?" said Monsieur Pelletier. "Can I speak to you in private for a minute?"

Leaving Angèle and Hélène in the little lounge, they went out into the street and lit cigarettes.

"I can only imagine, son, how hard it must be for you to have to give up your investigation. A story like that could make your name."

"It was more than that, I wanted to do it in memory of Étienne."

"I know that," said Louis. "It's a great sacrifice, and I wanted to tell you that I appreciate it. We all appreciate it."

"A fat lot of good that is to me."

He instantly regretted the words, but Louis shrugged them off.

"I also wanted to say . . ."

He nodded to the window of the small lounge through which they could just make out the silhouettes of Angèle and Hélène.

"About the École Normale Supérieure, and your job at *Le Journal*, I wouldn't want you to think that Hélène or Jean went behind your back . . . They weren't the ones who told us."

"I never thought they did."

"Of course you did! In your shoes, I'd think the same thing. I knew you were not going to Normale Sup very early. You wrote to tell us you'd been awarded an "honourable mention" in the matriculation exam. Well, you know how conceited I am when it comes to family, I requested a copy of the grades to show to my friends at the Café des Colonnes. I'm an idiot – you can say it, I won't be offended. When the university wrote back to say your name wasn't on their list, obviously, I lodged a complaint. So, they sent me the list of all those who had sat the exam, and your name wasn't on it."

"Why are you telling me all this now?"

"Because you're probably thinking I do more to help your brothers and your sister than I do to help you, that's why! You're thinking I paid for a car so Jean could work, and gave him money to open the shop with Geneviève. You're thinking I got Hélène a place at the École des Beaux-Arts, and found Étienne a job in Saigon, but I did nothing for you. That's why I'm telling you. I knew from the start that you weren't studying at the École Normale, that you never even *applied*. But I carried on sending you money and pretended I didn't know because I *trust* you, I trust your choices. And because I'm guessing you don't earn a fortune at *Le Journal*, I'll carry on sending you money, and I'm happy to. I just don't want you feeling we treat you worse than we do our other children."

François dropped his cigarette and crushed it with his heel; he wished he could hug his father or have his father hug him. Instead he said:

"Thank you, Papa."

"Come on, let's go inside," said Louis.

"Just one thing . . ."

François tugged his sleeve.

"I understand how you know about Normale Sup, but how did you find out I was working at *Le Journal*?"

"When I came to Paris looking for Hélène, I went to your apartment assuming she'd be there. There was no one in, but I bumped into your concierge – what's her name? Léontine? She could talk the hind legs off a donkey! So when I stopped to . . ."

"It's all right," said François, smiling, "spare me the anecdote."

They went back into the hotel.

*

Jean was so emotionally drained that he would have given ten years of his life to go straight to bed, but first he had to wait until Geneviève had finished what she sometimes called "her ablutions". Jean had rarely heard the word, and associated it with a private, somewhat shameful practice that he found too degrading to mention.

"I was right!" muttered Geneviève.

Jean squeezed his eyes shut. He had left the apartment this morning flanked by two uniformed policemen, and possibly destined for the guillotine. He had come back completely unharmed, but Geneviève had not said a word about it – not even an unpleasant one.

"I was right! I could just tell . . ."

Jean knew that she would keep repeating the phrase until he finally gave in, out of irritation or exhaustion, and asked what exactly she had been right about – but not this time. There were occasional moments when he refused to admit defeat, he did not know why. Perhaps because the terrible dread of the past days had faded, because the issue of his fingerprints was finally behind him. It made him feel strong.

"I knew it right from the start!"

Jean was determined not to give in.

He undressed, cautious not to glance – even inadvertently – towards Geneviève performing her ablutions, since, if he did, she would shriek and scream as if he had raped her.

He carefully folded his clothes. His head was spinning a little. He had had a little too much white wine.

Geneviève would always get into bed first, there would be much shifting of buttocks, twisting of shoulders and sighing as she pulled the blankets and the eiderdown up to her chin. Jean took what space was left.

"I just knew it . . ."

Jean groaned. He needed a little peace, he needed it now, so he relented.

"What did you know?"

"That your family had money. But they don't even invite us to stay for dinner, it's disgraceful!"

"Maman was tired . . ."

"And obviously they don't want to give us any money, even though they're rich."

For once, Jean was incensed. He felt his blood pumping.

"How can you say they don't give us money? They paid for a car so I could get a job, they gave us the money we needed to open the shop."

"No . . ."

"What do you mean, 'no'? Are you saying they didn't give us money for the shop?"

"No, they lent us money, there's a big difference!"

Jean choked. It was deeply unfair. Had the Cholet family ever given them so much as a centime? No, nothing. It was always the Pelletiers who were expected to cough up.

Angrily, he turned to Geneviève.

"Let me get some sleep," she said, closing her eyes. "I've had a hard day."

*

"It's a pity that Bouboule didn't stay," said Angèle.

They were sitting in a restaurant not far from the hotel.

"Would it be possible to get served quickly?" Louis had asked.

There were few diners. The Pelletiers simply ordered a main course and a bottle of wine. And, for the first time, it seemed possible to talk about Étienne without breaking down in tears.

A little later, Louis asked for the bill.

"Time to go, children," he said. "Your mother and I have an early flight tomorrow morning and—"

"No," said Angèle, "I've changed my mind, darling. I'm not flying back with you. I'm going to Saigon to get my son's belongings."

Hélène turned to her mother.

"I'd like to go with you."

42

You're right

Although he tried not to, and in spite of the traumatic events of recent days, François could not stop thinking about her. He had not heard another word from "Nine"; even the nickname she had given him was probably a fiction.

She had appeared before the magistrate, then vanished.

He had thought a thousand times of worming her name out of Juge Lenoir, but each time he got cold feet, and hated himself for it.

The worst of it was that even her exquisite face had dissolved; François could no longer picture it. The few details he could remember – the curve of her lashes, the fire in her eyes, her lips, dear God, those lips, her figure – briefly flickered into life only to fade. He could no longer see her as a living person. He was in love with a ghost.

He left *Le Journal* at the end of the day and headed home. He enjoyed taking the métro since it gave him the opportunity to read the pages he only had time to skim before they went to press.

Getting off the train, he turned right towards the exit.

There she was, on the platform, walking towards him. They both stopped for a moment. François stood, trying to calculate the odds of this accidental meeting. It was pointless. The young woman blushed violently. Their meeting owed nothing to chance. As if she had abandoned all pretext, she walked up to him.

Her voice quavered.

"I just wanted to thank you . . ."

Already the platform was beginning to fill with people waiting for the next train. They stepped aside.

"You're welcome," said François. "There was no need for thanks."

She was staring at him with the same intensity as in their previous meetings.

"And I was wondering . . ."

The train roared into the station in a shriek of metal that drowned out everything. As soon as it had stopped, she said:

"I thought maybe . . . I mean, if you . . ."

"Yes?"

She suggested a walk along the banks of the Seine. Or the Tuileries gardens. François would have been happy with whatever she suggested.

"We can meet on rue Bayard if you like."

It was near the Champs-Élysées, in a fashionable part of town.

"Is that close to where you live?" he asked and immediately regretted his tactlessness, but she merely laughed.

"It's not far, but you won't . . . How did you put it last time? You won't have to compromise yourself."

Meeting for a first date outdoors, on Armistice Day (when the weather report was forecasting fog), was hardly a typical romantic tryst, but François did not care.

"I'd like that very much."

She answered quickly – good, all right. She smiled. She did not shake his hand.

As he watched her walk away, she must have felt his eyes boring into her.

✳

François arrived forty-five minutes early. The weather report had not lied but, by noon, the heavy fog of early morning had dissipated.

The whole area was teeming with people. Veterans of the Great War were intending to lay a wreath at the Tomb of the Unknown Soldier, beneath the Arc de Triomphe. They had been joined by young communists from the UJRF, trade unionists from the UDS, wartime deportees and forced labourers from the FDT, together with sundry communist and feminist associations. François watched as the groups marched past, waving flags and holding aloft banners.

433

Since he had time on his hands, and was curious, he went to have a closer look.

As the groups converged on Franklin-Roosevelt métro station, the atmosphere was exhilarating and somewhat tense. François stopped a determined-looking young man who explained that the prefecture de police had barred the demonstrators from a large section of the Champs-Élysées. "But we're not going to stand for that," said the young man, as he melted into the crowd. François quickly realised that he was right; the demonstrators were not going to stand for it. Instinctively, he took out his notebook, and jotted down what he had just been told, information that he verified with other protestors when he reached the métro station. Protestors had been told they were allowed to go to the Arc de Triomphe, but were not allowed to pass Franklin-Roosevelt métro station. It was a preposterous decision that appeared to permit access to the Arc de Triomphe but blocked off any possible route. Before long, François realised that, for many of the demonstrators, the laying of a wreath at the Tomb of the Unknown Soldier was simply a pretext. Chants of "SUPPORT THE MINERS! SUPPORT THE STRIKE!" left little doubt as to the protestors' true purpose, and their anger was further fuelled by the blockade across the Champs-Élysées. There was a fearsome police presence, with heavily armed Republican Guards forming a blockade across the avenue. François jotted down the chants, the banner slogans, and tried to calculate the number of police units as he was jostled from right to left and deafened by the roar of the crowd.

He glanced at his watch. It was later than he thought, he needed to get back to the rue Bayard, and the crowd of three thousand raucous, riotous demonstrators was likely to make that more difficult now that some were suddenly waving the Tricolour and a number of militants had begun to use crowbars to rip up paving stones. Someone insisted that barricades were being erected on the rue George-V, and the rumour spread. A man who had just appeared, panting for breath, announced approvingly: "They've pulled down the scaffolding outside the Crédit Commercial on the rue Bassano!" This was some distance past Franklin-Roosevelt. François tried to understand exactly what was happening. Demonstrators had now massed at two opposing points on the Champs-Élysées, while the police cordon between them was supposed to prevent some from going down the avenue and others from going up. It seemed an untenable situation. He jotted in his notebook, though his pen kept slipping as he was jostled on all sides.

Then, suddenly, without warning, everything speeded up. "They're charging us!" yelled someone, and the crowd started running towards the adjacent streets, desperate to get back to the place de la Concorde. There were shots – was it live gunfire? François, still stupidly clutching his notepad, was running too. He tripped on a banner lying on the ground and fell heavily on his hip. All around, he heard racing footsteps echo off the granite pavement. A hand gripped him under the arm, someone hauled him to his feet and instantly disappeared. The police advanced, their batons raised. François was finding it difficult to run now, he was dragging one foot and clutching his injured hip. In a panic, he crossed the avenue, but police were coming from all sides; protestors were already falling hard, everyone was screaming. François came to the corner of a street whose name he could not read. Just then he saw a boy in a jacket and a turtleneck being grabbed by a small group of officers; the boy stumbled, got up again, but it was too late, his pursuers had already grabbed his sleeves and were dragging him to a doorway. François stood, poleaxed by what he had just seen. Then, without a second thought, he rushed into the building shouting: "Leave him alone, leave him alone!" The young man's face was streaming blood. One of the officers turned to François. "What the fuck are you doing here!" He raised his truncheon. François did not have time to reach into his pocket for his press card, so held up his notepad. It looked pathetic. "I'm a journalist!" The policeman snatched the pad from him. "You think we give a shit?" He brought the baton down hard on his skull, François fell to the ground, he tried to shield his head, this wasn't over.

From his vantage point on the pavement he could see four pairs of boots. The batons rained down, one hit him squarely on the back of the head.

He lost consciousness.

When he came to, he was lying on a tile floor, disoriented.

His head ached viciously and, bringing his hand up, he found it had been bandaged.

"He'll definitely need an X-ray," said a voice.

A calm voice. A man in his forties wearing a bloodstained white coat. A pharmacist. Propping himself on one elbow, François saw three men sitting on chairs set up between the shelves. There were bandaged hands, a leg in a makeshift splint, a man with a bandage over his face, and, everywhere, the smell of surgical spirit and liniment. The pharmacy was not technically open for business; the lights were low, the steel shutter only half raised. Outside, as far as he could see, the street was calm.

"What's your name?"

The pharmacist held splayed fingers in front of François's face.

"Pelletier. François Pelletier."

"How many fingers?"

"Four."

"Good."

François looked up at the clock on the wall: four o'clock.

"Jesus Christ!"

Nine! They had arranged to meet more than an hour ago. François managed to get to his feet, but had to steady himself on the pharmacist's shoulder. His head was spinning.

"Will you be all right?"

He staggered towards the door, stiff and hesitant, like a drunk pretending to be sober. Nine would be gone by now, he knew that. He was frantic, and furious with himself. He went back to the pharmacist, who was now treating someone else, and held out his hand.

"Thank you."

The man in the white coat stood up and shook his hand.

"What do I owe you?"

"Nothing. Just make sure you get an X-ray, you can't be too careful."

He found himself on the corner of rue Jean-Mermoz, and began to run. It was futile. This section of the Champs-Élysées was clear. There were groups of officers here and there, but the demonstrators were now several hundred metres further up the avenue, and there was still a lot of chaos and shouting. François did not stop. He ran to the rue Bayard, where, obviously, there was no one waiting. He had no way of finding Nine. She would simply think that he had not shown up. Of course, that was true, and at the same time, it wasn't ... He was choking with frustration.

As he boarded the métro, he was a broken man.

Why had he felt the need to go and see what was going on elsewhere when there had been a woman waiting for him?

François had never wanted a woman so badly, so passionately, and now he had failed to show up for their date.

How was it even possible?

As he headed back to *Le Journal*, he was struck by what had just happened. Never before had French police tried to prevent a journalist from doing his job, let alone beaten him. He thought back to how the police officers had been arranged. As so often, he was writing an article in his head. He regularly thought out his articles, coming up with sentences and whole paragraphs that only needed to be put down on paper. If he had a reputation as a fast worker, it was because he thought everything through before he sat down to write.

At his desk on the rue Quincampoix, he wrote out the article, then took it straight to Denissov.

"I've got something on the Champs-Élysées demo."

The editor-in-chief of *Le Journal* frowned.

"I don't understand ... We've got Vanacker covering that."

Denissov pushed a piece of paper across the desk.

"I've got his piece here."

From where he stood, François could read the headline:

BLOODY BATTLES ON THE CHAMPS-ÉLYSÉES. DEMONSTRATORS IN VIOLENT CLASHES WITH POLICE

Nearly 100 injured

He walked over to Denissov and held out several sheets of paper. "This isn't an article, it's an editorial piece . . ."

Denissov was so shocked he had to restrain himself from kicking François out of his office. An editorial? Since when did a junior news reporter write front-page editorials?

He took the document, put on his glasses and read.

WHAT KIND OF A REPUBLIC
DO WE WANT?

For some time, concerns have been raised about police brutality. Only recently, we witnessed the kind of savagery they can be capable of in Firminy. While we acknowledge that the police often face a difficult task when dealing with demonstrators, and even violent activists, it would be remiss not to point out that their duty is to restore and to maintain order, not to pour fuel on the fire, which is precisely what they did on the Champs-Élysées in Paris on 11 November. Setting up police barricades between two métro stations, thereby blocking a demonstration by members of the FFI, the FTP and the Federal Union of War Veterans, is not simply an idiotic and incendiary tactic, it is a strategic error that would be inexcusable in a tinpot dictatorship. It is easy to prevent a demonstration; you simply ban the march. But to give official authorisation for a demonstration only to later block the path of several thousand protestors is a deliberate act of provocation.

Were such a strategy simply to result in dozens of casualties, that would be grave enough. But when the police, empowered and indeed encouraged in their brutal tactics, seek to prevent the press from reporting on such events, snatching a notebook from the hands of a journalist, and knocking him to the ground and beating him senseless, that is an altogether more serious matter.

When police officers, the "keepers of the peace", are no more than brute forces, when freedom of the press is threatened and attacked, democrats of every stripe cannot help but wonder, is this what the hard-fought Resistance, the hard-won Liberation, was for?

Authorities would be well advised to reflect on this and to remember that we, the French, have not endured so much sacrifice in order to see our Republic trampled underfoot, to see the police act as an armed force intended to suppress dissent, to see our government adopting the tactics of authoritarian regimes.

Denissov took off his glasses.

"You're right, it's very good."

He set down the page.

"Front page, editorial."

François's jaw dropped. He simply nodded.

For the second time that day, he had been knocked senseless.

When the proofs landed on Malevitz's desk, François rushed over to look at them and there was his editorial, on the front page. But it was signed ... Adrien Denissov.

"Bastard!" muttered François and raced down the corridor only to be blocked by Malevitz.

"That's enough shit, kid! It's time you learned the rules. What did you expect?"

As François was about to push him away, Malevitz released his grip.

"You have two minutes in which you can either lose your job here at *Le Journal*, or you can get back to work and earn a front-page byline."

Malevitz calmly walked back to his desk and resumed reading the proofs.

"Now, you do what you like."

François felt the tears welling up.

His life seemed to career from one failure to another. He left the office without a word.

43

No *evidence, no investigation*

The temperature was touching thirty degrees, the humidity almost ninety per cent. Angèle found that she was utterly unprepared for the weather, for the mingled smells of charred pork, vanilla, smoked fish and exhaust fumes, for this raucous, bizarre bustle of people milling around the city, coolies on the docks, giggling schoolgirls crossing the street, shopkeepers standing in doorways, soup vendors grinning through the steam rising from their pots, women bent double under the weight of victuals, their children tugging on their vibrant skirts. All she could say was: "My God . . ."

Hélène, for her part, pictured Étienne when he first arrived, gazing wide-eyed at this brave new world. True, he had come here to be with Raymond, whom he would never see again, but, in the moment, Saigon must have seemed to him a wondrous city.

In Paris, the travel agent had told Angèle that in Saigon: "There are only two hotels, Le Métropole and the Crystal Palace, nothing else." Then, leaning across the desk to Angèle, she had whispered:

"Le Métropole is, well, it's a little . . . If you know what I mean . . ."

She sat back, satisfied that the customer had been duly warned. Angèle had elected to stay at the Crystal Palace.

"An excellent choice, Madame Pelletier, especially for a lady such as yourself."

Angèle would never discover why Le Métropole was unsuitable for a lady like herself because when she and Hélène went there for an aperitif on their first evening, she found the place quite enchanting: the huge hothouse plants, the all-woman orchestra, the exclusive, boisterous clientele, the balletic service. Had she not been there for Étienne, she would have thoroughly enjoyed herself.

Hélène turned many men's heads. This was the first time that Angèle had gone out not with her daughter, but with a young woman who just happened to be her daughter. What experience did she have of boys? That was the wrong question, thought Angèle. The right question was: what experience did Hélène have of men? Hélène was surely more confident in dealing with such advances than her mother had been. Was I as beautiful at her age as she is? At any other time, Angèle might have feared that the thought would make her seem old. But here it did not. She felt proud. And this made her realise that she was comfortable with her age.

Hélène also saw her mother differently now. She tried to square the image she had always had with what she had recently learned about her past. It was difficult for her to imagine her mother at twenty, fleeing the country with stolen millions, buying false papers to have a name with which to raise her children. She simply could not reconcile the two: that had been a different woman, one Hélène would never know.

The travel agent had been right: the Crystal Palace was an opulent hotel with a vast rooftop terrace that overlooked the whole of the city. Étienne would have visited these places, he so enjoyed going out and meeting people. Everything reminded Angèle of her loss.

She and Hélène decided that the easiest thing to do would be to go to the apartment where Étienne had lived, which was probably where his belongings were stored.

"If they were ever found," said Angèle.

She said it with a hint of fatalism that startled Hélène. It was as if, now that she was here, retrieving Étienne's trunk was no longer important.

They had no trouble finding the building. A storm cloud burst as they stepped into the lobby. Fat raindrops pounded the pavement, the cars, the rooftops and the balconies with a constant roar like an endless rumble of thunder.

So this was where Étienne had lived. Angèle looked around as if she might see something of his. It was a foolish notion. It was a large hallway with a wide stone staircase, broad landings, walls of peeling paint. The apartment building had a certain withered glory. Now it smelled of fried fish and rot, and the humidity of the rain.

Angèle knocked loudly because from inside the apartment she could hear voices, shouts, a heated conversation or an argument, she could not tell.

A boy of four or five flung open the door and when he saw Angèle and Hélène he ran off screaming as though he had seen the devil. After the gloomy corridor, the apartment room seemed large and brightly lit. They could see a window overlooking a terrace. What splendour the place had once had was now a distant memory. The floor was littered with clothes, rickety chairs were piled with kitchen utensils as though the family ate on the floor. Looming in the background, there was a huge American refrigerator.

A few steps inside the room, the floorboards had been blackened by a large dark stain.

A wary, worried woman stepped forward, calling to someone behind her. A man appeared. Several of his teeth were missing, and he spluttered and shouted. It seemed as if everyone was afraid.

"*Vous parlez français?*" said Angèle, smiling broadly. "Does anyone here speak French?"

She could not have been more affable had she been selling encyclopaedias.

The man waved gruffly, as though flicking dust away. It was clearly a blunt refusal. Go away.

"Étienne Pelletier," said Hélène. "He used to live here. *Here!*"

Two or three young adults came to the rescue, with a brood of children scurrying between their legs. With all their shouting and gesticulating, they managed to drown out the thunderous rain bouncing on the roof.

Angèle was startled and took a step backwards.

Hélène was prepared to try again, but her mother was at the head of the stairs, about to descend, glancing around at the querulous family as though afraid that someone might shoot her in the back.

The rainstorm added to the ambience. The downpour had begun just as they arrived and, just as they reached the ground floor, a

442

little stunned, it stopped. The two women did not speak. Had they come all this way only to have a door slammed in their faces?

"Maman!" Hélène cried suddenly.

Angèle whirled around.

"It's Joseph!"

Étienne's cat was terribly thin, but his eyes had the same gleam and already he was rubbing himself against their legs.

The two women picked him up and began to sob. Joseph closed his eyes and purred. All along the rue Catinat, the gutters were like rivers in spate, and the pavements shone.

＊

"Should we give up?" said Hélène.

Angèle held Joseph to her breast beneath her coat, as she might have held a baby. She was sobbing now.

"I can't give up," she said, fumbling for a handkerchief.

"Give Joseph to me for a minute," said Hélène, also in tears.

Angèle handed her the cat. By the time they had dried their tears, blown their noses, sobbed some more and whispered: "Joseph, Joseph," over and over, they were back at the Crystal Palace.

"I'm so sorry, madame, but pets are not permitted at Le Crystal."

The doorman cut a fine figure in his livery; he was proud of his role as gatekeeper. He was staring warily at the cat's head poking from beneath the coat.

"If you wish to throw me out, you will have to call the police," Angèle said wearily as she picked up her key. "They'll find me in my room."

Without waiting for a reply, she headed for the lift, then turned and leaned over to the receptionist.

"Could you have someone bring up some raw fish? I'll feed him while we are waiting for the police."

As soon as they stepped into the room, Joseph jumped down, ran over to the bed and curled up on the counterpane.

"He's so terribly thin!"

"No," said Angèle, "there will be no giving up."

443

It took a moment for Hélène to realise her mother was answering the question she had asked half an hour earlier. As she hung up her coat, Angèle continued:

"At first, I believed the plane crash was an accident. If the scandal Étienne had unearthed really was innocuous, I don't see why the government would have to go to so much trouble. I came here to fetch Étienne's things, but also to try to understand how he died. And why."

"Papa said the government had nothing to do with it ... Do you believe that?"

Angèle went to open the door. It was a chambermaid with food for Joseph.

"Yes, I do believe it. (Thank you, mademoiselle.) Come here, Joseph, come have some food."

As the cat sat down to eat, Angèle continued:

"I know Robert Andrieu very well ..."

She flushed a little.

"Time was, he would flirt with me when your father was not around ... Oh, he was always very respectful ... But I know he is not a man who would lie about such a thing."

"So ...?"

Angèle sat down on the floor and stroked Joseph as he ate his raw fish.

"So, it doesn't matter whether it was the government or the traffickers, what I want to know is whether they are going to find the person who killed my son."

"Yes?" said Hélène getting up to answer the door.

This time it was a bellboy. He proffered a folded slip of paper. Hélène looked through her suitcase for her pocketbook, found a coin and went to tip the young man. When she came back, her mother, who had read the note, said in a tone of amused solemnity:

"Hélène darling, apparently His Holiness Pope Loan, of the Siêu Linh, would be most honoured if we would grant him an audience."

*

444

Loan's invitation was for the end of the day. Angèle and Hélène had time to visit the Exchange.

They were told that they would have to take a ticket, then sit patiently and wait to be called.

"How long will we have to wait?" Angèle whispered to Hélène. "Surely there must be some other way?"

Everything about the Exchange portended an implacable rigidity, from the brass grille atop the counter to the serious faces of the clerks, from the wall clock ticking off each second with a fatalistic judder, to the dozens of people sitting stiffly in their chairs waiting to be summoned. Hélène remembered the director's name. "Jeantet is a strange guy, and rather disconcerting," Étienne had said in one of his letters. "On his desk he has a collection of photographs of dead dogs and ex-wives." It was a curious pen portrait, but at least they had a name. Summoning her courage, Hélène tiptoed over to a woman at the end of the counter.

"Do you have an appointment?" she said without looking up.

"Well, no . . . that is to say . . ."

"I'm afraid you will need to make an appointment."

"With whom?"

This question puzzled the clerk, who simply stared at Hélène.

"What is it?" said a voice next to her. "Can I help?"

The speaker was a tall young man in a garish shirt. He had a large nose, blond hair plastered to his head, and a supercilious air that had turned to a leer when he espied Hélène. He wore a number of signet rings on his right hand, set with stones of different colours.

"This lady is asking to see the director."

He was clearly the sort of man who would put his hand on your backside before asking your name. Intuitively, Hélène seized her chance; the young man was obviously a fool.

"My name is Hélène Pelletier, I'm Étienne Pelletier's sister, he . . ."

She trailed off. Gaston's face had changed.

"You . . . You're Pep's sister . . ."

You could have knocked him down with a feather.

"Come with me," he said, "come with me."

He felt like putting an arm around her as though she were an invalid, but he restrained himself.

"I'm here with my mother ..."

"Oh ..."

There was a sudden chill in Gaston's tone.

Angèle stepped forward. He took her hand.

"I'm so sorry for your loss, madame," said Gaston, unable to stop looking at Hélène, deflected like a needle by a magnet.

They walked down a long corridor. As they passed the single-minded clerks and desks piled high with dossiers, Hélène and Angèle wondered how Étienne had been able to bear such an atmosphere. "It's not exactly gay," he had written to his mother. "The Indochinese Currency Exchange looks more like the Indochinese Zombie Exchange." That was terribly well put.

"Monsieur le Directeur, this is Madame Pelletier, the widow of ... Oh, no, my apologies. Étienne's *mother* ..."

Jeantet got up and walked around his desk.

"Madame," he said, clicking his heels like an officer. "May I offer my deepest condolences. In losing your son, the Exchange has lost one of its most brilliant employees. You should be proud of the passion he invested in serving the Exchange, and through us, the colonial administration and Indochina itself."

Hélène wondered whether he would end with a stirring "Vive la République, Vive la France!", but no, he simply took Angèle's hands in his, tilting his head to one side to emphasise his commiseration, his eyes closed in mute anguish, and then, as if Gaston had flicked a switch, he changed the subject.

"Would you care for some green tea?"

It was disconcerting.

Gaston had stepped closer and was gawping at Hélène.

"Mademoiselle here is the sister of good old P ... of our late lamented colleague."

He smiled broadly, proud of this formulation. Jeantet turned to the young woman, grasping her hands as he had Angèle's. She feared he would repeat his funereal oration, but instead he said:

"Or, if you prefer, we have coffee."

Hélène surveyed the dizzying number of photo frames that covered the desk, but unlike her tactful brother, she did not hesitate, she picked up the one closest to hand and turned it around. Gaston choked back a startled cry of amazement and glanced anxiously at his boss.

It was a photograph of an utterly unprepossessing woman.

Far from being offended by this familiarity, Jeantet flashed her an admiring smile.

"My first wife," he said, "a bit—. A rare and precious jewel ... Now, take a seat, take a seat."

He had already forgotten about his offer of green tea.

"You've already met Gaston Paumelle," said Jeantet, pointedly staring at this junior, but Gaston was too enamoured of Hélène's presence to think of leaving.

Hélène recalled one of Étienne's letters: "My colleague, Gaston Paumelle, is one of those boring bastards you find in any agency like this. Though perhaps just a soupçon more cynical. And ugly. And stupid. I realise that sounds like a lot, but bastards of his calibre don't come along very often."

Angèle and Hélène sat on two chairs whose legs the director had had shortened so that, from behind his desk, he was always looking down on his guests, giving them an obscure sense of inferiority.

"My son died ..." Angèle began.

"I know, and in such tragic conditions."

"... while he was investigating a currency trafficking scandal. And I have every reason to believe that his death is directly connected to that investigation."

"Oh yes, yes, the trafficking business ..."

Jeantet suddenly looked very weary.

"It was a bit of an obsession," he muttered.

"And ...?"

"And ..."

He looked up at Gaston, who was gazing at the back of Hélène's neck. It almost looked as though he might take his trousers off.

"And ... I don't know, madame. I honestly do not know ...

He was going through the archives, compiling lists, what else can I tell you?"

"As the director of the Indochinese Currency Exchange, did this story of currency trafficking not arouse your suspicions? Or are you saying it was a figment of his imagination?"

"Your son never filed a report, Madame Pelletier. No one knows what he found. Indeed, no one knows exactly what he was looking for either, do they, Gaston?"

"Yes, yes," said Gaston, who had not heard the question.

He was craning his neck, trying to catch a glimpse of Hélène's legs.

Angèle was about to say something when Jeantet got up and moved his chair so he could sit next to her.

"It is an extremely murky story. And, if it is true, it must involve some very powerful, very influential people. Your son was under the protection of his friend Loan and the whole Siêu Linh sect. And yet, in spite of this . . ."

The director kept looking from Angèle to Gaston, who was standing by the door shamelessly detailing Hélène's body. He was sizing her up. Hélène abruptly decided that she had had enough. She whirled around and glared at him. Gaston simply smiled as though this were an invitation.

Jeantet laid a hand on Angèle's.

"Your son . . ."

There was a pent-up emotion in these simple words.

"I am deeply sorry, Madame Pelletier, but there is no one here who can help you."

Hélène felt a lump in her throat.

Her mother turned to her, tears in her eyes. "No one" was simply another way of referring to the Exchange and its director.

Without a word, the two women stood up. Jeantet picked up a photo frame and was about to hand it to them, but changed his mind. It was a photograph of his dead dog. Showing it to the mother of a dead boy would have been insensitive. He set it down again with a sigh, he felt misunderstood.

Angèle and Hélène went back downstairs, with Gaston hard on

448

their heels. As he bid the two women goodbye, he held Hélène's hand for a little too long. Oh, how he wanted to lunge at her. Instead, he flashed her an unambiguous smile; his teeth were yellow.

*

On the phone, the young official at the High Commission had been very sympathetic.

"It was I who had the doleful duty of informing you . . ."

It was he who had dispatched the telegram, which had been markedly lacking in compassion. It was he who had arranged for Étienne's remains to be returned to Beirut.

"Of course, if you come to Saigon," he had said on the phone, "I shall be only too pleased to take the time to meet with you, Madame Pelletier."

Courteous, perfunctory, efficient, bureaucratic; his physical appearance mirrored his language. He was about the same age as Étienne. Angèle was glad she had not had a son like this: buttoned-up, impervious to doubt. His name was Germain Rouet-Babarit. He rummaged in his desk drawer for his business cards. Angèle could tell he was more eager to give one to Hélène than to her.

"I'd like to know what is happening with the investigation into my son's death."

"Everything is on track, Madame Pelletier."

"What exactly does that mean?"

"We have managed to recover much of the wreckage. As you probably know, it was rather an old plane. Decommissioned. We are about to send everything to a specialist forensic agency. A highly reputable agency, I hasten to add."

"Why has this not been done already?"

"The workings of the administration are not always as swift as one might like, madame. The shipment will take place within the week, I promise."

"And when will you have the results?"

"There may be a bit of a delay, I'm afraid. Reputable agencies of this kind are far from common. This particular agency is in Bordeaux, and I think I can say that it is the finest."

He flashed Hélène a smile whenever he felt at his best.

Angèle persisted. "That really doesn't answer my question. How long?"

"Eight to twelve months. Probably closer to twelve."

The women were stunned.

"And . . . in the meantime?"

The young official peered at them interrogatively.

"In the meantime, are you pursuing your investigation? What are you doing?"

"Oh, no, no, no, mademoiselle! There is nothing we can do before we have the experts' report. We would not know which avenues to explore. But I assure you that as soon as we have their conclusions we will take all necessary measures."

Rouet-Babarit was not a complete fool; he knew that for these women this was terrible news. So, he decided he would try to "grease the wheels" – an expression he had learned during his civil service training.

"Did I tell you I had the pleasure of meeting your late son, Madame Pelletier?"

"Really? In what circumstances?"

"He suspected that people were trafficking in piastres to finance the Việt Minh. It struck me that he seemed to have rather a 'bee in his bonnet' about the subject. He wanted us to investigate, but he brought no proof that might justify such an investigation. So, I said to him: 'No proof, no investigation,' which, I'm sure you agree, is only logical."

"You give that same answer to every question."

"Excuse me?"

But Angèle had already stood up and was beckoning Hélène to follow. She would get nothing more here, any more than she would from the Exchange.

As they reached the door, Germain Rouet-Babarit said in a louder voice:

"Er . . . Madame Pelletier . . ."

He was holding an envelope.

"This is the bill from the High Commission. For the repatriation of your son's remains ..."

Angèle ripped it open, and Hélène, reading over her shoulder, flushed crimson. She opened her mouth to say something but her mother cut her off.

"I refuse to pay, monsieur," she said.

"It is simply to reimburse the administration for the costs incurred in the affair."

"You will never conduct a full investigation into my son's death," Angèle replied calmly, "you will drag your heels and then simply close the case. You send me my son's remains in a cardboard box and you have the gall to charge me 24,000 francs?"

She held out the bill without another word, and, when the official did not take it, she dropped it on the floor.

The young man stared at this calm, resolute woman.

And suddenly, he knew as clearly as she did that she would never pay.

44

Everyone did whatever was necessary to get by . . .

Louis took the métro to Montmartre. He had postponed his flight back to Beirut so that he could take Angèle and Hélène to the airport and then, since the opportunity had never presented itself before, he had invited his sons to lunch.

"With Geneviève?" asked Bouboule.

"Oh, I think a men's day out would be nice, don't you?"

The reader will have no difficulty imagining Geneviève's reaction . . . "Oh I see, so everyone leaves their wife at home? You'll probably end up at a boxing match! Well, bravo! Well, you tell your father for me . . ." There would be no end to it.

They had agreed to meet at Lamarck métro station. Not far from the station was a small kiosk where a war veteran in his sixties sold tickets for the Lottery. His profit could not be much more than a few centimes per ticket, little more than his military pension.

Jean arrived on time.

While they waited for François, they decided to order coffee.

"Or maybe not," his father said. "It's half past eleven, I think I'd rather have a Cinzano. What about you?"

Geneviève's permanent presence meant that it had been a long time since Jean was faced with such a choice.

"A glass of Saint-Raphaël, please . . ."

"How are things with Geneviève?" said his father, raising his glass.

"Good, very good. Thank you, Papa."

They exchanged an awkward smile, then took a moment to study the small café and the stairs that led down to the métro station.

He's put on weight, thought Louis. If it carries on, we can't keep calling him Bouboule. It was one thing when he was just heavy-set, but now ... This question of his son's weight intrigued Louis. He could not imagine Geneviève cooking little dishes, the woman did nothing but sit at one end of the dining room table like an Indian goddess, so how had this happened? Perhaps Jean stuffed his face in restaurants at every opportunity. He had downed his aperitif in one. Should Louis order him another?

"François should be here soon," he said.

Jean was regretting having accepted the invitation; he should have found some excuse; he hadn't thought things through. He felt uncomfortable here, alone with his father.

"There was something I wanted to say, son ..."

"Oh, what?" said Jean abruptly.

His hands felt clammy.

Louis furrowed his brow. He racked his brain and realised he and his son had not been alone together even once since Jean left Beirut. Or ever spoken of that dark period when Bouboule ... It was so difficult to put into words ...

Jean nervously toyed with his empty glass.

"About the soap factory?"

Jean blushed.

"I wanted to say that I'm sorry," said Louis. "It was my fault."

"No, no, it was me ... I should never ... I didn't realise ..."

Here we go, thought Louis, we'll all take the blame for everything, and it will be worse than if we'd never said anything. He turned to say something to his son, but immediately stopped dead. It broke his heart to see Jean like this. He was a ball of fear. How did he even get through the day?

Louis laid his hand on his shoulder.

"It's over now," he said, "it's all over now, son ..."

Jean looked utterly lost.

"You'll be all right now, won't you? You'll be fine ..."

Jean was crying softly, and seeing his large face, puffy with tears, Louis wished he could disappear.

He patted his son on the shoulder, mumbling useless words, fumbled in his pocket and gave Jean a clean, neatly folded handkerchief – Angèle took care of such things. Jean loudly blew his nose.

"I mean, this shop of yours sounds like a good idea," Louis said jovially.

Jean nodded, and blew his nose again.

"Yes, I think it will do well . . ."

He was unconvinced, everything in his life had gone wrong, he could see no reason why things would improve now.

This was all they could find to say to each other. Louis felt ashamed that he could not even talk to his son. He gestured to the waiter to bring another round.

"Oh, so there you are!"

François burst through the door, out of breath. He could sense that something had happened, Bouboule was snuffling and red-eyed. Oh, this family . . .

Since their father was present, the brothers hugged.

"Well . . . what's happened to you?" said Louis pointing to François's head.

He instinctively brought his hand up to the spot where the pharmacist had shaved a patch and put in three stitches.

"Just a nasty fall . . ."

He had no desire to explain things.

"Shall we eat here?" he asked, changing the subject.

"No. We'll find somewhere else. There are lots of restaurants in the area."

When Louis had paid for the drinks, the three men left the café.

"Actually," Louis said, "there's something I wanted to show you . . ."

He stopped.

"I don't know whether there will be anything to see now . . ."

Both Jean and François found this rather mysterious. They walked for a time and came to the rue Ramey.

"It's just there," said Louis, walking ahead.

François looked up. They were on the corner of the Impasse Pers. At the far end of this blind alley, behind a low cement wall and green wrought-iron gates, stood a buhrstone house of the kind common before the Great War.

"Back in my day, it was a wooden fence," Louis said.

The house did not face onto the street but onto a courtyard in which there was a sort of barn and a small vegetable garden which, though not very large, was neatly laid out. There were rows of vegetables, and the garden was carefully weeded. A metal watering can hung next to some garden tools.

Louis nodded to the smaller building. What had looked like a barn was in fact a lean-to shed. Though it could well have been torn down, it had been patched up. Louis was moved to see it: it was not a building; it was almost a sacred relic.

"That's where I lived with Édouard."

Louis turned to his sons.

"I don't want you to think that your father was a common criminal. Let alone your mother!"

1918. The return from war.

"Édouard and I rented the attic room. It was sweltering in summer and freezing in winter. At the time, just feeding ourselves was difficult, since military pensions weren't being paid. I don't want to bang on about it, I'd sound like some old fogey, but we had a pretty grim war ..."

Louis gripped the railings and placed one foot on the low cement wall.

His friend Édouard had been a *gueule cassée*, one of the many war veterans with terrible facial injuries scattered all over France. In Édouard's case, his lower jaw had been blown off.

"We were in a terrible state ... I did a few odd jobs, Édouard couldn't do much – well, his life was complicated."

It would take too long to tell poor Édouard's story.

It had been Édouard who first came up with the idea to sell non-existent war memorials, it had been Édouard who designed the catalogue; Albert had done the rest ...

Louis shook his head. He was saddened by these memories because, in a sense, this was where it all started. Thirty years had passed and now here he was again, with two sons he did not want to think badly of him.

"So, that's what we did ... At the time, everyone did whatever was necessary to get by, and that's the honest truth."

455

François and Jean glanced at each other. They had rarely felt so close.

"It was around that time that your mother and I met. Afterwards, we had no choice but to run . . . Édouard . . . Well, Édouard was already dead by then."

He let the memories wash over him, dismissing them with a shake of his head.

"Over there," he said, nodding to the main house which overlooked the courtyard, "that was Madame Belmont's house."

It was here that Louise had lived, Édouard's blue-eyed girl – eleven years old, pretty as a picture, but grave and serious. Louise was a war orphan, with no one in her life except a mother who had not spoken a word since her husband died in 1916. Louis had left a little money for Louise before he fled the country. But Louis kept this part of the story to himself. It was strange; he'd brought his sons here in the hope that they might understand the abject poverty he had faced after the Great War, but the house seemed pretty now. The renovated shed and the well-tended garden exuded a sense of happiness.

"Well, you know what I'm trying to say . . ."

François and Jean realised this was a question.

"Yes," said Jean, "yes!"

François laid a hand on his father's shoulder.

"Let's go," said Louis.

He was sick at heart from all the memories, so François took his arm and squeezed it. Jean hesitated, considered taking his other arm, but decided it would be impractical for them to walk like that.

"I'm famished!" said Louis.

He did not know what else to say.

They walked back to the rue Ramey. Opposite the Impasse Pers there was a little restaurant called La Petite Bohème.

"Why not?" said François to his father's unspoken suggestion.

They pushed open the door and were instantly enveloped by the aroma of boeuf bourguignon. The restaurant was busy, all the tables were occupied, all but one.

"This one has been waiting for you," said an elderly man wearing a beret as round as a manhole.

456

A grey, bushy moustache made him look like a walrus and his apron did little to hide the vast paunch that explained his shuffling gait.

The three men took their seats at the back of the room, near the telephone booth.

"For starters, we have oeuf mayonnaise and homemade liver pâté. I still have a couple of portions of poireaux vinaigrette – with home-grown leeks, I'll have you know!"

As he said this, he jerked a thumb over his shoulder and Louis wondered whether he was referring to the vegetable garden in the Impasse Pers. Did he live in the old Belmont house?

"For mains, it's boeuf bourguignon or blanquette de veau. Right, I'll leave you to decide."

He was a man with a deep, gravelly voice.

As he walked past the counter towards the door to the kitchen, he stopped.

"Did you really hate my blanquette de veau so much you're leaving it on the plate?" he said loudly to the younger of the labourers at one of the tables.

"Don't let him get to you, son!" said his friend, seeing the boy panic.

"I know where I'd like to shove that blanquette . . ." muttered the chef as he wandered into the kitchen.

It was one of Louis's great pleasures when he visited the city to savour the atmosphere of the Parisian bistros. He decided that he liked this bistro very much. He didn't remember there being a restaurant here, but perhaps that was because he had never had the money to eat out. A bottle of Beaujolais helped him drown his sorrows, and his sons were all smiles.

"Are you all right, Papa?" said Bouboule.

"This is good!"

They were not sure whether he was referring to their visit to the Impasse Pers or to the glass of Beaujolais he had just drained.

It was a joyous meal.

"Oh, I meant to say," Louis said to François, "I read the editorial by your boss – what's his name, Dirissov?"

"Denissov."

"That's him. The one about the protest march on 11 November. What an article – the man can really write!"

"Yeah," said François, "it wasn't bad."

Louis sensed that this was a touchy subject, so he said no more. There was some talk of Étienne, but it was not melancholy. And some discussion of Hélène, which was rather more awkward.

"Well," said Louis, "you do your best. She's a big girl now, there's nothing you can do."

La Petite Bohème had emptied, and by 2.30 p.m. they were the only customers left. They might have found the service infuriatingly slow, but the bistro provided more than enough entertainment. The owner, Monsieur Jules, was one of those cantankerous, irascible men who kept up a running commentary with everyone in the whole restaurant. Here at La Petite Bohème it was Monsieur Jules against the world. He had opinions about everything: rationing, war profiteers, the cost of living, the quality of tobacco, the arrogance of the Yankees, the taxi strike, rent controls, the Ideal Home Exhibition . . .

"He's more entertaining than a newspaper if you ask me," Louis laughed.

The owner had just appeared at their table.

"How was everything? I realise that service is a little slow . . ."

"No, no, it was fine," Louis said hurriedly.

"He's a strange fish, your father," said Monsieur Jules, looking at the sons. Then he turned back to Louis.

"It's because I'm standing in for someone. These days, I only work Fridays, so I've lost the knack."

"Not when it comes to blanquette," François said.

"Oh . . . a blanquette de veau doesn't take much thinking, it's something you have in your blood."

Louis paid the bill and they were just fetching their coats from the hatstand by the door when a young woman came in with a little girl who giggled and threw her arms around Monsieur Jules.

"Fatty grandpa!"

"I'm not fat, my little poppet, just well upholstered . . ."

"Could you look after Madeleine for an hour until . . .?" asked the young woman.

Before she could finish her sentence, her daughter was perched on the owner's shoulder. She smiled and turned to leave.

"Louise!" Monsieur Jules said.

"Yes?"

Louis was standing inches from the woman, his mouth open. It was her.

He recognised her perfectly. That solemn beauty, that ...

It was the eyes he recognised first, that look.

This was Louise. His little Louise.

He almost burst into tears.

"You're about to run out of coffee," Monsieur Jules said. "I've already told you twice!"

"Don't be silly, I bought some yesterday, there are eight bags in the shed."

"Oh, I see," said Monsieur Jules, looking up at the little girl. "Your maman never tells me anything, but she expects me to know everything."

"Allow me." Louise held the door open for the three diners who were leaving.

"Thank you," said Louis softly.

François and Jean could see their father's eyes were red-rimmed. As they walked down the street, he fumbled in his pockets muttering: "Where on earth did I put my handkerchief?"

*

Senator de Neuville had read Juge Lenoir's interview. It was devastating.

The magistrate's conviction that the last remaining witness had murdered Mary Lampson had been picked up by every other newspaper. The magistrate kept calling François at *Le Journal*. Sooner or later, he would have to call back.

"Monsieur le Juge ..."

"Ah, Monsieur Pelletier, Monsieur Pelletier!"

The judge was in a slough of despond. His voice quavered with emotion.

"Have we perhaps been a little precipitate?"

François would have liked to do something to help. All the poor magistrate could hope for now was that he would be proved right, that this last witness would turn out to be the murderer. Or for the case to drag on for so long that everyone forgot his rash statements.

"What do you mean, 'we'?" said François.

"Well, we made assumptions, but in the end ..."

"Monsieur le Juge, may I remind you that these are *your* assumptions, *your* words. I merely—"

"Yes, I know, I know, but you have to understand ..."

This was not a conversation, it was psychoanalysis.

By now, François had stopped listening, he simply repeated, *yes, no, don't worry*. His mind was elsewhere. A moment earlier, as he was thinking, "Let's hope for his sake the case drags on ..." an idea had occurred to him that he could not quite put his finger on.

When the poor magistrate had reeled off all his fears and doubts, when he had finally realised that he was now utterly alone and that his overweening need to talk to the press was about to cost him dearly, François replaced the receiver.

He spent the rest of the day trying to pinpoint a fleeting thought that had vanished as soon as it appeared.

He glanced at his watch.

A thought had just occurred to him. Was he right or wrong?

The only way to find out was to take a taxi to Le Régent.

The film was already playing, the ticket desk was closed. François made his way through the cinema and up to the projection booth where Désiré Lenfant greeted him with a smile.

"Ah, Monsieur Pelletier, what brings you here?"

Sitting at the repair table, Désiré's young nephew, who was splicing film reels, glanced up at this unexpected visitor.

"Give me a second," said François. "Roland, isn't it?"

The boy blushed. François smiled and stepped forward; the boy was once again bent over his work.

"How are you, Roland? Everything all right?"

Then he turned to Désiré Lenfant and said:

"Can I borrow him for a minute?"

45

It's hardly the ends of the earth

It was not exactly difficult to find the Siêu Linh in Saigon. The huge wrought-iron symbol of the sect mounted on the dockside cathedral could be seen from miles around, while the streets around the Holy See teemed with monks briskly striding with their hands hidden in the sleeves of their white robes. The wide double doors of the cathedral were closed, but opened as if by some miracle the moment Angèle and Hélène approached. A dignitary in blue robes and bonnet came towards them.

"You are expected, ladies. If you would like to follow me . . ."

They were mesmerised by the interior. Towering stained-glass windows cast an opalescent light that swathed the tables laden with oil lamps and incense sticks, while diffuse lighting discreetly highlighted the full-length portraits of the Great Heralds, which the church official greeted with a tiny genuflection as they passed. They were led down a seemingly endless green and gold carpet, a royal pathway that led to the high altar where dozens of faithful knelt in prayer, their foreheads pressed to the ground.

The boom of a gong brought the official to a sudden halt; he knelt and bowed his head. The Pope had made his entrance. Arms spread wide to welcome the two women, he moved towards them with calm and measured steps intended to highlight his tranquillity. Over his red robes hung a large necklet of gemstones and topaz, while his tasselled cap was taller than before and now looked like two superposed jelly moulds.

He looked nothing like the friendly, smiling man of Étienne's letters. His face was tense and focused.

Neither Angèle nor Hélène knew how to greet him and each

uncertainly grasped a hand. Angèle brought the Pope's hand to her lips, while Hélène briefly squeezed the one she held and let it go.

"Madame Pelletier, Mademoiselle Pelletier ... What can I say ...?"

His voice seemed a little choked.

"Come, come, let us not linger here ..."

He led them to a salon that owed much to the style of a Buddhist temple. Deep armchairs were arranged before a low dais bearing the throne. A monk on a nearby stool sat stoically waiting for the Pope. Reverently, he placed his hands on the tasselled mitre and removed it. It was now clear why the new mitre was so tall: Loan's crest of hair had grown to some twenty-five centimetres of twisted locks rising proudly towards the heavens. The Papal Cap had been redesigned so that it did not crush the great man's hair, which symbolised his elevated status. Hélène and Angèle were struck by this soaring, spectacular hairdo – all the more so because, as a stylist might say, it still "had movement": it gracefully swayed to each slightest gesture of the pontiff's head, underscoring his every utterance.

Once relieved of his tasselled cap, Loan led his guests to a more intimate space in a corner of the room, gestured to comfortable chairs with cushions and footstools. His expression remained ascetic; even his voice had not recovered its ordinary tone.

"When I heard that you were visiting Saigon, I took the liberty of inviting you ... Ah, Madame Pelletier," Loan took Angèle's hand in his, "what can I say? I loved Monsieur Étienne very much, you know? He showed me great kindness. If there is anything at all that I can do ... It is such a tragedy ..."

For a moment, Hélène thought he would burst into tears.

"I feel I must confess a grave wrong ..."

Although her mother was seated some distance away, Hélène felt her stiffen. Loan nodded, the crest of hair swaying like ripe corn.

"I did not believe your son, Madame Pelletier. That was my great failing, yes, yes."

Neither Angèle nor her daughter interrupted. But no more words came; Loan sat, staring vacantly into the middle distance. So Hélène spoke.

"My brother was trying to flee the country with the proof of the trafficking scandal . . ."

"And I did not believe him. It was a grave mistake, because if I had, then perhaps I could have saved him . . . I am sorry, ladies, this must all sound very confusing. What Monsieur Étienne called "trafficking" is in fact common practice here. Very common. Sooner or later most people profit from the system. If I am honest, even our church once took advantage of it. But Monsieur Étienne was convinced that the traffic in piastres was being manipulated to finance the Việt Minh. And I did not believe him. I helped him because he was my friend, but I failed to take enough precautions."

"But you now believe that he was right?"

Loan nodded for a long moment, the waves of corn fluttered and swayed.

"I now believe it is a certainty."

"What did . . .? Was it your plane . . .?"

Angèle gingerly felt her way, word by word.

"Yes, Madame Pelletier. And I do not believe that the crash was an accident."

"But it was an old plane?"

"Oh, yes, but it was regularly serviced and maintained and was absolutely flightworthy. It exploded in mid-air, Madame Pelletier! Oh, I'm so sorry, I'm so sorry!"

At these words, Angèle burst into tears.

Hélène went over and comforted her; Loan beckoned a hitherto invisible disciple, who appeared carrying handkerchiefs, a tea tray, and warm jasmine-scented towels.

"Thank you, thank you," said Angèle, shrugging apologetically.

Tea was served and Angèle blew her nose.

"I'll be fine, please don't worry about me . . ."

Loan marked a long silence, then he resumed his tale.

"Even had the plane not been perfectly maintained (and I assure you that it was!), in the event of engine failure the pilot would try to land. In this case, the pilot had no chance. Within seconds, the aircraft was lost with all hands . . . Yes, yes . . ."

Loan waited for the young white-robed disciple to finish serving tea and noiselessly slip away.

"But there is something else. It is my belief that Monsieur Étienne obtained his evidence from a young man who ... who lived nearby ... and was ... and was a sort of manservant, you understand?"

Both women understood only too well.

"He was the nephew of Monsieur Qiao, a Chinese comprador who had close ... very close ties to the Việt Minh."

"Did you say Monsieur Qiao?"

Hélène remembered François's puzzlement at the name Étienne had mentioned, which he had heard as "Ciao" or "Chow". François was sure that he had misheard, and had said: "We'll find out when Étienne gets here ..."

"Yes, Monsieur Qiao. It was his nephew who stole the compromising documents, and he was murdered only minutes before Monsieur Étienne managed to escape. I suspect that the Việt Minh knew I had made our plane available to your son, and when they failed to intercept him in Saigon, they sabotaged the plane ..."

Hélène could see the sequence of events as in a movie. The stolen dossier, the murder of the young man, Étienne's escape, the airfield, the plane ...

"And this Monsieur Qiao ..." said Angèle, tight-lipped.

"This is the third reason that, alas, leads me to believe that what I say is true. On the day after Monsieur Étienne disappeared, the body of Monsieur Qiao was found floating in a canal north of Saigon."

The movie was coming to an end.

The man from whom Étienne had stolen the evidence had in turn been murdered. All of the major characters were dead. The story was over; the screen was blank, the reel spinning empty.

"Did you know this Monsieur Qiao? Or his nephew?"

"I knew his nephew, yes, he attended our church, he was a gentle boy, calm and most devout, yes, yes. I did not know his uncle. I knew he had ties to the Việt Minh, so ..."

Confession had been good for Loan's soul.

"We often pray for Monsieur Étienne."

"Yes, yes," said Angèle irritably. Prayers would not bring her son back.

"Let me pour you some more tea."

"No. No, thank you."

Angèle got to her feet. The atmosphere in the room now felt oppressive.

Hélène, who had also stood up, could not help but ask:

"How did my brother get to the airfield?"

"That I do not know. I offered him the use of a car, but he chose to find his own way. I assume that he took a taxi. I never saw him again."

Loan accompanied them back to the cathedral, stopped briefly next to a stepladder on which was a blue-robed disciple who doubtless perched there for hours, and now replaced His Holiness's stepped mitre, whose tassels instantly twitched and shuddered.

Angèle felt increasingly overwhelmed by the grandeur and opulence of the cathedral, the quivering silence, its dense clouds of incense. She gripped her daughter's arm.

"If there is anything that I can do ..." said Loan.

"Perhaps there is. My mother and I have not been able to recover the things Étienne left at his apartment."

"Oh, I shall take care of that right away. I do not know whether we can recover everything, but I shall do the impossible, yes, yes."

He looked resolute, and the lively movement of his tassels confirmed his firmness of purpose.

"On Wednesday evening we will hold an evening procession to commemorate the anniversary of the revelation made to me by the Supreme Soul. Perhaps you will do us the honour of attending?"

Angèle pictured the procession, her son's spirit hovering over the crowd. It was more than she could bear.

"Thank you, really, but I don't think I could bear it ... If we could just get Étienne's trunk back ..."

"I shall deal with it, yes, yes ..."

As they stepped out, rain was lashing the square.

"I shall accompany you to your hotel," said Loan.

465

"Thank you, monsieur, but that won't be necessary."

They stood beneath the wide awning adorned with the emblem of the Siêu Linh, gazing at the torrential downpour that rumbled like a steam train.

Lurking cycle rickshaws were headed towards them.

In the cool freshness of the cloudburst, away from the oppressive atmosphere of the cathedral where no one, save the Pope, seemed truly alive, and shattered that their worst fears about Étienne's death had been confirmed, Angèle and Hélène no longer wanted the same thing.

Angèle wanted only to recover her son's belongings and go home, to leave this hateful city, this hateful country. She had come to find out how Étienne had died, and now that she knew, she had no idea what to do with this information; she longed only to go home and sleep.

Hélène, because of her age and her temperament, was not prepared to admit defeat and was still wondering what else might be done.

Back at the Crystal Palace Hotel, Angèle asked the receptionist to enquire about flights.

"Tomorrow or the next day," she said. It took more than half an hour to find flights leaving for Beirut.

Angèle could sense Hélène's mute resentment.

"What is it that you want to do, Hélène? The man who ordered Étienne's murder is dead ... Everyone involved in this story is dead."

Hélène refused to accept that it was over, but had nothing to suggest. She retreated into a sulky, stubborn silence that Angèle found childish.

Loan was as good as his word. By the end of the day, Étienne's trunk had been delivered to the hotel.

They instantly recognised the man with the missing teeth who had snapped at them earlier, but his manner now was very different, he walked with stooped shoulders, staring at the ground. The young man holding the other handle of the trunk had none of his elder's submissiveness. He held himself upright, striding with

466

the grotesque self-assurance of a toreador and staring intently at Angèle and Hélène.

Without a word, the two men set down the trunk and departed. The Pope of the Siêu Linh was respected and feared.

It was a metal trunk of the kind used by soldiers on campaign. Angèle had bought it in Beirut. It had taken many knocks since, but had looked surprisingly light when the two men set it down. Here, in the hotel room, Angèle and Hélène viewed it almost as a threat. Opening it would mean tears and grief and neither wanted to make the first move.

They looked around, hearing shouts from the hallway; they recognised the piercing, urgent, angry voice as the man who had shouted at them in Étienne's apartment. They looked at each other. Angèle was about to go and see what was happening when the door burst open and the younger of the men who had brought the trunk, flushed and furious, tossed an object into the room and disappeared, slamming the door before they had time to see what it was. It was Étienne's camera. Hélène opened the leather case. It did not seem to be damaged. She set it on the bed.

Then they lifted the lid of the trunk.

There was precious little left, and therefore little to cry about.

There were a few items of clothing, including a winter jumper that Angèle had knitted ("Maman," Étienne had laughed, "I'm not going skiing, I'm going to Saigon!"), a few pairs of trousers ... When the looting starts, clothes are the first thing to disappear. The statue of the Buddha was there.

"He mentioned it in one of his letters," said Hélène.

They also found the cat basket.

"Here, Joseph, this is yours ..."

The cat jumped into the basket, but rather than curl up he sat impatiently, as though waiting for the moment when they would leave.

Lastly, they found a Siêu Linh pamphlet from which a handwritten note signed "Your friend, Loan" fluttered out.

"Destination Phnom Penh then by commercial airline to Paris ..." As she read, Angèle was still wondering how Étienne had managed to get to the airfield. "If you need a car to get you to Biên Hòa, let me know," Loan had written. He must have taken a taxi, she thought. It was the only explanation.

Up to this point, they had managed to contain themselves; it was the bundle of letters from Angèle and Hélène that finally made them cry.

"You're going to laugh at me," said Angèle, blowing her nose. "I actually brought Étienne's letters with me to Saigon."

"So did I . . ." admitted Hélène.

It was so preposterous that they both smiled.

"Could you ring down and order a bottle of white wine?" Angèle said.

They spent the evening reading aloud from the letters Étienne had sent them. They drank, they laughed.

"Listen to this," said Hélène. "*I've made a lot of progress in framing my shots: it's very artistic to have half the subject cropped out. I think a new career is beckoning.*"

"And this," said Angèle. "*Pope Loan of the Siêu Linh is intent on forging relationships with other churches. Unfortunately, he considers Pope Pius XII and the Ecumenical Patriarch of Constantinople his subordinates, which is unlikely to help matters.*"

By late evening, they had fallen asleep on the bed fully clothed. Sometime around midnight, Angèle woke and tidied the room a little. Before going back to bed, she once again picked up Loan's note to Étienne.

"If you need a car to get you to Biên Hòa, let me know."

How did Étienne get to the airfield, given that he was being pursued by the men who had just killed the young man he lived with?

*

"What do you want to do?" said Hélène.

She was winding the film in Étienne's camera; she would try to buy new rolls of film in town. The camera was a Leica with a 50 mm lens and a satisfying shutter click.

"I had forgotten that you took photography lessons in school," said Angèle as she dressed.

"You could call it that," murmured Hélène in a voice too low for her mother to hear.

Did she have any interest in photography, given what little she had learned? Holding Étienne's camera she had a curious sense of familiarity, as though her fingers had finally found their place, as if these gestures were intimately familiar – which was preposterous, since she didn't even know how to develop a photograph . . .

"What do you want to do?"

"What else is there to do? See the sights?"

It was obvious her mother's suggestion was sarcastic; she considered Saigon a loathsome city.

Hélène was too tactful to say that she would happily go for a walk through the streets, down to the docks, maybe even take some photographs.

"The airfield is less than an hour away. It's hardly the ends of the earth."

46

It was tiresome

Only a few days remained before they were to open the boutique. This made Jean more nervous than usual. And Geneviève more spiteful.

"It looks like a flea market," she snarled when she saw the displays ready to be set out on the pavement.

The last delivery had just been delivered. Jean pretended he had sprained his back and stayed in the rear of the shop; he could not bear to face Monsieur Steuvels's steely gaze.

Geneviève tallied up the accounts, then called Jean out so they could watch the van drive off. It was then that they saw him, standing on the opposite pavement: Georges Guénot, his clenched fists stuffed into the pockets of his fur-lined jacket.

Jean, who was already exhausted by the morning, did not have the strength to face his former boss.

He was about to run for cover when he saw Geneviève, her arms folded, take up a defiant stance.

She was eager to have a showdown with the unexpected visitor who now strode across the street, stopped and said:

"It was you, wasn't it?"

Geneviève stared him straight in the eye.

"Someone grassed me up," he said. "I know it was you!"

Monsieur Georges seemed terribly sure of himself.

"Nobody else knew . . ."

Geneviève turned to Jean, who had no idea what to do. She bowed her head, as though in deep thought.

"Come with me," she said.

Then, without waiting for an answer, she turned on her heel and went into the shop, holding the door wide.

Guénot stepped inside and surveyed the dozens of boxes piled on top of each other. His eyes were instantly drawn to the sheets, the tablecloths and towels displayed on the counter. He knew his stock well enough to recognise fabrics that had once been his.

"All this is mine!"

"It's ours now," said Geneviève softly.

But she wasn't looking at Monsieur Georges, she was bustling about in the narrow space. It took a moment before Jean and Guénot realised that she was lining the displays up next to the door, and, even then, they could not fathom why.

"Yes," she said, "we are the ones who bought up your stock, dear."

She vanished for an instant and when she reappeared she was holding a length of wood that Jean recognised as part of a beam left by the carpenters. Guénot took a step back, preparing to defend himself, but Geneviève had already raised the beam above her head and brought it crashing down on one of the metal stands, which snapped in the middle.

"Oh!" said Jean.

Geneviève was not listening, she had stepped to one side, raised the beam again, and crushed a second display.

Jean was dumbfounded.

Guénot was already at the door about to leave when Geneviève turned to him.

"You came here and made slanderous accusations, then you flew into a rage and you started to smash things up."

"What?"

"You vandalised our boutique, my husband tried to stop you and you beat him, didn't he, Jean?"

Jean did not know what to say. But Geneviève did not expect him to do anything.

"You smashed so much that we will have to postpone next week's opening. We intend to sue you for damages."

"Hang on, hang on!"

Geneviève shattered a third display, then dropped the beam at her feet.

471

"We will file a complaint against you with Monsieur – what's his name again? Perret, Ferret, Terret? That's it, Terret. From the Committee for the Confiscation of Illicit Profits."

Guénot was ashen. How could Geneviève possibly know the inspector? But this thought was instantly drowned out by a voice inside his head. "*If, in future, we discover that you have been involved in a shady deal, a minor infraction . . .*"

"Stop," said Guénot, holding out both hands as though to prevent Geneviève from approaching.

"*. . . a simple blunder, that miracle will not occur again . . .*"

"I'm going, I'm going."

Guénot opened the door.

"*You will be brought before the magistrate . . .*"

"Ten thousand francs."

Guénot whirled around to face Geneviève.

"What?"

"Ten thousand francs."

She nodded to the shattered displays.

"We will not file a complaint if you pay us compensation, isn't that right, Jean?"

"But ten thousand . . ."

Guénot could not believe his ears.

"That's the price."

"It's . . . It's impossible!"

"Do you think so?" Geneviève glowered.

"*. . . and go straight to prison.*"

Guénot was devastated.

"I only have eight thousand . . ." he stammered.

Geneviève eyed him coldly and held out her hand.

*

François was expecting to be hauled over the coals. But while he could stomach a dressing down from Denissov, he felt less inclined to accept it in front of Baron and Malevitz. But that was what was about to happen, since all three were gathered in the boss's office.

Baron and Malevitz, usually bitter rivals, were on the same side now, and François was on the other side.

He was still reeling from the revelations about his parents' past. As he stood before the three men, he could not help but joke.

"Oh, I didn't realise. Is this a tribunal?"

Immediately, he realised his mistake.

"It may well be . . ." said Denissov in a brittle tone.

"About ten days ago, you questioned Arthur here about two corrupt private banks – Banque Godard and Hopkins Brothers. Both institutions we would be happy to write about. Three days later, without informing your colleagues, you interviewed Senator de Neuville, so I feel I have to ask: do you still work for *Le Journal*, or are you now a freelance journalist?"

François suddenly realised that his job was at stake. This had not even occurred to him.

Denissov had made a reasonable point, but François had no time to assess the situation calmly, ask the right questions, come up with the right answers. If he was fired from *Le Journal*, he was finished.

"Let's start again . . ." said Denissov. "Banque Godard or Hopkins first."

"No, that's not the way to think about it," François said. "It's all part of the same thing."

Denissov leaned back in his chair; go ahead.

"Out in Saigon, my brother was investigating the illicit transfer of piastres, financed by the French government, with profits being channelled to the Việt Minh."

The three veteran journalists instantly understood the devastating potential of this information.

"He suspected the funds were being routed through Godard or Hopkins."

"How did he know?" asked Baron.

His hectoring aggressive tone was an abuse of power. If I get through this, François vowed, I'll kill him.

"He didn't *know*. He suspected."

"Let's not split hairs. Why did he suspect this?"

At this point François realised he would have to steer away from the truth yet remain credible.

"Something he overheard at the Currency Exchange where he worked in Saigon. The problem was he had no concrete proof."

"Did he think Senator de Neuville was involved?"

François's room to manoeuvre was shrinking fast. One false move and he would be overboard and no one would throw him a line. The three men knew he had been to see Neuville; he had to assume that they did not know why.

"That's got nothing to do with the scandal."

"So, there's no connection between your brother's investigation and your visit to Neuville?"

"Yes, there is. Although my brother did not have any hard evidence, he died in a plane crash that we were told was an accident. Something I doubt."

"What had that idiot Neuville got to do with it?" Baron said snippily.

François would have to drain the cup to the lees. To wriggle out of this, he would have to make a fool of himself.

He glanced at Denissov. Here was a man he admired, one for whom he had longed to work. And he had achieved his goal. Unless he was prepared to make himself seem a fool now, he would be unceremoniously ejected and he would never be able to come back . . . He blushed.

"Someone told me he knew a lot about Indochina – he was stationed there for many years . . . I went to ask what he thought about the circumstances of my brother's death, whether he thought it might credibly . . ."

"You asked Neuville?"

This is what François had feared: Baron burst out laughing, Denissov restrained himself. Only Malevitz seemed uncomfortable. His protégé looked a fool, which was embarrassing for him too.

"Arrant nonsense!" said Baron. "The man doesn't understand the first thing about Indochina. Who could have given you such an idea?"

This was tricky, because François had no ready answer. Thankfully, Denissov saved the day.

"That doesn't matter. I hope you realise that it was a bloody stupid idea?"

"I realised that as soon as I talked to him, but by then . . ."

Were the storm clouds parting?

"When you know nothing about a subject," sneered Baron, "perhaps leave it to those who do . . ."

"Shut up, Arthur."

This was Malevitz's first intervention since the beginning of the meeting. He said it in the tone of a man who was prepared to accept defeat but would not be humiliated.

Once again, Denissov decided to calm the waters. Everyone accepted that François had kept it all to himself in the hope of unearthing a scoop.

"And you have nothing to show for all this?"

François had to choose between supporting Étienne and giving the government the green light to destroy the Pelletier family . . .

"Nothing. My brother had no documentation, no tangible evidence. Nothing that could form the basis of an article, or even an investigation . . ."

"What about his plane crash?"

"There's an investigation underway, but it was a decommissioned plane so it may have been badly maintained."

It was a rout. Everyone knew it. Even Baron was not prepared to kick a man when he was down.

François had fallen sharply in the esteem of Denissov and Malevitz. It was painful.

But he had one consolation.

"Look, I'm the first to admit that I behaved like a fool, but I'm not totally useless, am I?"

He handed his proposed headline to Denissov, who chortled.

"Bravo!" he said, passing it to Malevitz and Baron. "Well played!"

SHOCK REVELATION IN MARY LAMPSON CASE: "LAST WITNESS" WAS PROJECTIONIST'S NEPHEW

Eleven-year-old Roland secretly watched forbidden movies

François Pelletier was back to writing human interest stories.

47

He's a smart guy!

They caught a taxi outside the Crystal Palace and headed for Biên Hòa, north-east of Saigon. The driver chattered all the way in Vietnamese, pointing to monuments they could not see, or sights that had already flashed past, wagging his index finger and shouting warnings that Angèle and Hélène did not understand. After half an hour of this, Angèle and Hélène were exhausted. The taxi driver was obviously hoping to get a fat tip for acting like a tourist guide. Angèle opened her purse, took out a banknote – the first she found – leaned towards the front seat and gave it to him. "Please shut up," she said. The driver had his tip, he was satisfied.

There were trees of a green more vivid than they had ever seen, broad expanses of water, paddy fields, villages, roads that were little more than dirt tracks along which water buffalo drew carts filled with children who dangled their legs off the back and stared coldly at the foreigners while stroking the chickens on their laps.

Now and then, Hélène would tap the driver's shoulder and he would pull over. She would get out and take a couple of photographs. She was so pretty, smiling and graceful that nobody refused to pose for her.

Guynemer airfield was on the edge of the forest and had only one runway, which, at first sight, looked short and dangerous since it ran straight towards a line of tall trees. In poor weather, landing a plane would be something of a feat. A small, squat building clearly served as the control centre since there was no tower. The only plane was a tourist aircraft next to the lone hangar.

Angèle and Hélène went inside. Meanwhile, the taxi driver went in search of somewhere to park that would afford shelter from the downpour that had been threatening since they set off.

The building looked like an officers' mess. There was a bar, and the walls were hung with decorations, dusty trophies, faded pennants and moth-eaten flags. In a grimy glass display case was a brass cup with wings for handles. The low room smelled of tobacco and cheap cigars. It had the atmosphere of those places that miraculously survive long after their heyday is past and felt more like the bar of a failing fifth-division football club than the command centre of a private airfield. To the right was a control panel that looked rudimentary even to someone with no expertise: a microphone, a speaker, a few buttons and a large red fire extinguisher. It was manned by the flight-controller-cum-mechanic-cum-barman sporting a threadbare green cap, a Vietnamese man with a weather-beaten face and a mouth that always gaped slightly. His drooping lower lip formed a pout that made him seen condescending. He was about sixty years old.

"Yis?" he said.

His lips scarcely moved when he spoke. He had the gravelly voice of an incorrigible smoker.

Angèle introduced herself. She was unsure whether the man understood everything she said. As he listened to her talk about Étienne's flight, he became preoccupied by the fact that Hélène was taking photographs. This did not please him at all.

"Yis, yis," he said.

When Angèle had finished, he said:

"What do you want?"

Angèle was speechless. Had she not made herself clear?

"The young man on the plane . . . he was my son," she said.

"Yes, what do you want?"

This man was either an idiot or he had suffered a stroke. It was deeply worrying to think of him manning an airfield.

Hélène came to the rescue.

"How did he get here? By taxi?"

"In djiip."

They looked at each other, both wondering what language he was speaking.

"In djiip," he said again. "He come with ledjion. You want drink?"

"I'd like a beer," said Hélène. "So, he came here in a jeep, with the Legion?"

"Yes."

Angèle was stunned; she looked from her daughter to the barman.

"He came here with friends of Raymond. For safety . . ."

"Oh, I see," said Angèle.

"Yis," said the barman who had put three bottles of beer on the counter and had already started on his own.

Every order meant one for the house. His pendulous lower lip made it impossible to drink from the bottle, so he tipped his head back, opened his mouth wide, and skilfully poured the beer with great skill, making a sound like a gurgling drain.

Hélène had found the key to making conversation and, together, they were able to reconstruct Étienne's last moments, his arrival with a small group of legionnaires, the Siêu Linh pilot who had been waiting here for several days (sleeping in the hangar when not propping up the bar), the immediate departure, the legionnaires waiting until Étienne was aboard before heading back to Saigon.

And the limousine.

Parked between the control centre and the hangar.

"A limousine . . ." said Hélène, still smiling.

Her smile was a powerful incentive for the barman to keep talking.

"Yis."

Angèle was halfway through her beer, Hélène had finished hers, and the barman was on his fourth.

So far, everything they had learned (apart from the legionnaires) tallied with what they knew about Étienne's hasty departure. The limousine was more unexpected. Hélène went outside and had a look around. A car parked between the two buildings was not simply parked, it was concealed.

"Monsieur Qiao personally came to oversee the 'accident'," said Hélène as she went back into the bar.

Angèle sniffled and Hélène put an arm around her shoulders.

"Let's go back now, shall we?"

She turned to the barman.

"Thank you for your kindness, monsieur."

And, in that moment, everything changes.

"Wilcome, mam'selle," says the barman, genially raising his bottle.

The two women stare up at the ceiling.

The threatening rain has finally made up its mind. It is drumming on the roof so loudly they have to shout to be heard.

Hélène goes over and opens the door to find herself staring at a solid wall of rain. Bending down, she sees the taxi driver and beckons him to come in.

Meanwhile, Angèle is smiling shyly at the barman and clutching her handbag, trying to seem sober.

The bartender belches loudly, then leans across and says conspiratorially:

"No' m'sieur Qiao. See Loan. Tsieêu Li'h."

Hélène, who has no idea how she managed to hear what he said from where she is standing by the door, runs back.

"You're saying it was Loan? The Pope of the Siêu Linh? Are you sure?"

"B'solu'ly!"

He puts his beer on the counter and, with a broad smile, raises his splayed fingers over his head, mimicking Loan's flamboyant crest.

*

The car glided slowly along the road, like a boat. The roar of the rain made conversation difficult, but neither Angèle nor Hélène wanted to talk. They were both trying to understand the consequences of what they had just learned. Loan had been at the airfield when Étienne's plane took off.

Hélène leaned towards her mother:

"He said he never saw Étienne again."

"And that he didn't know how your brother got to the airfield," Angèle said. "But he was there all the time!"

"He was the one who threw suspicion onto Qiao . . ."

". . . who, conveniently, was dead."

As they thought aloud, Loan gradually shapeshifted from accomplice to assassin.

Why would the Pope of the Siêu Linh arrange to have Étienne murdered?

"There may be a way to find out," Hélène said.

*

Their first visit had not been enough.

"Do you have an appointment?" said the woman behind the desk.

Hélène's one hope was that they would not run into Gaston Paumelle again, but Gaston, like a bloodhound, picked up her scent from afar.

"Mademoiselle Pelletier!" he said, shaking her hand with nauseating insistence.

"Could you ask Monsieur le Directeur if he might see me for a moment?"

The presence of this young woman . . . It was almost too much for Gaston, who ran his long, beringed fingers across his fevered brow.

"Or shall I go and ask him myself?"

"Not at all, not at all!"

As they walked down the corridor, Hélène feared he might throw himself at her feet. He had a strategy. As they approached Jeantet's office, he fell behind so he could leer at her derrière in a floral printed dress that drove him wild. He thought that he could detect her perfume, and, better still, the smell of her; oh, how he longed to take her up against the wall.

"Monsieur le Directeur . . .?"

"Yes, yes, what is it?"

Gaston stepped aside and ushered Hélène forward.

"This is Mademoiselle Pell—"

Before he had time to finish, Hélène turned and gently pushed him back into the corridor.

"Thank you, Monsieur Paumelle, I can speak for myself."

She closed the door and turned to Jeantet.

"I needed to see you . . ."

By rights, Jeantet felt, she should have apologised for her intrusion, but there was an urgency in her tone.

"Quite," said Jeantet. "I was thinking the same thing."

"Excuse me?"

"He can be a little pushy, can't he?" He nodded to the door. Hélène smiled.

"Count yourself lucky," he added, "you don't need any favours from him because . . ."

He was busily rearranging his photo frames. It was like a game of musical chairs. Hélène stepped closer. Abruptly, he held up a photograph of a German shepherd.

"Itsou. I had to have him put down . . ."

"You should do the same with Monsieur Paumelle."

Jeantet was not listening, he rubbed the frame with his sleeve, put it down and picked up another one.

"This is about your brother, I assume . . ."

"I thought that perhaps without Monsieur Paumelle present you might feel you could tell me a little more . . ."

Jeantet opened his desk drawer, took out a piece of chamois leather and began a major cleaning operation, taking each frame, wiping and replacing it.

"Yes, yes . . . A little more, I see."

Hélène was convinced the man had a screw loose.

"This is about Monsieur Loan," she said, "the Pope of the Siêu Linh."

"Ah, yes, dear old Loan . . ."

"Do you know whether he knew Monsieur Qiao?"

The name of the Chinese comprador had a startling effect on Jeantet. He dropped the chamois leather, laid his hands on Hélène's shoulders and forced her to sit in the deep armchair. Then, as he had done with Angèle, he sat next to her, placing himself in a subservient position.

"Your brother . . . Incorruptible! Absolutely incorruptible, mademoiselle, you should be proud of him!"

Was he about to launch into his funeral oration again? He glanced towards the door, then lowered his voice.

"Thick as thieves, that's how I'd put it."

Hélène was finding it hard to keep up.

"Loan and Qiao, thick as thieves. They did a lot of shady deals together. Then later ... When old Diêm, I mean, when Loan set up his church, he didn't need the Chinaman as much, you know? But before ... Yes, a pure soul, your brother!"

Hélène knew that she had to let him ramble on, or risk him losing the thread.

"Now Qiao, he was a wealthy man, and Diêm – I mean Loan (I still can't get used to that) – was a small-time operator. He used to bring clients to Qiao, who'd give him a commission. Remind me why you are you asking me these things?"

"I'm simply trying to understand what my poor brother was looking for. And you are by far the most well-informed man here at the Exchange ... So, I've been wondering about Monsieur Qiao ..."

"He's dead, didn't you know?"

"Yes, that's my point. There is a curious parallel between Étienne's death and his."

Jeantet was puzzled, his eyes darted around the room looking for some place to rest.

"You thought very highly of Étienne, didn't you?"

"A noble soul!"

"So, help me to understand. Was Monsieur Qiao arranging currency transfers to finance the Việt Minh?"

"Oh dear!" Jeantet groaned and got to his feet, flapping his arms and glancing around the office like a drowning man.

"What do you want me to tell you?"

Hélène said nothing.

"Everyone in Saigon traffics currency, you know? It's a nightmare. Absolutely everyone. So, it's hardly surprising the Việt Minh would want to get in on the act ..."

Hélène got up. Jeantet peered at her, she suddenly looked very tall.

"Tell me ... Would it be in Loan's interest to maintain close relations with the Việt Minh?"

Jeantet stared at her, wide-eyed. Then he laughed.

"Of course it would! His church needs to keep on good terms with everyone – the French administration that grants him territory, and the Việt Minh for whom he can be a powerful ally when the time comes. Old Loan always has a finger in every pie! He's a smart guy!"

*

Angèle and Hélène went to Le Métropole for an aperitif. Two sombre women in a dazzling setting. They had spent a long time talking in the hotel before going out.

Loan had lied to them over and over.

He knew Monsieur Qiao intimately.

He "obviously" had a relationship with the Việt Minh.

He had been at the airfield when Étienne took off in his plane – a plane he had the best possible opportunity to sabotage.

He knew how Étienne had made the journey from Saigon to Biên Hòa and had lied about it.

Étienne's investigation threatened to cut off one of the Việt Minh's most important sources of revenue, and Loan had sided with his associates over his friend.

Everything fell into place. Right down to the way in which Loan had tried to frame a dead man who could not be questioned, let alone prosecuted ...

Angèle sipped her cocktail.

"I want to kill him," said Hélène.

"So do I, my darling, so do I. We still have a day left here. Then we will go home and it will be over."

She took another sip.

"It will all be over."

48

It's over

Hélène spent the night in a furious rage. When she slept the shadowy figure of Étienne cried out for vengeance, pleaded for justice, she heard him calling to her . . .

Over and over, she killed Loan only to wake with a start, bathed in sweat and utterly lost. Despite the extreme cruelty she used, she could never manage to kill him completely, he was a phoenix, he kept rising from the ashes, smiling, the shadows of his great crest casting serpentine shapes on the walls of the cathedral.

Three times she got up, staggered to the bathroom to splash her face with cold water; she was exhausted.

As she passed her mother's room and heard her relaxed breathing, saw her sleeping figure, she was appalled. How could she sleep after what they had discovered?

Joseph, who had had enough of her constant comings and goings, curled up in his basket, too fearful to go back.

Angèle closed her eyes and yielded to the night. This, surely, was what it was like to die; you surrender and allow death in. How many times had she wondered what her son had felt, whether he had been afraid? Why could she not take his place?

Three times she had heard Hélène get up, pause at her door and gaze at her. Lying in bed, Angèle could feel Hélène's resentment, the anger and hostility towards her mother that had abated during their mourning and now returned with even greater intensity. Angèle had not moved, she tried to adopt the calm shallow breathing of a sleeper. She needed to be alone.

But even endless nights come to an end.

Hélène's ended as day was breaking, just after 8 a.m. Her

mother's bed was empty. She washed and dressed. Still Angèle had not reappeared.

"Madame Pelletier said to tell you that she is in town," Hélène was told at the reception desk.

The receptionist spoke curtly through pursed lips; his resentment had not abated since Angèle had insisted on taking a cat up to her room.

"Did she say where she was going?"

The receptionist found it difficult to fulfil his role with such people.

"She requested an address for a company called Lecoq & d'Arneville, that is all I can tell you."

Having done everything he could, he turned back and stared intently at the rack of keys.

Hélène had just finished breakfast when her mother returned. She had bought a bright yellow raincoat, an umbrella and a handbag.

"Where did you go?"

"I went shopping."

Hélène thought her mother looked drawn, despite the fact she had seen her sleeping deeply.

"You visited Lecoq."

Was this a question? Her tone was reproachful, but Angèle pretended not to notice.

"Yes, I needed to withdraw some money."

"But we're leaving tomorrow."

"This hotel is more expensive than I expected. What are you planning to do today?"

Angèle bit her tongue. Hélène always reacted to these questions as if her mother were invading her privacy.

"What about you?"

It was just like being back in Beirut, the same sardonic questions.

"I'll leave you to do whatever you like today, darling. I'm very tired . . ."

"It's not as though you didn't sleep well!"

Angèle smiled. Yes, she had slept well.

"I may take another tour of the city, I'm not sure. I'm not likely ever to come back, but this was where Étienne lived, so . . ."

Hélène looked dubious; she had no idea what this meant.

"We can meet up for dinner, what do you say?"

The suggestion that they go their separate ways suited both women.

Hélène left the hotel, camera in hand, and set off to buy some film. But she was still fretting about Loan. What should she do? Stab him, creep in with a knife like one of the ones in that shop window, bury it in his stomach and watch him writhe in pain.

She could never do that, and she knew it. What then? Punch him? It was absurd. Loan was more than capable of defending himself, besides, his disciples would come running, she would be beaten up, thrown out and reported to the police.

This was what she despised about her mother, she thought, her passivity. In crude terms, her weakness. And it was something Hélène had clearly inherited, since she was not prepared to do anything. She wandered through the city streets.

This was the only sunny day of her whole stay. The rain clouds had drifted north, the sky was pale, the air humid, but the city was unchanged; the shifting weather did nothing to change its rhythm.

Subconsciously, her feet had led to the cathedral of the Siêu Linh, where, even at midday, preparations for the evening's procession had already begun. Banners were being strung across the streets, pennants and flags were mounted here and there, the Siêu Linh monks bustled about like mice.

Hélène's whole body trembled as she remembered the bastard's words: "I have decided to dedicate the procession to the memory of Monsieur Étienne."

She felt bitter, vengeful, sick at heart. She snapped pictures as though slapping the subjects. The camera embodied her state of mind.

She walked along the docks, through the suburbs, back down to the river, then headed to the hotel for a nap. She worried that she might run into her mother, but she did not. She lay down on the bed fully clothed and slept for two hours only to wake up

487

still bleary. Night was drawing in. She lay on the bed, unable to summon any strength. She wondered what her mother was doing. She had not seen her all day.

It was an evening of missed opportunities. Hélène had waited for her mother in the hotel lobby only to leave just before she arrived back, so they narrowly missed one another. By the time they finally met up, it was late and the mood was less than gay.

They dined at Le Métropole, ate too little, drank too much, avoided talking about anything that mattered, sat through awkward silences, then walked back to the Crystal, passing beneath the awnings of the Siêu Linh while pretending not to notice, then went up to their room. They had ordered an airport taxi for 5.30 a.m.

"I'm worn out," said Angèle as she finished her toilette.

For the first time, she kissed Hélène on the forehead, as Louis always did.

"Good night, Maman."

Now here they are, each in her own room, the connecting door is closed. Hélène is aware only of her aching legs, she does not realise how tired she is. No sooner does she lie down, than she sinks into sleep.

What time is it when she wakes again?

The curtains glow with lights from the boulevard. It is 10.45 p.m. She has been woken by the music from the cathedral, the dull, monotonous rhythm, the booming gongs. This is the procession.

Hélène lets her head fall back on the pillow. She needs to get up, go to the bathroom, pass by her mother's room.

She moves on tiptoe, closes the bathroom door behind her, then tiptoes back. Her mother's bed is unmade but empty. Joseph is curled up on the coverlet at the foot of the bed.

"Maman?"

She hears her voice echo. Hélène glances at the chair, steps forward, opens the cupboard. Has her mother gone out? Her raincoat is gone. So is her handbag.

"Maman?"

Her spectacles are not on the bedside table.

Where could she have gone?

She has gone to see the procession. Of course she has. She will cry all night.

She will have been woken by the muffled noise of the procession and gone out. She will come back when it is all over. She will not bother to go back to bed; soon it will be time for the taxi, the airport, the flight.

It is the word "flight" that prompts Hélène to go into the hall where the luggage has been stacked. She opens Étienne's trunk. There is the Buddha wrapped in newspaper, her letters, Étienne's letters. They are all jumbled now. On top is a letter from the early days of her brother's time in Saigon. Hélène turns pale, she looks up.

What was it he wrote . . .?

"*It's a very violent country. They say that everyone here has killers, that you only have to go to Cholon to find someone who, for a few piastres, will get rid of just about anyone you want.*"

Her mother visited Lecoq & d'Arneville.

She has been absent the whole day.

Hélène does not waste a second. She rushes to get dressed, she grabs her things and is already hurtling down the stairs to the lobby, but this time she does not stop, does not ask whether they have seen her mother because she knows . . .

Hélène races through the streets, elbowing her way through the crowds without a murmur of apology, she runs as fast as she can.

The streets are filled with a mournful, funereal music. Still, she runs. The lights by the cathedral are bright. Countless torches illuminate a vast crowd in silent prayer. Drums, gongs and tambourines. The faithful are lined up along the pavements. The middle of the street has been cleared for the procession of monks and dignitaries that she can hear in the distance. The procession has begun.

The music grows louder.

Hélène does not know which way to turn. She edges forward, weaving her way towards the square in front of the cathedral, which she can now see is where the dignitaries will emerge.

Glancing around, she sees two wooden crates discarded on the pavement. She runs over, stacks them, and climbs on top: over the

489

heads of the crowd she can see Loan, in his flowing red and gold robes and his tall tasselled mitre.

He leads the procession, closely followed by five disciples in blue robes. Behind them, a vast crowd of worshippers slowly streams out of the cathedral, carrying banners and flags, beating drums, moving to the slow, solemn beat of the tom-toms and cymbals, the piercing flutes. The smell of incense floods the street. The crowd kneels as Loan passes, his ecstatic gaze trained upon some far horizon, some ideal.

He is about thirty metres away when Hélène sees her mother in her yellow raincoat, the only person in her tiny group not to kneel as the Pope draws level.

Angèle remains standing; she feels strong.

Loan treads slowly, then his eye is caught by the flash of yellow and he turns slightly.

When he sees Angèle standing in the midst of the kneeling worshippers, he cannot turn away, he slows his pace, recovers his pace, his eyes still fixed on the woman staring at him. Something is about to happen.

From the moment the Pope of the Siêu Linh slows his pace, everyone can tell that something is happening.

He is the first to react. His mouth opens. Is he about to scream?

The gradual slowing of the procession reaches the timpani, and one by one the drums cease to beat. The flames of the torches quiver.

Angèle and Loan look into each other's eyes.

Loan wants to say something, and Angèle clearly senses this because slowly she shakes her head.

At that moment, the bullet hits the Pope.

The gunshot echoes around the streets.

There are wails even before Loan, clutching his head, crumples, falls to his knees, reaches out for help, blood gushing through his fingers. His tasselled mitre rolls onto the pavement and is trampled by the faithful as they surge forward.

Heads turn towards the buildings on either side. Did a sniper shoot from one of these windows? There are so many. Was it a long-range shot? Did it come from nearby?

The crowd rushes to the Pope, now lying on the pavement in a pool of blood.

Hélène looks around for the yellow raincoat, but it has disappeared.

She steps down from the crates and tries to run, but she has to move against the tide of disoriented worshippers all waving, shouting, wailing.

It takes almost fifteen minutes for her to get back to the Crystal Palace.

Suddenly, she stops in front of the large picture window. Standing at the reception desk, her mother has just handed a bulky envelope to the night porter. She tells him something; the man nods, takes the envelope and turns to open the wall safe.

For a long time, Hélène stands there on the street, the city is filled with voices, people hurrying towards the cathedral as though afraid they will get there too late, shocked, worried faces quiz those heading the other way – a gunshot? Really? The Pope of the Siêu Linh . . . he's dead.

Ten minutes later, Hélène watches a man dressed all in black walk into the lobby of the Crystal Palace Hotel, unruly hair sticking out from his grey felt hat.

He stands in front of the reception desk. The night clerk gives him a long look.

The man waits patiently, takes out a pack of cigarettes and lights one.

The night clerk turns to the wall safe, opens it and hands the man the thick brown envelope he has just been given by Angèle.

When he comes out, Hélène sees the icy look in his eyes; his lips are so thin they seem not to exist.

With a practised gesture, he pockets the envelope and melts into the crowd.

Back in the hotel room, Hélène creeps into the bathroom but does not linger.

In the semi-darkness she can see her mother's body.

She feels devastated.

Her mother has done what she could not.

Overwhelmed by emotion, she feels tears sting her eyes, but manages to check the powerful urge to hug her mother, to tell her ... Silently, she sobs, then goes back to her own room.

Joseph is sleeping on the counterpane.

Without bothering to undress, Hélène lies down.

It is over.

Epilogue
18 November 1948

49

You did the right thing

There was nothing else that Louis could do. After many days' absence from the soap factory, a lot of work had piled up for him, and also for Angèle, and since he had come back to Beirut on his own, it all fell to him. So, when he heard what time his wife's flight was getting in he thought long and hard: there was no way he could go. He sent his most trusted foreman to the airport, then raced off to check the consignments and the deliveries.

He had not reckoned on the fact that the plane would be delayed. Louis was at home by the time Angèle finally arrived shortly after 11 p.m. As the foreman put Étienne's trunk in his old bedroom, Louis looked away.

After hugging Louis for a long time, Angèle took off her hat and hung it on the coat rack.

"Did it go well?"

"Yes, yes, it went very well."

"You must be tired . . ."

"A little."

Louis had prepared a tomato salad, the only thing he knew how to make.

"Don't worry, it's perfect," Angèle said.

He had opened a bottle of white wine. Angèle took a seat.

"How did things go with the boys?"

"Yes, it was . . . It was fine."

They had been together for almost thirty years. They had always been happy.

The past few weeks had been appalling, marked as they were by the death of a son and the resurgence of a past they had hoped to bury, but their relationship was as strong as ever.

"I wanted to tell you . . ." said Angèle, careful not to look at her husband as she helped herself to more tomato salad.

Louis nodded.

"I went to Lecoq & d'Arneville."

She sliced some bread, still careful not to look at him.

"I spent a lot of money, Louis."

Louis took a moment and then asked calmly:

"When you say a lot . . . You mean an awful lot?"

"Yes, my love, that's what I mean."

Louis nodded. Images flickered through his mind but none of them really tallied with what Angèle would call "a lot of money". Especially since she had always been frugal, or even miserly – not to insult her. She did not seem inclined to explain what she had spent this small fortune on.

"Did you at least spend it wisely?" said Louis.

She looked him in the eye.

"Yes, I think so."

"Then you did the right thing, Angèle."

"I love you, Louis."

"I love you too, my darling, you know that."

✳

There were two stories that any journalist could have turned into front-page headlines, a series of articles, maybe a whole soap opera: the Albert Maillard affair ("MAN IN 30 MILLION FRANC WAR MEMORIAL SCANDAL FOUND") and the currency trafficking scandal ("POLITICIANS' ILLICIT PROFITS FROM PIASTRE TRADING SCAM FUNDED BY FRENCH TAXPAYERS"), yet both these stories had slipped through his fingers.

Even his lone editorial had been stolen from him.

Since 1941, François had seen others rise while his star faded. Was he cursed?

It is a courier who brings him the purple envelope, with its looping, cursive feminine hand. Instantly he knows. He tears it open.

"64, rue Rambuteau. Now?"

François rips his jacket off the hallstand, almost falls on his face on the landing before taking the stairs four at a time. He is panting by the time he reaches the corner of the street . . .

Nine is there, hands folded in front of her. He stops.

"I'm sorry if I made you run . . ." she says.

"No, no, not at all! I just wanted to say . . . I'm sorry about . . . Let me explain . . ."

But she does not let him, she leaps forward and kisses him with a passion that leaves him breathless. Her lips are warm and silken, her mouth like a small ripe fruit. She presses against him, then gently pushes him away.

"Come with me . . ."

Her accent is more pronounced now. François looks up. Number 64, rue Rambuteau is the Hôtel Mercator.

Nine takes his hand and leads him.

"Do you have a room?" she asks the receptionist.

The young woman is smiling as she asks. The receptionist takes down a key attached to an unwieldy pyramidal key ring.

"Room 12, first floor."

Already they are climbing the stairs, Nine still leading him by the hand, quickly, quickly . . .

She is so flustered she cannot get the key in the lock. She laughs, François tries to help but finally the door opens. "Come on," she says, feverishly they undress, shoes and clothes flying everywhere, Nine unbuckles François's belt, everything is chaotic, clumsy, urgent, François undresses her, and, as though he cannot do it quickly enough, she bends down to take off her panties, "Come on," she drags him towards the bed, pushes him so that he falls back, then climbs on top of him, reaches down to grip him, guides him inside her, screams, bites his shoulder, "I'm coming," she says in a whisper, crying at the same time.

*

Two hours later, the room smelled of tender love and cigarette smoke; Nine smoked with an elegance François found delightful.

497

Silken was the word that came to him, everything about her was silken.

She was sitting up in bed, with beads of perspiration still glistening between her breasts. François had bitten her too, near her armpit. She stood up.

From François's jacket, which lay on the floor, she took a copy of *Le Journal*.

FOLLOWING IDENTIFICATION OF "LAST WITNESS" JUGE LENOIR OFFICIALLY CLOSES MARY LAMPSON CASE

"You really tipped him up," said Nine, pulling on her cigarette.

"He didn't need me to fall flat on his face."

"They'll appoint a new magistrate ..."

"No."

"That is what it says in the article ..."

"They'll appoint someone else for form's sake. But now that all the possible witnesses have been interviewed and there are no more suspects, a new investigating magistrate will have no choice but to close the case. Unless there's some startling revelation, nothing will happen. Mary Lampson has died a second time."

"Oh," said Nine.

She had got up and started to get dressed. She had put on a blouse but nothing underneath; it was both brazen and wonderfully natural.

"No, I've never been to this hotel before."

"Why did you say that?"

"Because you were bound to ask, it was only a matter of time. I chose it because it is close to your office. I waited until you went into *Le Journal* before I gave my message to the receptionist and told him it was urgent. That's why."

Still gazing at him, she finished dressing. François decided to do the same.

"You can stay," she said. "I have to get home, but you can stay for a little while."

She spoke again so softly that he barely heard her.

His heart ached as he watched her leave. She scribbled something in the margin of the newspaper.

"That's the phone number of my concierge, she's a good messenger," she said in a whisper. And her breath still carried the perfume of their violent ecstatic lovemaking.

"Wait," he called after her.

He hugged her to him so tightly that she choked.

"I have to go," she said.

He loosened his grip.

"I . . . I don't know the first thing about you."

It was absurd. In the past two hours he had learned more about her than many people who had known her for years, but Nine did not smile.

"We have time."

She moved to the door then turned.

"You know, I'm not that kind of girl . . ." she said, pre-empting a question that, in François's mind, had already begun its insidious, poisonous path, the one many men would ask themselves: was Nine "that kind of girl"? Easy. Prepared to sleep with the first person who came along.

She looked François in the eye, as if she was waiting for an answer. He stared back, still prisoner of an embarrassing, chauvinistic presumption that, in the glare of Nine's forthright gaze, felt petty and shameful.

A kiss on her lips and Nine was gone.

The corridors were carpeted, he did not even hear her footsteps on the stairs.

The sudden silence felt strange and oppressive.

François got dressed. There was something going round and round inside his head; some word, some idea.

"The lady paid for the room," said the receptionist.

Out on the pavement, François paused. He would never know quite how the pieces of the puzzle suddenly fell into place.

Nine spoke softly not because she was afraid of being overheard, but because she was afraid of speaking too loudly. François felt

499

his chest tighten. He was standing in the middle of the pavement, passers-by had to walk around him.

Her accent was not foreign. It was a speech impediment.

And the reason she had come to his office rather than leave a telephone number was because she could not answer.

And the reason Nine stared at him so intently was not because he was handsome; she was reading his lips.

Nine was deaf.

*

Hélène pegged the eighth photo to the piece of wire. This had to be Vĩnh, a handsome, shy-looking boy. He was posed next to a huge refrigerator – was it the one she had seen in Étienne's apartment when the new tenants opened the door? There could be no doubt her brother had taken this photo; Vĩnh was bisected at the left shoulder, he was even missing an ear.

At home, the bathroom was cramped, she had to be very careful not to spill anything and tidying up afterwards was quite an undertaking. Time was, this would have caused friction with François, but the tension between them had eased, events had meant they were starting over. It was agreed that Hélène would only develop photos when François didn't need the bathroom.

Hanging on the wire were other shots from the roll of film she had found in Étienne's camera: winding streets, half of Joseph's head peering into half his basket, coolies carrying bags of rice . . .

In the developing tank, the next picture was already emerging. It was always a magical moment, when shapes seemed to appear from nowhere.

Hélène stared at it in horror. It was Loan, wearing his tasselled cap, riding some sort of chariot, a small, smug smile playing on his lips . . .

François had asked what had happened in Saigon. Bouboule had too. Hélène told them about their meetings at the Exchange and the High Commission but nothing else. As far as they knew, Étienne had been targeted by the Việt Minh because of his investigation.

All things considered, it was not far from the truth. Hélène did not feel she could say any more.

She turned on the overhead light, sealed the bottles and gathered up the sheets of photographic paper; she had to carry it all back to her room.

She had spent almost everything she possessed on this makeshift, temporary development lab. Now she would have to start looking for a job.

François had just arrived home. Had he come straight from *Le Journal*? He looked tired and preoccupied, but there was something about his smell she did not recognise.

He opened a bottle of wine, engrossed in his thoughts.

"Would you like a glass?" he said.

"My God . . ."

Hélène came and sat at the table. Joseph jumped up onto her lap and curled into a ball.

She held out her glass.

They made a toast.

"There's something I've been meaning to ask you," said Hélène. "Do they employ photographers at *Le Journal*?"

*

On 18 November, the day the boutique opened, Jean set the display rails out on the pavement beneath the wide awning. "Like the ones you see at the greengrocer's stall in the market," muttered Geneviève.

The similarity to a market owed something to the little slates on which Jean had spent much time painting the name "Dixie". Geneviève glared at him as he painted the letters. She thought the slates were vulgar. Like the name, *Dixie*. Jean insisted it would encourage trade: "It sounds American, and people like that." He had chosen slates so they could chalk up the prices and change them from day to day.

The pavement displays encouraged passers-by to browse. Only bedlinen and larger pieces were displayed inside the shop.

"We keep prices low, we make a small margin, but we make money on the volume."

It was something of an understatement to say that the prices were modest; the first thing that customers remarked on was the prices.

"We'll never make a profit," Geneviève whined.

Jean could see no other solution.

"We don't have the means or the products to pitch ourselves as a luxury boutique, so people do what they do at a market, they rummage around, they choose something, they pay. They buy towels and tablecloths the same way they would buy potatoes and cauliflowers."

To Geneviève, this comparison was nothing short of insulting; but she did not think so for long.

They opened at seven every morning. Commuters heading to the métro would pause as they passed and call back on their way home. They closed late, at 7.30 p.m. During the day, passers-by would hesitate, but as soon as they began to rummage in the baskets, they were hooked. Every second pedestrian quickly became a customer.

Within two days, they had run out of napkins, within three days they had no towels or flannels. By the evening of the fourth day, they had only a third of the bedsheets and a few pillowcases left; everything else had been sold.

By the time Jean and Geneviève closed up, there was barely anything left to sell. They were exhausted, and dazzled by their meteoric success.

Geneviève did the sums. Purchasing fabric for a third of the going rate, selling from market stalls and maintaining low prices had borne fruit: They had made 800,000 francs. Twice as much as Guénot had predicted.

"Why don't we go to the restaurant?" Geneviève suggested.

All the carping about sales techniques and the fact that the shop looked like a flea market was forgotten. The Pelletiers had found a business model. They would seek out cheap fabrics, buy in bulk so they could keep prices low, and sell at a modest profit.

"The secret," said Jean, "is turnover."

In order to find fabric and subcontractors, he would have to travel a lot, he thought.

Geneviève smiled beatifically as she ordered half a bottle of Muscadet for herself. Jean, who preferred red wine, demurred – was he allowed to order wine for himself?

"Of course you can," she said. "Enjoy! It's not every day we get to celebrate a big event."

"That's true," he agreed. "It's not every day we make a profit like that!"

"That's not what I meant, Jean." Geneviève smiled at him, she had "put her face on" before leaving the house. She was not simply having dinner; she was holding court.

Jean did not really understand, but he had long since resigned himself to the fact that, when it came to Geneviève, he rarely understood.

"Well, let's say that as events go," he continued, "it was an event!"

"I have much more important news, Jean."

Jean's smile froze.

Geneviève placed her hands on either side of her plate.

"I'm pregnant, Jean. We're going to have a baby."

Jean's face fell; he turned as white as chalk.

"That ... That's ..." he stammered.

He reached forward and grasped Geneviève's hand.

"That's ... That's wonderful, my darling."

Acknowledgements

I am indebted to the historian Camille Cléret, who, from beginning to end, provided me with assistance, advice and documentation. In particular, she pointed out my incorrigible tendency to take poetic licence with historic events. But I persisted in the error of my ways.

My thanks to Valérie Tesnière and all the staff at La Contemporaine who allowed me to immerse myself in the archives of *France-Soir*, which this remarkable library on the Nanterre campus makes available to its users.

In terms of bibliography, I would like to acknowledge my debt to certain works.

First and foremost, *L'Indochine* (Grasset, 1997), a trilogy by Lucien Bodard that documents the First Indochinese War. To be honest, I did not expect to respond with such passion to this book, which is sustained by the sheer ferocity of Bodard's vision, his ability to sketch pen portraits and his immense talent. It is to him that I owe the "Việt Minh factory" in chapter 25, the Saigon killers, and many other things.

Jacques Despuech's book *Le Trafic de piastres* (Deux Rives, 1953) was a mine of information on a currency trafficking scandal, which, though it seems fanciful, is so well documented by historians that I did not need to invent much ...

The death of Étienne Pelletier was inspired by the accidental death of François-Jean Armorin (*Son dernier reportage*, Véziant, 1953, preface by Joseph Kessel).

The events of 11 November 1948 come partly from a letter sent by the president of the Étudiants Catholiques, Georges Suffert, to the editor of *Combat*. François Pelletier's editorial was directly inspired by Claude Bourdet's article in *Combat* on 12 November 1948.

For details of the torture practised in Indochina, I have drawn on the famous testimony of Jacques Chegaray ("Les tortures en Indochine", in *Les Crimes de l'armée française*, La Découverte,

2006), the writings of Andrée Viollis (*Indochine S.O.S.*, Gallimard, 1935), Colonel Trinquier (*La Guerre moderne*, Economica, 1961) together with an interview with Marie-Monique Robin (*Hommes et libertés*, Ligue des droits de l'homme).

I gained much from my readings of *La Nuit indochinoise* by Jean Hougron (Robert Laffont, 2004), *Soldats perdus et fous de Dieu* by Jean Lartéguy (Presses de la Cité, 1986), *Rue de la soie* (Le Livre de Poche, 1996) and *La Dernière Colline* by Régine Deforges (Le Livre de Poche, 1999), but also a number of more comprehensive works, including: *Indochine, la colonisation ambiguë, 1858–1954* by Hémery and Brocheux (La Découverte, 1994), *La Guerre d'Indochine* by Jacques Dalloz (Le Seuil, 1987), *Indochine 1945–1954* by Patrice Gélinet (Acropole, 2014) and *La Guerre d'Indochine* by Ivan Cadeau (Tallandier, 2015), *La France du marché noir 1940–1949* by Fabrice Grenard (Payot, 2008).

Le Métropole and the Crystal Palace in the novel are clearly different from the real establishments that inspired them, but owe their atmosphere to books such as *Continental Saigon* by Philippe Franchini (Olivier Orban, 1976), *Saigon 1925–1945* (Autrement, 2008) and *Le Roman de Saigon* by Raymond Reding (Éditions du Rocher, 2010).

Hélène's brief stint at the École de Beaux-Arts in Paris echoes the experience of Isabelle Conte, "Les femmes et la culture d'atelier à l'École des beaux-arts" (Livraisons d'histoire de l'architecture, 35, 2018) and some of her wanderings in *Le Plus Bel Âge?* by Ludivine Bantigny (Fayard, 2007).

Inspiration for the misadventures of Georges Guénot comes from *Les Françaises, les Français et l'Épuration* by François Rouquet and Fabrice Virgili (Gallimard, "Folio histoire", 2018).

In the scenes set in *Le Journal du soir*, I have drawn on *Lazareff et ses hommes* by Robert Soulé (Grasset, 1992), *Histoire de la presse en France* by Christian Delporte (Armand Colin, 2016) as well as the memoirs of Jean Ferniot (*Je recommencerais bien*, Grasset, 1991) and Daniel Morgaine (*L'un d'entre eux*, Jean Picollec, 1983).

With regard to issues relating to Vietnam, I am grateful to Sylvain Ouillon, who not only answered with kindness and erudition, but never laughed at my questions, something I greatly appreciated; and to Pierre Josse who gave me the benefit of his remarkable knowledge of South-East Asia.

When it came to Beirut, Alexandre Najjar, the author of *Dictionnaire amoureux du Liban* (Plon, 2014), was kind enough to be my Cicero.

Finally, I owe the precious details concerning the Siêu Linh sect to my Vietnamese translator, Nguyên Duy Bình.

My sincere thanks to all of the above.

More than once, I have had occasion to quote H. G. Wells's *Apropos of Dolores* (Jonathan Cape, London, 1938). Let me repeat it: "You take bits from this person and bits from that; from a friend you have known for a lifetime, or from someone you overheard upon a railway platform while waiting for a train, or from some odd phrase to a thing reported in a newspaper. This is the way fiction is made and there is no other way."

Doubtless there are many other ways, but Wells's way is also mine. So it happens that in the course of writing I acknowledge the origin of some of the "odd phrases". In this novel, some are due to Louis Althusser, Louis Aragon, Margaret Atwood, Gérald Aubert, Saul Bellow, Michel Blanc, Pierre Bost, Georges Brassens, Jérôme Cahuzac, Alexandre Dumas, Maurice Druon, Gustave Flaubert, René Goscinny, Elizabeth Jane Howard, Eugène Ionesco, Michel Jobert, LSD The Documentary Series, John le Carré, Jean-Pierre Melville, Lisa Moore, Yolande Moreau, Claude Nougaro, Marcel Proust, George Sand, Cécile Scordel, Antonio Scurati, Gédéon Tallemant des Réaux, Bertrand Tavernier, Heimito von Doderer and Deric Washburn.

His readers will appreciate, I hope, the nod to Georges Simenon.

As usual, a number of friends: Pierre Assouline, Gérald Aubert, Catherine Bozorgan, Nathalie Cohen (to whom I owe "Les années glorieuses"), Thierry Depambour, Camille Trumer and Perrine Margaine kindly agreed to read the book in manuscript and offer astute reflections and wise advice. I would like to thank them very much.

Finally, my thanks to Philippe Robinet and to Caroline Lépée, my editor; my gratitude to Camille Lucet, Patricia Roussel, Anne Sitruk and Valérie Taillefer, and, more generally, to everyone at Calmann-Lévy.